SOLDIER XVII

TODD BROOKS

SOLDIER XVII

FORGED FROM FIRE

TATE PUBLISHING
AND ENTERPRISES, LLC

Published by Tate Publishing & Enterprises, LLC
127 E. Trade Center Terrace | Mustang, Oklahoma 73064 USA
1.888.361.9473 | www.tatepublishing.com

Tate Publishing is committed to excellence in the publishing industry. The company reflects the philosophy established by the founders, based on Psalm 68:11,
"The Lord gave the word and great was the company of those who published it."

Book design copyright © 2014 by Tate Publishing, LLC. All rights reserved.
Cover design by Rtor Maghuyop
Interior design by Jimmy Sevilleno

Published in the United States of America

ISBN: 978-1-63306-697-7
1. Fiction / Christian
2. Fiction / Action & Adventure
3. Fiction / Drama
4. Fiction / Superheroes
14.10.13

THIS BOOK IS dedicated to Diane Brooks. It is a very small way of saying thank you because she has dedicated her life to her family of which I and all seven of her children are the beneficiaries. I cannot even begin to try and express the amount of devotion, sacrifice, and love she has given to us for the last twenty-five–plus years. Whether it is the 9,100 meals she has made for us, (and they have all been fabulous), or the 1,800 loads of laundry, or the 3,240 days of homeschooling she has put in, or the 1,300 times she helped the kids and I get to church on time, or the 16 years of preparing for every-other-Friday-night Bible study in our home, it has all been, and continues to be, a gargantuan effort of service from one humble human being who does it all to bring glory to her Savior, Jesus Christ. I love her very much.

PREFACE

ONE OF MY earliest childhood memories is watching the landing on the moon on our probably-twelve-inch black-and-white television set (perish the thought!). My father was a film editor in and or near Hollywood, California. My grandmother was in postproduction working for a film lab. My brother is currently a music editor. One of my best friends going back to the third grade, which was a long time ago, works for a major television and motion picture studio. I still live in Southern California. I think it might be fair to say that I am a child of the entertainment industry, good or bad (at least that is where my three squares a day came from). But the simple truth is that there is a dearth of good wholesome current entertainment. Many people would argue that, I am sure. But my experience as one who has and is raising teenagers is that it is a very small section of action-packed current material that isn't about Greek mythology or wizards or killing each other in a game or all of the aforementioned, and then there is the whole subject matter of dealing with heavy romantic themes. So my goal was to entertain with a purpose.

I am hoping that people of all ages, from the young teenagers, both boys and girls, to adults who go back as far as the Depression era, will enjoy aspects of the story. My hope is that you will laugh, cry, and get mad at times, but most of all that it will make you think. Then after you put it down, you will say, "That was unlike anything I have ever read," and I would be most grateful if you then would pass it on to your friend or your child.

CONTENTS

PROLOGUE

C LYDE WAS AT the point of no return, yet he would not quit now. He was not willing to sacrifice the lives of the eleven men under his command nor give back Colonel Davies.

The cliff at this point jutted out about ten yards above his head. The total free climb up so far had been around two hundred feet. He was on a ledge the size of the curb. The thought kept nagging at the back of his mind that this entire campaign was a setup. It was too easy for his unit to sneak into this very southern portion of North Korea and grab the kidnapped Colonel Jonathan Davies. Now they were pinned in with probably five hundred North Korean soldiers dogging them. As soon as daybreak came they were all going to come down the one trail that led to their little holdout beneath this cliff. It was a mesa with no way down. It seemed as though they had been herded here like cattle. Their global positioning data indicated there was a way out, but it didn't identify the hundred-foot chasm of free airspace between the two mesas. There was only about a mile free fall down to a river.

The idea he had was that from this ledge he might be able to swing his rope and lasso a sharp pointed rock maybe fifteen feet above him. It looked like it had just enough upward thrust to hold the rope and carry his weight. He could swing across the ravine and get out from underneath this overhang to continue free climbing. *Clyde Gareen you are nuts,* he thought. He fashioned the rope and let it go. He pulled it taut. Backing up about four steps, he ran across the ledge like a gymnast on a balance beam. He jumped. Two seconds and then his hands slammed on the ledge, but they were slipping, and then he caught the edge and it held his swinging weight. He climbed up on the tiny little precipice. At the top of the cliff, he switched his shoes to a pair of moccasins, a little trick he learned growing up. He was able to slip into the camp of the North Koreans and identify one of the pilots. After a few seconds with his hands on his proper pressure points, he knew the pilot would no longer be in need of his identification card and his key to unlock the control panel of the helicopter. The startup of the chopper would wake everyone up, but they would think it was time to start moving. He thought maybe fifteen seconds until they would know.

Still in stealth mode, Clyde edged closer to the helicopters. It looked like there were about ten MI-26 Halos, and then he saw what he thought was a UH-60 Blackhawk. He looked at the ID card and then the key ring on which there were seven keys. The ID card let him in the Blackhawk twin. He had noticed it was loaded with a dozen Hellfire missiles. *That will work,* he thought. He unlocked the panel with key number three and strapped into the pilot seat. Clyde actually got forty-five seconds, and he was far enough away to unleash four missiles at the Halos.

Then he shot four more into various makeshift depots around the camp. No need to wait any longer and he pulled back on the throttle going backwards and turned the helicopter in an arc. Then he shot forward out of the hot zone. As soon as he was out of range from the enemy camp, he communicated with his team and said he was coming in a little blind. There was a pretty thick fog over the entire part of the mountain where his team was waiting, but Clyde had a pretty good feel for the mesa and the subsequent cliff. He landed on the mesa with a pretty good margin, and the boys piled in like a bunch of high-schoolers running out to a late night drag race.

Johnny Walker took over the controls on the Blackhawk and Timothy Koh took over as co-pilot. He was fluent in the North Korean tongue as well, which might prove helpful in case the enemy decided to send an F-15 after them or they needed to order take out. Clyde was in position to shoot off the remaining four missiles that the chopper was equipped with. The helicopter was off, and they used the ravine as cover and followed the river. From the time Clyde stole the helicopter to their move down the ravine had only been about three minutes. They knew that the North Koreans were already after them. It was helpful that they were flying one of their birds so it was hard to identify.

The really good news was that Johnny Walker was as confident and daring pilot as they had in the US Special Forces.

"Clyde?" asked Johnny. "When we get to South Korean airspace, do you want me to just hang out the white flag and say, 'Please don't shoot us, we are friendly'?"

Conner Griffen came over the com saying, "Stay on task, fellas. I have the general on my secure line. He is going to communicate with South Korea and let them know there is an unfriendly bird running like a scared cat from a pack of dogs out of the hills and headed to the demilitarized zone.

General Myles turned to the ambassador of South Korea and said, "Crisis over. We got back our kidnapped Colonel and all of our marines will be over the border in five minutes. No harm, no foul."

"How did they pull that off?" asked a bewildered ambassador. "I thought they were pinned in on that mesa?"

"It looks like one of our soldiers free climbed a five-hundred-foot cliff, snuck into the enemy camp, stole a helicopter, unleashed eight missiles right into their bellies, and gave our boys a joy ride back home," said a proud Kirby Myles.

"Better give that boy a medal!" exclaimed the ambassador.

"Medal nothing." Smiled General Myles. "I am going to buy that marine a beer."

In a parallel conversation from a North Korean general, the comment was made to a silent investor that unfortunately Clyde Gareen had slipped away.

RUNNING ON EMPTY

THE BURNING-HOT WOOD-FIRE pizza oven was now stone cold. Until just recently, it took chilled lumps of hand-tossed dough and transformed them into savory and aromatic delicacies. It just did not matter anymore. What exactly does desperation look like in living color? What is the essence of sheer helplessness almost to the point of lunacy? The tidal wave of hopelessness that can crash down on a whole country, a village, and on individuals has no favorites but comes when unbidden and covers absolutely.

It seemed like the whole world had come smashing down on one poor, forlorn soul sitting on the curb of a busy New York City street. With his head on his knees and his arms folded over the top, Clyde Gareen was never so completely alone as in that moment. Even though hundreds of very busy people frantically hurried by on the cracked and dirty sidewalk, dozens of yellow cabs comingled with other would-be vehicles that were all crawling by in midday stranglehold traffic. A jet slowly flew by overhead, and somewhere near, a street vendor was yelling about his infamous product.

Clyde was transfixed with the pain of being wiped out. So this was financial ruin. He had never felt failure so strongly. It was like a pungent taste in his mouth. He honestly could not believe that he had lost everything. On the heels of the greatest personal crisis he ever faced. He winced at the very thought of Ilyaina, or Laina, as he had always known her. Two years of seventy-two–hour workweeks later, and he had nothing to show for it. Everyone told him that owning and running a restaurant was next to impossible. Everyone told him that it would suck the life out of him, and he wouldn't be able to devote much time to his family. He knew all of these things and was willing to accept defeat.

The hard part to swallow, of course, was that his restaurant was successful. People loved it, and they made bookings every night. When Charles Walls decided to abruptly pull out his half-a-million-dollar investment, there was nothing Clyde could do. He did not fully understand how quickly the end came. He tried to borrow money and get a loan and show that he was covering his overhead and making profit, but the equipment wasn't paid for, and the lease was only guaranteed with the capital, and he could not purchase his food on credit.

Man, it unwound quicker than a paratrooper getting out of his chute in enemy territory, Clyde thought.

What was he going to do now? To whom was he going to turn to? The hardest part of all—with the foreclosure of the business—was now having time to think. He just did not want to think about Laina. It was too hard to imagine. He just threw himself into his work for the last three months and refused to even believe she was gone. He had known her for twenty years. They had been married for the last fifteen. She was only thirty-six when she, when it, when the fateful catastrophic event happened in the streets of Palermo as she was home visiting her parents.

Thinking about her made the pain so awful Clyde was short of breath. How could someone he had been so connected to on so many levels be gone? They had childhood memories together, they were totally in love, they had four children who were now busy making new memories—the only woman he had ever been with, and she was gone. It seemed like he could just turn to her at any moment and talk to her, yet he could not. From the moment of the explosion to the burial, it had been less than three days. It was surreal, it happened so fast. He had never known anyone so healthy, so vibrant, and so full of life to be gone. It was almost as though she had been vaporized. In fact, that is exactly what had happened.

The guilt was unfathomable. Clyde felt completely responsible. He was supposed to protect her. Everyone had said this has nothing to do with protection; that is why they call it an accident. That event he had replayed over and over in his mind, and with the restaurant and the kids and her being gone, was so painful he thought he was going to retch. He was a pathetic soul.

Somehow he had to gather his thoughts, pull himself together, go on despite the pain; he had a family who needed their dad. What they needed was a provider, and he hadn't done very well. This had all the smell of overwhelming devastation, not only to experience the near-suicidal scope of financial failure but also to be on the heels of losing your life mate who had been your constant advocate and companion for twenty years. How on earth was he going to pull himself out of this hole?

Clyde lifted his head and put his arms out and simply prayed, "Lord, you are going to have to throw me a rope, because I can't do this on my own."

He had been through enough military operations to know there were no atheists in foxholes, but at this moment, having never been an atheist, he knew that life had outfoxed him, and he simply needed outside help. To say that Clyde Gareen had bet the farm on his restaurant was not only an understatement; it was an exact commentary on what he had done. He had sold his beautiful Connecticut farm to put up his capital in the business. Twelve years of military life after college, and they had saved every dollar possible to buy the farm.

Farm was not really the exact word; it was really a ranch. It was a ranch with sixteen acres of awe-inspiring beauty. Clyde and his family had a fishing hole, a vineyard, and room for their six horses. Laina loved to ride and would take off into the woods every morning. As soon as Katarina was old enough, she began to ride as well, and her brothers were quickly becoming avid horsemen as well.

Clyde smiled when he thought of his young vaqueros. They had sold the home and taken the money to put into the restaurant. They had enough money for a little flat in the city that was a walking distance from the restaurant. Wow, life had changed so drastically.

Laina was adamant about making the sacrifice. She realized how dramatically different life would be and accepted the challenge with zest and enthusiasm. She was a staple at the restaurant. Always hosting, always talking, dealing with the staff, and, most of all, dealing with the investor.

Charles was a stuffy old friend of the family. It was really Laina's family. Laina's father and Charles went back thirty years when they had met in Italy, as Charles was there with the military. The military connection did not translate between Clyde and Charles. For some reason, Clyde never was in sync with Mr. Walls, as he referred to him. That dramatic pullout was characteristic of Clyde's feelings for the man. He always felt it was an issue of character and that there was some deep, dark inner secret he could not quite put his finger on. It did not seem to at all factor.

The Gareens had put up two hundred thousand of their own money. Most of that was used in the renovation of the lease site and to purchase equipment, so he realized, even at the time, that most of his capital was being spent, and the other capital—oh, it did not matter. Why had he not just taken the SBA loan? That would have been harder to get yet so much easier to manage.

Now Clyde—the ex-colonel, the ex–restaurant owner, the ex–happily married man—was formulating a plan as he sat there on the street, watching life bustle by him. He was going back for the coins, and he just needed to make sure he had all of his x's and o's in place. He always went back to the chalkboard and diagrammed everything in his mind. Eighteen years of soccer had done that to him. The only thing he loved more than soccer was cooking and, of course, flying planes.

Some people called him a modern Renaissance man, but he just felt like he was a schizophrenic. Speaking several languages only helped to exasperate the feeling. He was so comfortable living in many different cultures that sometimes he felt like a man without a country. He had finally quit the military after the background checks from marrying an Italian national became so ludicrous. He really wanted to open his own restaurant. He always tried to explain that she was actually born in the United States and she was the daughter of missionaries, but she had lived and been schooled her entire life in Italy and attained citizenship there. She was perfectly happy being there and wasn't coming back to America other than to follow her husband.

Clyde wrestled with these feelings and was worried at times that he would act on them. Trained in espionage and the use of highly specialized weapons, it was never a good thought that he might slip over the edge and turn ugly. Thank goodness for his mentor, Gen. Kirby Myles. How many times had he pulled Clyde out of the mire he found himself stuck in. Kirby used to say, "It is only because I am twenty years older and did the same stupid stuff." Both *stupid* and *stuff* were, of course, paraphrases, but Clyde did not miss the point. One of the frustrations of failure is knowing that you gave up on other paths. This was particularly excruciating for Clyde. Ever since he was a boy, he knew what he wanted to be. These other things had become more important, but Clyde had always wanted to be the seventeenth warrior in a succession of war heroes in his family dating back to the first-century AD.

Somehow Clyde had to wrestle with being ambitious or being this ultimate in-his-mind war hero. Lots of guys had been in the military. Many family members through the years had served their country with the willingness to lay down their lives. His father had been briefly in Vietnam and then served during the Cold War. His brother, Brad, was still in the military. He was a graduate of the Naval Academy and was now a captain stationed in Washington, DC. But the feeling of being named the next warrior—hero, soldier—had crystallized in Clyde's mind when he was twelve. He could remember it like it was yesterday.

REELING BACK
THE YEARS

F AMILY GATHERINGS CAN be a real bore when you are twelve. Mostly because the adults just want to sit around and talk. What is the point of all that useless conversation when you can go outside and shoot some hoops, climb a tree, swim in the stream, ride your bike through the forest, or even take your slingshot and try to peg an unsuspecting flying black rat otherwise known as crows? It might even be better to have to talk with one of the neighbor girls than sit inside and listen to all this squirrel chatter.

Clyde Matthew Gareen, for so this twelve-year-old had been named, was lying on his stomach on the living room floor. His head was propped by his hands connected to elbows which were digging into the soft shag carpeting. The wood floors lined about 60 percent of the room. Almost no other seventh grader would make a mathematical accumulation of the carpet area, but to Clyde, it just came with his very inquisitive mind. Clyde was absolutely glued to the proceedings that were taking place. Of his seven brothers and sisters, Clyde was the youngest and, for the most part, the only one who seemed to care about this family event.

It was the proceedings of a ritual very ancient yet so very twentieth century. Families had been getting together for five thousand years and bestowing honor to one another. This was, of course, a little different because this family had grown from the regions around Western Europe and migrated to Wales around 400 AD. This is where it had maintained its history for the next 1,400 years until they had moved to the New World.

For the next two hundred years, they had occupied a little valley just south of New York in New Jersey. It was an amazing place because it had a lake and tons of trees, and the ten acres had a view of the ocean. It was here on this hot and sultry July day—the Fourth of July—where they had been gathered to celebrate their country's independence that they were honoring Clyde's uncle. This was Clyde's only uncle with the surname of Gareen. His father, Robert, had one brother, Turner Patrick. Clyde had what seemed like an endless array of aunts. He had three on his dad's side and four on his mother's side. Clyde only had three cousins named Gareen. All the other twenty-nine cousins had some other name. It was hard to remember them all.

The family was about one hundred people. His grandfather's home was large. Quietly after their evening meal—which his grandmother called supper, for whatever reason—they had eaten barbecued hamburgers, watermelon, and corn on the cob. The best part was the homemade strawberry ice cream. Clyde had gone to Gramma Gareen and offered to help, and she asked if he would take out the trash. He thought it was a splendid idea because he had to walk down the driveway about a quarter of a mile, and their German shepherd, Lightning, always followed him to the trash bin. He threw old walnuts, and Lightning chased them and brought them back, eager for more.

Then a bell sounded, and Clyde knew it was time. He had been waiting almost an entire year. And while his older siblings feigned courteous attention, he knew that none of them really cared. Maybe Brad cared. He was Clyde's oldest brother and was number two in the pecking order. Silvia was the oldest, and she had recently been married to Shawn, and she was expecting twins. But Brad was just back from college, and he was bound for the military. He wanted to fly airplanes, and he had a knack for understanding Clyde's complete absorption for all things military related. Clyde could recite every conflict that the United States had been in since the Revolution. He knew the finer nuances of the battles and each of the pros and cons of the decision that were made both on the macro and micro levels. At the current time, he didn't use the terms *macro* and *micro* because he was only twelve.

Today was a very significant day in the Gareen family clan. They had emigrated from Whales back in the early eighteenth century. Patrick Matthew Gareen was 106 years old. He was ninety four years older than Clyde, and Clyde had been born in 1984. So that meant to Clyde that his grandfather had been born in 1890. Clyde knew fully well that Grandpappy Patrick, as he was affectionately named by the Gareens, was an adult by the time World War I had come along. In fact, he was a major by the time they actually experienced real conflict. Patrick was Soldier XV. He was the fifteenth in the line of war heroes that had held the name Gareen, or its similar derivatives, for 1,500 years. He was named Soldier XV by his great great-grandfather, who was ninety-two at the time.

This was the kind of math that was confusing, but Clyde had penciled it out. Pappy Gareen was thirty at the time. So Soldier XIV had bestowed the honor upon him in 1920. So Gareen Soldier XIV had been born in 1858. This was so totally mind-boggling that it made Clyde shudder.

At this very moment, Pappy was handing his uncle a key, and it was on a ribbon and could be worn discreetly on a uniform. It very clearly was marked *Soldier* and then *XVI*. This was a key to a trunk. Clyde had heard what was in the trunk and couldn't believe that Uncle Turner was now getting this key. Just think that it had a sword that Soldier II used in defending Rome against the Huns and the Ostro something. It was said that Soldier II, or Rominus Gareen, had fought off six men to keep the emperor safe. Just recently back from battle, Rominus had been recruited to be the king's bodyguard because of his skill in fighting, along with his steadfast character. They knew they could trust Soldier Gareen, and the political landscape of Valentinius was short on trust. Rome had just finished repelling Attila the Khakan or great king of the Huns, at the battle of Chalons, and now he was dealing with internal strife in his own court.

Clyde could see it in his mind, lying right there on the floor. Rominus was standing by the emperor and fighting off these usurpers. They were men who had entered the palace and were trying to take the emperor. Rominus was fighting two at a time and not waiting for the attack but being the aggressor. Taking one by the neck, he turned him so the soldier was stabbed by his own man, and then he hooked the other soldier with his feet. Rominus jerked him off the ground, sliced through him like a tomato, and finally turned to face more oncoming attackers. The story went on that he had flipped a third onto a beleaguered fourth and then pierced two with their own sword, shish kebab style.

Clyde was always awestruck when he was told that story. His mother would argue that it was not good to be fascinated with such gruesomeness. "Fighting is always ugly" was Clyde's response, and as he grew older, he would change that to say that fighting was the darkness of humanity revealed. Right there in front of his eyes, he was looking at Soldier XVI. Grandpappy Patrick was recounting that it was rare for a soldier to be handed the honor by another living soldier, and that only once from nine to ten had it been in consecutive generations.

Clyde knew right then and there he wanted more than anything to break the cycle again and be a consecutive generation. He wanted more than anything in the world to be Soldier XVII. Clyde knew the names and the acts of valor each soldier was responsible for. He knew that it covered the War of Independence, which he didn't quite understand because weren't they all from England. Nevertheless, he knew that prior to that, there were the many battles of the English and French. His thoughts got interrupted as Grandpappy was talking about Turner. He was talking about Vietnam. He had been shot. He had cut the bullet out of his thigh, put on a large band-aid, wrapped it as best he could, and carried two wounded soldiers out of some kind of three-tiered jungle. He had to make two separate trips under heavy gunfire. He then was captured, had escaped, and was able to give his commander the coordinates of the Vietcong's stronghold in that area. He understood the land mines and the tunnels, and saved thousands of lives with this new information. From Vietnam he had become a pilot and had flown countless missions during the Cold War. Even while he was a top stick air force colonel and instructor, he was still manning combat planes and going on missions.

Well, you don't become Soldier XVI in the Gareen family because you just volunteer for the corps, Clyde thought.

YOU'RE SIXTEEN,
AND YOU'RE BEAUTIFUL

W HAT WAS HE thinking? He had a couple of dollars in his pocket. He had the rest of the day, and he could use an espresso. He walked over to the nearest café and ordered a double shot, and sat down in the quaint little open-air patio between two high-rises and faced the street. He picked up the daily *New York Times*, and as he sat down, he was again flooded with the thoughts of his wife. Would life ever have the same vitality? Would he again be able to face the days ahead? And how on earth was he supposed to raise a nine-year-old miniature version of his wife along with her three siblings? Nuts.

A single dad with four kids, Clyde thought. *I am nuts.*

He could not help reverting back to the time he and Laina had met, as he thought of his little girl. At fifteen, Clyde discovered two of his greatest passions at once: food and women. It was problematic for the latter that he was at the time spending the summer with a friend in Italy whose parents were missionaries. But he found that a little discretion was in order and the secret could be all his. That is at least what he thought. The use of the word *women*, which was plural, was not actually right. The right word was *woman*. Clyde Gareen, at fifteen, was a one-woman man, although at the time he did not realize it yet.

He was playing soccer all summer on a traveling team with Ivan Del Amo and Conner Griffin. Conner's parents actually were missionaries too in a Middle Eastern country, for the moment unnamed. Back then, Clyde remembered it was such a big secret. Yet Conner spoke Farsi and Arabic, and how many countries spoke Farsi? Clyde—whoever named him that, he thought—was getting schooled in the art of *futbol* and, unbeknownst to him, was learning Italian from his teammates and a smattering of languages from Conner.

It was Ilyaina del Amo, or Laina, who held his attention. She was a year older than Ivan and much better looking. She also spent a lot of time preparing the family meals. She didn't have to because Mrs. del Amo was a really fine cook as well, but she loved it. It probably helped that she had twelve-year-old sisters, twins, who did the entire cleanup. But Clyde loved the aroma that came from the kitchen. It was akin to therapy for him. At fifteen, he didn't really have need for the word *therapy*. That would come into play later in his life.

Something about the way the Italians cooked their food. It took longer. Whether it was the garlic simmering in red wine or the fresh mozzarella or the homegrown onions and tomatoes sliced and added to the oversized stewing pot, it was really incredible. Somebody was up early in the morning, grinding their own coffee or smoking some of that fabulous prosciutto on the stove. Then the girls were out in the garden picking the fresh herbs, and those were brought in and washed. They were making their own pasta and then rolling out handmade pizzas. Clyde said that he felt like they were running a restaurant.

Between feeding their family of seven and the three boys staying with them, and people from the church, they were literally feeding hundreds of people every week.

"The church is increasing in size because you stuff everyone with all your amazing delicacies and then roll them into the building next store," Clyde said. "Culinary evangelism at the del Amo household."

Mr. del Amo smiled and said that the Lord works in mysterious ways. It is funny how things influence you, and in that one summer, Clyde grew three inches and gained fifteen pounds. He came back to high school as a six-foot-one sophomore who weighed two hundred pounds. It was helpful that he had raw natural speed; he was tall and had just spent three months playing with all-star European players.

But his whole palate had changed. He enjoyed his food more and was not afraid to prepare it himself. His soccer buddies at high school thought he was one exotic dude.

"Who else goes out and buys a cookbook, shops at different grocers, and then makes the food?" they would say, although when Clyde did pasta, sausage, and garlic bread—which was his own version of spaghetti—they all sat in stone-cold silence eating the meal, and no one ever uttered anything defamatory about Gareen in the kitchen, not even with Dinah.

Clyde never stopped cooking. It was an art and a science to him. He really wanted to understand how things worked and the processes that made food different in so many different ways. He enjoyed it through high school and kept on learning and experimenting through college. He played four years of soccer, double majored in chemistry and languages, and spent all kinds of weekends doing ROTC. Yet all of that was secondary to cooking. He knew all of the food staff in each of the kitchens at Duke University. He knew what the ingredients were to all of the items and what was on the menu. He really liked trying to feed thousands of people. He understood the dilemmas involved in prepping, cooking, and holding so many meals and then doing it all again for the next day.

He listened to the manager of the meal service team, and then the manager listened to Clyde. Based on a few suggestions and the new herb garden he helped them plant with the help of the botany program, the food at the cafeteria was unbelievable. Oftentimes the senior staff of Duke would come down and sample the food—in their private room, of course—but they were not ordering off the menu or having their own food made.

By this time, Clyde had finished his espresso and had sauntered down to the subway. His mind had been wandering all over the globe. It was not easy to focus when so many things caused so much pain. One kind of just bounces from one memory to the next, avoiding real pain like one would avoid a traffic collision. He was going to go back to his folks.

No. First he was going to find an apartment and reestablish life on his own. He dearly loved his parents, but he felt it would be better for him to live on his own and raise his children, and they would move on with their lives. The diagram from the chalkboard in his mind was complete. He could rent an apartment, and he would take the job offer from Darla Esperanza to be their executive chef. It was a fabulous restaurant.

PASSAGE TO BANGKOK (ACTUALLY EGYPT)

C LYDE WOULD START the lease and the new job in the beginning of June which gave him two weeks to get into Egypt and see his old friend Conner Griffin. From there he would travel maybe by boat down the Nile to one of the coastal towns and then on to Kafr Jallu. Reaching this little piece of the desert by camel was unnecessary because there was a road all the way into the town. He would have to go in through the cave and probably do a little tunneling, but two weeks would give him time, and he could pull out enough of the coins to maybe buy a little home outside the city if he saved his pennies and proved his work history at the new restaurant. Katarina could have a horse, and he would have no choice but to send the kids to school. Well, he could circle back on that issue a little later. Of course, he was going to have to devise a way to off-load the coins without too much undue investigation. This might take a little time, and it would be fun for the five of them to live in the city for a period.

How on earth was he going to work and raise small children? Laina's sister—not one of the twins, Angelina—had been living with them for a few years now, and she was very helpful, but it would be awkward without Laina. This was a complication. He knew it wasn't complicated for him because he would be single the rest of his life. Nobody would ever replace Laina. He knew in his heart he was done. The kids would like the open space, of course, like at his parents', but he felt it would be naturally difficult for Angelina. It would be too much proximity. What did his daughter say? "We will have to stick that idea on the mirror and come back to it."

If Clyde could talk his folks into coming up from their place in New Jersey, he would really love it. Dad would drill him about the money. He knew everything had gone into the restaurant. The best thing with Dad was his honesty. He had discovered the coins on a mission. They had taken some fleabag the military wanted and were transporting him to their base in Kuwait. The fleabag, as it turns out, befriended Clyde because they could converse in Farsi. Clyde had spent enough time in Iran to learn the language, and it was pretty customary that Middle Eastern guys could speak multiple languages.

This guy, though, was not really Middle Eastern. He was from Pittsburgh, and his parents had emigrated from Egypt. They had fled from Iran during the days of the shah and then went to the United States. Only problem was they had sired a traitor. The guy had nominal intentions as a teenager. College had turned him into a radical. He had some complete knucklehead of a professor of whom he followed his teachings. He became a Muslim extremist. He operated out of Iran and was using his family ties in Egypt as a covert operator. Among other things, he was trading weapons on the black market. The American government had funded this dude's education.

Sa'id, as he called himself, was buying Russian SAMs and selling them to all kinds of characters in the bazaar of underworld freedom fighters.

"Freedom fighters nothing," Clyde had always said. *Freedom suppressors* and *gangland third-world mafia* were much more appropriate terms. After a couple of days, he told Clyde about the coins and how he had traded them for some "equipment." The coins dated back to a sixteenth-century Spanish ship that had "confiscated" them from other voyagers. Clyde knew Sa'id was telling the truth because it was his way of trying to seduce Clyde into helping him escape.

Unfortunately, Mr. Sa'id was never going to get back to those coins because he fell two hundred feet trying to escape from the military base in Kuwait. Conner Griffin had overheard the conversation and had said to Clyde that, in fact, this human being was, without question, a seasoned highwayman and a lifetime pathological liar.

"So you don't like him?" Clyde asked rhetorically.

Conner literally made no reply, except for a little roll of the eyes. Conner went on to say that he had a premonition that this guy was really telling the truth. The tone of Sa'id's voice changed, and his Arabic got really clear as he spoke about this treasure. The fact that he didn't just say buried treasure but was specific about sixteenth-century coins gave credence to his little story. In fact, Clyde, who was not a betting man, thought that there might be a 10 percent chance that the coins were, in fact, actually buried there. Most likely other so-called partners had laid claim to it, or that per chance some wandering pirates passing by might have stolen it. It was worth a chance, so they decided to go find this property.

So on a short leave, Clyde and his longtime friend and fellow marine special ops comrade had taken that risk, and they travelled back to Egypt. Not easy for two combat marines to travel in and out of Middle Eastern countries, but they had visas and passports and were, for the most part, travelling commercially. They flew into the El Nouzha airport on the northeast side of the city of Alexandria.

My, what a city. Clyde thought to himself.

They felt like they had just jumped back about a thousand years. And then just around the corner, they felt as though they were right back in the modern era.

"We need to spend more time in this city," Clyde mentioned. "The history of this city is unbelievable."

The city was designed and created by Alexander the Great around 300 Bc and through the early periods was one of the most culturally inspiring and thought-provoking places on earth. There was a fusion of British, French, and Middle Eastern architecture, with ancient buildings that heralded from the pre-Renaissance era and then modern hotels with all of the current amenities.

"We don't have time for a tour," Conner said. "I feel your pain, though. I would love to spend about two weeks here."

They rented a car and then traveled out of town on the international coastal road. It was closed from time to time, but their ability to speak the language and willingness to depart with a few pounds when necessary allowed them to travel around 140 kilometers to a little city called Kafr Jallu.

What a name for a town, thought Clyde. *It would be fun as a kid just to write your address* Kafr Jallu.

Clyde and Conner went to work and drove into the city to find the Egyptian version of the county clerk's office. They wanted to get public records and didn't want to start digging in someone's backyard. If, in fact, their little hailed-from-Pittsburgh-turned-Muslim-extremist mina bird—who sang all that he knew in order to gain his freedom, or at least put together a story that they would buy into—had, for some tiny reason, cleverly devised this tale and was lying like a Persian rug, then Clyde and Conner could wind up in a very hard jail cell somewhere in the center of town, and it might take a few weeks or months to process the paperwork and clear them of any wrongdoing.

So they found the county or regional courthouse, and they got the public record showing the deed to the property. Yes, it was owned free and clear, and it was owned by one Michael Sa'id Abraham Halim. They asked what the process was to buy this property since they knew the owner had passed. The people in the government office asked if it was possible if they could notify the next of kin, and then it was possible they could sell it.

"What is the other alternative?" Conner asked.

The people in the government said they could publish it in a newspaper and see if anyone came forward, but it would take around six months and a court order for the property to go through the legal equivalent of probate. So Clyde looked up the Halims in Pittsburgh and found two who had the name of Abraham in it. He took a stab and dialed the number direct because he had an international calling plan on his cell phone.

An older gentleman picked up the phone, and Clyde asked him if he had a son by the name of Michael Sa'id Abraham. The man said that, in fact, they did. Clyde broke into a little bit of Farsi, and while it wasn't fluent, it was helpful enough to let the senior Abraham Halim know that Clyde was not your average American guy making a sales call. Clyde asked directly if the United States military had contacted Mr. Halim for any reason. Mr. Halim said that, in fact, a gentleman had come over in the morning and had discussed the recent events in detail.

"I was there," Clyde said. "And I am sorry, and my condolences to you and your family."

Mr. Halim's voice grew a little hoarse, and he was certainly speaking from a humble heart and with all of the compassion of a father who didn't understand the decisions his child had made. "I tried to tell Sa'id that the professor was wrong, that this country we had migrated to while, of course, it has its flaws, is the one of the greatest countries to allow us to immigrate here, to give us all unprecedented freedom and then afford us the systems in which we can work hard and prosper. But Sa'id turned his back on all that and wanted to get back to his roots and took off for the Middle East. We don't know what he was doing, except he was tied in with some radicals and they were involved in fighting against anything Western. He learned this all from his college professor, who, while working in an American university, was teaching everything contrary to the very reasons we immigrated here in the first place. I guess there are bad apples in every crate, right? You just have to have the backbone to walk away from their errant philosophies."

"Again, Mr. Halim, I am really sorry," Clyde said. "And the reason why I am making this call is that Sa'id owned property in a little town in Egypt. It is a good location, and it is close to the Suez Canal and to Alexandria, and we think it would be a good investment. Would you be interested in selling it by chance?"

Sa'id's parents wanted nothing to do with ties to the Middle East. They had left behind a severe culture in Iran, and they were never going back. Through Skype, they were able to walk through the legal process with an attorney and sell the property. The process was a little longer in Egypt, but Clyde and Conner paid the attorney, deposited the amount of money for the negotiated sale, and made copies of all the legal paperwork. While they would not technically be owners for a few weeks, they, in fact, had purchased the land and were soon to be the rightful owners.

"Let's go see what we bought, brother," Conner said.

They drove out to the little lot and found the tiny house all boarded up, not because of damage but to keep the home secure. So after a few hours with the hammer, they got enough of the wood off so they could get into the house and have enough light to look around and see what they were doing. Between the flying, driving, and dealing with the property and now the physical labor they had already spent two days—dirty, unshaven, and hungry—

the guys asked themselves if it was better to finish now or to find a spot, get some food, and try to get a little sleep.

"Nope," Clyde said. "I have a portable light in the car, and I am going to finish this deal right now. Either he has coins or he doesn't."

So with that, they began to search the home. Underneath some carpet in the hallway leading to the master bedroom—well, at least one of the bedrooms—there was what appeared to be a cut in the floorboard. After some prying, pulling, and tearing apart at the floorboard, they came to another doorway. It was about the right size for a hobbit, Conner said.

Sa'id, on one hand, was philosophically out to lunch with his jihadist holy war terrorism for all things Western while, on the other hand, he was pretty savvy about safekeeping his household goods. Imbedded in the door was a pretty secure combination lock.

"How are you at picking a combination lock?" Clyde asked.

"I am really good," Conner said. He pulled out what looked like a can of WD-40, and he sprayed the lock. Clyde knew that he was freezing it. Conner took a sledgehammer, and the combo lock exploded after one roundhouse swing.

"You might have some aggression issues," Clyde said after he watched Conner swing that hammer.

"This is my big boy hammer," Conner said. Clyde agreed that he wouldn't want to be on the receiving end of that bad boy.

The door came open after the two of them pulled on each end until they had just about turned blue. It finally creaked and groaned and then swung open and revealed a staircase going down into the ground. Clyde grabbed the light, started down the steps cautiously, and found himself at the front end of a long narrow tunnel.

Conner and Clyde crawled through the tunnel for about two hundred feet and came to another door. This one had a good-size single-key lock on it. Conner, to Clyde's surprise, pulled out a key and inserted it into the lock. Clyde looked at Conner with a "Wherein heavens did you get that key?" kind of look.

Conner said, "I was the first one to the body when Sa'id fell, and he had it on a chain around his neck. I didn't think the US military would have need of it, so I grabbed it for safekeeping."

"On behalf of the United States Marines, I, for one, salute you for your service to the country and saving them all that trouble," Clyde remarked sarcastically. "Imagine the quandary they would have been in. What do we do with this key around his neck?"

It is possible that this anti-American radical may have a vast load of treasure lying somewhere unnamed on planet Earth, Clyde thought.

"Yeah," Conner said. "Which trash can does it go in would have been the only serious question they would have pondered."

The lock opened underneath his hand, and then Conner pulled the door open. They were looking at a storehouse of weapons, C4, computer equipment, and what looked like a pre-revolutionary war chest. It was all hand carved, with large metal bands or straps around it and a latch on it, but it was, to their surprise, unlocked. It was full of coins. They looked like they could be eight or nine hundred years old.

"Strike me with lightning, and hit me over the head with a pot of gold." Conner laughed.

"Or, in this case," Clyde said, "with an ancient wooden treasure box full of rare coins."

"He shouldn't have tried to escape," Conner said. "I think he would have negotiated a better deal than his parents did. But we paid enough for the chance, and we have come up all sevens on this spin."

"Well," Clyde said, "what do you want to do? Pack it out of here and declare it in customs? Or should we come back and just take these out in stealth mode and fly under the radar of the current Egyptian regime?"

"Which, by the way, do they have a regime at this moment?" Conner asked. "It has been a little crazy in this country over the last few years, and I don't know who will stop us and what will be on their agenda. But in order to get them out of Kafr Jallu and Egypt undetected, we might need some more time."

They decided to put everything back in place, and they took two coins each from the chest.

"At least we will not doubt what we have after some years," Conner said as he began to think the event might be more of a fantasy.

"It is hard to believe, and I am standing here," Clyde said.

So they locked the room up and crawled back through the tunnel. They went up the steps, shut the door firmly, and Conner put a padlock on it.

"Not as good as the combo lock, but unless you have the right chemical agent—which, of course, they didn't sell at the local home improvement store—you will probably not try to go through this," Conner sort of mused out loud.

"What about the weapons, the explosives, and the equipment, now that we own the property?" Clyde asked.

"That is a risk, Clyde, but I can come back after our tour of duty and get some of these unsavory items out," Conner said. "I might even begin to have some collectors start looking at our newfound assets while I am at it."

So they boarded up the house and staggered wearily back to the car. On the trip back to Alexandria, where they were hoping for a good meal and a shower, Clyde said two things that would stick with him for a long time. The first was when he was just chatting with Conner. "I am starving. Where can we go in this huge town to get a really good meal? I don't need fine dining, I need good eating. I am starving. Not like a Ruth's Chris kind of hungry or Morton's, but more like a 'Mom and Pop, feed me till I burst, and charge me reasonable.'"

Clyde carried on with his soliloquy. "I am in Alexandria, and I just need to know the three best places to eat. Let's start with, first, when I am starving and, second, when I want to go on a date with my wife—"

"Or just a date," Conner interrupted.

"And finally," Clyde went on, "the last place I need to eat is when I need to feed my family. Could someone please tell me that?"

"It would be useful information," Conner said.

The other item that was noteworthy was that as Clyde was looking at the coin, he thought it might be from, like, India in the ninth or tenth century.

"I am not even going to ask you how you know that," Conner said begrudgingly.

"I think that from the inscription it looks like Sanskrit before any Muslim influence in the twelfth century," Clyde said. "I think it is a picture of one of their early temples before the invasion of Mohammed of Ghor."

"You know," Conner said, "I didn't ask, and you didn't have to tell me. I was going to take it at face value."

"I wonder what a twelve-hundred-year-old coin is worth," Clyde said.

After they got back to Alexandria, Clyde had given his coins to Conner because he had his leave coming up first, and then he could start to do some research in that part of the world.

Might be helpful, Clyde thought. At the moment, he was really ready to get back to his wife and growing family.

Who knows, Clyde thought. It had been four years since that trip to Egypt, and he probably had lost the coins to some pirate. He was pretty well aware of the development that went on in the city because he read the publications from their city building and safety departments on the Internet. It was rough reading Arabic, but he could get by. So by any stretch of the imagination, this, of course, was a long shot. He probably had better odds playing the lottery.

He could hear his dad this very second: "Egypt! Coins! Explosives! Clyde, this isn't going to go well for you."

No, his dad was right. No dad would listen to such nonsense. It wasn't reasonable. This was the kind of thing to actually just do and then ask for forgiveness later. It was a whole lot easier to say, "I am sorry I didn't tell you when you are sitting on a hundred thousand in coins that you nearly gave your life in securing." He would need another reason to go out of the country.

Actually, Clyde was not well versed in coins. He thought they looked old, but it was Conner who felt like the stash was actually valuable. Conner had said that while he knew most of the coins were, in fact, Spanish and probably dating back to the Ferdinand and Elizabeth dynasty, he also thought in a few of the subsequent conversations that they had had about the coins that Clyde was right, and there were some older coins from India.

TIME FOR A COOL CHANGE
PHONE INTERRUPTION

A s C LYDE SAT waiting for the train, his cell phone rang. He did not recognize the number, and he really was not in a real talkative mood. He reached down to hit the end button, but his knuckle hit the screen, and he inadvertently answered the phone. Oh, those blasted phones were far too sensitive. What happened to the good old days when you had to open your cell phones first? What was that like? It must have been at least two years ago or something.

He could faintly hear a woman's voice on the speaker, saying, "Hello? This is…"

He couldn't quite hear the name but was embarrassed to hang up the phone. "Good morning, this is Clyde."

The caller was Anna something, and she was too awfully happy this morning. "Thank you for taking my call. It is a pleasure to speak with you."

Clyde was waiting for the sales pitch. He was about ready to say, "No, thank you, I don't need the newspaper" or "I already give to my church, but I wish you luck in your fundraising efforts."

But to his astonishment, she said, "I am a reporter for the *New York Times*, and I do a food column every week, and this week I am going to do a spotlight for Channel 6 news, and I am going to critique local restaurants, and I was hoping to get your expertise analysis."

Clyde thought she better take a breath. "Okay, wait a minute," Clyde said quickly. "I know you actually liked our restaurant, but you misquoted me saying food is the love of my life."

Before he could get in another word, Anna defended herself, saying, "Well, you did say food was the love of your life."

In mock seriousness, Clyde retorted, "You forgot my preface! So you are going to do critiques on camera? You must be really moving to the big time. You would like me to give my opinions as well? You must be crazier than I thought."

"Let me answer your questions," Anna replied. "Funny, I thought I was the one doing the interview. This is the first opportunity I have had to take my column on the air, and yes, I am a little nervous and, for that matter, giddy. But it will take the same format as her column, only on TV. It was a real shot for her."

She went on to say that she really wanted Clyde to come down to the studio to do an on-air interview. "The column I wrote about Del Sol was probably the most widely read from what our analysts say, so I figured that you might be the first candidate to go on the air."

Anna, who spoke perfect English, had said her last name was CiFuentes, which she said with an accent. She asked if he was busy this afternoon.

Clyde, in a moment of transparency, said that obviously time was one of the things he had a lot of. Anna, being a reporter, and having that lead shoved in her lap, did not pass it up. The tone of her voice dropped lower as she got serious and with true sincerity asked about Del Sol. Her follow-up comment regarding the irony of one of the best new restaurants in the city going out of business led Clyde to talk.

"I really can't explain it all," he said. "I was just back there this morning, signing over some of the final papers. I guess I didn't realize that we had a lease backed by significant capital, and when that large chunk of money was removed, we immediately lost the lease. My argument was that the restaurant didn't need the capital, that we could handle the lease on our own, obviously since the cash flow had proven itself out over the two years, but they were concerned that without that safety net and with my 'growing responsibilities' it would undoubtedly hurt the product. They said that I was only one guy and I had lost my most valuable asset."

Clyde was trying to talk, but it became apparent in the conversation, as the tears ran down his cheeks, that he was really choked up. He cleared his throat and sniffed away from the phone and then came back, saying he was sorry. He went on to recount that without the lease, they would have to move the restaurant, and that was when he found out that part of the startup costs had gone into the equipment and Mr. Walls was going to sell that at auction to recoup some of his investment money.

As Clyde spoke, he remembered a conversation he had with Charles regarding that very issue and that Charles had said that the equipment was on a two-year lease and the balloon payment at the end was to be paid from the cash proceeds, yet Clyde felt for sure that there would have been enough money.

Anna replied in the same questioning fashion with the same sentiments. "It would seem to me that the restaurant was successful enough to generate an equipment balloon payment. That equipment loses most of its value in the first two years, anyway."

Anna smelled a story. It was instinctive in her training. She could hear Professor Moreno saying, "Read between the lines. You have to follow your feelings. People only tell you half the story, or they are spinning it to give you part of the story." But as she heard what Clyde was saying and read between the lines as well, she realized that even some of the really smart good guys can be trusting. The other thing, for the moment, was that she had a bigger fish to fry. She had one of the best chefs in the industry, a true rising star, on the line, and she wanted to interview him today.

Anna said to Clyde that she really appreciated his candor and was wondering if 1:00 in Studio 5 on Central would be okay. She said that it would be better if he hadn't eaten a big lunch because they were going to taste several dishes from two restaurants and he might get his fill. Clyde said that was okay because he had spent his last few dollars on an espresso, and he was going to eat light by design. Anna thought that for one who had been through total turmoil, he was in pretty good humor. Clyde said that he was happy to do it. It was such short notice that he must have been the pinch hitter, and he said as much to Anna. Anna relayed the story to him about her having an alternative plan, but she was really the pinch hitter for Channel 6. They were supposed to run a series of stories on searching for hidden treasure for their lifestyle segment, and it was being preempted for lack of really anything interesting. Clyde was about to comment on the irony of the situation but held his tongue—not literally, of course, because he had the phone in one hand and the espresso in the other.

GRAND ILLUSION

IT WAS JUST a simple gesture of kindness. Three months before that desperate scene on a New York street corner, Laina had run into Karen on her way to the dentist to deal with an emergency dental problem. She was in Italy, back for a quick trip to see her youngest sibling graduate from college. He was fifteen years her junior, but he was her baby brother, and she was so proud of him. He had graduated with a double degree in psychology and economics. He had very diverse tastes and had really done well and enjoyed the university atmosphere. He was close to his oldest sister because she had spent a lot of years taking care of him. When she was fifteen, she was old enough to watch him, and she had done it regularly for five years.

While she and Clyde were first married, her brother had been a regular part of their lives, and it was often in the beginning that she would stay at home with her parents because Clyde was on tour with the military. She couldn't miss his graduation, so she had jumped back on a late-night red eye to Palermo and was just staying for a few days. The graduation had come and gone, and she had just gone into town shopping with her twin sisters. It turned out that her sisters were going to catch another ride home because she had to deal with an emergency dental issue. At the moment, they were at a store in the fashion district when she had gotten lost looking for the restroom and had inadvertently walked into the warehouse back room, the place with a lot of boxes.

Laina was just turning back around when she stopped cold. Charles Walls's number two guy was meeting someone. Who was that other man? She knew him because Clyde had mentioned that he was an international war lord, drug lord, Mafia-style thug. She couldn't ever forget the name Kjarstifatyupol, with the *k* silent, like most Thai names. Why would Fritz Reckonboeder be meeting with this known criminal? She was going to bolt, knowing that vanishing in thin air was out of the question. But she froze for just a split second.

That hesitation forced Fritz to look directly at her.

Laina knew at that moment she had been recognized, and while any other time it would have been perfectly normal to say hi to her friend Fritz, it was if a cold wave of reality had just washed over her. In the span of 2.9 seconds a piece of the puzzle fell into place. The tumblers spun in her head, and the lock clicked open, and the thought imprisoned inside was free, and it said that Charles was in league with a lot of bad people and was, for whatever reason, in negotiations with the likes of Kjarstifatyupol, and it all spelled third-world collusion. Charles was not in pursuit of what most of these guys offered in the way of financial remuneration; he was after some other avenue of destruction.

How did she know that? What was it that told her deep in her soul that Charles was all about pure and utter destruction? Clyde had always said that Charles was behind some big and dark secrets and that he was just the type of human being to want to gather ultimate power and seek vengeance on all the people who have forced him into his loneliness, his seemingly constant battle with working to create the next product. Thousands of scenes over the years fell into place, and Laina knew that for all those years, she couldn't put her finger on what it was about Charles Walls. It had all just unfolded before her like a fuzzy or garbled TV picture that had just become crystal clear.

And in the very same moment, she also knew thoroughly that her life was now in danger. She thought of calling Clyde and discussing it with him, but she knew that her phone lines would be tapped and all access to New York would be somehow watched and or blocked. Charles was the type to hate and to know exactly what to do her family. This was an issue to big to come to the surface, and whatever it was that Charles was involved with would blow a long and well-planned cover-up. She was in real trouble—deep trouble.

STRANGE MAGIC

AS CLYDE GOT on the train to leave the city, he said good-bye and hung up as the train proceeded in the opposite direction. He dialed back Anna from his cell and got a voice mail. He really had no idea what to wear. He couldn't make it back to his folks where he had been staying and had put on some jeans from this morning, a T-shirt, his leather flying jacket, and a baseball cap. He needed a quick shower, a new shirt, a tweed coat, and a haircut and a shave. He jumped off the train at the next exit and walked one block to the gym. The great thing about New York City was everything was on top of each other. The worst thing about New York City was that everyone and everything was piled on top of each other. But in the moment, it worked to his advantage.

He stole a quick glance at his watch. Man, he loved that Navy Seal dive watch. They were a great group of guys to have on your side, and they put their name on a great timepiece. It showed exactly eleven o'clock. This gave him enough time to run into the barber, shoot next door and grab some clothes, and shower at the gym. Lorenzo would set him up with the right attire. He had been begging Clyde to come down and get an outfit. He woulda really a appreciate ifa he coulda come and getta some of his outrageous newa stuff. He could hear the man now. How would Lorenzo feel ifa his a newa stuffa was a going to be on TV? Clyde loved to speak to the man in Italian and cracked up when he wanted to be heard by all, so he spoke his broken English. Wasn't that America, though, people from everywhere getting a new start on life? It was the only place, after all, that had the American dream.

Clyde, you are an incurable romantic, he thought. *You have just lost your shirt, and now you're blubbering about some other guy who you're hoping will loan you another one.*

As he hopped up the steps two at a time to street level, he had pulled out Lorenzo's business card from his wallet in his jacket and had accidently fumbled with the card, and as he reached down for the card, he shot a backward glance and saw a guy in the same khaki trousers with saddle shoes that he had seen in the plaza outside the café.

Strange that he would be followed. Who cares what he is doing? He hadn't been on a mission with the unit in almost three years. Who wants to follow a guy without a shirt? There has got to be important guys to follow who actually know what they were doing. Clyde wasn't born yesterday, though, and this guy was bad at what he was doing, which means he was probably just a private detective and was on an hourly dime. Well, no use to have him in all his business.

Clyde picked up his speed, made a quick right at the top of the stairs, headed down the street, picked an alleyway between the first two buildings, and then ducked down a private flight of steps that led to someone's basement. He hid there for a moment, heard some feet shuffle past the alley, and was glad he had yet to shower as this person's trash can was here, and now he smelled like last night's dinner. Back up the steps, back out the alley, a quick left past the train entrance and up the street, where he made an immediate left down a very busy street and jaywalked in front of all the cars and heard the cabbies yelling at him in multiple languages "May your mother put rocks in your turkey-day Thanksgiving-chicken-and-dumplings feast."

Clyde loved being able to speak Arabic. These guys were cursing him in run-on idioms. He should stop and write a book about what he heard that people didn't know he understood. Across the street, and he walked into the barber. Fortunately, at eleven fifteen, no one was waiting for a cut. He grabbed the nearest chair and said, "Trim it up, and give me a shave."

"Yes, sir," the barber said.

"I will take a wash since it has been under my hat all morning," Clyde said. He loved his Jets cap. Too bad they couldn't win a game, but he still pulled for them, nevertheless. He loved the name of football for a game you played with your hands. He should try out and kick for those guys, although the oblong ball was so different than a round one.

The haircut was fast. Clyde had dialed Lorenzo and put him on alert about the clothes, so he paid for the haircut with his Del Sol American Express. He would enjoy the accountant asking him about that. He walked out of the barber and over to his fitness club. He hadn't lifted weights in two days. He couldn't stop his early-morning regimen of sit-ups, push-ups, and the Stairmaster. He thought it would be a good idea to start rowing again. He loved to row, though, and didn't have much competition for the machines. He sat down for a quick ten-minute workout after he put on some shorts. The room was quiet, except for the TV in the corner.

Clyde walked over and found the soccer channel, and it was a rerun of the Chelsea vs. Barcelona champion's league final.

Oh, what a game, he thought.

Chelsea, down by three goals, came back to get the equalizer in the eighty-ninth minute, only to give up a Pique to Iniesta to Messi attack that ended in a cross to Henry, which, in French, was pronounced *On-ree*. Clyde was breathing pretty hard in a quick span of ten minutes and could barely pull himself away from the rerun, and he finally headed for the showers. He made a quick left and headed for the elevator. They had a track on the roof. He knew he needed to run. Eight laps was a mile, and at forty seconds a lap, he did the mile in five minutes and twenty seconds. He knew he needed to run a little more because he was breathing hard. His best time in the mile was four minutes and fifteen seconds. It was not world-class time, but it was very helpful in his former line of work.

Making his way down the stairs, he wondered if Saddle Shoes knew about his gym. There was nothing like a haircut and a shower to make a man feel like a million bucks. A little gel and some aftershave and a quick glance at the hairline—still there and yet no gray.

I am okay for thirty-six, he thought. *Don't look a day older than thirty-five.*

Lorenzo was thrilled to see him. He gave him a bear hug that was going to squeeze the mascarpone cheese right out of him. But he was thrilled to get some clothes. Lorenzo had picked out four outfits for him. Clyde said that he just needed one set for today, and Lorenzo looked like he was about to cry, so Clyde quickly added that if it was okay, could he hold the other three and he would be back after the taping and pick them up. Lorenzo was thrilled.

Clyde asked Lorenzo how much he owed him, and again that same look of sadness crept into his eyes. And then Lorenzo burst into laughter and said, "No worries, I already charged your account."

Clyde didn't know he had an account with Lorenzo, so he went along with it and said, "Do you have my new address since Del Sol has closed?"

"The way you cook, it doesn't matter if you work in a Denny's," Lorenzo said. "I will find you and eat your food. Just let me know where you land. I can't get real authentica Italiano food anywhere in the city like yourza."

Leaving, Clyde thought, *Is it my city or my food in this city?* But he knew what he meant. What did his pastor always say? "Context. You have to understand the context."

His context had taken a huge turn. He was down in the dumps this morning with a situational hangover, and now he was going to go on be on the air. Only one million people or so were going to see this spot. Fortunately the camera could not look into the big gaping hole in the middle of his soul. If it could, it would see a lifetime of memories gone with the passing of his sweet Laina and the Herculean effort to start a restaurant in this huge metropolis, all gone in a New York minute. It felt like the buildings were burning down all around him and he was stuck in the middle.

Clyde turned down the street and entered the building that housed Channel 6. It was not hard to find. He headed for the elevator after giving the doorman the correct information. As he waited for the doors to open, he looked at his reflection, and a thought from Conner's recent text message flashed through his mind: "You lost a spouse and it tore a hole in your soul because of the love you had for each other. Think of how many people out there are toiling in loveless marriages that would give their left arm for one night of what you shared for twenty years."

NOBODY KNOWS
THE TROUBLE I HAVE

L AINA DARTED OUT of the warehouse, and she actually didn't know where to turn.

I will just go on with my day as planned, and I will have to think and pray and get a plan, she thought. *I can't go home, I can't go to friends, I can't go into hiding. That is it, hiding. But where?*

Just then she heard, "Laina, what are you doing?"

That was a pretty poor translation of the Italian phrase, because it really meant not just at the moment but also what has been going on, and now, what are you doing? Laina forgot her thoughts for the moment and lost herself in her long-lost pal whom she had been friends with for years.

"Karen, what are you doing in Italy?" Laina asked. "I thought your family had relocated in South America with your father's business?"

"Yes, it is true we were there for five years," Karen said. "And when I was done with school, I came back here."

As Laina stood there, she realized that while Karen was probably the same age as her, all of thirty-five, she looked pretty worn-out and tired, maybe more like fifty. Nothing wrong with fifty, of course, but when you are actually still in your thirties…

The thought just kind of fluttered through Laina's mind, and then she asked if Karen was hungry and would like to get a bite and they could talk. Karen was thrilled. She was beyond worrying about how to pay, and she was just thrilled to catch up with Laina.

They sat down in a semiquiet little restaurant—more like a deli with tables—and the waitress came to them. They ordered a bite, although Karen ordered a piece of lasagna ala carte and an espresso. Laina, who explained that she was on her way to the dentist to deal with an emergency crown issue, just had coffee. She liked it with cream and sugar, something she had come to appreciate from Clyde.

Laina was absorbed in her conversation with Karen, who had married against her father's wishes and it hadn't gone well. Karen had moved back to Italy with her husband, and he was not what he had made himself out to be during their dating days. He had left her after five years, and Karen had not done well. She was out of money; she didn't have any real skills and had a little more than trouble with substance abuse. How Laina had gotten all of this out of her in fifteen minutes was a little amazing.

Karen had been in jail and was actually living on the streets. Laina understood, and it became clear to her what that her initial reaction was correct. This was a hard life. Laina reached out to Karen and grabbed her hand and asked what she could do to help. Karen said that she had a cousin who lived just outside of town and had been asking her to come live with them. She really hadn't wanted to impose on him and his young family and bring her troubles to them, but they had really asked her if she would at least come over and talk with them. Karen asked if Laina could take the drive with her. Laina knew that this was a really big step for someone who had reached this level of society. Laina said that she would be thrilled. Laina also remembered that one of the churches in this area was going to have a giant secondhand sale in the morning.

"Karen," Laina said, "the Bible Church of Palermo is going to have a big, huge sale tomorrow. I have seen what they are selling, and there are terrific secondhand items and some very nice clothes. Would you be interested in going over there and seeing what they have?"

After a bit of hesitation and cajoling by Laina and a promise that she would call the pastor's assistant and she would be expecting her, Karen actually smiled for the first time and thought this was a good idea. She asked if she could pay the church back.

"Don't worry about it," Laina said. "Karen, can you drive?"

Karen said that of course she could drive. Her license was expired, but she still remembered how to get in a car, turn it on, reverse out of the driveway, and move forward into the street.

"Not a big deal!" she exclaimed, like a teenager getting a new iPod.

"Look, I have to go across the street and see my dentist," Laina said. "Here are the keys, and the car is in the garage around the corner. It is the first garage at Antilles parking. Give him this ticket, and he will show you to the car. Tell him you are a friend, and he can call me if he needs to. Take the car, and go to Avenue DelaReche, and follow it out of town till you come to Guillermo's farm. It isn't far and in the front of the house they are setting up for the sale. Talk with Angelina, and she will show you around. I will be done in about two hours, so take your time. We can talk then, and I will drive you out to your cousins."

Karen walked out of the café and down the street. Laina looked at her watch and finished her coffee. She had a couple of minutes. All right, back to her trouble.

I will go to the dentist as normal and then drive Karen to her cousins, she thought. *And then I will keep going. I will drive up north to Milan and then catch the train, probably to Moscow. Oh, there is a lot to think about.* She just knew that she was in danger. This was a real problem.

She got up and paid her bill and walked out and crossed the street. She had just walked into the area preceding the hallway to go the office for her dental emergency, and she turned to see her car going by. Karen looked competent and fine driving an automobile.

It is really like riding a bike, Laina thought. *We all learn the skill and then never forget it.*

She saw Karen brake for a pedestrian. Laina thought it was kind of unusual for a man to cross right in front of a car, and then she absorbed the fact that Karen was going to miss the light and was now waiting at the intersection. A moment later, as Laina started to turn, she heard a terrible explosion. She turned back in horror as she saw her car in a ball of fire, which was now heading up into the air. Not her car, per se, but the ball of fire. She could actually feel the heat a half block away. She started to scream but then stopped. With a sudden wave of cold reality streaming through her, she realized—but how so quickly—this was meant to be her. Nobody knew Karen. Cars don't just explode. Explode nothing. That car was virtually gone. Nothing even landed in that spot.

There is nothing, Laina thought. *Nobody will know. They can't even identify the car.*

Just then she remembered her old bridge with the crown, sitting in a box. Somebody might find it and think it was her by the dental record.

"Oh, Lord," she prayed. "I can't worry about my tooth. I have to get out the country, the world, the planet and hide somewhere, but I am going to need a little help with my departure."

LIMELIGHT

THE SET WAS incredible. Everything was laid out to the nines. Clyde's life had been completely flipped upside down in half a day.

Okay, spanky, cool your jets, he thought. *This is a onetime unpaid interview.*

At best, it was a little promotional event that might solidify a new job with the owner of a very chic upscale New York restaurant. It did not hurt that a five-foot-ten blonde was walking straight at him. She was breathtaking and had a smile to light up the entire room. Too bad she was not a day over twenty-five.

"Hi, I am Anna," she said.

Clyde looked questioningly at her. "CiFuentes?"

She immediately started cracking up. "Oh, you are pretty fast." She then added that her family was from Argentina and a lot of people were very light skinned in the Hispanic culture. "Please come with me. We have a lot to cover. Since you don't have an agent present, we have to do things a certain way, or we can be in legal hot water."

As they made their way over to a set of offices offstage, Anna said, "We can go over this human resource stuff, and then we will talk with the producers in the storyboard room, and we will shoot live at 2:00."

Clyde froze. "What do you mean live? We are not taping this and then you edit it, put in the music, etc., etc., and only keep the good stuff or, in my case, semigood stuff?"

"Nope," Anna replied immediately. "The whole world will see exactly who you are and what you are going to say."

"Well, that puts me at ease," Clyde said.

As they approached one of the offices that said Payroll, Clyde got a funny feeling. They pushed through the door and met with a guy who looked like a lineman for the Jets. Clyde shook Samuel's hand and asked if it would be okay if he called him sir. The big bean counter laughed and said that accounting was his second profession, after he blew his knee out at Ohio State.

Anna had excused herself. Samuel went on, "I tried out for the Packers, but my knee was not going to allow me to take the punishment. This was a standard first-time contract. It was regulated by SAG and that it would be a onetime payment, unless it was going to be shown in other paying shows, or syndicated, but since this was live, it probably wouldn't get picked up and or used around the country."

They will probably just burn it in the dumpster, Clyde thought.

Samuel said that from time to time, another network or cable station might pick it up and make it part of their show and then they had to negotiate that pay scale with him.

"Look, I am happy to do this for free," Clyde said. So whatever they were going to pay him was fantastic, it was really his honor."

Samuel said that he hoped Clyde's cooking was better than his negotiating skills, but his honesty made this actually pretty simple. They were going to pay him twenty-five hundred for the live spot, and that was really on the lower end, but it was his first time and all. Clyde picked up the pen before Samuel had finished and signed the paperwork. Clyde chatted with Samuel for another minute and then shook his hand as they parted, and Clyde meandered a little bit out in the hallway. He watched as the afternoon news anchors were doing their reporting. They were so natural in front of the camera. It was almost as if the gray-black gun with a light on it was not even there. Yet it was there because they would look straight into it.

Clyde turned as he heard Anna call out his name, and she motioned for him to follow her. They walked into another room just offstage, and now he could see all of the food being set up so it was ready to be brought right into the studio. Clyde forgot how hungry he was as the smells hit him like a wave.

Clyde and Anna walked over, and before Anna could say anything, Jacob Otealy said, "Clyde, it is so good to see you, and I was very sorry to hear about Del Sol."

Clyde genuinely appreciated the sentiment and told him so, and Jacob looked at him and said in his very South African accent, "Clyde, there is more than meets the eye to this whole business, because in my experience, successful restaurants are rare and they are not hard to recapitalize when the cash flow is very strong."

Anna knew it. She had sensed it earlier, and now Jacob was confirming it. Clyde looked at her, thinking that she looked like a lion ready to pounce on her prey.

Anna relaxed and smiled at him. "Okay, we go on in thirty-five minutes, so let's stay at the task at hand. Let me introduce you to our producer, Nina Pearson. She will walk us through the segment."

For the next fifteen minutes, Clyde listened as everything was laid out for him. They were going to spotlight Jacob's for ten minutes, and then they were going to deal with MKEA. The locals pronounced it *Makea*, with a long *a*. It was Hawaiian, and nobody really knew how to say the name or what the initials stood for, but it did not matter. They had a great gig going on. The fresh-roasted Hawaiian-style pork cooked right in the banana leaves in the center of the restaurant was a show in itself. The food was always so good. They had probably the best fish in New York and a sushi bar as well. Clyde had never seen the restaurant empty even at two in the morning.

Clyde's role was simple: he was going to taste the food that the owners presented as Anna talked and walked them through it, and then they were to look to him for analysis.

"So in reality, I am the color commentary," Clyde quipped. "Like on a football game, Jacob makes the play, as Anna calls it, and then I taste the food and give some insight into what Jacob has prepared."

Anna said the point was to lend third-party credence to what Jacob was saying, and that was really the hook on this segment."

"What if it is not very good?" Clyde said. "No offense to you, Jacob, just a question."

Jacob laughed, saying, "I would need a new chef, if that is the case."

Anna looked straight at Clyde. "You are to give your honest opinion. It really would not be authentic if we were saying it is wonderful just for the show. I believe people really want to know. Clyde made the comment, kind of like, 'This is a great restaurant, and mostly everything is delicious, but don't dare order the fillet of soul.'"

Napa, as they called the producer, said, "I think that is good camera. Clyde, have you ever been on camera before?"

Clyde said that in the military he actually had to do all his mission-complete briefings on tape, and then they would watch and critique the film. In truth, he had seen hours of his reports on video or on the computer in an MPEG file.

"Okay, then just do the same thing," Nina said. "Taste the food even while Anna and Jacob are discussing it, and then give us a report."

They finished going through the final rehearsal, and then they were called to the green room. Final touches were made on each person's wardrobe and makeup, and the wardrobe consultant asked Clyde where he got the terrific tweed coat. He told her, adding, "You have just made my friend's day." Then they just casually walked out onto the studio.

Anna, whom Clyde knew was nervous, was void of thought the minute before the camera went on. They were seated on a sort of stool-height low-back chairs, and then he heard someone say, "Thirty seconds, and we're live." He could see from the monitors that they were on a commercial.

Why on earth did I ever agree to this? he thought to himself. As he heard them say "Ten, nine..." he glanced over at Anna as she was just lifting her head up, as though she had been praying.

Now there is a good idea, Clyde thought. *I could use some prayers right now.*

Well, it was too late because just then, the lights came on for Anna; as soon as the camera went red, she looked straight into it and welcomed everyone to the first segment of the *Cities' Upper Crust*. "I am delighted to bring before you two restaurants that have been featured in the newspaper version of *Upper Crust*, and the feedback from my readers was so dramatic we thought we would bring these two restaurants to you first. I have Jacob O'Tealy with me today who owns Jacob's, which is one of the finest long-standing restaurants in the city, featuring mostly American cuisine. And I have also with me Peter Ono from MKEA, which we all pronounce *Make-A*. We might talk about the name a little if we have some time, but we really want to talk about the food.

"As we discuss those two restaurants, I have also with us, to provide some professional analysis long-time international food connoisseur and chef, Clyde Gareen. How are you doing today?" Anna asked with a twinkle in her eye and a big smile on her face.

Clyde felt for a second that she was almost taunting him with all that was really going on, but he smiled right back and said, "I honestly could not be more excited to taste this very aromatic food." His hand waved back and forth to signify the smells. "And since no one would let me eat today, it lends to all the more anticipation."

Everyone in the audience laughed. This almost threw Clyde for a loop, the magic of television; somehow, they had transformed the newsroom studio into a live theater, if you will. Obviously not that big of a deal stagewise because the whole set of the news team pulls off on rollers, but where did the crowd come from? Somebody must have been out on the streets bringing in a crowd of people, offering them who knows what, but it made an entirely different atmosphere altogether.

For a person trained in supposedly seeing the finer details in a given situation, he had missed the elephant in the room on this one. It just goes to show you that when the mind is focused on an entirely different set of circumstances, you can miss five hundred people in a live television audience. Anna, who was really a natural despite the limited time in front of the camera, had a great series of very quick questions for Jacob first. As they sampled the dishes, Jacob was explaining what they were eating and how he had prepared it. Obviously it was a little bit of a setup because this was a very popular restaurant in Manhattan.

Clyde, who was completely absorbed in the food and the conversation, utterly forgot about the camera. He was able to talk expertly with Jacob on some of the exotic spices on the rub of his pork ribs, and as they started for another dish, Clyde asked if he could get a "dozen of these to go." Clyde, not realizing it once again, had brought down the house. From Jacob's food, they brought out the owner of MKEA and discussed the marvelous array of food that Peter Ono had prepared. What Clyde thought was the very best dish was the mahi-mahi. This fish was lightly pan seared and had an organic honey-and-citrus glaze over crusted pecans.

Clyde said that it was amazing how fresh the tuna tasted and how the texture was firm yet flakey and melted in his mouth. There was no hiding the ingredients of the glaze on the fish either, and Peter quipped for an Italian master, he wasn't missing any of the finer points of his recipe. Clyde said the truth was that he had tasted this dish at the restaurant and wasn't nearly as impressed as he was at the moment.

Peter didn't miss a beat. "You taught me that if the dish doesn't work, recreate it, and I did."

Clyde said to everyone's delight, "Recreate it nothing. Peter, you have resurrected this one, and it is now a heavenly meal."

What Anna was getting couldn't have been scripted any better. The shooting of the show went fantastic. They had taken a couple of questions from the home audience watching it live, and the response was overwhelming. Clyde was, without question, an instantaneous hit. The show was immediately picked up by the Food Network and run nationally that evening. Anna was fantastic on the screen—charming and natural, and an excellent journalist—but Clyde was charismatic, and his natural authentic style made you want to listen to what he was saying. It didn't hurt that, of course, he loved cooking, loved eating, and was an expert at providing insight into the subject matter.

Clyde sat down after the shoot and had a ginger ale. Laina said it was too sweet, but Clyde had liked it since he was ten, and it had never left. Lots of his friends had moved onto adult beverages, and many of his churchgoing brothers were big on diet Coke and iced tea, but ginger ale, very dry and strong, was his drink.

As he sat down and chatted with Anna, the president of Channel 6 television Charles Seger (*No relation to Bob or to my old enemy Charles Walls*, Clyde thought) came over and asked if he could talk with the two of them.

"Quite frankly, I don't do this myself, and never after one taping," he said. "But that may have been the most energetic and delightful talk show they had done in years. Both of you are really good. You both have very good careers in front of you if you want to pursue more television. But together, there is really quite good chemistry. Rupert from production, who you know, Anna, put this segment together, tells me that the two of you have never actually met."

Clyde said that he had read Anna's column almost every week.

"Well, that is funny," Anna said. "I have been to the restaurant and had seen Clyde, but we had never actually met." She had called Laina and tried to get interviews with Clyde, but for some reason, that had never materialized.

Mr. Seger actually laughed out loud at that comment, and Clyde felt like he had missed something, but then Charles—who was probably in his early fifties, with a shock of white hair—said, "Anna, if you were trying to interview me and you were asking my wife's permission, I can see her stonewalling you as well."

Charles, who asked to be called Chuck, went on, "If you two can find it in your schedule tomorrow, I would like to take you two to lunch in our executive dining room downstairs and discuss and idea I have." He looked at Clyde and thought, *What on earth am I thinking?*

Charles spoke aloud. "Why don't we have lunch at Bonaparte's on the water at 1:00? And if you will indulge me, I would like to share this concept I have of a new show. I need both an expert and a journalist for it, and I think you guys would be terrific."

The look on Clyde's face must have spoken a million words. *He was thinking, Mr. Seger, you have got to be kidding. I am a run-down guy without a shirt—well, in a borrowed shirt on a credit card I am not sure how to pay for yet—and I am hoping not to be homeless in the next few weeks*—this thought was more ironic than Clyde could ever imagine—*and you, of all people, want to talk to me, have lunch with me, discuss an idea with me.*

Although he hadn't said any of that to Chuck, before the words could materialize, Chuck Seger let a brief sigh. "Look, I realize you think I am dropping a bombshell on you, but if you would just say yes to lunch, we could put all the cards on the table tomorrow, so to speak, and you may speak freely and ask any question you like. Trust me, though, you will like the figures we will be using, and I am not speaking of waistlines either."

I have been around a lot of dignitaries in my time, but this is a very compelling man, Clyde thought. *I might take on one hundred guys in the middle of an Iraqi desert with nothing but a pistol if he asked me to.*

Clyde looked at Anna with smiling eyes and said, "I think I can arrange my schedule for 1:00."

Anna—trying to hold back the big, huge happy face as she was being shown through the biggest open door of her short four-year—well, almost five—career, said she would be there, no problem. After Mr. Seger had left, Anna looked at Clyde and started to speak, but there were no words. She reached out inadvertently and grabbed Clyde's hand, and her eyes were welling up with tears.

Then she said in Spanish, "Es muy grande tiempo por mi vida." (This is the biggest moment in my life.)

Clyde was really blown away at the sincerity of this beautiful, articulate young lady and her willingness to be transparent with him. He put his arm around her. "Anna, you are going to have mas tiempo grande en su vida. Believe me, it is la verdad." That means "It is the truth."

She looked at him with a little suspicious eye and wondered how good his Spanish was because he rolled his *R*s perfectly and didn't sound like a white guy speaking Español.

"Look, it is almost four," Clyde said. "And my mom is picking up my kids, and we are having dinner together at their place outside the city, so I need to get a move on."

"Of course," Anna said. She wanted to ask a thousand questions but simply said, "How old are your children?"

Clyde hesitated, because he heard the reaction a thousand times. "My children's ages are nine, seven, five, and Josephine is six months old." He was waiting for the gasp and the "You have four children" comment; it was inevitable.

Anna smiled. "It is obvious you are very blessed."

"I didn't anticipate that reaction," Clyde admitted. "Most people can't believe in today's world I would have four children."

Anna looked at him, stuck out her hand, and said, "Okay, I will see you again tomorrow. By the way, thank you for your time to today. It seems as though it may have opened a few doors for both of us. I can't imagine that the president of Channel 6 walked downstairs and wants to have lunch with us. Life is so crazy."

Clyde really liked her accent. She was like so many second-generation Americans, with perfect English but at different aspirant points. There was a definite hint of her original tongue.

As she turned and walked away, Clyde found there was a definite feeling, for the first time since he was fifteen, that he wanted to know more about another girl.

LONG-DISTANCE RUNAROUND

GEN. KIRBY MYLES was a lifelong military man. He had fought in Vietnam and had seen things he would have never imagined. He was a hell for leather-flying helicopter pilot. How he had survived was something he couldn't imagine, and definitely the bulk of what still woke him up in a cold sweat in the middle of the night forty, no, almost forty-five years later. He had taken incalculable risks in that conflict. But he hadn't any choice; he often was going after trapped and wounded soldiers, brothers, Americans on the ground fighting for their lives. He had come out of that war having been promoted to colonel with a bunch of jewelry pinned to his uniform, and he really didn't want to do anything else.

From Nam, he had been overseas in a variety of places, and now here he was in Washington, DC, and he had been fighting a brand-new battle: politics. This was a war without guns. This was a war over money, power, and something else—values, or really a lack of values, human ego over all else. He didn't always get it. He was glad to have resigned from being the chairman of the Joint Chiefs of Staff. Boy, was that a stuffy gig. War or military conflict he understood because there were good guys and bad guys. The bad guys wanted to kill the good guys. The bad guys were the ones who wanted to kill you, and now they were ones who just wanted to hurt Americans and or their allies and do whatever to hurt the American way of life wherever they could.

He had fifteen minutes, and he was going to jump in a car and meet with the president. Nobody knew he was going to meet with anybody. This was really a private venture. He knew that this would be the last meeting with the president. He could read what W had wanted, and he really got along with his sidekick, Mr. Cheney. He knew what Clinton was about, and Mr. H. W. Bush had been a former military guy, so they saw things much the same way. Reagan, although he only saw him from a distance at that point in his career, in his mind, was a genius. He was a politician; he was sharp, funny, and brilliant, but he wanted one thing: American values—the dream, freedom—and he wanted it for the whole planet.

But this guy, General Myles couldn't read him. It made him nervous. Barak's agenda was different, and he couldn't tell really what it was about. Maybe it was purely egotistical selfishness, like the conservative talk shows said; maybe it was a different goal for humanity than others before him. Myles couldn't quite tell. It made him as nervous as a captured soldier in a Vietcong prison before dinnertime. It wasn't getting a meal that scared you; it was what you were getting.

As he stepped into the backseat of his newly arrived car, he shuddered at the thought of some of those meals. Thank God for a weak stomach. He knew now that he had been so much better off by throwing up 90 percent of that food rather than allowing it to wreak havoc in his digestive system. Boy, the parallels were a lot the same with the gig he previously had in the capitol. Much of the stuff that was given him to digest was really better not being left internal.

The car pulled up and showed the correct documentation. General Myles walked to a back door and was quickly ushered through some side rooms and then to an elevator and then downstairs to a private room next to the situation area. He thought he would be in the oval office, but this was much more clandestine, to be honest. He saw the chairman of the Joint Chiefs of Staff walking toward him, and he genuinely liked Ian Kilpatrick. He was a soldier. No question about it.

Kilpatrick made his way over to Kirby, shook his hand firmly, and motioned into the side room. There was the president's chief of staff and the head of Homeland Security. Myles cataloged without thinking and noted that there was no vice president. Whoa, this was a power meeting.

President O. walked in, and everyone stood. He looked at General Myles and said, "Nice to meet you. I have heard a lot about you. Thank you for your service to our country, both in the military and in this arena as well. We have a serious matter to discuss, and quite frankly, this meeting is off the books. Not that we are trying to hide anything, but sometimes, a public forum is the wrong place for such discussions. I will let Kilpatrick fill you in on all the details, but he assures me you are the right liaison to stem the tide of a very interesting set of intel we have."

As the president made his exit, Kilpatrick looked at Myles and said, "That was huge. Obviously, he can't be tied into what we are about to discuss, but it is nice to know he wanted to send you this is a high-priority message."

As they turned to get settled in the room, the head of Homeland Security made his exit as well. With a firm handshake and a smile, the ol' Washington tap dance was well under way. The game, of course, was that people, or the wheels of bureaucracy, were putting their agenda in motion yet being careful to keep their hands clean so they wouldn't be tied to the very things they started if they were to go wrong. Myles had a gut feeling this was going to be something he didn't like.

General Kilpatrick simply laid a napkin on the table. It had a list of names. Obviously with this list, there was an order of priority. It was interesting because he had Bin Laden maybe sixth or seventh down the list. His name was crossed out. Not that big of an issue. He used to be the puppet master, but it seemed that some of the puppets had gotten to the point where they were far more dangerous now.

Well, Kirby thought, *I am jumping to conclusions. Let's hear what the chief has to say.*

Kilpatrick said that they had gotten some sporadic information on several occasions, which led them to this list and what these people were targeting to do. "There is some kind of coordinated effort going on here, if my hunch serves me right. Too much data is centralized around some of the same themes. These guys are extremely well funded, and from what we can tell, their money isn't coming through the usual nomadic channels, if you follow what I am saying."

Myles spoke up and said, "You mean through Iran, or Libya, or Pakistan?"

"That is exactly what I meant," Kilpatrick quipped. "This money is finding its way from somewhere else. The equipment that is being prepped is for some Super Bowl–size parties, and we don't prefer the outcomes of those."

Myles made an off-the-cuff remark about stealth bombers, and neither Kilpatrick nor any of the other superheroes in the room found his comment funny.

"Wow, this is serious," Myles exclaimed.

Serious?" Kilpatrick exclaimed. "We can't imagine that kind of money being put behind these independent contractors." Kilpatrick ran his hand through his hair and looked at Kirby straight in the eye. "They are working for the man!"

Now Myles knew enough to know what that meant. They didn't have the man, or the group who was strategizing this, but somebody somewhere was playing with billions and had just hired the Joker, the Penguin, and the Riddler to do his dirty work.

"What is the end game coming out of Gotham City, and do we know where Gotham is?" the retired former chief asked.

At that moment, each of the other guys from the bureaus, the Armed Services, politely told General Myles it was nice to see him. It included several invitations to dinner, and one for the Super Bowl without the B-52. As he sat there and looked at the chief, he mentioned that he had taken a shower, but that may not account for the curry that was still in his system from dinner last night.

Ian Kilpatrick, longtime mentor and friend—they had been in foxholes together, they had saved each other's proverbial tails that had been in the crack—looked right at Kirby and smiled. The twinkle in his eye told Kirby that what he was going to say was put on pause as he asked, "Are you dating somebody new?"

Now there was a loaded question. In the military business, they didn't much care for pillow talk. Kirby personally didn't care for it at all. Having been married for thirty-five years, he didn't date much and had only recently stepped out of his shell, as they say, to get to know a very nice lady, who had also been widowed after twenty years of a successful marriage. So he looked at Ian and said dryly, "What is this all about? I feel like you're about to exile me to Antarctica or, worse, Texas."

Oh, that hurt bad. The look on Ian's face completely went aghast. "How in the world could you talk trash about God's country with such irreverence?"

Myles laughed out loud and said, while he was getting more coffee, "Okay, what do you need me to do? You want me to get a guy and begin to eliminate this list? I am guessing there is a price tag for each of the guys, and you would prefer them in order. But it is not mandatory because while each of these guys is significant in and of themselves, you want to know who is running the cannery and has put together this kettle of fish."

Ian smiled and retorted, "Well, there is not anything wrong with your math. You added this up pretty fast."

"Come on, Ian," Kirby responded. "I have been at this too long not to know you want to smoke out somebody. I also know with the firepower that was in this room ten minutes ago that this is not idle banter over a couple of beers at the officers' quarters, and we, you, they need to get wheels on the Corvette and start chasing this data."

Ian looked at Kirby. "I realize you are from another part of America. Translation: I wasn't from Texas, but do you always have to speak in parables. You must have spent a little too much time in church." Ian got that three-star-general look and squared his shoulders while sitting up perfectly straight. "Let me tell you as directly as I can, soldier. Your country needs you at this moment. You aren't going to get a silver star for this and or a Purple Heart, and, if fact, no one will ever know, unless somebody writes a book thirty years from now, and you and I will both be in glory by that time. I have got to have the very best possible guy on the planet systematically eliminating this list. I know you are the finest and have relationships with some of the best operatives we have ever trained. I can't go get them because of my position here currently, and I am not sure they would come to work for me, anyways. I don't know who you will get or how many, I only know that no one will ever know about this. We need to move quickly, and the money we are earmarking for this is above your salary and mine. And, of course, if we screw up, it will be a scandal then a book then a movie, and it will drag our names through the mud forever."

He took the napkin, and he wrote a figure by each name, and he wrote another number at the bottom. "Let's call that the incentives plan if the whole group goes away," he added.

There must have been a bang in the room as Myles's jawed dropped to the floor while looking at the amount of money that had been arranged for this project. As someone who wasn't surprised by anything anymore, he just couldn't f Since the beginning athom that the government was actually willing to secretly spend $12.5 million to deal with this. It wasn't like a small line item on the budget. This was actually real money being spent for "contract" labor. Kirby was reluctant to say the very least. He didn't want to do this. He was actually really enjoying civilian life. With seven grandkids who were playing baseball, doing cheerleading, doing plays at local theaters, in the Boy Scouts, singing at church, he had more than enough to fill his time. He had no more satisfaction than to take one of on his sons and their boys fishing in the Adirondacks for the weekend at the cabin. But his sense of duty was also there, and Ian knew it. He knew that if the president walked into the room, he would have Kirby at the handshake.

Myles took the napkin and knew that all ties were gone with it. There was an operating bank account that had been set up, and the operation could start with that. Kirby shook Ian's hand. "It will be done. How would you like me to communicate with you?" This was Kirby's final question.

They made the arrangements, and Kirby knew that most likely he probably would never talk face-to-face with Ian again regarding this matter. In fact, as he sat there, it would be a pretty good shuffle to get him out of the White House and back into the city without really anyone, from the staff to the press, knowing. But he froze for four seconds and then quickly called Ian back into the room.

"Okay, wait a minute," he spoke fervently. "You want me to chase down this list and then eliminate them?" *I understand that part.* On a side note, the thought quickly went through Kirby's brain on whether or not it was an act of war, which could be argued over or seen as semantics at any time. "But really, what good will this do? So conventional wisdom says we eliminate these poster children for small-town terror, and we might smoke out the driving forces. But really, what is going on? I know you told me what you can tell me and the same old rhetoric, but I know a few names on this list. You have a guy known for arms dealing, another known for terrorist training, a third on the list who might be responsible for huge amounts of drug sales into third-world countries, along with his funding of local governments and moving drugs into Europe, Asia, and America. First of all, if you lose one character, they will probably fill in that role before the body is buried, or a rival character will absorb the shocked troops and take over leadership for these guys. So why not get the real information? What is going on in these camps? Okay, if I find one of these underworld snake-infested maggots, why don't we actually document what is going on?"

Kirby let out his breath for a second while Ian sat back down and looked like he was smiling. "Let's find out if uranium is being made or tested and where is that coming from. Actually, get real data and find out who is behind these characters. Who is selling and or dealing with biological terror. Getting a guy in there to sit in a tree and use a high-powered sniper rifle and then get out, I admit, is no small trick. I have a few guys who are the finest on the planet who could handle this. But what if we actually get in there and get the real data on what is happening and get some inside surveillance to allow access to mission-critical data that points in the direction of who is actually pulling the strings?"

Ian had negotiated a deal with the government. Yet he knew in his heart—and in his mind, for that matter—that this was not another typical operation. Since the beginning of espionage, which probably went back to the Trojan horse, it had been one country or region going in and eliminating the adversary. This, as Kirby had pointed out, had a lot more merit. Without question a much tougher task. Because ultimately you had to get closer to the source, plant the technology, and then get out. But this drove straight to the heart.

As Ian looked across the table, he smiled first and then shook General Myles's hand. "This is why I brought you into the equation. I knew that you would elevate this task from another down-the-road Iran contra affair to a brilliant discovery of who the players are in what looks like a very sophisticated grossly funded global plan that could erupt into something that may make us feel like we are in Armageddon." Ian looked at his longtime friend and colleague and said, "Kirby, I am going to need that napkin back." Kirby unclasped the brad that loosely held the envelope closed and reached in for the napkin and handed it to Ian. Ian took out his marker again and doubled the payout. "If you can acquire the data we need to pinpoint the 'central banker' or the silent force behind this worldwide collective collusion. If you also help us avoid a global holocaust we would happily double the reward."

Now it was Kirby's turn to talk again. "General, let's face the music, we may literally get a two-for-one deal on this. You can't get a guy into these kinds of situations without having some kind of collateral damage or at least local, maybe regional and, at times, national repercussions. Am I right? So we might as well go the extra step and get ongoing intelligence at the same time."

Kilpatrick grinned as he got up and gave Kirby a thumbs-up, and, as he started to walk away, turned and said, "From time to time, I like to eat a little pastrami, if you know what I mean."

Myles knew what he meant as he watched the chairman leave the room. Why in the world did he commit to this, he wondered, as buyer's remorse was quickly setting in.

"I must be crazy," Kirby said aloud. *Well, to be honest, I am a marine.* Second of all, as he stared out the window at the leafless trees lining the sidewalks of downtown Washington, DC, he thought, *How else can I get a job done and pocket millions of dollars?* Forty-eight years in the military and a retired general with a bunch of stars on his shoulder. Well, to be perfectly honest, he wasn't missing any meals, but goodness gracious, he could send his grandkids to college pay off the cabin. Wow. At least it was fun to think about.

Now the analyst part of his mind was taking over, and he thought, *If I want to make that money, I have got to get the right people to take care of this. No, I don't need people. That would be too many loose ends. I just need the right guy. I need someone off the grid who can slip in and deal these underworld characters and get out without anyone on either side of the equation knowing about it.*

To be honest, General Myles was extremely pleased with himself. He had taken this gun-for-hire situation and elevated it to what could be one of the most important data-gathering and or intelligence missions in the history of military conflict. Because if this super organization was left unchecked, there might not be much of the world left. Or anyone to make history. He was no superhero, but they had just embarked on smoking out the super villain. He was seasoned enough to know that gloating was really not an option. Just when you thought you were brilliant, you found that you overlooked a detail, and in his line of work, that meant a marine died. You only had to tell a grieving family that once to realize what an idiot you really were, and you sure as heck ought to thoroughly analyze your game plan and check and recheck your details.

Well, that shouldn't be hard. He needed to find an out-of-work contract operative who can't be tracked, is highly skilled, is capable to use any kind of weapon, speaks multiple languages, is able to think on his feet for all kinds of scenarios, won't fold under pressure, and can slip into an enemy camp with all kinds of high-tech security, dogs, people etc. Furthermore, the operative must be able to eliminate a terrorist cell leader and get back to safety with the red flag.

Actually, Kirby thought, *I will just pull over to the phone booth and look this up in the Yellow Pages. With the unemployment rate being what it is, I am sure there are lots of guys willing to do this particular job for this amount of dough.* Well, all sarcasm aside, he thought, *I need the right liaison between myself and this list.*

As he came to his home in Arlington, he thought of the one guy who had all the ingredients. How on earth would he ever convince him to take up the vigilante call? Maybe it was the meet and greet like he had just had with the president? No, that would neither motivate this player, nor allow him to keep hidden from the bad guys he was chasing. He would have to appeal to this guy's sense of duty and be straight with him on the level of how critical this mission was maybe even for life as they knew it on earth.

All right, maybe I am extending the hyperbole a little far, Kirby thought. But one thing was for sure: the guy he wanted would play it lean and clean. He wouldn't let a soul know he was involved. He had too much at stake.

I will just have to put a feeler out and see what is happening, Myles thought.

ALL MY LOVE

SITTING ON THE couch in Mom and Dad's living room never got old. Dad worked on the fire and Mom read something to prepare for Sunday school that she had been teaching for forty years. All of the kids were asleep or at least in bed, and Mom and Dad were listening to Clyde discuss his day. They had been doing that for as long as Clyde could recollect. Before he had much to say, he remembered them listening to his siblings. He was recounting that it was probably the most juxtaposed day he had been through in a long time. He had some pretty interesting days in the last six months, had some interesting days in his life. Crawling inside a marble bath tub as a bomb went off in a safe house in Eastern Europe, the births of his four children, his wedding day, scoring a goal to clinch Barclay's premier league for Aston Villa—these thoughts flooded through his mind, but today, he told his parents, he started out at the very bottom. He was ready to quit. The overwhelming grief of losing the restaurant and losing what he and Laina had started together was literally unbearable. So he was mentally and physically in the gutter. He finally decided to drown his sorrows in a couple of shots of espresso. He had accidentally answered his cell phone in the midst of trying to shut it off, and he miraculously had run across an opportunity that could start an entire new opportunity in his life.

Dad turned from the fire and looked directly at Clyde. "Clyde, I am never one to say that the Good Lord doesn't still act with miracles. Every time I see a human being go from a complete and utter disaster to finding a newfound hope in their Savior, I realize God is still in the business of miracles, but if you are trying to tell me that you ran across an opportunity today because it is miraculous, I have got bad news for you. Sometimes what seems like a miracle is simply timing working itself out. The president of the network has seen in you something that because of diligence, perseverance, combination of your giftedness has already been there. Clyde, your mother and I and fifty-three of our closest friends on speed dial all watched you on Channel 6.

"Son, I am not saying this just because I am your dad. Well, not mostly, of course, but when you start to talk about food, you are totally engaging. That young lady that invited you on to her show is no slouch either. She kept the whole thing on pace and asked you good questions, interacted with the other restaurant owners, and really maximized your expertise without letting you ramble on about professional stuff that the average Joe on the street may not care about. I think it was pretty obvious that you two are a dynamic duo on the set. This guy whoever he is—president or CEO, or commander in chief—wants to have lunch with you guys because you are good. It may well be that he has an opportunity for you that with the restaurant you may not have wanted to be a part of.

"By the way, if he wants to move you to LA so you can be closer to their Hollywood studios, your mother and I have already decided that you can't because you are not taking our grandkids across the country. These last few months taking care of the kids have been some of the most precious times I have had as a human being."

"For an old crusty military guy, you sure are getting all emotional on me," Clyde said.

His mom, whipped up from being buried in the midst of her Noah's Ark craft, defended her husband, saying, "You your watch your mouth, Clyde. Your father is neither crusty nor old. Well, at least he isn't crusty. Although I will admit this time he is right, because we surely do love those kids. And because they are here all the time, then your brother and sisters drop off the cousins quite a bit more."

"Listen, Mom," Clyde said. "I can't imagine they are going to run me off to Hollywood or anywhere else for that matter, but I want to make sure I am not wearing out my welcome with you taking care of my four little ones."

"First of all, Katarina is nine and would be offended at being called little," Mom fired back. "And Cody is very tall for six, almost seven, and as for Vanessa, she will be in school in a few months. And that little Josephine is our delight day and night. Really, Clyde, with your niece, Alexandra, coming over every day after school and twice a month on Saturdays, it has been a blessing for everyone. You know your sister and her husband love you, and their daughter is getting paid good money to help. What more would you want? You are still Dad. Everyone is here, school is close, and we can stand beside you during this time." She started to tear up as she spoke. "Don't forget, young man, that Italian beauty queen you married was in our lives one way or another since you were fifteen years old. We loved her too. And this has been the best healing process for all us. Nothing better than fixing a peanut butter and jelly sandwich for a starving six-year-old after school and running off to grab a diaper to help you forget about the pains of yesterday. No, you do what you need to do as a father and a provider. Your father and I have our health and as long as our heavenly Father sees fit to keep us on this earth, we want nothing more than to be a part of your family."

Well, Clyde was speechless. He didn't think this was stuff one hears on *Dr. Phil* or on *Oprah*. He quietly said thanks to his mom and dad. He heard the baby crying in the other room and went down to check on her. Little did he know that commitment from his parents was going to pay big dividends for mankind.

ALL I NEED IS A MIRACLE

OW DOES ONE disappear? Where does one run and hide to? She had an enemy. No, it appeared like he was a nemesis. All the resources in the world at his disposal, coupled with and an overarching desire to not be exposed. All these years, and she had never known. Clyde knew. He had always said he didn't trust Charles Walls. There was something that did not add up. Laina had felt that Clyde was wrong and had said so; she, of course, did not think this was a jealousy issue, although Charles had been enormously successful. He had a real, at least it appeared, deep relationship with her father; she always thought maybe that was it. Her problem at the moment was not that her spouse was right and she was wrong. The critical mass issue for her was that her enemy could probably tap into any telecom company in the world, get data from satellites, have access to all the intelligence agencies, and obviously have a mass network of underworld allies that could be his eyes and ears on the street anywhere in the world. Her only advantage was that she was dead.

Oh my goodness, Karen, she thought. What a tragic end to such a devastating life.

Laina started to get philosophical and pulled up short in her mind. *Focus now.* She couldn't bring Karen back, but obviously, if that was a planned incident and it happened that fast, then she did not have much time.

Hide normally in an abnormal place.

Where did that come from? It was a voice that spoke to her and said clear as day, "Just be normal in an abnormal or uncharacteristic place."

Simple. I will be homeless. This was an inspiration from her few moments with Karen. *Where should I be homeless?* That, of course, was a very odd question. It was not like planning a vacation. But nevertheless, it had to be somewhere unexpected and mild and busy. Los Angeles?

That is it, Laina thought. *How do I get to Los Angeles without anyone knowing? Well, I can't just hop on a plane and go there. I will leave an electronic trail from here to the next galaxy, and one that even a blind rat could follow.* This one wasn't even blind but smart and dubious. She had no doubt in her mind that if she was still alive, her family would be in trouble. They might come, after all, and they might just use the kids to get to her.

Wow, this is really scary. How to get to LA without using any documented paperwork? Can't get on a plane, right? Pay cash for a plane? No way can that work, with all the security issues. That is impossible. What about on a cargo ship?

She slipped into a little secondhand store and bought a rough very 1970s scarf, big sunglasses, and a large hat. The hat was mostly straw and really ugly, but it covered her head and the scarf. She also grabbed a very large oversized black raincoat, and at the last second, she grabbed what appeared to be large-cut blue jeans with more holes than a gopher-infested golf course.

Perfect. Now she just needed to roll in garbage for three days. Making a quick pit stop inside a dark parking garage as it was just approaching twilight, Ilyaina Teresa del Amo Gareen— wife, daughter, mother of four beautiful children, member of the church, co-owner of a New York City restaurant—was going dark. She was going off of the grid. She had about $500 cash on her, and she kept her New York driver's license and one Discover card that had a $5,000 limit but was really still in her mom's name. Why they had never closed that account, she really did not know. The rest of her stuff she had already put in the mail all inside her purse. She put all the correct postage on it, but it was marked Return to Sender. The sender was an old friend of Clyde's in Idaho. Yes, they had been friends a long time, but he was still as old as the General Sherman tree in Yosemite. He was, like, late in his eighties or something and had fought with Clyde's grandfather in the Civil War. Okay, she was being silly because that was 150 years ago, but it was probably even World War 1. He would get the package and hold it for Clyde. She had put Clyde's name on the return address as well. This would take a while, and it would give Clyde a clue.

She kind of scurried down to the river, which was a half block away, and paid for a ride down in a gondola, and they headed for the port. It took about fifteen minutes, and she did not utter a single word. She was able to think and she was not panicked, but she did not want to be recognized. She overheard the gondolier saying that his dad was busy tonight with the last-minute preparations of shipping his olives overseas. There had been a storm, so the boat was already three days behind schedule. The ship was going to skip South America and head straight through Panama for the ports of Mexico.

Perfect, she thought. *I have to get on that ship.*

The gondolier was a chatty fellow. Laina thought it must be a girl he was trying to win on the other end because this guy wouldn't shut up. The boat was sailing around 5:00 a.m. That meant the crew would all have to be back by 10:00 p.m., she heard him saying. Yeah, they will all be bummed to leave the docks, dives, and clubs so early.

Well, once it gets dark and they are all out having their last port of call, maybe I can slip onto the boat," Laina thought.

Laina did exactly that. She was able to remain near the vessel well after sundown, and she found a little spot underneath the street that was running parallel with the marina. She had bought some jerky at a local liquor store where she was going to buy a beer to pour over her clothes for the smell, but couldn't bring herself to it. She figured that after missing a few showers she won't need to increase the essence of living on the streets. Sitting there, watching the cargo ship—which, except for one light in the control room up top, was dark and ominous looking as it gently swayed with the tide starting to come in—she heard a little noise and then a growl. Startled, she peered into the back of the overpass cave she was sitting in and saw two little beady eyes and a small overbite of teeth. So she held up some of the jerky and then tossed it to the back. That did the trick. There came an undersized terrier. The prospect of food being far too overpowering to worry about a new trespasser in his cave, he quickly came forward, wagging his tail and all hoping for more food. He sat right down on his back paws, waiting patiently for the dried beef.

Laina had a new friend. This very young dog she quickly named Monster, partly for the irony and also because he was a wild thing in the back of the cave who curled up right on her lap and went to sleep. When it came time for Laina to move, she gently moved Monster aside, and then she walked straight up the ramp. She was fully expecting to get turned away, but it was a ghost town. Dark and unguarded, she was sure there was a security camera, but they may not check it for a while. She knew her way around ships. This wasn't the first time she had been on a ship.

As she tiptoed around the deck looking for a passageway, she heard a noise and ducked into a tiny space behind some sort of rigging. A man appeared on the deck and saw Monster, who dashed away. She slipped out from where she was and was able to grab the door where the man had come out of that didn't latch. She was down the stairs and below deck and found another set of metal steps that led to the cargo hull. She buried herself in as deep as she could among the crates. She settled in after making sure she could not be seen or squished by the crates. Not more than twenty minutes later, she heard shouts and then footsteps as men were making their way back onto the ship. They were getting the ship shaped for an early sail. After what seemed like an hour later, something crawled right onto her lap. After suffering what seemed like cardiac arrest, she looked down at Monster, who was lying down. Pretending to be homeless for six hours, and she already had the dog. Monster had already helped her get on the ship, so the least she could do was hang in there with him. It was a long way to across the Atlantic. She was frightened, scared, and worried. Ironically enough, Mr. Walls had taken them several times on short journeys and a few cruises on medium- and large-size ships. As she thought about it, she finally fell asleep.

EVEN THE LOSERS
GET LUCKY SOMETIMES

BONAPARTE WAS A great restaurant. It was small, down by the water just off Second Street near Battery Park, but that lent to its ambiance as well as its intrigue. With only about twenty tables, one couldn't just walk in. Not even for lunch.

Chuck Seger had a standing table and was there probably about three days a week, and he paid for that privilege. But it served him well since his guests were impressed. The food was always perfect. It was a combination of creative, imaginative, with impeccable flavor, and, well, very expensive. Clyde knew the owner and the chef, and of course, with his background, time spent in Europe, and marriage to an Italian national, he could talk shop.

Beid Sorre was keenly interested in exactly what Clyde had to say. Clyde always said that he was no expert in French cuisine.

Beid didn't care he wanted to know. Chuck was impressed at the attention Clyde got. He was a very well-established client but had never just sat for fifteen minutes in the middle of the day and exchanged ideas and banter back and forth with the head chef of his very favorite lunch spot.

After the meal was cleared and they were drinking lattes and sampling a new desert Beid had brought out, Chuck Seger put his large forearms on the table and signaled he was ready to lay out his vision. "Here is what we call Traveler's Delight. Know the best local spots to eat when you are travelling. Look, we all like to travel, and we have seen different food shows, but when I am in London, where should I eat?" As he spoke, he laid out a kind of storyboard-slash-brochure that had been kind of mocked up, and it looked very cool, even in its sort of rough format.

"We have been throwing this idea around of a journalist or host, along with a food expert travelling and explaining where to eat when in Rome or Moscow or Athens," Chuck said. "But we want it to be interesting and helpful, but we just couldn't get it off the ground with the producers until yesterday. One taping of the two of you, and I got five calls during the show, saying they were interested. All of them had the same caveat. You both had to be a part. Watching the two of you interact on TV was like magic. I actually don't even know what it is, but the chemistry is there, you are both engaging and energetic."

Chuck went on, "Here is what I would like to propose: we initially do six shows over the next twelve weeks, and we will pay you each one hundred thousand per episode."

Clyde sat back and folded his arms and shook his head, all communicating "Absolutely no way." He later revealed to Anna that it was like an out-of-body experience, but something took over, and Anna was so shocked she couldn't speak. Six hundred thousand for six shows or twelve weeks of work, and Clyde was saying no? Didn't he just lose his restaurant from lack of funds?

Chuck read Clyde like a dime novel and immediately said, "Okay, a flat million, but it might take a little longer if we need a couple of shows with double segments."

Clyde leaned forward and said, "Okay, fine with me, but I don't want to speak for Anna."

Anna smiled. "I was in at six hundred, but I will work with a million."

Chuck pulled out his tablet and hit the calendar icon and up popped a very impressive multicolored layout of the next month. "Okay, today is Wednesday. Can we shoot for the following Monday, ten days from now, and leave for Rome? If we can do the show in five days, you guys can leave on Friday and be in, say, Belfast on the following Tuesday. Shoot four days and then three days off and then back in say Moscow. Does that work? I mean, the format?"

Clyde was speechless as the realization of a job just hit him. He was going to take a job at a restaurant because, well, he was out of work as of two days ago, and he would have been paid $150,000 a year top end, with some bonus as well, but this was a tad bit more lucrative. Along with an exotic opportunity, to say the least, to just fly around everywhere and see the world on Channel 6's tab. Looking over at Anna, he also realized it wouldn't be the worst thing in the world to have to work with her nonstop for the next six to nine weeks.

Chuck then said to Clyde, "I know you are very close to your family and the heartache you have gone through over the last three months, and I know your kids are young, but at any point you feel your daughter is able to go with you, just call Mary in my office, and we will book another seat for the both of you."

Wisdom was shouting from the rooftops. Clyde thought, *How better to hook a guy in than say his family is welcome?* Katarina would love being on the set and seeing Rome. Her grandparents would be thrilled to see their oldest. Although, knowing his in-laws, they would lobby to have her stay with them for at least a month. Lord knows they deserved it. They were absolutely heart-broken over Laina.

As the tears welled in his eyes, he said quietly to Chuck, "Thank you. That means a lot. Heartache is a really good word."

"I have been in television production a long time," Chuck said. "But the both of you are so transparent, and what we saw yesterday didn't change in front of the camera, and that is extremely rare. Losing yourself in the moment and forgetting that we are taping is not easy to do because most people become self-conscious."

They all shook hands, and then Chuck said that he would have Mary e-mail the contracts after he got them from legal, and itineraries would be forthcoming. "Let me add one more item. If you don't mind, we are going to have Yeager Bierson do the directing. He is very accomplished, and we think his viewpoint will be refreshing, but he has an ego, if that is okay?"

"Thanks for the good word on the young buck calling the shots," Clyde said. "I know it won't be an issue for me, but he better be careful trying to run over our headstrong young journalist here." He winked at Anna.

With that, Chuck gracefully exited out the front door. Anna just laughed out loud and looked right at Clyde. "Aren't you glad you took my phone call yesterday morning?"

"It was an accident," Clyde shot right back. "I hit the button on the screen, and it automatically answered. I really wasn't in the mood to be interviewed, and I just wanted to drown in about six cups of coffee and figure out what to do with the rest of my life."

"Well, Mr. Gareen, that is off of your to-do list," Anna said. "A million dollars? You have to be kidding me. I can't believe you actually said no at first."

"Well, you just got enough to cover your taxes on that million," Clyde responded.

"I knew the taping went really well, and all my colleagues at the newspaper were reaching out and saying they thought it was brilliant," Anna said. "But I had no idea that we would get this kind of job offer the next day."

Beid came up to them. "Chuck is one of customers' best. I mean best customers, I can never English, get it correctly. It is such a strange language coming so late in the history of time and then being spoken everywhere, it seems, in every country. So that went well? I watched you two on TV last night. I record anything with cooking in it, and boom, here you are, interviewing two of my competitors. I think you are trying to put us out of business."

Clyde looked at Beid and laughed out loud. He had known Beid for a long time. They had played against each other on the pitch both in Europe and in college. Beid could have played in League One in France, but he severely tore ligaments in his knee. He didn't mind, though, because he actually liked cooking better.

"Beid, nobody can put you out of business," Clyde said. "You can't even get a seat in your restaurant. Booked for lunch and dinner for the next month, five-star chef, and James B. award winner. Come on, friend. By the way, that was a really good meal. I could eat your fondue for a month. The aroma is tantalizing, and then the sauce with the white wine, garlic, and pepper. Is that cayenne? It has a nice bite. It isn't hot, though."

The three of them talked for a few minutes, and Anna realized that Clyde was the real deal. His friendships were deep, and people genuinely liked him because he was interested. No, he liked them too. He knew people and who they were and remembered details.

"I have to be going back to the work now, but I wanted to take a moment and tell you how sorry Chloe and I are for your loss," Beid said. "Laina was one of true treasures in the world. She was our friend, delightful in every way, and we loved her. God bless you, my friend." He then turned and walked back to the kitchen.

BORN TO RUN

K IRBY SAT IN his favorite diner reading a newspaper and waiting for one of his emissaries to come in from the early-morning chill. Kirby liked this dive because it was open when he started his day at zero four hundred hours. He couldn't sleep past 4:00 a.m. if his life depended on it. It didn't matter if he went to bed after midnight. Bam! At 4:00 a.m., and he was awake. Like it was Groundhog Day or something, without Sonny and Cher singing, though. It was 5:35 a.m., and he had read the *Wall Street Journal* and the *New York Times* and finished his coffee and was ready to head to the office.

In walked the young upstart Sergeant Kelly and sat down opposite General Myles and said, "Good morning, sir!"

"At ease, marine," Myles said, and asked Kelly if he would like some coffee.

Kelly said that he would and asked Myles how he was doing.

The general replied cordially and then remarked that the Red Sox had given a pretty good beating to the Nationals last night, and that hurt Kelly deeply, he could see.

Kelly said that he was at the game, and he knew the pitcher should have come out in the sixth. "The skipper left in him in one inning too long, in my humble opinion. He was chased for seven runs. All of a sudden, a 5–0 game is 7–5. I am going to tell you, management is not as easy as it looks. Even though you have multimillion dollar payrolls, you still got to make the calls at the right time."

Myles casually asked about Gareen.

Sergeant Kelly rolled his eyes. "That boy still has the goods. I couldn't even tail him. He knew I was on him, and I lost him twice. I hired a couple of gumshoes to help me out, couple of guys I worked with in Iraq. You have no worries, General. In my opinion, the colonel hasn't lost a step. Word on the street is that he is out of his restaurant, lost his wife, and, of course, we all saw him on television."

"What are you talking about?" Myles exclaimed.

"Yes, sir, he was on Channel 6 with a smoking-hot reporter, with all due respect, talking about all these restaurants I can't afford on a military salary," Kelly said. "Taco Bell for me and the kids is in our budget, with an occasional upgrade to Applebee's if I am able to find a coupon."

"That is just perfect," Myles interjected with a tone of sarcasm. "I send you to New York to see if our man still can recognize a tail and evade a couple of guys, and in the meantime, six million of our best friends in the greater metropolis of NY City see him live and up close." Myles couldn't believe it. He needed a job done quietly and quickly, and the number one recruit on his list is like Visa, recognized everywhere you want it to be. Oh well, he must go to number two.

"General, if you don't mind me saying, I think it is kind of odd to have a guy hiding in plain sight," Kelly said. "But for your money, he hasn't lost anything. He is completely aware of his surroundings and still moves like a marine on reconnaissance. Thanks for the trip, and if I can help you out with anything else, let me know. I will add this as well: I think there was somebody else keeping a sharp eye out at the same time. Someone who knew his schedule a little better and could keep his distance, but I recognized the guy a couple of times from a distance."

"Did he spot you?" Kirby asked mildly.

"No, sir. I highly doubt it because I was three guys, remember. We compared notes pretty well and found Ole Round Eyes and Stiff Pants a couple of times in all the same places as Clyde—excuse me, I mean Colonel Gareen."

"Now you have lost me," General Myles said.

Kelly went on, undaunted. "Oh sure, sir, the guy was unmistakable. Flat head and round eyes, couldn't get a date at an all-girls school picnic, and he walked like he was sore, like an old injury or something."

Myles took a deep breath. "Okay, marine, you are off duty. You did your job well and earned your keep. Keep up the good work, and I will catch up with you later."

The truth of the matter was that the sergeant was dead-on. Imagine that the man in your living room talking to you about Tilapia is slipping out at night and was the number one asset against the war on terrorism. The beauty was in the simplicity.

CLOSE TO THE EDGE

C LYDE TOOK A deep breath. The train ride would not take that long, and then he was meeting his dad for the rest of the trip back to his parents' farm. Relieved was the sensation he was feeling. Most people, of course, would be ecstatic. You have been toiling for years in a job and the thanks you get is that you are paying your mortgage and keeping your kids warm, healthy, and fully engaged to run off and do something behind your back, and then all of a sudden, out of nowhere comes a huge game changer, and you get a pay raise, or now you're heading a new department, or the boss who always liked you gets a promotion and you become his or her number two. This kind of thing where the job lottery hits those who have worked hard and the stars align and they get a sudden and severe increase in income happens all the time. And most people run home, take their spouse out to dinner, order a bottle of champagne, and really celebrate.

Not Clyde. With this newfound career opportunity, he was just relieved. He had felt this way before. He had been in the middle of a cave in a godforsaken hell of a desert staring at a gunman who had the drop on him, and he knew he was about to eat a full round of AK-47 for breakfast and his life was over when his Special Forces partner, Jackson Sinclair, had just snuck around the corner and dropped the gunman into the next life. That he should be dead but have been given a new-lease-on-life moment had not come that often in Clyde's twelve-years-or-so military career, but he remembered that instant and one other like it was happening before his eyes.

No, Clyde wasn't ecstatic; he was fully engaged and knew that he had once again just dodged a bullet. It was plain and simple because he knew that yesterday morning he was ready to fall on his sword. "In times of want and in times of excess." This was the concept that Paul had talked about in Philippians. This was the same notion in his wedding vow. Rich or poor, it didn't matter. We are to stay committed to the ones we swore allegiance to. Clyde couldn't keep the vow any longer because that person was gone, but he wasn't breaking his vow either. But he certainly was not thinking of going home and celebrating. He was just simply, at the moment, thankful. Thankful that once again, with no effort on his part, that God had provided. The Creator of the universe had reached into his world in time and space and continued to orchestrate events. Clyde knew that all of it was ultimately to bring Him glory, but he was glad at the moment that this turn of events had been positive. He had faced enough very difficult trials, and all of the burdens or consequences were not over, but there was light at the end of his tunnel. Well, maybe more like a big huge flaming sun at the end of the tunnel. He just hoped it was not connected to an oncoming moving vehicle and this was going to be a train wreck of a show.

As he stepped off of the actual train at his stop and walked over to the car, he opened the door, and his dad asked, "Well, how did it go?"

"Nice to see you also, Dad," Clyde said.

His dad looked at him, like, "You know, it is nice to see you, but I have been waiting here for twenty minutes, and we have been wanting to know all day."

"You know, Clyde," his dad said very sarcastically, "they invented these little devices that you press a button and they dial another device, and you can get connected with someone a long distance away and communicate ideas to one another."

Now it was Clyde's turn to be a little sarcastic. "Sorry I didn't call and give you the news. It has all been a blur, and I have been trying to synthesize the events of the past few months with this new opportunity to shoot six or nine restaurant-critic-type shows in exotic international places over the next three months for a million dollars."

His dad looked at him. "You know, Clyde, that was a run-on sentence. But if you are going to be grammatically incorrect, you might as well have that kind of unbelievable news. Nice work, son. Nobody deserves to pull all aces in his hand than you at the moment."

Clyde couldn't have agreed more.

"We actually don't believe in luck, but you fully know what I am saying," his dad said. "That is so awesome, and I don't know whether I am happy for you or proud of you." As he turned onto the highway, he said that he was both.

Just then Clyde looked into the backseat and into the eyes of a little six-year-old hiding on the floor. He said with a smile, "My seat belt is still on, but you didn't know I was here did you, Dad? I was being as quiet as you were when you infil…snuck into those bad guys' place in Baggad and rescooded those newspaper people. Maybe even more quiet." He made an "I really did good" kind of smug, slightly cocky face.

Clyde reached over and grabbed his son and pulled him into the front seat. He buckled him in between himself and his father, and three generations of Gareens laughed hysterically for the next five minutes.

"Oh, that felt really good," Clyde said. "To just laugh hard. I am not sure there is more of a remedy than that. I don't think I have laughed that hard since I was in college and Fannie Tomkins was singing some scenes from *Porgy and Bess* just a little off-key and Sam Turner, Hardy Epston two old soccer mates, and I started to crack up, but we were trying to hold it in and how that never works."

Dad asked when the shooting started, and Clyde said in ten days.

"Hey, we have enough time to go hunting up in Idaho," Clyde's dad said. "Norv Adkins has been asking me for two years to come back to his place, and just recently, he has kind of turned up the heat again to get us to come out there."

Clyde said he didn't want to leave his kids because he would be gone for so long.

"Nonsense," his dad said. "Let's take the kids."

Cody couldn't have agreed more. "Dad, can you teach me to hunt? I want to shoot a gun. You know, I am almost seven."

His dad went on to say, "You know Old Norv, though he is like ninety-four or something now, and sharp as a tack. He served with your great-grandfather and has been a friend to my dad and to me and has followed every step of your career. He is the best Gareen historian but yet isn't a Gareen. But getting pulled half-dead out of a foxhole with enemies closing all around and dragged for three miles will attach one human being to another and his kin like probably nothing else ever would. He has been a long and loyal friend."

Just then Clyde's phone rang. It was Anna. *What on earth could she possibly want?* Clyde thought. But he relaxed. *She probably just has a little itinerary data for me. Maybe she doesn't have my e-mail.* "Hello, this is Clyde."

"Clyde, I am so sorry to bother you," Anna said. "But Chuck Seger's office just reached out to me and said that they want us to go on the *Tonight Show*."

Clyde's reaction was immediate and clear and cut through the cell phone waves as a bell cuts through the evening ranch for dinner. "No!"

Anna was caught totally unaware. She had thought this was terrific news and actually extraordinary that so quickly they wanted to put their new show as a highlight on the major media outlet as such was this "national" platform. "Um, I am sorry. I heard you, but I don't believe you."

"Anna, I am not intending for you to understand this, but I absolutely refuse," Clyde said. "It isn't up for negotiation, and I wouldn't do it in a hundred years. So tell Chuck's office that I will not. You are welcome to do as you please, but I am not going to sit there and make banter with a bunch of left-wing radicals who represent everything I am opposed to. No. I will not do it, and besides, I am going out of town for nine days. Is there anything else?"

"Let me get back to you after I talk with Chuck's office," Anna said with deep disappointment and bewilderment.

Robert Gareen said with all the sarcasm intended, "That was gracious."

"I am sorry, Dad," Clyde replied. "I need to be less terse. There is just something that takes over in me, and I speak a lot quicker and with more force than necessary when I can just as easily say no."

"A harsh no or a kind no is still no," Clyde's dad said. "The force of the refusal will play itself out."

Clyde knew, like a million times before, that his dad was right. Clyde learned this lesson early in his life. He didn't want to admit until after college, but Robert Gareen was a humble, kind, gracious man and was well liked by all. But he had his core principles and wouldn't bend this side of the millennium.

"Clyde, you are going to need a representative, or what do they call those legal guys?" his dad asked.

"Lawyer?" Clyde asked.

"Yes, I know they are lawyers, but also when they are negotiating for you or on your behalf, I mean?"

"Oh, you mean an agent," Clyde said.

"That is what I mean, exactly," Clyde's dad said. "You should talk with Thompson Brannigan. He is an excellent attorney, and he will know exactly how you should go about these contracts, etc."

"Dad, that is the last person I would want to talk with."

Robert looked at his son questioningly. "He is a good man and an elder at the church and very successful in the legal field."

"Dad, he is a disdainer," Clyde said calmly but with a measure of force.

Robert could see Clyde out of the corner of his eye. He turned the car to amble down the dirt road from the highway that led to their home in upstate New Jersey. He had had this conversation with Clyde before, and he had to admit that Clyde was more than right, although he really hated to admit it. Clyde didn't feel like many of those in the church, especially guys who had been insulated for many years in leadership had much room in their lives for mistakes or imperfections.

"I know they mean well, but so often, you get the feeling they are looking down their nose at you with disdain," Clyde said. "They are 'leaders' they are highly revered in the church, and they get confused about their own rightness."

Clyde thought that life was far too complicated and situations were much more involved than to say this person did this wrong and this person didn't do this right. Clyde had commented about millionaire guys with two kids and one dog who lived in their little world of perfection. He and Clyde had discussed for hours that God had left them a manual, and they could know how to live life in this world, and they had good indications of what a person who had submitted to a life being filled by the fruit of the Spirit looked like.

"I know guys who are convenience store managers by day, and they have more integrity and kindness and humility than a lot of those very 'successful' guys who give a lot to the church," Clyde said. Charles Walls crept into his mind. Clyde knew full well that he was stepping on toes, but he quite frankly couldn't care.

"Dad, all of us are sinners," Clyde said. "This is why God had to come to earth and deal with this issue in a drastic way. But we are still sinners." Clyde went on to say as he had said it before. "Dad, you know how I feel, that we have a dying—literally dying—world, and we sit by and collect our pensions and drive motor homes, and we do nothing to take in the orphans on this planet. If 5 percent of Christian families took in one orphan, we wouldn't have any issue whatsoever."

As the car pulled to a stop in front of the house, Robert had that look of experience and exasperation on it.

Clyde relented. "Okay, Dad, I am sorry. I need to get off my soapbox, and I need to get the log out of my own eye. I know we are not perfect people, and each of us need to be moved and convicted by the Holy Spirit as what is right for our individual families."

"Thanks," Robert said to Clyde. "That means a lot, and I know you are also right and that each of us could do a lot more to give, love, and sacrifice for the body of Christ. All of us, at times, want to go back and bury our parents rather than make the sacrifice daily to deny ourselves and follow Christ, which means making the hard decisions."

"You know, Dad," Clyde said, "the thing I find remarkable about you is that at your age, with the long and winding road you have been down, you are willing to admit mistakes. But at the end of the day, I would bet the next week of salary that there is something up with that Brannigan character."

"I wouldn't throw in next week's money because it might be around twenty thousand bucks," his dad quickly added.

Clyde smiled. "Point well taken."

HOME BY THE SEA

THREE WEEKS AT sea, and Laina thought she was going to be absolutely sick for the rest of her life. She had actually gotten better over the last two days. She didn't have any worries about looking homeless. Oh, what a mess. She was very fortunate because there was about thirty minutes in between the shift change of guys posted to watch below deck between 3:30 a.m. and 4:00 a.m. She could use the restroom at this time. Get some water, and she just had to wash her face. She couldn't stand the grime. She was able to dispose of Monster's droppings and get him some water. He was actually in pretty good shape as well.

She was starving. She had eaten out of the trash several times. It was amazing what an entire day without food will do to what one once thought was utterly detestable. It was shocking that she had just spent the last year running an exquisite restaurant in the tony Manhattan district of New York. Her husband—oh, her poor husband. She missed everything. She broke down into tears for the ninety-eighth time. She wondered if it was bad for her system to lose this much fluid. It was like an endless well of tears. She missed her children so bad it ached deep in her belly. The big dilemma, if she ever got out of this mess, is how she was going to stop from choking Charles Walls and getting thrown in prison for murder because she was going to grab on and not let go until—

Wow, she had changed. This was no Sunday school answer. Crumbs and water were her daily dining experience. She felt like they had been through Panama and was up the Central America coast somewhere headed for Mexico. How she would get from Mexico to Los Angeles was an entirely different riddle she was going to have to solve. This ship had come by perfect providence, and she was very thankful. While miserable aboard her floating prison, it gave her time to think. She was hoping that at some point Norv Adkins would connect with Robert Gareen, and they would put the whole package item together very discreetly. In fact, she knew Norv was so discreet he might not give the package to Clyde, unless he saw him in person. That would mean a trip to Idaho. They would jump the train and ride to some unknown destination.

"Canny old coot!" That was all Clyde ever said about Norv. Some kind of code or symbiotic communication was between these war-hero guys. Made a lot of sense, though. They had learned not to trust anything but each other in all the conflict that they had seen. She also realized that, without question, as painful as this was, Walls, as she referred to Charles, had come crumbling down. Walls would have her killed. She knew that whole incident in the street was no accident. How he passed that off in less than five hours was very telling of the strings he could pull.

Crap, she thought.

Whoa. Three weeks in the belly of a boat, and her language was in the garbage. Well, that was where she was eating from, anyway. But the panic was sudden and severe, and she knew that

Charles was going to pull his capital from the restaurant and, with all his financial muscle, would block any bank in Manhattan from doing business with Del Sol.

That can't be possible, Laina thought. *People rave about the restaurant. Now that couldn't happen. No way. With me gone, what is the harm? Why alarm my father? Charles had a plan, and it wasn't good.* The man she saw with Fritz Reckonboeder was a full-blooded underworld maniac who would make death-row inmates look like Sunday school teachers from the *Leave It to Beaver* era.

Quiet, she thought, as he put her hand on Monster. *Someone is coming. No, it is two people, and they are carrying on.*

"No way is it possible," the one man said, lurking in the shadows. "These containers are foolproof. Each one contains 120 pounds of unprocessed olives."

"That is a lot of olives," the second man said, with a very deep, almost Darth Vader kind of voice.

"You bet," Lurker Man Number One said.

There isn't a chance in the world, which was the edited thought Laina captured as she reinterpreted their filthy language, that they will ever find the containers inside.

"We are running drugs of a very high caliber that came in from Russia via the Netherlands. It is so easy to move contraband in Europe. Straight down to the docks of Southern Italy, where they were loaded right in the plant that made these crates. Then we ship the crates to the processing plant right at the farm, and then right here on the cargo ship."

"What is this issue with the storm off the coast of Mexico?" the Darth Vader double asked.

"Yeah, unfortunate break. Now we don't get to dock in Mexico, and we have to deal with the border patrol of the United States. I am sure they will find us another way and search the ship. They are really good at this stuff. They have all those canines too. I tried to feed one of their dogs one time, and he looked right at me and said, 'You want jail time, Sinbad?'"

They both had a really good laugh. Monster got along well with other dogs. He wasn't frightened and didn't make noise. He quickly befriended even the fierce-looking bulldog they had on this ship. Laina guessed that Enoch the bulldog was around 102. He was past his prime and probably his purpose as well. But they liked him and didn't get challenged much down here at sea. She overheard them saying for a second time that they weren't going to port in Mexico but straight to Long Beach, California.

This time it registered.

Oh, Lord! Laina thought. *Thank you. This is a huge break. I needed one too. Aside from an asteroid dropping right on Charles Walls, which would be a Get Out of Jail card. Man, I went from the frying pan to the fire. An unexinstinguishable grease fire.*

Great. She was almost killed by a maniac for seeing one guy, and now, knowing that, she was aboard a floating narcotic container headed for the streets of Los Angeles.

So much for safe passage if she gets caught down here.

CAN'T ALWAYS GET WHAT YOU WANT, BUT IF YOU TRY, SOMETIMES YOU CAN GET WHAT YOU NEED

M YLES KNEW HIS man. But his man was now seen by millions. And the word from his friend in the studio industry Doug Love was that this show was a go and they were going to air on the food network. Chuck Seger, from a pretty large local television station in New York City, had sold the show to the Food Channel and was still in charge of producing it. Seger's team had high hopes, but the Food Channel still wanted to see a little more proof in the pudding although the original live segment that was taped earlier in the week was really good. He didn't like food stuff much, and in this offering, he was completely engaged. It was the two people doing the show. They were both good, but together—it was for lack of a better word—magic. They had a hit, and they knew it.

The thought that came back to Kirby as he drank his coffee was "hiding in plain sight." The sergeant had it. Who better to carry out a secret mission that very, very few people knew about than the guy everybody knew? It made him cringe. It was such a good thought. He thought he would pick up the phone and say, "Hi, old buddy old pal. This is your mentor, Kirby Myles, and we need a for-hire assassin to fly around the world and pick off some major targets and gain intel as he goes with the real goal of smoking out the big fish who has some kind of major master to plan to do real damage, maybe even nuclear. Big money is involved, so don't worry about that, and we can give you access to transport and get you back to your day job."

Sure, he thought, that will work. Not a chance in the world. Better chance to bring back the dodo bird than to get Col. Clyde Matthew Gareen to be his on-the-ground operations guy. He better go through his folder one more time and get plan B. As General Myles went through the folder, he knew there were a lot of really good guys. Top soldiers whom, by just looking at their scores, he knew were at the pinnacle of their field in so many different arenas. Hand-to-hand combat, marksmanship, infiltration, communications, endurance, multilingual, quick studies, aviation, weapons expert, and explosives.

But there was another ingredient that Clyde had. Well, as long as he was dealing with the food concept like a unique curry flavor that was a conglomeration or fusion of awareness, competitiveness, and intuition. He hadn't see anything like Clyde in years and hated to lose him. But he knew that Clyde was right. Laina's nationality and living abroad was a total hang-up in the quagmire of government relations. And Clyde had other talents. But what had Clyde told him once after a successful mission and a late night beer? Soldier 17. That was what he wanted to be.

Clyde had told him the story of Soldier IV, or maybe it was V, in the fifth century, protecting some early Spanish bishop named Isidore of Seville as he was challenging a monarch in a stronghold of what is now Southern Spain. *Challenging* is the wrong word; the correct word is *confronting* the monarch. The monarch was going against the church and advocating some sort of heresy, and Isidore was the representative sent to accuse this despot and get him to recant from his heretical viewpoint. This was a Moorish monarch, and he wanted to kill Isidore, and he attacked him on the road to the palace after assuring him of safe passage. There were eleven men in the party sent by the king to attack Isidore and his party, which was largely unguarded. Soldier Gareen Numero Cinco, as Clyde had said, fought off the initial attack and killed five of the men with a sword and a small makaira or large knife. He then proceeded to chase, catch, and kill the other six. He was a warrior for the ages. He came back with their steeds and money sack, and Isidore quipped, "I have been granted safe passage with Centurion Gareen on duty, and on top of that, we have found a gift for the church."

Kirby sighed. *I will have to appeal to the very depth of the mission and the duty he has for the country and, in this case, the world. It is true we are at the superhero level because there was a super villain, and according to the intel, coming in him—or them, for that matter—was or were depending on whether this was a person or a group poised to wreak havoc. How do I reach out to Clyde? I get so worried about the phone. Too many people have the ability to pick up on the communique.*

It wasn't that they would be able to get the conversation because they could speak on encrypted phone lines, but what he knew was the phone call from point A, and it is Kirby Myles to Clyde Gareen, who is in point B. The wrong people would ascertain that a high-ranking government official is reaching out to this former combat marine who was a colonel in special ops. He knew Clyde and his whole family had left town. Where did they go, and how did they get there? Clyde was a magician, and he had disappeared with four kids and the grandparents.

I wonder if Clyde drives them all crazy, Kirby thought. But Clyde could fly, and that was a major help. Go to a private airport, rent a plane, and boom, you are gone. You have to file a flight plan, but if you don't know where to start, you can't figure out where he began. and there are just too many airports. Kirby picked up a brand-new mobile paid for strictly in cash and dialed Clyde. But before he finished, he figured, *No, that won't work. Well, let's finish it, anyway.*

Clyde answered.

"Clyde, this is—"

"Go to the nearest pay phone and dial a number I will text you," Clyde immediately said.

Kirby did as instructed. Why had Clyde responded so quickly? Did Clyde know something? He drove about five miles and found what appeared to be an old pay phone still in use. It looked like Superman didn't need to change in this one because there was no booth anymore but a bench and phone. So General Myles dialed the number, and he heard some clicks, and then Clyde said, "Hello. Sorry about the private detective stuff, but I have reason to be a little suspicious."

Kirby followed by saying, "Hey, Clyde, I need a man for a job, and I wanted to run it by you. I like your secure line and all, but I would rather meet with you in person."

"How about the Olive Garden in Coeur d'Alene at 6:00 p.m. tomorrow night?" Clyde asked. "General, can you get here without the world knowing you are coming? Or Homeland Security, the CIA, multinational companies. I think you know what I mean, Mr. Walk into the Pentagon at the Drop of Your Hat."

"I can assure you that will not be a problem," the general responded. "See you tomorrow night."

Just before Clyde clicked off, he shot off the following, "I know you have seniority on me, but I am thinking since you did the inviting, you got the tab, General."

GOING OFF THE RAILS
ON THIS CRAZY TRAIN

C HARLES WALLS WAS not just a bad guy. He was an idiot. He was a man entirely without scruples. He didn't hold a grudge against one person or one nation, he hated the whole world. He had one very simple goal: eliminate people. Earth would be better with around fifty million as opposed to five billion. It wasn't a hard goal. But the execution was a little trickier. Now that was a play on words. He called it the elimination of the nations. Whittle them down to a handful apiece. He didn't have a list or a reason or who was on the needs-to-go list or needs-to-stay roster. He was just going to play an unconcerned god and let the chips fall where they may. He was willing to live out his years quietly and peacefully and with a whole lot less of the hoi polloi, which meant the common people in ancient Greek. It was on the one hand a matter of getting nations to fight against nations. He was convinced on that front he could potentially rile the Muslims against the rest of the Western world. They were already ripe for picking off the low-hanging fruit of holy war, or jihad, against the "infidels." With someone in the driver's seat fomenting one little imam here or another little cleric there—*e, i, e, i, o*—and he could see driving down the populace quickly. The big explosion could be the Chinese against the rest of the Asian countries. With all of those little expenditures turning up the heat and with the scoring losses on both sides, in reality, civil war was the best. Imagine all those people in the same country wiping each other out. What could actually be worth dying for? One man's political agenda, as opposed to another, really added up to the price of giving one's life.

Charles thought people were so ridiculous. He couldn't imagine someone's philosophy actually being worth dying for. You can't have a religion or a conviction lying six feet under a pile of dirt. Charles knew that the final straw to population elimination was biological terror. He had a little bit of trepidation with this because it had a few unknown factors. In other words, it could come back to bite him in the butt, as the saying goes, and that really wasn't something he was up for. Charles was like most other hardened criminals: seared in his conscience yet completely absorbed in self-preservation. It was like there was some sort of groove in his brain where the neurons of self-analysis couldn't connect. A genius of a human being and totally immersed in his own longevity, he couldn't see the irony of how other people want to have the same self-existence he prized so dearly.

It was no wonder that Charles's efforts to love had been rebuffed. He was a war veteran, a brilliant physician and scientist, not a bad-looking man who had enough money to play poker with the oracle of Omaha and the Seattle software wunderkind, and still buy out the sappy built-her-fortune-out-of-nothing network guru goddess who turned, of all things, an afternoon talk show into media gold. Yet for the likes of it, he couldn't get a date with a middle-aged divorcee who did Christmas all by herself. Why? It was simple enough. Because even those, while they were temporarily a little down on their luck, had enough self-respect to want to be loved. Oh sure, he had women around from time to time, but the problem was the women he wanted around to superimpose the image he had created didn't give him their attention for more than three days. His first and only wife had left him after three weeks and asked the church if she could have an annulment because there was only love enough for one man.

What makes a monster? Some people say that people are born tabula rasa, which is Latin for "a clean slate." Others would say no, they are all born sinners. Has anyone met a perfect person? So somewhere along the line, everyone has problems. But men like Charles Walls go the way of Hitler, and one wonders how that happens. Charles grew up in a loveless home where his father brutalized his mother in his early years and then was killed in an auto accident. His mother went from place to place and finally succumbed to her addictions, and Charles was placed in foster care at thirteen. He finally found his way into a group home for teenagers and had to deal with some pretty mean and nasty foster brothers and sisters. He said at times he felt like a lab rat. College and the military were his escape. It didn't hurt his cause that he was smarter than most of his professors, and he quickly rose to the top of his class. He was always something a little different than everyone thought.

While people thought he was a medical doctor, he was really a research doctor and finally became a full-time scientist for a pharmaceutical company. He quickly found that religion offered him a real camaraderie he had always lacked. But nothing ever said from the pulpit in any way, shape, or form ever reached his heart or, for that matter, his mind. So while he seemed like a churchman on the outside, he truly didn't believe a word that was ever spoken. All along, while he seemed like a company man and that he was very content working for a pharmaceutical giant and simply not worrying about anything but using his genius to develop the latest lifesaving medicines for the betterment of humanity, he was secretly keeping back much of the research for his own private use later. He was doing his job, and the company was paying him upward of $300,000 a year to spearhead their research unit.

He had in five years put three new drugs on the market. He was single-handedly changing the cardiac market and improving the lives of human beings. He had walked out on his company and immediately opened his own brand and put no less than six new drugs on the market. His pharmaceutical company quickly became the powerhouse on the planet. Two initial investors had also risen to billionaire status in a five-year period because these two individuals had spotted Charles a quarter of a million each to face some start-up challenges.

Charles didn't regret these two comrades. They were in and of themselves very successful humans. They quickly discovered that despite the fact that they lived on different continents, their annual business meetings became a meeting of the minds. Three minds all bent on the same goal. None of them really liked the fact that they had to put up with five billion people. This is really remarkable, if not even a tad bit ironic, for it was Alberto Johnston, the former South African who had relocated to New Zealand, who made a living buying and selling goods from one country to another on a global scale. He had initially invested with Charles and Zeuterfeld Labs when he had met Charles off the beaten path in Australia. Charles and his female companion du jour were vacationing and had met Alberto on a forty-person sailing yacht as they toured the islands of Polynesia by day and ate sumptuous meals at night.

The thing that struck Charles and Alberto, who shared the same vision, was in these areas there were very few people. It was a sound utterly devoid of the chaos that the masses created while scrounging for a living and trying to make something of their meaningless boring lives. Charles couldn't understand for a moment why the mass throngs of people elected to live together. Why not buy a house in the surrounding areas of New Delhi and not live in the overpopulated, noisy, filthy, and chaotic city? For a man of sheer brilliance, he was blinded by simple human plight. He should have been able to sympathize with the struggle because of his early childhood experiences, but for some reason, his success had only calcified his opinionated misdirected callousness toward other individuals. In his absolute superiority complex, he simply couldn't identify with the fact that he had hit the proverbial lottery and very easily things could have been different. Everyone else knew the margin between success and failure was a very thin line. But because Charles had experienced several successes in a row, he was beginning to think that everything was directly related to his own innate abilities. He didn't appreciate for a second that he had been given a gift that very few people had received.

Yeri de Angelo was really born Gerhard Angelo Van Gelderal. He dropped the last name early and added the *de* to *Angelo* and shortened the Gerhard. Yes, he was Argentinean, and yet he was a full-blooded German. His grandparents had fled Germany in the mid-1940s, and he had always been enamored with all things Third Reich. Charles and Yeri were cut of the same cloth. The fabric of their character consisted of monstrous egos stemming from an innate inferiority complex. Yeri had grown up in Argentina with very stern grandparents, a father who went back and forth to Germany all the time, and a mother whom he never met. He never asked why Hitler wanted to exterminate the Jews, but he had always wondered why Hitler didn't take the Asians, Africans, and Moslems with them.

Charles Walls had found kindred spirits with these two other investors who had become part of a little billionaires' club. It was ironic that their money isolated them and insulated them from people altogether, and yet that wasn't enough. These three amigos together made the Joker, the Penguin, and Two-Face look like kids in the sandbox. The fusion of these heartless and cold-blooded crackpots and their schemes were exploding to make a nuclear holocaust look like a cheap Fourth of July firecracker.

Charles was very comfortable living in his Sicilian estate. He had vineyards and a garden, horses, sheep grazing on a hillside, a beautiful pool where he could sit on the veranda and overlook his forty acres and watch the sun come up over the mountains and turn the other way and see the sun go down on the other side behind another set of mountains, and a dramatic ocean view. It was beautiful. He received his morning reports from a couple of sector managers as he called them and made a few notes and then called for the helicopter to be ready. He was going into town to meet with Fritz.

Charles thought that Fritz had handled that situation so beautifully with Laina Del Amo. He refused to call her by that stupid man's last name. What a total idiot that boy was. Charles hated Clyde for so many reasons, and at the end of the day, it was mostly because Clyde drew people to himself effortlessly. Charles wouldn't admit that, and he would never dream that because Clyde gave of himself through caring, engaging, asking simple questions, and being interested—which others might call love—that Charles was actually the exact opposite, and because of his total lack of interest in others, he repelled most human beings. It was a complete shame that Laina had seen Fritz in that compromising position meeting with one of their network operators. Of all people, why did it have to be Laina, who, from the time she was little, Charles had always adored?

But Laina recognizing the connection would have had immediate repercussions. It would not only pierce the façade Charles maintained in his private life but also it would have sent alarms to many people in the global security forces. Fortunately those "international" forces were not at all international; they were very national and kept each other at arm's length. At a time when you could transport, FedEx, Skype, and penetrate any border anywhere through normal business channels, catching criminals was much harder to do with very little country-to-country cooperation. This, of course, would work to Charles's advantage.

Fritz had immediately seen the solution and had called for authorization and had carried out the "accident" flawlessly. The flight was simple into town, and Fritz had sent over a car. They were meeting a local trattoria, and Charles had said hello to the provincial delegate of the state senate. He said he was doing a good job and Charles was very supportive of his agenda, which, translated, meant "I will continue to contribute." Charles was amazed at the access he was granted in Italy, in the United States, or anywhere because of his wealth.

He and Fritz walked to the back of the restaurant. There was a very secluded table where they sat. They took off their overcoats and were brought a bottle of very good cabernet. Fritz saw that he piqued his boss's interest with a couple of items that Charles had been watching carefully. The team had picked three major centers to establish facilities where they would eventually manufacture Tierdon P53. The infrastructure surrounding these facilities, as far as stability went, was important to Charles, Alberto, and Yeri.

Yeri de Angelo was their partner who had originated from the very southern Americas. They had worked hard at putting these third-world regions into the hands of local despots who controlled their little corner of the world and were obligated to work the team. It was seemingly so effortless to stay in the graces of the team that Charles didn't feel like there was any compelling reason for them to be alarmed or for anyone to connect back from these petty anarchists to Charles and his group. Northern Africa, southern Philippines, and some very remote regions of South America were regions where the group had laid the foundation through arms dealing, narcotics, and other legal export and import activities. These were places where they were very influential in the balance of trade.

Fritz had waited to bring the news to Charles, and it appeared like a pretty normal business meeting. But the table had been cleared, and the espresso had been served, and the staff was informed to give them their space after they received dessert. Nobody had taken a bite, so all were keeping their distance when Fritz casually said that his inside contact at the White House communicated that there was a meeting the president had with Ian Kilpatrick, who was the Joint Chiefs of Staff. What wasn't normal was that some money was earmarked through external channels for a special project to the tune of twenty-five million and retired general Kirby Myles was brought in through back doors to meet with Kilpatrick shortly after.

"Did the movement of the president and Myles overlap?" Charles asked.

Fritz knew that his boss was a quick study, but he had put his finger on the trigger. "Yes."

"Did you follow Myles?"

"We did, and he met with a couple of low-level military guys. For what reason, we did not know."

"He also has flown the coop?" Charles asked. "Where did he go?"

"He must have caught a private plane somewhere," Fritz said. "And we can't know where he went. Because we don't know where he originated."

The other item of note was that shortly after subject number eleven, because Charles would not hear Clyde Gareen's name in his presence. Few things elevated the boss's blood pressure, like bringing up that name, so they referred to him as S11. S11 had met with Chuck Seger of Channel 6, and he had quietly disappeared.

"We know S11 can fly as well, so he must go to a private airport and slip out of dodge. Or go to Dodge in a dodge?" Charles said.

Fritz said that S11 was really good at catching a train or switching cars and getting lost, even with his family.

Charles looked at Fritz. "I know where he is."

"How can you possibly know that?" Fritz asked. He liked to set up a little drama for Charles as well, but he was surprised because his local trader-for-hire espionage network had lost him.

"Idaho" was the reply from Charles.

In conversations at the Del Amo household when S11 was a younger jerk, he had mentioned that his great-grandfather had a friend in Spirit Lake, or near some little town, called Newport.

"Yes, sir," Fritz said. "But couldn't his parents have friends all over the United States, since it is an old family, after all?"

"Yeah, sure," Charles said. "I know, old family, and they go back all the way to the Roman Empire. That is such a bunch of hogwash and fairy tales, and I can't believe that anybody believes that this guy has heritage past the turn of the nineteenth century. Oh well, it doesn't matter. I have had enough of this. It was all I could bear to see him featured on the news. Send a crew to Idaho, and let's put out this unfortunate blight on humanity."

Fritz knew that Charles was now very irritated. He never mentioned in all his meetings a direct or blatant order to kill. This was a first. Fritz told Charles that he had the right people and would get them in place. Fritz was about to tell Charles about the crown found at the scene of the accident and the latest news regarding S11's refusal to go on late-night talk shows when Charles slammed his fist on the table.

"All members, do you hear me?" Charles asked. He decided to wait.

"I hear you," Fritz said, and was astonished that the hatred for S11 from his boss was so deep that he wanted S11's family as well. Fritz had, quite frankly, never completely understood this antagonism. Clyde was perfectly amiable although, like most fundamentalist right wingers, he was self-righteous. But Fritz had known many ex-military card-carrying NRA guys who wore their religious cross on their arm band, and while Clyde could probably speak at the prayer breakfast, he was a reasonably intelligent unimposing human being. On a side note, it always kind of

struck Fritz funny because he was supposed to hate these neanderthals who were antidrug, anti-abortion, and, really, anti–all
human pleasures. His boss certainly painted the death row image
of this young man, but beneath it all, Fritz saw a caring and lov-
ing father who worked hard, kept his nose clean, adored his wife,
and cooked the finest pot of bouillabaisse he had ever eaten.

GO YOUR OWN WAY

ANNA CIFUENTES WAS confused. How do you take a huge gift and then throw it away? Where was Clyde, and why was he not answering his phone? It had been two days, and she couldn't get a hold of him to talk sense to him. She sat in Nina Pearson's office. Nina was the producer of *The Seasoned Traveler*. They had thrown around a couple of other names like *Cities' Key Ingredient*, *Traveler's Delight*, and now, finally, they had chosen the one she liked best, which was *The Seasoned Traveler*. But nevertheless, it looked like Anna was going to have to go Los Angeles and make the rounds on the talk shows as well as here in New York all alone, and it may well be that she would be putting out fires. She could hear Nina talking with Alex Bodejo in the next room and saying stuff like "It makes no sense," "I am shocked," "This has taken me completely by surprise," and "I would have never imagined in all my years in television," so Anna was preparing for the wrath of God.

Oh well, she thought. *It will make excellent conversation around Happy Hour.*

Nina came in with her hands on her hips. She sat down next to Anna, put her feet up on the chair, and said, "Clyde has become the number one news item all over America, and no one even knows where he is." She grabbed the remote control and flipped on the flat-screen television lining her wall opposite the chairs, and swiveled around to face the broadcast. Leading the segment was a picture of her and Clyde on the set of Channel 6 and the word *controversy*. Sam Flour was saying that the new celebrated talk show segment turned new national television show that will be filmed and aired in the fall possibly has taken a very funny twist. As is common with new formats and new shows, oftentimes the star or stars of the show are invited to make guest appearances and introduce the show. But what is so very odd is that Clyde Gareen, the celebrated New York City super chef, has refused to be interviewed whatsoever on any show at any time on what appeared to be political differences from the "liberal mass media outlets."

Sam went on to say, "What appears to be the real news is that Channel 6 may lose its deal with the Food Network because of this sudden and very strange controversy. I am going live to Riann Surrey, who is with Charles Seger, the president of Channel 6."

"Thank you very much, Sam," Riann said. "And with that, I would like to ask you, Mr. Seger, what is the actual latest on this breaking story?"

"Thank you very much," Charles Seger said. "It has come to my attention that Clyde said in a phone conversation, which was relayed to the people in Burbank and to the Tonight Show, that he 'refused' to discuss the new show with anyone at the present time."

"But didn't he say in that same conversation that he wasn't going to 'banter back and forth with the established liberal media?'"

"Well, I think the gist of the conversation made reference to political ideology, but you are relying on third hand information, and I don't know exactly what Clyde would say if he were here. Although I believe he does have some core political views that might run opposite many of us in the media who voted for the current administration. Let's face it, Riann, I didn't hire him because he was a dyed-in-the-wool Republican or card-carrying member of the NRA or doesn't advocate ObamaCare and or any other government largess that you and I might think would solve some of our country's current problems." He went on to add, "I hired him because when he talks about how to cook ono or the spice rub needed for beef ribs, he has a particular set of skills that I am not sure anyone since Bobby Flay has portrayed. We gave Clyde ten days to be in Rome, where we will shoot our first segment in a city where I want to know where I should eat when I have to fly through there in three days."

Nina said that Chuck was actually pretty good in the interview and was accomplishing the same thing that you want to with talk shows: coverage, which equates to publicity. She flipped to channels 2, 4, 7, 11, and then on to CNN, MSNBC, and, finally, Fox News. They all had different takes. One reporter was saying that Clyde Gareen is a throwback to the 1950s. While he could cook, he lived a life right out of *Leave It to Beaver* or *Mayberry R.F.D.* He didn't smoke or drink or cuss. He was a regular church attender at a Baptist Church, and he dated then married one woman in his life. Clyde was, in fact, a square.

They cut to a segment with a former member of his elite marine unit who said, "That is not completely true. I saw Clyde drink a half a glass of chardonnay one time at a farewell for General Myles."

This brought the studio to a full roar, and when it happened, the anchor went on to say, "Well, there you have it. But we would like to get Clyde's take on this, but he is nowhere to be found. In fact, they think he might have literally snuck out of town. Nobody knows where he is!"

Anna couldn't believe it. Clyde was more popular than the pope. All of this publicity was due to the fact that he had made a decision to not go on television. Just then Nina's phone rang. "Give me five minutes, and we will walk downstairs."

"No, Nina," Anna said. "I am not unwilling to be interviewed, but I am completely booked all day, and we will have to do this in the morning. How is nine o'clock?"

As Anna turned and walked out of Nina's office, she felt sick to her stomach, like she had just eaten something terrible, and then her phone rang. She answered to someone, saying, "I would like to say I told you so."

"Where on earth are you, Clyde Gareen?" Anna couldn't contain herself, and she bolted for the elevator and then thought better of it and made for the staircase.

It is only six flights, she thought. "The entire world is trying to track you down, mister, and we can't find a flight or rental car, and your parents' car is in the driveway."

Clyde rebutted by saying, "So everyone is stalking me now?"

Anna threw up her arms and sighed. "They are not stalking you. They want to talk to you. You are the rage of the industry, and the networks are mad at you—"

"But Chuck seemed to enjoy all of the press," Clyde broke in.

Well, Anna thought. *He is still in the country.* "Why does your phone say untraceable?"

"The cellular networks can't find a code for where this call is originating," Clyde responded quietly. "It is a secure line, and more importantly, no one can find where I am. Anna, I am fine. I wanted you to know, and since you will probably have to go fight these wolves without your partner in crime."

Anna, with a little exasperation, said, "You kind of up and left me high and dry, and I don't know you well enough to have guessed any of this."

"My apologies for running away as it seems," Clyde said. "Sometimes it is just nice to be gone and having no one able to find you."

"Isn't that kind of paranoid?" Anna asked. "Well, I guess in this case, it works out that the media can't find you," she conceded.

But as she was mentioning this to Clyde, her instincts as a journalist took over. She may have been writing a food column for two years, and now she was going to be an on-air host, but her training was in finding the scoop, and there was a reason why Clyde had skipped town untraceable. Somebody was looking for him, and he didn't want to be found. She needed more information, but in the meantime, she just told Clyde to take care. "I will see you in Italy, if not before."

DOES ANYBODY REALLY KNOW WHAT TIME IT IS?

Rico Del Amo was not fooled for ten seconds. He had worked as a pastor for forty-five years. He was considered a missionary being sent from a large church in the United States. But other than his father, who was American, he had been born, raised, and had lived his entire life in Italia. His mother was a full-blooded Italian, and they could trace their roots back to the Etruscans. She was eighty-two years old tomorrow, and she would probably outlive Methuselah. His wife, Maria, adored her mother-in-law, having lost her parents early in her childhood. Yes, Rico knew that he was blessed beyond measure, and he knew people very well. He didn't believe from the moment he heard about his daughter's tragedy that it was an accident. He had mentioned this once to Clyde, but Clyde was so grief stricken that he didn't want to even hear it.

Furthermore, Rico was not convinced it was his daughter in that car. Maria said that he had absolutely no evidence to the contrary.

Rico said, "I can feel it in here," as he rubbed his stomach.

"That feeling in your gut is hunger pains because you need to eat more," Maria said. She had been complaining that he was too skinny and needed to put on a few pounds, but secretly she was proud that her sixty-five-year-old husband still played futbol and was coaching their grandchildren. She knew over the years that her husband might have a hunch, and while all others talked down to him or were condescending, he ended up being right. *A man of prayer gets inside information from on high* was the thought she had. She bantered with her husband from time to time, but she would not hear anything else about this and stated emphatically that the death of their daughter was really a tragic accident. It was more than she could bear to think about it for more than a minute, and couldn't keep the tears from rolling as she thought of the joy and love her daughter brought to every occasion and situation. She knew from the minute Laina laid her eyes on the bronzed athletic, gangly, and goofball of a fifteen-year-old that she had bought it hook, line, and sinker. They had raised Laina to love one man and give her life to him, but they didn't think it would happen at sixteen.

Five years later, they got married, and Clyde finished college and went into the military, and Laina lived all over the world for five years. They didn't have children for four years, even though they were willing. And then the floodgates opened, and four children in the next eight years, although it was one every year, or so it seemed for three years or so, and the little trailing baby girl who looked so much like her mother it literally floored her. Maria del Amo had always thought her mother was beautiful and yet Maria had barely known her.

But looking at Laina's youngest, Josephine, was truly a miracle, and while Maria knew that reincarnation was a misguided religious belief, it was hard not to think about the mother Josephine would never know that well and the four or five pictures Maria kept in the family Bible of her own parents. Rico had been right before, but the thought of her daughter being alive and where on earth would she be if—no, it was ridiculous.

Rico waved his hand at her, and with that, Maria knew he wouldn't debate it anymore. But Rico thought the failure of a very successful New York restaurant and the death of his daughter all within a few short months couldn't be coincidence. As he read his newspaper, he glanced at the short little column about a childhood friend of Laina's who had become distraught over a failed marriage, losing a child in infancy, and now she had disappeared. Life was hard, and this was the only sanctuary many people were going to get before they faced a godless eternity.

Rico looked at his watch and realized he had to pack. He was headed all the way to Los Angeles for a conference. This is truly the last thing on earth he wanted to do. They had made him promise last year that if he couldn't come, he would this year, and now he was the keynote speaker. They had asked him if he wanted to postpone the event in light of the recent tragic events, and he said no. "It is painful, and we are grieving, but we rejoice in the tough times and know that God has a greater purpose than we can ever imagine. The great redwoods are not born until the fire burns, and what looks like it destroys is really the provision of the maker to bring about a greater good than could have ever been imagined."

He kept his hunches to himself and quietly went about his business. He packed a book about dragons his grandchildren were reading. They would laugh when he knew what a werecat was. It was not his nature to be suspicious, but there was a member in his congregation for many years that he knew was a flatliner. It was an annotation for those that existed. They were in the right places, and some, like this particular member, gave significantly, but they didn't really serve, and they didn't really grow in their faith. It was never about theology or their personal relationship with the Lord. It was always about the local futbol club or the latest movie or who was getting elected and what he or she was going to do for the country. And, Rico thought, in most cases they never talked about sharing their faith with a friend or a neighbor.

Rico's flight was not direct, because he was flying to meet with a young man whom he had taken as a disciple and then who had planted a church in Argentina. Who would have ever imagined, but his young protégé was originally from there when his dad had business assignments in Europe, and Italy became their home for his later primary school years. He had gone to college here but waited until he got back and married a local. His heart had always been home. Home was where he had been born and his cousins still were. Ed de Angelo had a thriving church in Buenos Aires. Fifteen hundred Argentineans called Iglesias de Gracia their home. They were growing daily right in the belly of one of the biggest Catholic bulwarks on the planet. Every day people were being rescued from the works based religion of the Virgin and coming to receive faith in the risen Son of God. He was thrilled to meet with and worship with these zealous believers who faced ridicule and persecution in school, work, and at play but didn't care. Rico did not find it the least bit coincidental that he was going be in Argentina at the same time as his old friend Charlie Walls.

GHOST AND THE MACHINE

Norv Adkins appeared. There was no other way to describe it. One minute Clyde was alone in the forest of Northern Idaho, and the next he was looking at Norv Adkins fifteen yards away.

"You know, Norv, we could use a good guy like you in the Special Forces," Clyde said. "The Nez Pearce would say that you are a spirit, the way you came out of nothingness. They would say that you have big medicine and are not to be trifled with."

Norv said it really wasn't that hard because he knew this area better than any human on the planet and there was a system of caves in the mountains you just had to know. He turned and whistled. "It is okay, Shep."

A big bear of a German shepherd, as old as Norv, came slinking out of the same path Norv had come but was wagging its tail. He walked right up to Clyde, and Clyde squatted down and rubbed the dog along the sides of the face and played with him for a minute like he was a puppy.

"I have never seen him take to anyone before," Norv said.

Clyde said that he remembered. Norv said, "It has been what, ten years?"

"Follow me," Norv said. He turned and literally ran down the path and into the darkness of a mountain cave that Clyde had not seen. Norv pulled out what looked like a little glow stick, and they were jogging, practically climbing, now running, and then jumping from spot to spot as they moved through the underground caverns. And then there was an opening, and bam, Clyde was in the light.

Norv checked his watch. He turned and said to Clyde and Shep, "Okay, stay right with me and jump when I jump." He was gone moving swiftly in a half-jog down the path through the trees under large bushes, through plants that didn't look like they had trails, and then around a hill.

All three of them jumped and landed and then fell because they were on the move having just landed on a train.

"You fall well when you face the unexpected," Norv said. "That isn't easy to do. It is only three minutes, so get ready. We are going to climb up as soon as we get out of this part of the tunnel."

They waited about one more minute and then stood and walked, and then they were looking at the forest again, but they were a little higher and had a spectacular view. Norv stepped around the door and then leaped. He grabbed hold of a ladder-type rail and pulled himself up and then found footing and was climbing up onto the car. He disappeared on the top, and Clyde followed right behind. As soon as they were up, Norv said, "Stand on the far-right corner facing the mountain, and jump when I do."

Clyde was looking straight into a wall, and then Norv jumped, and so did Clyde, expecting to hit the wall and then die. But he had been trained too long as a soldier to not follow orders. They hit an opening and then rolled and hit another side of the wall although the impact had broken their speed. They rolled gently into the other wall. Clyde told Norv there wasn't much room there. He looked up at Shep panting and ready to go. He asked Norv how Shep made the climb.

"He didn't," Norv said. "There was a little opening in the back of the boxcar we were in, and he scurries out and climbs up one of the log cars and has to jump a little up, but his timing is impeccable."

"How long did it take you to teach him that?" Clyde asked.

"I climbed up on top one time, and he found his way to the top of some logs," Norv said. "And I jumped, and three cars later, he followed. Darndest thing I ever saw. I have been trying to get rid of that dog for years, but he keeps on finding me." He said those with a laugh, and Clyde knew that was not true.

"Are you okay to keep going?" Norv asked. "We only have about five miles."

Clyde said that he didn't mind the hike, but he wasn't in for being gone all day as he wanted to spend time with the kids.

Norv said that it wasn't five miles, it was only about five minutes. "But I want you to see this. It is important."

Clyde walked into what looked like a modern-day war room or situation room. There were two big flat screens hanging from the ceiling, four computer monitors, and a host of other electronic devices. Then there were too-large "bulletin" boards, for a lack of a better word, with newspaper clippings all over them, and then one giant map. It had pins in it with various colors.

"Look at the big screen to your left," Norv said.

Clyde said, "Hey, Norm, we are in the middle of exactly nowhere, and—"

Norv cut Clyde off midsentence. "Generators and satellite."

"You packed them all in," Clyde retorted.

"I didn't need mules because there is a longer way around, and the train at one point is virtually at a standstill as it climbs," Norv added. "And I have a wagon."

Clyde wanted to know if at some point he would reimburse Pacific Northwestern Rails for all of the free rides and de'ivery.

"Why pay myself?" Norv said. "I own the train!"

"Look at that," Clyde said. "Ask a stupid question, get a stupid answer."

"Your dad isn't sarcastic," Norv said. "Where did you get it from?"

Clyde was about to remark that it must skip a generation when a YouTube video was about to play on the screen. The title of the video was *Kung Fu Panderer*.

"The Internet is amazing," Norv said. "Something happens in Los Angeles, and you capture it on your phone and then upload it to the Internet, and we can see it from every corner of the world."

"From under the world as well," Clyde said.

So the video began to play, and it is of a homeless woman with a dog and a baby.

Poor lady, Clyde thought. *I wonder what led to her plight.* "We have so much, and these people lose their minds from addiction or mental disease or both, and they wind up on the streets," he spoke out loud.

So the lady is standing next to her stroller against a wall. A homeless man comes by and grabs her, and it looks like he is going to try and accost her, or worse. The homeless lady doesn't seem to react. She isn't standing but leaning against the wall, almost in a half-crouch, and Clyde sees her slightly move her leg to hook behind his ankle. A half-second later, she stands up hard and runs into his chin. The perpetrator goes to grab his mouth as he pulls away. This causes him to trip as her foot is already hooked behind his ankle. He hits his head on a brick or hard object while he appears to be bleeding from the mouth. The woman flips the man over and seems to take something out of the man's pocket.

Clyde realizes this is a simple self-defense move, just like he had taught Laina if she ever got attacked. The kung fu mom gets up and leaves with stroller and a cute little dog in tow.

Clyde looked at Norv. "Why did you show me that?"

"It fits the description," Norv said. "And who else knows that move but a Special Forces's wife? And it was executed flawlessly."

"She has a baby and a dog, and it is Los Angeles," Clyde said. "Norv, what are you insinuating?" He was incredulous. "I can't believe it, even for one tenth of a second."

Norv was expecting this reaction. "Clyde, that is not the only thing."

Clyde looked at Norv, almost without speaking. "There is more?" he finally said.

"It ain't much, but it is something," Norv said. "It is kind of strange." So he handed Clyde the unopened package. The handwriting was in block printing, but it was obviously feminine, and the return address was the same as the delivery address. Both of them had the words "Grandpa Norv in Newport, Idaho."

"I don't have any kinfolk," Norv said. "And the only family I really have is yours because your great-grandpa and your grandfather and I served together, saved each other's lives, and spent forty years all over the globe fighting for Uncle Sam and against all the bad guys. It is a woman's writing, and you know she calls me grandpa, and it makes me cry every time one of your kids calls me that. Live to hear it, and I am your guardian angel, and most folks think I already came back from the dead. But if this is what you look like when you come back from the dead, then I want a trade-in. I have been old and ugly for thirty years. I want to look more like Tim Tebow."

Clyde opened the package and fell to the floor. It was Laina's purse. Credit cards, wallet, her driver's license, and passport were all in the purse. Clyde knew that she had an old charge card that was still in her grandmother's maiden name. This card wasn't in the purse currently. Farousia, which seemed more Eastern European than Italian, but for whatever reason, she had kept the account separate from Del Amo and had put Laina on the card as a coborrower.

Clyde looked at Norv. "She is hiding. She has a secret."

"I knew it," Norv said.

"How long did he have the purse?"

"Maybe three months. It is postmarked the day she died."

Clyde didn't have to ask the obvious because he knew that if Laina had a secret, it would have to wait until Clyde came. It was too precious to utter electronically.

"Did they go back the same way, or did he have a rocket that launched them home?" Clyde asked.

Norv turned and walked to a panel and pressed in a code. A door opened, and Shep ran ahead, and Clyde followed Norv.

BLOODY, BLOODY SUNDAY

T HEY DID THE same train trip as before with a few exceptions, one of them being that they jumped from a different location to board the train. It was really more like a step as they walked onto a flat car and into a boxcar. They exited at the same spot and made their way through the forest to the path that split to each of their locations. Clyde said they were fly-fishing in the morning and Norv was welcome to come. Norv said he would grab his pole and meet him at the docks at first light.

"Sounds good," Clyde replied.

At that, they turned down separate paths, and Clyde was immediately put on notice. It was late and dark, but the pine tree nearest the trail just off the intersection where the path met Norv's path was displaced. Well, it really wasn't Norv's path but one wherein the direction led to his home. The other path took a direction that went to a small lake around three miles away if one continued to follow it. There was a turn off for the Gareen vacation home in another six hundred yards or so. Clyde had set the pine tree to flip back if it was dislodged by anything larger than a dog. Now Clyde knew that a moose or bear could have come this way, but he saw no track for an animal. He backtracked down the path and saw nothing. Clyde had no weapon on him but a two-edged hunting knife. He stood motionless, all his senses alert.

Clyde went from dad to warrior in thirty seconds. He knew this wasn't Kabul, so it was very different, but this threat to his family elevated his adrenaline immediately. He had seen a smudge of what looked like a moccasin print or from a combat boot, since they were made for walking long distances. He thought about the immediate terrain and asked where he would go. The spot that gave this place the best ability to see what was coming was too easily identified, and Clyde ruled it out. But the next spot was up ahead behind a tree, and one could hide in the half cave and see both ways. Clyde knew how to go to that spot from behind. He backpedaled slowly and got onto the path that led to Norv's home. He listened because it was dark, but while he hadn't been here in years, he played a great many days here as a kid. He could move with his eyes closed, but they weren't, and the moon was bright, and he could see a lot.

Over the rock, careful not to drag clothing and onto the hill and around the tree, and there was his trail and the other spruce and behind a notch. It was dark, but Clyde could just catch a small reflection of probably night-vision goggles. Clyde started to slide, and the body, waiting, turned and looked at his last sight. Clyde's hunting knife penetrated just below the Adam's apple, almost to the hilt. Clyde went to work quickly, first digging out the earpiece and then putting it in so he could hear. He disarmed the man as so he was: blond, German looking. East German, Clyde thought, which meant probably a five-man kill squad. They didn't take any chances. Last guy will be close to the house.

Clyde shivered with the next thought. These guys wanted him first, but they were sent to eliminate all. As a parent and a protector, it is one element to fight for the country you serve and what it stands for, but Clyde's motivation for mayhem just went up a notch. He was a professional and knew this business, but now he was mad. The next two attackers were probably two hundred yards east of his position, which would have been about two hundred yards from the house on a triangle, as he was more like 350 yards straight to the house. But it was a steep climb up, and it was much easier to move east and then back to the house. But he felt like the interception point would be near the riverbend and where the river touched a corner of his property. He heard the others ask questions of Number 5, although he remembered later it was more like the fifth letter of their alphabet. He gave a slight command to wait with just one brief word kind of whispered, hoping they would think he was waiting for the target.

As he worked his way just off the path through the trees, he got close to the river, slipped off his coat, and went in. It was really cold, but he moved under with the current for about ten seconds and came out slow and lifted his head up and moved toward the shore at the bend. He could see Number 2 crouched behind a tree, a rifle aimed on the path. That would have been a bellyful, thought Clyde. He wasn't in the right clothes, just in a pair of blue jeans and a T-shirt, but he was going to have to move as silent as Sioux on the hunt for his first deer. Three steps, using the timing of a crane leaving the river, he rose out of the river almost silently, and as Two turned, he met the same fate as his comrade, with a double-edged hunting knife through the center of his heart. He also suffered from a broken neck, but that wasn't the fatal wound. That was just pure anger.

Clyde didn't care. These boys were after his family, and there might be some collateral damage. Number 3 was trained enough to know that this recent scuffle and no communication from one meant trouble was afoot and the target was in their midst. They had been fully informed and knew that Clyde was no beginner but a full-fledged marine combat Special Forces member and to be respected and feared. But Three wasn't fast enough, as Clyde came out of the brush and picked him off with the AK-47 he took off the first assailant. Clyde knew that he would be heard, but this was his plan. He quickly thought that if he got Three, then Four and Five would come away from the house and move toward the fight.

But he was wrong. Five decided to go into the house, and it was a mistake. Robert Gareen was no kindergartner. He had been up waiting for Clyde to return because he knew Norv wasn't playing show-and-tell just to run Clyde up to the cave. So Robert had moved into the porch-slash-mudroom and had taken a position on a bench next to the door that led into the house. He was looking out the open door through the screen at the dark night and was wondering why the crickets had stopped. This allowed him to take the two shotgun shells out of his pocket and load his favorite double-barreled gun that had been given to him by his dad. It was an old-time Remington but he had hunted a lot of fowl with this gun. Lady, his full-blooded springer spaniel, was holding her head up, listening too. While Robert was silently sitting in the dark, he was armed to the teeth and ready for a bear.

Only it wasn't a bear. It was a fully trained, fully armed senior member of a death squad, dressed head to toe in black, who had silently slipped through the door. Robert heard the first step, which was barely audible, on the deck. He put his right hand down on Lady, and his left hand depressed the trigger ever so slightly. As the former East German came through, he was met with both barrels of shotgun shells that, at a seven-foot range, didn't leave much left of his upper body.

Clyde Gareen was a chef, a soccer player, a recent husband, a son, a father, a former marine combat colonel, and, at the moment, exactly like a tenth-century madman fighting for his former Welsh clan against the tyranny of the English lords and while he had only been in Idaho for almost two days, he had whittled two spears from five-foot branches. They were crude, with the bark still on in most spots, but the tips were sharp and strong. And he could pierce a hay bale at forty feet. But he didn't have to throw this one because on his way down into the yard of the house, he picked one out from behind a bush where he had left it and slid into a little rain runoff ditch just off the path. As the night-vision man slipped quietly down the walkway with automatic weapon ready to blast, he never saw the spear as it was thrust into his stomach and up through his vitals and out the back. Death wasn't instantaneous, so Clyde knew to roll away from the reaction the trigger finger had as it depressed the gun and shot aimlessly into the moonlit night.

This happened about five seconds after he heard the shotgun and knew that Dad couldn't sleep. They gathered the bodies and burned them in the trash cave at the base of their property. This would send a message, but Clyde didn't know who in the wide world of clandestine activity would want him and his whole family dead. Who would know he was here, and would have the audacity to send a kill squad that had to penetrate the borders, get weapons, and position themselves to be in place where Clyde was coming back home? Standing in the middle of a crisp Idaho late evening, Clyde had a vision of a blacksmith pulling the burning-hot orange-and-red metal out of the forge and then smashing it with his hammer.

"The fire allows the metal to be turned into something useful," he thought aloud.

Clyde did a couple of things that evening. He changed his meeting with Kirby Myles to be at a little restaurant in Agua Dulce, California. There was a private airstrip there, and Clyde could get a fly in without anyone caring. This was partly his dad's suggestion because he had a sister—with a different last name, of course—there in the area, a big house, and a pool, and they had all never been there before. The other item Clyde did was reach out via protected and or encrypted communication with his old friend, Johnny Walker. He inquired as to whether or not Johnny

Walker could find out any information on this crew. He sent over photos of passports and as much information as he could.

Johnny wanted to talk, but he knew it wasn't the time. He said, "I am on it, and good to hear from you, old friend."

The kids loved to fly, but Lady wasn't crazy about it. Although without the Tramp, she seemed to be kind of a sourpuss of late anyway, or, actually, a sour dog. They had lost the Tramp to a mountain lion the last time they had been hunting. One swipe was all it took. But without the Tramp, it might have been one of the hunters. A cornered cat and a dog barking up the wrong tree, and it was probably going to pounce on one of the hunting party.

After fly fishing in the morning, they gave Norv the information that they would be leaving sooner than they thought. Norv mentioned, "He heard the shotgun and could see the fire and knew something had gone down. But he figured that if you needed him, he would have heard from them."

"Thanks for keeping the package and for the Internet surveillance," Clyde told Norv.

And then Norv said, "Hey, Clyde, the person Laina is running from I am betting is tied to the party you had last night."

Two hours and fifteen minutes was all it took the NetJet Clyde had rented. It seated a dozen, so it was actually a big plane. They moved pretty quickly, and they broke into the Santa Clarita valley, a suburb of Los Angeles, on a 95-degree day in May. Clyde hadn't felt this heat since Iraq. Although it could get pretty hot and humid in those crazy New Jersey summers.

Clyde's aunt Sherri, short for Sherri Anne, was just thrilled to see everyone.

"Sorry it was so last minute," Robert said, "but we had to do some real cleanup work on the house in Idaho, and it was better to not be there. And besides, the kids really wanted to see the sights." She said her youngest, Clyde's cousin Tyler, was on location shooting a movie for a month in Holland. He was a cameraman, and she said the house was empty.

As everyone in the family knew, her husband, Evan, had finally succumbed to a three-year battle with cancer. So with the youngest of four gone for a month and the others all busy with their families and careers, she was super excited for the company. Clyde's mom and aunt got straight down to talking and catching up on everything. Clyde was always so amazed how women could be so engrossed with every detail. He was always thrilled at getting the Cliffs Notes version of everything, after his wife had talked about with a good friend or family member for two hours. He could glean all the important information in fifteen minutes. Man, he missed Laina, and the idea that she might not be gone—unbelievable. He could not even foster that emotion, but it was really thrilling to think, maybe!

So after getting settled, he told his parents that he had to run out to a meeting. They didn't ask because they knew he couldn't tell.

Mom said that they were going to get ice cream with the kids after Aunt Sherri's grill cheese feast.

TO THE POINT OF NO RETURN

KIRBY MYLES HADN'T changed in twenty years. Although Clyde had only known him for a dozen, he was darn sure Kirby hadn't changed in twelve, so it was pretty easy to ascertain the other eight.

The general said Clyde, "What on earth are you doing, tracking me down? I did my tour and a couple of extra. Honorable discharge is what the paperwork said. I am a civilian."

Clyde said that as he thought about the spear he had made and used, and had actually relished in light of the evidence to bring harm to the entire Gareen clan.

"I wanted to discuss some very interesting data that we have and what our plan is to deal with it," Kirby said.

Clyde knew that the general was too military not to cut to the chase, but they were old friends. "You know I owe you my life. I was in a dark place after that last tour. You don't see what we saw and do what we do in the line of duty to not feel like you have given your soul."

"I was glad to be there for you, just like Ian and a few others have been there for me," Kirby said. He went on to add, "The truth of the matter is that you have a really good support group with your family, and you would have been fine."

"Just like Cleveland without Lebron," Clyde said.

"You know," Kirby said, "I was going to pick up the check, but if you bag on the Indians, the Browns, or the Cavaliers, you will be on your own."

Clyde laughed and raised his hand. "Okay, fair enough. I know you don't live there anymore, but having grown up in Cleveland, you will always have a first love even if there is only, like, one championship in the last one hundred years."

"Tell me something I don't know," Myles said. "You think they could win at least one World Series!"

Kirby talked with Clyde about the restaurant issues, losing his wife, and then, finally, about the new gig on television.

"I know it isn't easy, and television, like many things, has its finer nuances and idiosyncrasies, but I think you will be a big star," Kirby said.

"What on earth makes you say that?" Clyde asked.

General Myles paused a second, took a sip of his beer, and continued, "Clyde, you are camera friendly. That was obvious in the training tapes we made. You are funny, and you actually know a whole lot about your subject. Those seem to be the right ingredients. But if I may diverge for a second, I want to show you some data." He pulled out a world map. It had three large red circles and then five smaller, not so much smaller, orange circles.

Funny, Clyde thought, that Norv seemed to have these same areas mapped out as well.

Kirby outlined his thoughts and started with saying, "On the surface, this will all look like the same gangland style underworking: arms dealing, import and export of narcotics, money laundering, and even some human trafficking. But I think you will find some regional data that takes this to a higher level."

Clyde listened for thirty minutes, but there was no arguing the facts. In each region—North Africa, Uruguay, and the Philippines-Malaysia-Singapore triangle—Clyde could see that there was a recent proliferation of the crimes aforementioned, and in each case, a single guy was rising up to consolidate power. The same was true with the other five circles: Central America, Jakarta, Bangladesh, Istanbul region, and, believe it or not, the areas just north of Gdansk. Suirillite, Ildefongwe, Woo, Kjartifarstiyupol, and Harimarillo were the top five he saw on a napkin the general pulled out of an eight-and-a-half-by-eleven clasped manila envelope.

"These are the guys who are amassing power and buying people out and who seem to be on late-night Vegas roll," the general said. "But in each case, we are sensing, or the data suggests, that they have a banker. I am almost convinced that they have a think tank. I mean, some of the stuff they have recently done: manipulating local currencies, squeezing out other warlords, buying up small towns for planting, and then wanting to give back to their local areas. It is incredible, with the backing of local politicians, giving to cultural awareness, building infrastructure, and starting charities. One would think some of these guys were going to run for congress or, worse, start a Hollywood movie studio." He paused for a second and rubbed his beard.

"This is what has us perplexed," Myles continued, "and here is what we do not know. Why are they building in each location a massive million-square-foot warehouse?" He pulled out the map again and pointed out some of the locations. "They seemed to have buildings with multiple levels, and in all cases, trains go underground. Our major concern is not nuclear because the launch aspect of those is the tricky part, and then they can also be shot down or blown up in the air. And while no one wants radioactive fallout in the atmosphere, it is better than obviously a nuclear strike. We might be dealing with Peter Gabriel's song 'Red, Red Rain' but far better than the actual continued repercussions if it hits. No, our concern is biological, and not just from a regional standpoint. Someone, or a group of someone's, are manipulating regional conflicts and then laying the red carpet for a carte blanche approach to manufacture something nasty."

This was serious business, and the general wasn't outlining a Bonnie and Clyde scenario. This was the real deal.

"I don't use the phrase *something nasty* lightly," the general quipped. "I am not talking about my aunt Helen's stew either, although I wouldn't wish that on the barking dog next store. *Nasty* is the operative word for what we think is a biohazard pollutant. What it is and what they want to do with it is what we intend to get at."

Myles was a straight shooter and knew the best approach with Clyde was to come at this thing with both guns ablaze. Myles, who was all in at this point, was set for a terse no and finally said to his number one recruit, "So let me lay it on the line: eliminate the top five guys. But get any data that is available along with the job. Here is the figure for each specific job detail."

Clyde looked at the three zeroes after the five hundred number.

"Clyde you are the only one I want for this job," Myles said. "I don't have a backup plan. In fact, I am pretty confident I would not want to do this without your help." He looked up at General Myles and said with a stony face, "Television pays better, and it is all you can eat. There is a double the mileage, double the figure bonus if you get all five. But we also need to unlock the puzzle: what are they doing? If we can figure out the endgame, then we can double the double which means ten million."

"Done!" Clyde said.

One could have hit the general over the head with a Louisville slugger. For about five seconds, he was speechless and then said, "Of course there is no paperwork. Just my word. Period."

"I was surprised you had the napkin," Clyde said.

They shook hands, and the general let out a sigh and smiled while Clyde, reading the general's thoughts, mentioned his motivation.

"Who in the name of Franklin Delano Roosevelt would actually do that?" the general rhetorically asked. The general didn't like FDR, and it wasn't the man per se because he was only pushing sixty and he had never met FDR, but he hated the entire new deal. He could tie in the whole social security card in with taxation and with Big Brother and with knowing too much about free men to make him feel comfortable.

Kirby Myles smiled and quipped, "You know you should have gone on the talk show circuit like they asked, and they wouldn't have had to hire a former Soviet death squad to teach you a lesson. Let me ask you a question, how on earth did you kill five?"

Four was the reply, and Myles questioned, "You let one get away?"

"Dad got the fifth," was the reply, and Clyde went on to add that it was with a 1963 double-barrel Remington.

"No getting away from that," Kirby offered. "I am afraid you are right about that. Lots of cleanup, but not too much left of the fifth."

Clyde added without being asked, "I don't want to kill, and I certainly am no fan of lying in wait, but somebody has raised the level and has brought the war to my doorstep. Now I am not going to sit here and say that these provoking-nation type of super villains armed with biological terror or nuclear weapons are related to my little nighttime escapade, but from what I picked up in rough German last night, it was the elimination of my family. It looks like someone already got my wife, even though it was deemed an accident. They want me, and now, it appears, along with the rest of my family. It isn't about revenge as much as it is about protection. The best defense is great offense, and if you take it to them, they have to spend their resources repelling the attack. Somebody somewhere thinks I must have information, and they came after me. I have a feeling they may not do that in the near future because it might get traced back to them since we have already begun to identify and follow the trails of these five Neanderthals. How much help can I get from you transportation wise, or am I completely on my own?"

"You have all my resources at your disposal, but it has to be discreet," the general said. "Here is a secure URL address, and your inside guy can request what you need, and we have ways to fulfill that."

"Who knows?" Clyde said.

Myles looked around like he was being watched and drew on a corner of the placemat. "POTUS, Joint Chief, Homeland, CIA, and their links are strictly just me. They don't know who or what or if, but you know Ian Kilpatrick from some of your former posts, and he would guess I would go after you first."

Clyde said it was good to know he wasn't the pinch hitter. But honestly, if it hadn't been for the incident last night, he probably would have been very reluctant to even think about being in situations where he could die. Clyde outlined that this was the real issue here. Yes, we all think about the morals of being hired by a government to do a job. Especially jobs such as this where oftentimes you look down the barrel of the carnage you create. Obviously it makes it simpler when someone is coming at you, and you have to shoot or die, and it gets fuzzy when you lie in wait for a person the government has said needs to be removed, but the truth of it is he didn't want to die. Something happens to you when you get older and you have children. You want to be around for them.

Clyde knew all the classic arguments about self-defense. Whether it was the side of obeying the government based on your duty. He had heard from the pacifists until he was blue in the face, and they always quoted the passage in Romans that said, "Vengeance is mine thus saith the Lord!" He understood that was taken out of context. Others had reminded him, and he thought often about taking a life that was going to be "damned" for eternity. Each of these biblical or moralistic arguments had merit. He wasn't going to deny that. He also was keenly aware that the "Let's sit around the coffee table or the big blazing camp fire and banter right and wrong away from the realities of being in the midst of conflict" also had flaws. But if he had not noticed the overpatch in the snow or the brush back of the low-lying fern, there would have been a slaughter at the Gareen household. This would have included Mom, Dad, his four kids, himself, and Lady.

"Oh, dear God, please forgive me now," Clyde prayed. Then, with resolve, he thought, *Well, we are going after these petty crime lords, and we are going to find out who the boogeyman really is.*

"Clyde," Kirby said. "One more question, if I may?"

Clyde knew what was coming. He said, "Sure," and he took a deep breath.

"Are you sure you are going to be okay?" the general asked.

"I think so." Clyde paused. "No, General Myles," he remarked carefully. "I am going to be fine. I am not going to ever think about it, and if it were to happen again, which I highly doubt, then I will go through the same process as before and recount it to you. Think about it honestly, write it down, and take it from there."

Clyde was recalling a pretty painful event that both marines knew happened. One of his colleagues had frozen in a terrorist situation. Clyde couldn't blame him because the "enemy" was around twelve. But he was loaded with explosives and heading right to a bunker with a dozen navy seamen. After the soldier froze, Clyde had to take the shot from his location at almost twice the distance. It was a good shot, but when you watch the effects of a couple of pounds of C2 embedded in a fledgling teenager's coat, it can have psychological repercussions. Compound this scenario with a marine disobeying a direct order, and it can get really convoluted.

"People are going to be human, sir."

"Sounds like you have come to grips with it then, Clyde."

"It is what it is, sir, and no matter how much I think about it, it isn't going to change what happened."

"That is simple truth, Colonel." The general sighed reluctantly. "Okay then, marine, let's go to work!"

Clyde fully understood the imperative. "Roger that, General."

OH, BLACK WATER, KEEP ON ROLLING!

T HE THREE OF them were sitting on Yeri's yacht just outside of Buenos Aires. It was a beautiful day, and the ocean was calm, and the fish were jumping, and the people were moving about their business on the shore.

"Charles, you can't let your dislike for one human being get in the way of the big picture here," Alberto said. "You have worked long and hard, and we are going to bring a new day to civilization. This will start time again. It will be BCE, before the common era; ACE, after the common era; and NDD, a new day has dawned. We will have one fifth the population, my dear friend. We will have turned history on its head. All of that puritanical thinking gone, all the world is getting better gone, and all of mankind will start fresh. But we will have the same technology and the same entertainment but less mouths to feed. We can consolidate governments and run the world correctly. Three nuclear explosions, and it will erase the Tierdon P53, and the world weather systems will virtually restart. Hawaii might be a desert after that. Can you imagine a rain forest might pop up in the middle of the Sahara Desert? Why must this one young man get so under your skin?"

Charles smoked his cigar casually. "I have hated him since he was fifteen and lovely little Laina turned her affection to him."

Yeri said that it can be rough. Charles was only fourteen years her senior, and she just needed maybe four or five years until she was of age. But the truth is, and Alberto sensed the distance in his longtime companion, we can never gauge where a woman's heart goes. They have been singing about this since the *Fiddler on the Roof*. Well, actually, Ruth turned her affection on Boaz four thousand years ago, and probably at the birth of civilization, the good mother of us all scorned the first walking man and waited another one thousand years for a soul mate. Oh, they all laughed at that. This is the interesting thing when you have bought into the lie that you are more important than the next person. That your self-interests outweigh the next guy or the other person. You are impervious to the plight of your neighbor. "Let them eat cake" was the feeling at the table as employees brought them more coffee and dessert.

"Well, I will eat my cake," Charles said out loud. "Hey, Yeri, this is very good, and I am sorry for getting emotional and jumping the gun. I was out of line. It will not happen again. Nobody deserves to die quicker than the other four billion people. If my calculations are correct. And then again, my calculations are always correct. Then next step is to build our incubators where the spores can be absorbed in the water molecule, and then we spread them through the oceans and allow nature to take its course. The key to this, and if I may say the genius, as it works itself out, is that we are literally putting out three different types of molecules or isotopes as it were that in and of themselves are useless, but when the three of them cross through evaporation, you get the synthesis that will rain disease on the human immune system. It is about a thirty-six day cycle to put all three of 'hem in the air. We need about twelve days apart, and the first is ready to be launched from our facility in Punta Arenas in South America.

"If you guys have been on your regimen, we will be totally vaccinated against the virus, and so we can move freely and be seen normally, and it will not be an issue for one of us to be involved. The first twelve months will be chaos, and we will have to mitigate against that. Be a voice of calm and reason. Having liquidated all of our money into gold, silver, and diamonds, we will have access to capital when the banking systems fail. We can easily reinvent the banking system. We can work with governments, get peace-keeping forces into place, and be ready and available. *Time* magazine will vote us Men of the Year for Alberto Johnson, Yeri de Angelo, and Charles Walls."

Charles mentioned that he was going into town to meet with Rico. Charles really liked Rico; he was a man with genuine sympathy. If Charles hadn't known better, he could almost believe Rico. It never crossed his mind, not even for a millisecond, that Rico didn't believe him. Charles felt like it was so simple to talk the talk and move in and around the church and to be part of the "chosen." Oh, how he hated that term. Can you imagine or begin to think that there was a god who chose some and not others? This was impossible for Charles to believe. He had read and listened and talked about it, and they called it one of the great mysteries of Scripture. These were good "God-fearing," people but they didn't have the first indication of what the future held. Charles held the future, and there was not a single prayer they could utter that would change that.

Yeri hated talking with his son. He didn't know how Charles could move in and out of the church like a chameleon.

"I am not white on Sunday and black on Monday," Charles said. "I am gray on both days. So it is so very hard to see any difference. I am normally pretty conservative as far as choices with cars, music, art, etc. That part is easy. I listen a lot, and I don't say much. It works out well. They think I am a sage because of my desire to hear and understand."

"Well, don't let them see you with me because I think it is all a crutch," Yeri said. "Religion is strictly for the needy. They are simply insecure and looking for a higher power outside of themselves. Same as mankind has done for thousands of years before the enlightenment. They have found it all right, and it is the church who accepts their offerings and turns it into a machine."

"I fail to see why you are bitter, Yeri," Alberto commented. "You have turned goods and services into a machine, and you are minting your own money. Thirty-three billion was the latest total according to *Forbes* magazine as of last week. That is only the money I report. The other thirty billion is beneath the surface."

Charles said that was all not a problem. "I have church relationships, and then I have business relationships. As far as the church is concerned, I have to do business with the world so I can move freely into the pagan culture and conduct business affairs. That is pretty normal. What the church can't see is what I really believe on the inside. That is really their problem."

YOU GOTTA KNOW
WHEN TO FOLD THEM

C HUCK SEGER SAT in his corner office in downtown
Manhattan and looked over the New York skyline in one
direction and the bay in the other. He could see the boats
and their sails, freighters and ferries, and the fisherman going
out to get their catch. He couldn't believe his luck. In most busi-
nesses, missing your star and having people mad at you was not
good for commerce. You were holding meetings and finding out
how to solve the problems and putting out press releases to show
you were being forward thinking and taking the bull by the horns
and working through your finance people, and talking with the
analysts to show that this wasn't going to hurt your bottom line
in the effort to keep your stock price from taking the elevator to
the basement in a free fall. Well, this was not the case in the television industry, and certainly not in the news and or pop culture

or lifestyle segment of the industry. This was an industry where attention was tantamount to gold. All of the morning news shows were featuring a segment on Clyde Gareen and his side-kick, Anna CiFuentes. Anna was in Chicago to do a segment on the OWN network, and in the meantime, she was sitting down with Bett Grunch of CBS, who went to her and was being interviewed live. *Grilled* is the better word, but it was all in relation to why on earth would her cohost refuse to be on any talk show.

Why was Clyde Gareen so anti–talk show? Who was this guy? All of them knew his food, and all of them were shocked to find out his restaurant had gone out of business. But what didn't add up was how such a brave soldier and an American hero—Clyde detested this label because he said that doing his duty didn't make him a hero—be so against something as iconic as late-night talk shows. All of the big names made the rounds on these, and you didn't have to agree with all of the ideologies of the individual hosts, but to flat-out refuse was contra Americana. It was so ingrained in society that to say I "hate" those talk shows and what they stand for was on par with, well, bigotry.

Chuck sat there on his coach looking at the clock on the bottom of the flat screen on the opposite wall, holding a scalding cup of black coffee. Five in the morning was the time, and he was catching up on the morning news shows in London. He almost choked on his bagel when the lead for the morning telecast was a shot of the three of them together at their after-taping meeting in the sixth floor studio, and they were saying that Chuck Seger, president of New York's Channel 6 news, was doing a very fast tap dance to endear the American public to his really new international food critic who had gone rogue and was defying the likes of Reif Lemonhead, Jasper Mikkel, Sackett O'Neil, and the new one from *Saturday Night Live*, Tommy Jenkins. The defiant Clyde Gareen has stated emphatically that he refuses to grace the late-night talk shows because "they are strictly an outlet for the liberal democratic agenda and debase of any moral values."

Then they cut to his recent interview where, of course, Chuck said Clyde, who was on a little vacation before they started shooting, being a food critic as well as a master chef, didn't really see the need for the hobnobbing on the late-night talk show circuit.

The Brits were saying that, obviously, Mr. Seger is downplaying this immensely. One late-night host has stated emphatically that it is typical of the right wing to get so caught up in their philosophy that they would rather wage war than sit down at the table and have a dialogue. So while most had begun to anticipate a backlash from the Food Network over the programming of this new show featuring Clyde Gareen and Anna CiFuentes just recently, the Food Network has come out strongly in favor of doing the shows. Food Network has stated it is really about the product and not the political views held by the personality. Now if we were a news station, it might be different, but if you enjoy knowing where to eat in Europe because of this new show, then we don't see the harm.

A few hours later, while Chuck and a few of his key staff sat down over fresh coffee and scones to watch the interview Bett Grunch was doing in Chicago, Chuck said, "This is unbelievable. I haven't seen this much press since that football player drove his bronco through Los Angeles. Who gets Bett Grunch to fly to them because she wants to do a morning interview and it can't wait until she gets back to New York?"

"Nobody, really" was the common response. Heather Pearson introduced the segment with "Now we turn to some really very interesting developments in what is being called 'Take my dolls and going home' controversy. Well, maybe it isn't being called that everywhere, but we certainly feel that way about this upstart food critic who is severing ties with all late-night talk shows because of their quote-unquote liberal bias. Here is Bett Grunch with Clyde Gareen's partner, as we speak."

"How are you doing, Anna?" Bett asked.

"I am fine, thanks for asking," Anna remarked. "Although it is a little early, I will admit it has been a hectic five days."

Then Bett got right down to it. She asked straight out, "So where is your cohost right now?"

"Well." Anna paused. "I know this much: he was at his vacation home in Idaho but has since left, and I actually don't know where he is today. He is a private pilot and can get out of Dodge pretty quick."

"Do you know why all the mystery?" Bett asked. "Why doesn't he want to be found? He was spotted in Coeur D'Alene, Idaho, a couple of days ago, and then he is gone."

With a smile that lit up the camera, Anna said, "Like a big game of hide-and-go-seek, right?"

"Well," Bett says, "not exactly, because in that instance, both sides know they are in a game. In this case, the local and national media outlets have been trying to get a hold of Clyde, and he is nowhere to be found."

Anna went on to defend Clyde a little. "I don't think he is actually hiding. I just think he wanted a few days off. We have a big schedule coming up at the end of next week, and he has been through a lot."

"His wife is killed in an explosion in Italy a little over three months ago, and now his restaurant gets closed because of some sort of fall out with his investor," Ms. Grunch said. Do I have this all correct? Can you tell me if there is any or what is the relationship between his wife and this investor?"

Anna looked at Bett like she was insinuating something terrible, and Bett retracted her comment and said, "I am sorry, that came out wrong. What I was trying to ask, and it came out kind of lame, was we know the investor was a family friend of Mrs. Gareen. Why would he pull out, especially after the terrible tragedy?"

"I would love to answer your question or give you an answer because I think it is a really good question and something I have wondered and many of us in New York were wondering when we ate at Del Sol," Anna said. "But I am not sure that I can speak with any knowledge of this family relationship and as to why in light of certain events that one so close to the family would pull his money out. Especially when the investment looked like it was going to play out in spades. I think the question would be a really good one for that investor. Maybe he needed the money for another project, or maybe he doesn't like Clyde. Which I think is hard to imagine because everybody likes Clyde."

"Except for four late-night talk show hosts who feel like they got the middle finger from your cohost," Bett quickly inserted.

Anna commented rhetorically that it didn't take her long to recover from the previous foot-in-mouth question. And then they both laughed, which was ironically enough great television, and everybody in the studio, as well as here in Chuck's office, was laughing too.

"I can't honestly tell you what Clyde thinks on all those subjects," Anna said. "I know that he comes from a very long history of soldiers, and he has relatives that fought with Washington in the Revolutionary War and with General Sherman in the Civil War. He has living relatives that fought in both world wars, and I think they have a way of thinking, along with his very personal relationship with Jesus Christ, and on all these things, Clyde is very forthright about. I don't know these things from Clyde personally other than hearing him in conversation at Del Sol and then some brief exchanges in the last few days."

"So is it fair to say he is a right-wing fundamentalist?" Bett asked.

Anna remarked, both as a friend of Clyde's and as a journalist, "I do not honestly know. That phrase sounds so terribly harsh. I actually don't know if I could define it for you. We throw it around as somebody who has a fanatical bent or maniacal conservative approach to government, taxes, spending, social issues, but I have spent the last couple of days with a super nice guy. He loves to cook, he dearly loved his wife who died in a tragic accident three months ago, and a man who tears up when he speaks of his kids." As she said all of this, she looked down at her phone, which was on the table along with her plate and cup, which made it look like she had been eating as the interview was supposed to be live and as you were.

"Right now I see his picture from my angle," Bett commented. "You aren't getting a text right this second, are you?"

Anna reached down. "Which I am sure the CBS gods were all thrilled to relate firsthand to the planet. 'Dear Anna, please tell your friend Bett that I will answer that question in a blog post this afternoon. I don't have anything against the late-night talk show hosts personally, and I wish them all the best. I just really don't want to go on their shows. There are a couple of people I would sit down with in an interview.' End of text."

"Text him back and simply ask who," Bett said.

Anna hit the phone and flipped it to one side and with both hands typed in, "Who?"

The reply was instant. "Not saying until after our first show!"

The conversation continued, but back in the office, the staff was howling. It was a mix of cheer and laughter. Clyde had just bought them unprecedented continued coverage, and what was a national story for a few days was now becoming a cultural phenomenon. Anna CiFuentes had, in many ways, cut through all of the stereotyping that the media was trying to give Clyde because he was not playing their game, and she had made Clyde out to be super likable and a normal guy whom most people could connect to.

DESPERADO

I NA DE ANGELO reminded Rico of his Laina, and it hurt him to look at her. Ina could sense something in Rico's deep black eyes and asked, "Everything all right, Pastor?"

He said that she had a keen sense of awareness. "No, Ina, you have always reminded me of Laina. Your bubbly, easygoing personality and the way you make everyone feel comfortable is so much like Laina."

"Is?" Ina said.

And Rico said as Ed walked into the room from a phone call in the home office, "I am the only one on the planet who doesn't think Laina was in that car, and my wife forbids me to mention it because I have no proof, and she says I am in denial. Which, well, maybe, but I will hold out for a few more months." He turned and said, "Brother," to Ed and gave him a warm embrace. "You look like someone just stole your wallet."

Ed nodded and looked at Ina and then replied his father was in town and wanted to have dinner. Rico responded by saying that was great news.

"He is always so antagonistic about me and the church and what we are doing," Ed said. "It gets old."

"Ed, I know you are too close to the fire on this, and it hurts so deeply because of your relationship with him and the past, but keep in mind that he is just one person who doesn't realize that he is a sinner and needs a savior to pay his debt for offending the Creator of the universe. You know this, and you say it every week, and people respond to your pleading as though you were pleading for God! Ed, I know, I know—and I have known, and I will know—the pain caused in these close personal relationships is the greatest pain of all because we are highly leveraged and highly invested, and it is what makes us human. Besides, our rational thinking, it is the love and the care we have for each other that makes us who we are made in the Imagio Dei. Go to dinner with your father. Love him as you would any visitor that came to su Iglesia. Don't think about his shortcomings as a father and whatever he thinks of you now."

"Rico, my brother, five years apart, and you are still my mentor."

"I am not your mentor anymore. We are brothers, and I would say this to any brother in the Lord. You are my fellow bondservant toiling in the work of seeing people repent and then grow, or sometimes not grow, and we get all of the blame, and the Lord gets the credit, and it is okay."

So Ed said to Rico, "Are you hungry? Can you eat South American cuisine, or does everything need to be pasta?"

"I am starving," Rico said, "and looking forward to breaking bread with you guys. I have had a long flight and I just finished reading the very long book called *Inheritance*, which my grandchildren have read. That young author has a vivid imagination."

They ate and talked the night away. Ed and Ina had five children, a nine-year-old boy whom Rico knew as well as the seven-year-old twin girls, but the three-year-old and one-year-old brother-and-sister set were adopted from a local orphanage where the need for parents was unprecedented. Argentina was yet another country with an alarming birth rate to unwed and very underage girls. It was the crime of this culture to propagate intimacy outside the bounds of commitment and not provide rock-solid advice to the kids about what happens as a result of all of this promiscuity.

"It is the biggest problem on the planet right now," Ed said. "We can't unteach fast enough what the world is advocating since they get to start in on their lies at five years old when they start in the school system."

The nine-year-old was a big soccer fan, and he wanted to talk about Messi and Barcelona and the Argentinean national team. Pastor Rico, as the kids called him, said he needed to buy fourteen long-sleeve Messi jerseys, which was a request made by his grandson's soccer team. His oldest grandchild was thirteen and currently playing in the Inter Milan club system. But all the boys would come over, and when they heard Rico was going to Argentina, they asked if he could get the jerseys. The seven-year-old wanted to know all about his granddaughters and if they liked riding horses. They had horses and rode with Mommy every day. "When I am ten, I get my own horse, but mi padre says I have to clean up after it, or I cannot keep it."

"Hey, my cousin Antonio plays for the one of the local clubs here, and it looks like he will make that national team you are talking about," Ed said. "Do you want to go watch his game and then we can ask if he can get some autographed long-sleeve jerseys about adult small?"

Rico responded, saying that he would be the hero of all grand-fathers if he could. "And yes, I would love to be outdoors, see all of the people, and of course, I love the beautiful game, even if they play it a little sloppy here."

At the game, it was a de Angelo family reunion. Antonio was actually getting really good. He was *diez y siete*, or seventeen, and in the last seis meses, he had averaged a goal a game. He was an emerging superstar and a super nice kid. His father, Cordero, was at the game, and so was Ed's father, Yeri. Ed introduced Rico to Yeri, but they reminded each other that they had met over the years although Yeri was frequently gone. Yeri had an air about him as did Rico's friend Charles Walls. Rico knew that they were business partners and had done some international ventures but that was about all Rico really knew. He didn't know the half of it, or so did anyone think, but Rico had his suspicions, and talking with Yeri confirmed a lot.

Rico said to Yeri, "You know my friend Charles Walls?"

Yeri said he did and, in fact, had just recently had dinner with him. And Rico said, "Or you are that friend who owns the yacht."

Yeri said that Charles needed to keep his whereabouts a little closer to the vest, and they laughed, but Yeri wasn't kidding. Rico said that he was pretty unhappy with Charles at the moment and was going to tell him as much, and Yeri kind of frowned, and Rico said that Charles had pulled a lot of money out of the restaurant his daughter and son-in-law owned. One would have thought that Yeri just heard the click of a land mine but hadn't let his foot off yet.

"I am sorry," Rico said. "I have said too much. I am always opening my big mouth."

Just then Yeri gathered himself and said, "I am sorry, I didn't know it was Charles. I knew that it had happened because I saw the broadcast news in New York this morning, and your son-in-law is the most famous guy in the United States right now. He gets more coverage on prime time television than the president. He is going to have to unearth another scandal to get some more coverage."

Rico said that the corruption in Italian politics made the United States look like schoolchildren, and Yeri erupted with a howl. The United States has nothing on either Argentina or half a dozen South American neighbors. Then fans stood on their feet. River Plate had just stolen the ball and was on a counterattack run straight up the middle of the field, and it was three on one and one very lonely keeper. The ball was passed right, and he took a shot from almost the opponent's goal line that was going over the head of the keeper but was going to miss the goal until the left striker, who was Antonio de Angelo, was sliding to meet the ball with his outstretched foot. He got it and redirected the ball just past the diving keeper firmly into the back of the net. "Golaso" was the scream, and everyone rejoiced. The hometown team ended up winning two to zero over their archrivals Racing Club. Once again Antonio had scored the game winner.

Antonio changed, and everybody went out for dinner and coffee. Antonio said to Ed that he saw Uncle Yeri at the game. "How come he didn't come to dinner?"

"I never know what Papa was going to do," Ed said.

Antonio said that he was the new sponsor for the national team, with one of his companies, Comtigo, which was a huge multinational food distributor, and now it looked like Ed had heard the click. Rico was, like, "What is it about tonight that everyone seemingly is getting startled? This is not a group of folks who, by any means, would scare easily."

Rico asked Ed if the name of the company meant anything. Ed said it was nothing. What Ed knew couldn't be repeated because he had been told in a private meeting with a young worker from one of the distribution centers and said he had come back to work late at night one evening because he forgot his tickets to the match, and there was an entirely different shift working, and they were packing what looked like an entirely different product line than the one he was in charge of. He skipped getting the tickets and appealed to a friend who was a vendor and got into the game anyway and knew no one would be in his seats.

Yeri de Angelo was the owner of about thirty different companies. This was one of the ways that he had done so well, buying and remaking the companies mostly in the food distribution arena so profitable. And now Ed knew what he had suspected. His dad was probably making in the billions through illegal drug distribution. Rico didn't need to be told. He knew. He could see straight through Ed de Angelo and knew for a fact that he had another piece of information regarding that company that he couldn't share because it was privileged. Someone could lose their life if he told what he knew, or that oftentimes was the level of information as a pastor you were given when people were unloading their burdens. Tonight a terrific soccer game, and tomorrow church and then a late lunch with Charles, which could be quite interesting knowing what he knew. Confrontation was not his favorite agenda, but deal with it he would.

As they got up to leave the restaurant, a man came in with a big box. "Señor Delmo" was the cry. Rico stood up because he heard *Del Amo* pronounced a thousand ways to Sunday and wasn't worried about it. He like the *señor*, though, and was wishing his señorita was on this trip with him. He hated being away from his family although seeing Ed and his family was a real bonus.

The man with the box came over to Rico and asked him to sign for the delivery. Rico was so surprised that he got a package, but he was even more taken back when he opened it and there were a dozen or so Argentina National Jerseys with the number 10 on it and all signed by Lionel Messi.

"Wow! I can't believe it."

Antonio came over and gave Rico a big high five. "We would do anything for you, Pastor Rico. All you have done for us vicariously through what you have done for Cousin Eddie. Next year, hopefully, the young Italian soccer stars will want numero vente y dos."

Rico smiled. "I will see you at church in the morning?"

TAKING IT TO THE STREETS

L AINA GAREEN HAD been living for the last eight weeks in a halfway house. She thought that was a living hell. She is on the earth and she is alive, but nothing was real. Well, she couldn't go back to reality, or her family will be dead. Being alive was nothing short of a miracle. She wanted to be careful with the concept of not dying in the streets of Palermo being a miracle because too many people abused it on an almost-daily basis. But she had been caught red-handed on the ship. Shortly after they docked, she had just come out of the restroom when a powerful hand grabbed her. He said in English, with an American accent, "What do we have here? Trying to sneak on the ship, are we? Well, your ride finishes before it begins!"

And that was how she snuck off the ship. They kicked her off. Mistakenly they assumed she had just snuck on in Long Beach. She was to find out that she was in the port of Long Beach. She had made it to Los Angeles and was walking in the streets of downtown Long Beach. She might blow her cover, but she and Monster were both starving. She walked into a homeless-women's shelter. Checking in right at eleven in the morning, she found she was able to secure a spot. They let her keep the dog, and she got a hot meal and a shower.

A counselor came in to do an assessment on her, but she knew that talking would blow any kind of chance she had at being seen as actually homeless. She wasn't high or incoherent like most homeless people because of mental illness. But her silence was perceived as though she was a victim of the most terrible sort. A young woman who, despite the baggy clothes, couldn't hide her beauty, and the worst was assumed. Laina overheard one counselor say it was not uncommon for victims of violence or worse to be in denial and almost in a walking comatose state. It was a sad place, where the downtrodden had come to be anonymous and had come to be in a permanent altered state so they didn't have to cope.

After two nights at the shelter, she felt like she wanted to make her way into the heart of Los Angeles. She actually didn't know why. Well, for the most part, she had a feeling that this shelter would ask too many questions. She got on the metro and rode it straight to the skid row area. Lots of people—strange place to be in—and for the most part, she wanted to work in some Lysol to the whole bunch. Clean them up and their belongings. She still had all her five hundred dollars in cash and in almost a month hadn't had to spend much at all.

Laina, who found a small corner of her own, was settling in on one of the permanently homeless encampments when a young lady came up to her. She was dreadfully young and had what looked like maybe an eight-month-old infant boy with her in a very rusted and decaying stroller. For whatever reason, this young mother found something she could trust in Laina. She asked Laina if she could watch her baby for ten minutes while she used one of the public restrooms. Laina said, "Of course," without thinking, and the girl moved off down the street. Just at that moment, she heard a tall foul-smelling man come up from behind her and grab her by both arms and while sort of whistling was saying that if she was quiet he wouldn't hurt her too bad. Well, she wasn't married to a special ops military man for nothing. She immediately relaxed her body, which gave her some space between her head and his chin. While sliding her right foot back and behind his right foot, in the meantime, he misinterpreted the moves as though she was going to be a willing accomplice. When her feet were set, she thrust upward, and her head went straight into his chin.

Unfortunately for Mr. Predator, his tongue was in between his teeth at the moment, and the blow made him bite down hard, slicing through his tongue. As he released his grip and started to step backward, his foot caught her foot, and he started to fall. In an ironic twist of events, he crashed hard on a rock and passed out. Lying there in a pool of blood, it became apparent that he would probably suffocate or choke or both. Laina simply rolled him over so the blood could drain out of his mouth. She quite frankly wasn't that concerned whether he made it or not. Seeing a large bulge from his back pocket, she reached in and found a wallet. She grabbed this instinctively and turned to find the nearest officer.

As she turned, she saw the entire encampment was clapping because this was not the first time Mr. Predator had attacked someone. It was nearly sundown when she tired of looking for an officer. So she just sat down on a bench not far from Pershing Square in downtown Los Angeles. She examined the wallet and found it had 440 dollars in it. She found that remarkable for a man who was "homeless." There was nothing of importance in the wallet, except for a driver's license and a bank debit card.

Now that is odd, she thought. *Why would Egan Sooers have identity and a bank account? He had cash on him, and well, she had both also, so maybe he really wasn't homeless, just preying on the homeless.*

She didn't miss the coincidence of his name as she thought he was truly living in the sewer. She was about to make her way down the street when the sweet young girl came back to claim her child. Laina had a million things she wanted to say to this high-school-aged child and wanted to ask her as many questions. She just said, "I hope to see you again," and turned and walked aimlessly away until she stopped near a vendor selling hot dogs and couldn't resist buying one. She was just tired and hungry, and it was the smell that got her. It actually wasn't a hot dog; it was a bacon-wrapped polish sausage that came with jalapeños and onions.

As she and Monster sat down to eat, Laina began to cry. Oh, not again! She dreadfully missed her family. Actually, *dreadfully* wasn't even the beginning of the description. It was overwhelming pain, and it made her short of breath. The other very quirky detail that had slipped her attention at the time of the attack was that the entire episode had been caught on a smartphone and was instantly uploaded to YouTube. She wandered down the street and caught a bus and knew she was headed for one of the local shelters. She got off the bus about a block away, and the people were glad to see her leave. Dirty from a few nights in the streets and her faced caked with tears and sweat from her ordeal, she looked homeless. In fact, truth be known, she *felt* homeless. She longed for a shower, her family, and she just wanted to sit in church. She missed Sunday morning, singing praises to her heavenly Father, praying with the congregation, and hearing God's Word articulated, which always made her contemplate on how she should change. In fact, these things she took for granted, and it made her think of her brothers and sisters in countries where it was illegal to gather in Christian worship.

At the moment, she had stopped in an alleyway between two apartment buildings, and she heard a little crying coming from the Dumpster. "Oh my goodness," she said aloud. "I can't believe what I am hearing!" She opened the trash lid and reached way down into the bin and grabbed a bundle of loosely wrapped T-shirts and towels. She sat down next to the Dumpster and held the bundle and unpacked a tiny little baby boy. She thought it was maybe only hours old. To her astonishment, a shadow crossed in front of her, and she looked up to a police officer.

"Officer, I just pulled this baby from the trash," Laina said.

The officer looked at her and didn't take the baby from her as she handed it to him.

"Ma'am, please hold onto your baby and let me help you up," he said.

"Officer," she cried, "I am not the mother!"

He looked at her like he had heard this many times before and repeated, "I understand. Let me get you some help. We can walk just around the corner to a shelter, and they can provide for families."

Well, one could have hit Laina over the head with a flatiron skillet. She couldn't believe what she heard. Stunned, she walked meekly next to the officer, holding a life that was crying and obviously hungry, and Monster was following right behind. As they entered the shelter, the officer explained to the intake coordinator that the reluctant young mother needed some resources and access to formula. The counselor looked at Laina and spoke in Spanish to her. It didn't faze her a bit, she was of a dark complex, and the baby had lots of dark curly hair, with large black eyes and very olive skin. Nevertheless, Laina responded in Spanish and said only, "Ayuda, por favor." She repeated the phrase and then went silent, and they brought her in and gave her diapers and formula and very small onesies. Because she was a young mother and had children, she, of course, was very adept at dealing with a small little body and tiny little toes. Oh my, this baby was hungry, and so extremely gorgeous, and her heart melted. She fed the child, and the baby slept next to her on the padded cot.

Laina passed out because it had been one heck of a day. Monster kept watch under the cot. Laina woke up to a crying baby and sat up and fed the child.

I can't keep calling him baby, she thought. *I can't keep him. Someone needs him or wants him, or I know there is a process. Okay, I will get cleaned up as best as possible and go to social services. They will know what to do.* "Hi, my name is Laina Gareen, and I am homeless, hiding in Los Angeles from a psychopath who killed an old friend of mine in my car, and will probably kill my family. And in the meantime, I almost killed a man yesterday, who tried to molest me, and shortly after that, I found Ricardo in a Dumpster." She envisioned briefly through this scenario and concluded, "Yes, that should go well."

They will say, "Well, Mrs. Gareen, you are a hero. Thanks for bringing in this child, and we believe every word you are saying since you are homeless, living on the streets, and you 'just' found a baby which looks just like you." She made her way to the dinner line, and they heaped rice, large pinto beans, squash, and what looked like carnitas onto her plate. As she held the baby in one arm and ate with the other, someone from the shelter came up to her and gave her a small baby carrier. Laina placed the baby in the carrier and strapped him in gently for safety, although she didn't seem him jumping out anytime soon. She had changed his diaper already, and he looked like all systems go. Hadn't made a peep since he had eaten, and was already sound asleep. She also was given a piece of paper for a family shelter in Pacoima. It came with bus fare and directions.

So that was it. From that arrangement they had moved her from the family shelter to a halfway-type house to get homeless people back into permanent living. It was her second halfway house since she didn't want to get to know anyone too well. She had managed to say very little, but in the ensuing two months, through what Laina attributed to the providence of God, she had reconnected with that young mother who had asked her to watch her baby. The young mother called her baby James and had asked what Laina's baby's name was.

"Ricardo Gareen, and I am Laina," she said. She thought it was crazy. Living on the streets or in the system, and she was raising a child, ministering to an unwed teenage mom, and taking care of a dog. Well, Monster was taking care of her, in reality. James was six months old and moving. Tonya, as the teenage mom said her name was, didn't know the father or who the father was and had been clean since the pregnancy and birth of her child. She just didn't have any family because her dad was in jail and her mother was a prostitute and an addict. Laina asked Tonya if she played cards, and Tonya's response was negative because she had never been taught. Furthermore, since she couldn't read, it was hard to learn the rules on her own. Laina's heart fell through the floor, in a manner of speaking, and she began to encourage, teach, and instruct Tonya.

I LOVE LOS ANGELES!

RICO LANDED AFTER a long flight from Argentina. He had flown most of the night. But it was still only 7:00 a.m. in Los Angeles. He proceeded off the plane after grabbing his carry-on, which was really a working case. He had a couple of books in it, his Bible, and his laptop. His new tablet was a thing of unbelievable equipment. He could write on it, listen to music, stream sermons from other ministries, and read and communicate with blogs all over the world. It was truly incredible. He thought back to Wycliffe wanting to get the Word of God into the English language so that everyone could read it. Here he just clicks on an icon and his software asks him what language.

He was speaking at the conference tomorrow, and he was more excited than he had been in years. The message on his heart was simple: our people look like the world. Big business, two kids, public schools—it was crazy. We are not to be conformed but transformed. This meant if the world was doing it, we probably shouldn't be. But most importantly, we were to be separate; different. Raise our own kids, love the unloved, reach out to the downtrodden, share ourselves with the hurting. We need a fresh paradigm. Freedom had too many downsides.

Rico was so lost in thought that he didn't realize he was already in the baggage claim area. He could hear one man with his back to him speaking to another in Italian and he said, "I know that voice." The baseball cap and the awful-looking sunglasses from the *Star Trek* era were serving the purpose of keeping the Italian local incognito. Just then the man turned, and Rico couldn't believe it. The man had his hands up to his lips so that Rico wouldn't blurt it out. The problem with television is now everybody knew him.

"I didn't know you were in Los Angeles," Rico said.

Clyde said that they had made a quick trip from the family vacation home in Idaho. "We are staying with my dad's sister Aunt Sheri Anne, and you are welcome to join us."

Rico said it was a great idea, but he would like to stay at the conference accommodations but certainly would love to come out and see everyone for dinner. "Let's forget dinner. How about breakfast? I would love to see the kids."

They drove pretty easily through the west side of Los Angeles as it seemed like millions were pouring into the city. They were all the way up the 405 or the San Diego freeway from LAX in about twenty-five minutes. The 405 ended into the 5 Freeway, and they were through this juncture and back out to Agua Dulce in another fifteen minutes. Easy trip, thought Rico, and they pulled off the 14 freeway and drove into Agua Dulce.

Aunt Sheri was so pleased that Rico Del Amo had come out to the home. Grandpa Del Amo hadn't even waited for the car to come to a complete stop before he bolted out of the car and ran to hug his grandchildren. Aunt Sherri and Clyde's mom had cooked a feast. Pancakes, thick slices of ham, scrambled eggs, and lots and lots of coffee. It was a sight. It had been a long time since Rico had seen the Gareens, and he had such a great time sitting and talking to the children. The funeral had been fast, and it was so hard on everyone.

Clyde asked Rico what his schedule was and when he had to be at the conference. Rico said he had a few meetings later that afternoon and then the conference started in the morning around 8:00 a.m. Clyde didn't know what to do. He hated the thought of false hope. He was also very nervous about letting whatever cat might be held out of the bag. He decided to wait. He didn't have any proof. He wasn't sure himself. It was not time yet. All of Clyde's training told him that if there was a threat, it could be inside a very close circle. Obviously it wasn't Rico, but it could be someone inside the immediate family circle.

Clyde thought of aunts and uncles and then of associates close to the Del Amos. The problem was there were people he didn't like and maybe people willing to kill him, but what was a threat that could be so immediate and pervasive that it would drive his wife into hiding and not tell her special ops trained husband who had just been contracted to eliminate four or five of the worst bad guys on the planet?

"Connect the dots, Clyde," he said softly under his breath.

Rico left that evening for a preconference meeting, and then he went on to his hotel. Everyone packed up early and spent the entire day at the "Happiest Place on Earth." Clyde thought it might be the most expensive place on earth, but his kids grinned from ear to ear the entire day. With Josephine back at his aunt's, it made for a lot of happy people. Sherri Anne was thrilled to have the baby all day, and the kids were old enough to really groove at the amusement park. Three adults and three kids work out well especially when his mom enjoyed nothing more than being with a four-year-old granddaughter on It's a Small World, although Mr. Toads Wild Ride got a little dicey, but the older kids were rocking on Space Mountain and Indiana Jones.

Clyde enjoyed the day with his family. He knew that there was a storm a foot, well maybe more like a Florida-coast category 5 hurricane. But he was going to be out of the loop for a little while emotionally and physically with his kids. So he took time to talk with them and hold them and laugh with them. To hear the echo of his daughter's laughter inside the caves of the Matterhorn, so hauntingly just like her mother's. The juxtaposition of just cracking up with his daughter and the emptiness inside of him missing Laina was enough to send somebody straight to a bipolar designation without passing go and without collecting two hundred dollars. They rolled back into Agua Dulce around 11:00 p.m. and carried three sleeping children straight to bed. They were going to have giant lollipop dreams, Clyde thought, as he tucked them in and headed off to his room.

Clyde checked his e-mail and saw one from Red Horse. The story was that Red Horse had killed a ten-horn buck, and while he went to get the kill, both a spotted leopard and a pack of coyotes were moving in, but it appeared that one lone wolf might have his back.

That is pretty good, Clyde thought. They had worked out their cryptic messages in boot camp and in officer training school. Clyde had always said that his friend Johnny Walker was a horse of a different color, as his great-grandfather like to say, and since Walker Red was a well-known label for scotch.

Or was it whiskey or turpentine? Clyde thought.

Red Horse was moving and could be found near Saint Louis which he gathered from the *s* and *l* in the second animal. He also knew it was within a ten-mile radius of the center, and it was at 1300 hours on the clock. Which, of course, is one, and looking at MapQuest, he saw that there was a zoo. Where else do you find a lone wolf? He replied that the lone wolf had trapped the leopard and scared away the pack and was happy to help with the buck, but it would have to circle twice before the leopard moved on. This, of course, had to mean 3:00 p.m. in the afternoon because Johnny wouldn't be awake that early. He was a rock and roller and could party late into the evening, and typically, he never saw the sunrise. Things were different in the military, but it has a way of making you conform really fast.

At breakfast, Mr. Gareen told Clyde that Rico had invited them to Italy. Laina's sister was going with them to help with the baby, and the seven of them would fly out and stay for two weeks. "This makes a lot of sense because everybody gets to see the kids, and you have to shoot for the next ten days, anyways."

Clyde thought that verb was a wonderful play on words in light of his new arrangement with General Myles. Clyde said that would work out fantastic, and he said that he didn't want to put his parents to the trouble.

"Really, we get lots of help with the kids, and we get to go see Italy," Robert said. "I know you have spent a lot of time there, but we are thrilled to go."

So it was settled, and shortly after breakfast was cleaned up, Clyde and his father drove down to the convention center for what had to be the largest conference of evangelical pastors Clyde had ever seen. As they were making their way downtown, Clyde told his father they better get gas, and they exited off the freeway into downtown Pacoima. It was pretty close to a town called Van Nuys, but as Clyde pumped the gas into the white Suburban, he looked across the street at the Guardian Angel halfway house. He wondered what life was like for the people to be coming out of the system and trying to get their lives back together.

As Tonya looked out the window while she was holding James and helping him burp after his morning meal, she saw a man filling his new rather-large Yukon and staring at their apartments. She thought she recognized the man from TV. It looked like the guy whom they were all fussing about not willing to go on all the talk shows. She thought the last thing in the world she would want to do was go on TV and have somebody ask her a bunch of questions. Although she would love to go on that singing show with the judges and see if she could go to Hollywood.

That is funny. She smiled. *I can take the bus to Hollywood. But why would I want to?*

Clyde saw Tonya in the window and gave her a thumbs up. Clyde headed back into the car, and they jumped onto the freeway for downtown. What he didn't see was the woman sitting next to the window who was busy changing the clothes of a newborn infant. It would be sometime later before Clyde would know that he had been across the street from his wife.

As they entered into the main auditorium for the convention center, they could hear Rico Del Amo speaking in English, although with a thick Italian accent, and he was in full preacher's mode. He spoke with passion, and he spoke clearly. "I am an older man, and I have lived a long time, friends, and I know this: if you look like the world, and you talk like the world, and you think like the world, and you do the same things as the world, then you have not been transformed. You are still conformed to the world.

"Christ told the rich young ruler that you must sell all your belongings and follow me. Well, this was too high a price for the prince. He needed to spend the summer on the country estate and help his new wife with the baby. No, maybe he needed to spend his days managing his vineyards and making sure the next crop was right to be harvested, bottled, and cured before it went to sale all over the world. This is important stuff, and he couldn't drop everything and follow Christ. He was willing to accept and add the newly articulated Christian ethic to his life and to be kind and gracious and live life with some humility, but he really needed to finish building the rocket ship."

Pastor Del Amo paused, looked at his audience, and smiled. Putting his hand to one side of his face, he whispered, "I changed illustrations on you. Hang in there with me. So this engineer says to the Lord, 'I can't follow you today. I have to finish building the rocket ship because if I don't, then my country can't be the first to colonize the moooon!'"

Everybody in the audience howled with laughter.

Pastor Del Amo went on, "How ironic that we are going to send people to the moon and the God of the Universe says, 'Hey,

I am here, follow me,' and we say, 'Excuse me, but at the moment, I got really, really important stuff to do today.'"

Clyde sat there, stunned, and then he thought, *I wonder how it would play in this gathering with me deliberately ending the most nefarious of human beings life? For humanity or for country or for whomever, I am going to do the best possible job I know how, and I will have to the let the chips fall where they may.*

HAVE YOU EVER SEEN
THE RAIN?

S ITTING IN A Midwestern town, waiting for Johnny Reb, as he called him, Clyde couldn't even begin to think about getting out of his rented convertible BMW. He thought he would have a little fun driving through Saint Louis, only he didn't pay enough attention to the forecast. It wasn't raining, he thought. It was a cloud burst. He couldn't see ten feet out of his windshield, and it made it impossible to see, let alone drive. He felt like the rain was an indication of what he was feeling inside at the moment. It was all gray, dark, and foreboding, with enormous rain clouds on the horizon and no end of the storm in sight.

He found the zoo and was waiting in the back of the lot. He had to pay $5 to park. *Not unlike Los Angeles or New York*, he thought, *but it would have been double or triple that. Here I am, sitting in the parking lot where all of the wild animals are caged so they won't hurt the public. What about the animals that are running loose that fully intend on hurting the populace? The only difference is that these animals at the zoo can't reason. Well, I am being paid to be the zookeeper. Just on behalf of a different kind of animal.*

A white Scion pulled up, and the window came down a crack.

"Hey, Clyde, how are you?" Johnny yelled. "Let's do this meeting inside my vehicle. You aren't set up for a wheelchair, and we need to keep this session dry."

The side door opened from the modified car, and Clyde scurried out of his car and into Johnny's. He quickly closed the door behind him, and Johnny turned his seat completely around, and Clyde slid into a half-height bucket seat that was next to the table and opposite of Johnny. They had a regular conference room.

"What is up, bro?" Johnny said. "Life has had its moments for you lately. I can't tell you how sorry I was about Laina. As you know, I never felt for a moment that was an accident. I evaluated the footage, and to me, it looked like the upward thrust of the blast indicated it had been preset. It got a little sloppy around the edges, but more like the bomb technician knew what he was doing and tried to make it look like an accident. You got an enemy. And why he would go after that pretty wife of yours makes no sense to me, unless she saw or knew something that would have been dangerous to the wrong people. I am sorry for all of this, you know. Of course you do, because you are Clyde Gareen, the most hated guy of all the talk shows, by the way."

"Hey, Johnny, do you ever shut up?" Clyde asked.

"Sorry, man," Johnny said with a hint of remorse. "It is just good to see you!"

Clyde retorted that it was great to see him also. "Listen, I would love to chitchat, but there is a lot we need to cover, and I am on a really tight schedule. I am due to fly out of New York in the morning with the crew, and we start our ten-to-fourteen-day road trip. We are trying to shoot three shows. But I am not here for that, as you probably well know. I had a meeting in Los

Angeles, and besides the person I met with, only five people know the purpose of that meeting. I will lay it out for you in a second, but I have to ask if you are willing to be the back-office technical guy as I do this job. It is tough-as-nails military ops—black ops—off-the-grid stuff where we will get no support if we are compromised and the bad guys could turn on us and come back and bite down hard, if you follow what I am saying."

Johnny held up his hand. "Clyde, I am in full throttle. Stop with the nefarious bad-guy disclaimer stuff. You know I won't tell my dog any of this stuff. You will have all of my resources at your disposal. Please do not say it, I know you are going to offer me money to reimburse for my resources. I don't want your money. I pay enough taxes already, and quite frankly, I don't want to pay any more despite what the popular rhetoric of the day is that the 2 percenters are able and willing to pay more. I can use the expense write off. This is a perfect plan, and I am all in. You have been asked by Myles to eliminate the likes of eight or nine despots, and I can list the top fifteen, but they are all FBI poster children for their most wanted, and they make the CIA, Homeland Security, and Interpol lists. The simple and elegant plan is you will hide in plain sight. It is beautiful. Your face will be on the tele, as the Brits say, and by night you will put on the Caped Crusader routine."

Clyde, flummoxed with Johnny's soliloquy, simply said, "Thank you." Then he blurted out, "Johnny, they came after my family in Idaho."

"No kidding," Johnny said. Well, he didn't use the word *kidding*, but he was pissed. "Who knows already?"

"That is the thing," Clyde replied. "I hadn't met with Myles yet."

"Somebody hates your guts, Greenie," Johnny responded. He used the nickname, which was the shortened version of Gareen from their old vet days and adding the *ie* that everyone liked to tag on.

"Well, the pool isn't that large, friend," Clyde said, "because they knew I had a family home in Idaho. My whereabouts was on the serious DL, as the teenagers say."

"Do you think it is that idiot Walls? Johnny said. "Clyde, if he hadn't been a friend of your wife's family, I would have rearranged his face personally years ago. You would think that a foster kid gone bazillionaire would have a little bit of a soft spot for the down-on-your-luck types who also occupy the globe."

"What do you mean foster kid?" Clyde asked.

"The scoop on that fat cat was bad dad and addicted mom," Johnny said. "One died, and the other was put out to pasture for failing over to many rehabs, and he went into the system at thirteen."

"I wonder why I never knew that," Clyde wondered out loud. "Yes, that is weird, but no, I don't think it is him. He is a first-class jerk, and I may beat you to the punch literally the next time I see him, especially after the crap he pulled in New York, but I don't think he cares one way or the other about all this country fighting and global nuclear-war stuff. Plus I don't think he has the connections to an East German death squad."

"You said five man when we talked on the phone earlier," Johnny quipped. "Did they carry AKs or modified Uzis?"

"It felt like an AK," Clyde said. "Maybe manufactured somewhere in the former Soviet Republic, because they were a little heavy and tighter on the trigger. And they were super quiet, which became their problem, after I got the first two men. The next two ran straight back at me and between my knife and their guns. Well, need I say more?"

Johnny shook his pinky and asked again about Numero Cinco. Clyde told the story again of his dad getting in on the action with a shotgun.

Johnny laughed for five minutes. "You have got to be kidding me. Don't mess with old man Greenie. He is packing bird shot and shoots from three meters." Johnny changed faces and pulled out a little thumb drive. "This is what I will need."

"Are you getting hooked up with Gray Eagle again for the military resources?"

"Yes."

Clyde nodded. "Good."

"I like working with her," Johnny said. "She is tight-lipped and all business. You know, I have a feeling she is totally hot. That is why Myles won't let us meet her."

"Johnny you need to settle down, get saved, and get married," Clyde pleaded.

"In that order, preacher boy?" Johnny laughed. "Look out, world. Johnny is going to church."

Clyde interrupted, saying, "You know you are going to reach out to me from the wrong side of judgment and say, 'Why, Greenie, didn't you help me?'"

This was an old conversation the two friends had bantered with each other with since their first night as bunkmates in boot camp twelve years ago.

"Look, I have really matured and slowed down," Johnny said. "I don't drink nearly as much, quit smoking cigarettes—just mostly cigars now—and I am down to one pipe a week. I had a girlfriend for two months. Same girl. Clyde, we actually talked, and I met her parents. How about that for progress? In some states, that is considered common law, man. I will make you a very simple deal, Clyde, and I am totally serious. If the Big Man upstairs heals my legs, then I am all in. I will go to church, I will get baptized, I will take notes, I will serve on the sound team that sets up the music and slideshow and whatever else they need."

"One girl?" Clyde asked. "Dude, you are killing me, man."

"Look, I already came across the aisle to shake your hand," Johnny retorted. "You got to leave me with a little something."

"Johnny, I will leave you with this," Clyde said. "You know more than anybody on the planet that I love you. You saved my life at least twice, and the last time I was shot up and left for dead and without you, my obituary was written on the stone already. But it isn't about doing stuff, and it isn't about your legs. It is about—"

And then Johnny finished the sentence. "I know it is about the heart, and my heart isn't there yet. But enough of the Bible talk, man. We got work to do. I will send you encrypted communication devices so we can talk all over the planet untapped. We will piggyback on some of the NSA stuff and some of the military stuff. They won't know because I won't let them in, and we will talk Tennessee to Africa, or South Am, or the Malaysian corridor. Yes, you know me. I already know, dude."

"Okay," Clyde said as he gave Johnny the list, which he had copied straight from the napkin and slipped it into an eight-by-eleven envelope.

"These are the guys," Johnny said. "And are they in order?"

"Not necessarily in order," Clyde said. "But since I will be in Italy, we will cross the Med and get northern Africa first."

They shook hands, and Johnny the Rebel said, "Red Horse out." As he spun his chair around to get situated again, he said, "Hasta luego, mi amigo, and don't forget, when we get to the nineteenth, you are buying the suds. Clyde." He paused.

"Yes?" Clyde said, before the door was opened.

"You are the finest operator on the planet!" Johnny exclaimed. "Be careful. Trust your instincts! Double plan your escape! And when it becomes necessary, run like a bat out of hell!"

Clyde chuckled and retorted, "Vaya con Dios, esse!"

IT'S STILL ROCK
AND ROLL TO ME

T HIS IS THE *easy part*, Clyde thought. *I feel like a rock star. We are flying on a private jet to Europe. Check in was thirty minutes from curbside to takeoff. Lunch is being served. The bags are packed, but my bills aren't paid. The kids are in Europe. Not every father of four children below ten says that very often.*

His mother-in-law was so excited she couldn't see straight. She needed the change of pace. It had been some really dark months for her. Rico was working, so she had no outlet for her pain. She had been really quiet all these months, and that was unlike her. She was a good soldier, and her faith was deep. But it is a lot. Parents were not supposed to outlive their kids. Humans were not programmed that way. Parents raise their children, love them, give them their start, and then enjoy their friendship and watch them learn the lessons of parenthood. Parents guide from a distance, and children consult them as much as they wanted and watch the next generation go through childhood.

No, to Mrs. Del Amo, losing Laina was literally like losing a part of her. This was her firstborn and her first daughter. The kinship was connected on too many levels. Clyde wasn't prepared to tell anyone about what he knew of Laina. He wasn't prepared to begin to accept it at all. It was just too many variables. For now, there was hope. He would leave it there. He would do his job and build his new career, and hopefully, this contract work might uncover the issues.

Anna asked Clyde how he was doing. "Did you have a nice time visiting your relatives?" she asked. "Were the kids glad to be flying and experiencing all that new stuff?"

Clyde said that he had a fantastic time and he got to spend time with his father-in-law as well.

Anna had a questioning kind of look on her face. Clyde said, "They are still my kids' grandparents, and unlike a divorce where everyone takes sides, there is no sides, no animosity. I still love them to death."

"That makes a lot of sense," Anna said.

"In fact," Clyde said, "they are all in Italy right now. My in-laws live further south than where we will be, but my folks and the kids all went for two weeks. But my guess is that it will be three. Between the grandmas and the sisters and all the cousins, it will be super busy. How it was going at the newspaper? Do you have a plan in the meantime?"

Anna said she had taken a leave of absence and still wanted to write. She really liked the journalism side of asking questions and uncovering facts, even if was just from a human interest type of story. "I am an interested human. I like to inform. I enjoyed my ten days too."

Clyde asked if she did anything that was different from the normal two days off on weekends.

"That between spending time with some friends and doing a couple of interviews in Chicago," she said. "And by the way, thanks for letting me hang out there all alone with no one to have my back."

"How was the Oprah interview?" Clyde asked. "I saw it, by the way, in LA."

Anna frowned. "You didn't tell me you were going to LA. In fact, you didn't tell me nada."

Clyde thought that when she used a Spanish word that her accent was so beautiful. His smile gave that away. Anna didn't miss it but didn't think it was flirtatious. She knew Clyde wasn't flirtatious; he was just himself, and Anna knew that with her being so young and Clyde having kids that there was no way on earth his eyes would ever roll her way. What Anna didn't know was that she was completely wrong. But Clyde knew in his heart that if there was one millionth of a chance that his Laina didn't go up in that blast and she was alive, he would stop all time, hold back the Roman legion, and cross the Sahara in a Fisher Price Cozy Coupe to be with her again.

Anna continued, "The interview was super, super intimidating. I am the one who is supposed to ask the questions. She grilled me about you, and I don't even know you and about the new job, and everyone wants to know why there favorite restaurant is closed. She had been there, you know?"

"Get out!" Clyde exclaimed. "You are lying. Oprah Winfrey was in Del Sol, and I didn't know it?"

"She does that regularly," Anna remarked. "She has a few things that she won't say that make her incognito."

"I find that really hard to believe."

Anna went on, "She asked me a really good question. Well, you know, you saw it."

Clyde thought he knew what she was talking about. "The whole did I plan to say no to all the talk shows to create a buzz?"

Anna nodded. "Well, you saw my response, but is it true?" She went on to add that Clyde had said he wouldn't ever have dreamed of going on those shows if he was the last man on the planet, or something like that.

Clyde shook his head. "No, all I said was no. It was emphatic, and I will admit that. But you know it wasn't planned."

Anna had said to Oprah that it was simply a reaction. It wasn't premeditated, from what she could tell. She just didn't think it would go viral, so to speak, on the grapevine.

"So what is our gig looking like here?" Clyde asked. "Go into the restaurant and eat and talk to the people and the owners and all that jazz?"

Anna said that she had been thinking and talking with production. "They wanted to be different."

"Let's go in undercover," Clyde said. "I mean, not undercover, but just as normal people going to dinner. The camera crew can film from backpacks, and then once we are served, we can bring out the whole entourage, but it will add a live element to it and then a real see-what-you-get kind of deal. We can break out after the meal with talking with the shop owners and that kind of pizzazz. In fact, like most tourists, we can walk in with our own video recorders and just act like foreigners enamored with all things Italy."

One of the producers turned around and started chiming in. He thought it was brilliant. "It will add a reality aspect to the show. It will be real people, in real time, without a whole lot of actual canned or contrived footage. We can go back and narrate after the fact. We will take them by surprise, and we may not get the owners, or who knows? But we can also provide a follow-up visit."

"I don't even think we need the follow-up visit," Clyde said. "That whole approach to seeing the restaurant and talking through ingredients is kind of old, isn't it? You are probably not going to make the food, anyway. You want to eat the food. And I simply think you really want to know where to go and why. Look, when I am in Venice, I want to know what are the three must-eat-at places or go-to venues. Is there also a place to avoid? Can we even do that? So in summary, fellow travelers, I would go to A, B, C, and for my money, I would skip D, E, and F."

At the hotel they met with Yeager Bierson. Clyde thought he couldn't be a day over thirty, but he was super sharp and seemed to just have an easy way about him. Clyde was thinking back to the whole "has an ego" thing and didn't seem to sense that about this guy. Maybe he got mislabeled somewhere down the line, or maybe after dealing with various personalities in the restaurant world and having been through the ranks in the military Clyde was just kind of impervious to a person with a large ego. He didn't think so. He could read people, just like any other guy, and had to in a lot of situations. No, Yeager was good, and asked questions. When the executive producer mentioned the whole going in live and incognito thing to Yeager, he absolutely loved it. He told Clyde that it was brilliant. "It was the thing I couldn't put my finger on. It is the angle we need."

So he sat down with a legal pad, and they began to scratch out some ideas. "Okay, this sounds great. Let's meet for dinner at 6:00, and then we will call it a night, and tomorrow we won't have a meeting till lunch. In the afternoon, we will discuss our show, which restaurants, and we will be done, then have dinner and call it a night. No need to kill ourselves on the first leg of the trip. We will see how much we get done on the first day of shooting and what it looks like. We are supposed to do one show per five days in each location." Yeager turned to Clyde and Anna. "There is such a beautiful spot outside which overlooks the vista of the city. Would you mind if we kind of do an informal interview and welcome to the show?"

"I look like a kind of weary traveler rather than a seasoned traveler," Clyde said.

Anna popped right up and said, "Sounds like fun to me, let's do it." And she was off to the powder room.

Clyde wasn't sure what she had done in there, but when she came out, she had a baseball cap on with a ponytail and sunglasses, and looked like she was ready to spend a day at the beach. She walked up and said, "Hey, Clyde Gareen, we are being paid to travel the world, and would you look at this? We are in Venice! What do you like most about this city?"

Clyde didn't even blink but, as was his way, got lost in the question and forgot about the camera. He kind of half-turned and pointed and said, "There is no place in the world like this with all their canals. You feel like you went back in time fifteen hundred years and you're living the really simple life of waking up, providing for your family, and working hard. The smells of the ocean water, the vitality of the people, commerce happening right before your eyes. It is so incredibly fascinating to me."

Anna followed his gaze. "I can only imagine the food is incredible."

To which Clyde replied, "It is Italian, but yet it is Venetian. They eat some things only here and prepare others dishes which are naturally Italian but in a certain way. Fantastic from start to finish, and in fact, you haven't lived until you have had a cappuccino from one of the rolling carts."

Without even rehearsing, they both turned and looked straight into the camera.

"Welcome to the first episode of the *Seasoned Traveler*," Anna said. "I am Anna CiFuentes, and this is Clyde Gareen, and we are thrilled to have you along as we discover Venice."

DO YOU BELIEVE
IN MAGIC?

CAN'T BELIEVE YOU guys," Yeager said. "That was the first take. I find that amazing. I don't even need to be here. You are going to put me out of a job. Hey, by the way, is one of those carts close?"

"Yes," Clyde said. "Let's just walk down those steps, and you will see one in the first alleyway."

So they all followed Clyde and Anna and came to man sitting in a chair, reading a newspaper next to a cart with an espresso machine. Clyde spoke to him in Italian, and the man's eyes lit up, and he started chatting with Clyde out of sheer enthusiasm and began tinkering with the coffee machine. Clyde turned and translated the essentials and spoke back to him in Italian, and within a minute, they were all drinking hot steaming cappuccinos. The man could tamp and fill and pour and steam milk like

Picasso with a paintbrush. It was magical, and the espresso with the hot, frothy milk was so good. Clyde was serving the crew, and everyone was talking and laughing, and Yeager was grabbing the entire scene on film, and he knew right then and there this was going to win him an Emmy.

His father had told him that his career was over. He said, "By thirty, you should be doing feature films." Yeager was doing something he hadn't done since he was a boy: he was having fun. They were making it up on the fly. It wasn't scripted, it wasn't over-rehearsed, it was traveling to a foreign country with a guide and doing what the locals have done and enjoyed for years and now capturing it on film.

Anna, through Clyde, was talking with the vendor. "How long have you been selling espresso here on the corner?" she asked.

"Thirty years," the vendor replied.

As Clyde related it to the hearers, Anna asked graciously, "May I call you Giorgio?"

"That would be fine since that is my name."

"Giorgio," Anna went on, "your cart is pretty new. How often do you have to get a new one?"

Without even waiting for the translation, Giorgio jumped in and said, "Never."

Well, that was pretty surprising, first of all, to realize he at least understood English, and second of all, from the looks of the cart, it certainly didn't have thirty years of wear on it.

Clyde asked rapidly in Italian and then a little slower in English, "I am not sure I understand if you have been selling for thirty years. How does your cart look so new?"

"Parts new" was the response from the vendor who called himself Giorgio. "Assembled in my garage, I made it from, how do you say, scratch."

Yeager couldn't believe it. Here they were, standing before a seemingly relaxed unambitious, just-let-the-world-go-by kind of vendor, and ironically, he was a master craftsman. The cart was beautiful, and the machines were obviously very capable. Clyde asked Giorgio how and where he made it. He replied in Italian, and Clyde translated that the frame of the cart was original. The translation continued, as he spoke with a relaxed yet conversational manner, "And if you looked closely at the handle that pushed the cart as it was connected to the frame, you could see the almost-patina-like finish and the well-worn brass handles. The rest of the frame was a very sturdy carved wood that was well worn yet had been rubbed and polished and looked authentic. My son is a better machinist than I could ever dream of being, and he makes carts and sells them all over Europe. We ship around six a month. We could expand and get a warehouse and hire people, but no need. We are happy, we are comfortable, we live on the canal. All of our family is here, and we enjoy really good espresso!"

It was spontaneous, but the crew all clapped for Giorgio, who said he was really astonished and said he felt like a man running for office. As the group turned to head back up the few steps to the hotel, Clyde stayed to chat for a few more minutes. As they shook hands and Clyde gave Giorgio a hug, as was customary on that side of the Atlantic, Giorgio said to Clyde in perfect English, "Johnny asked me to relate to you that you should be careful."

Now it was Clyde's turn to be astonished. He muttered a barely audible "How?" Giorgio's hands spread out next to his legs, palms up, and he just shrugged. "That is all I know."

Clyde said thank you and turned to go, but all his senses were on alert and knew that Johnny had picked up some traffic. While Clyde thought there would be no more attempts, it was obvious that Johnny had a little more information.

How on earth did he find the cart guy? How did he know I would talk with him? Maybe the cart guy was a plant? No, he was the real deal. How did he know me? His English was perfect. Maybe that was the line. Wow! Even Clyde was amused. *How did Johnny do it? How could he have reached out to me through a local vendor without the entire world knowing?*

Clyde thought it didn't matter. He needed to be careful. They weren't meeting until tomorrow at lunch, and Clyde now had a sixteen-hour window.

SMOKE ON THE WATER, FIRE IN THE SKY!

T SEEMED LIKE he had been sitting in this tiny little ditch for hours. He was waiting for Omad Mahman Suirillite III to show up at his country fiefdom. It was not really a home or a palace; it was like a working plantation or a series of homes surrounding a castle overlooking a lake, with crops and livestock and even some type of manufacturing going on in some outlying buildings. Getting to this spot was what one had to do in this line of work. To sneak into this compound and get past dogs, guards, and various different groups of people, one had to know what they were doing. He was sufficiently trained in this counterespionage type of work, and the truth was he was beyond all the experts in covert operations. His uncle had taught him about the apaches and how they could literally steal a rifle right from the campfire full of cowboys or soldiers and nobody would know.

The trick was blending with the surroundings. The other trick was not moving.

He probably hadn't moved for an hour. He had already been in the house and had already planted the bomb in the bathroom and, with a remote camera, was able to see who was going into that baño. Funny, why he thought of the Spanish word at the moment, he could not give an answer to. His mind was wandering. He refocused on the available data around him, and then he heard the car coming up the road. From the slight depression noise and the engine revolutions slowing, he could tell that the car stopped at the bottom of the hill where the sentry was posted, and he heard the electronic gate rumbling over the tracks as it opened. The engine was revving a little as the car started to move slowly forward, and by the gentle hum of the engine, it had to be a Range Rover. Odd that it wasn't a Mercedes. He knew that this dictator was made of money. It was probably the heroin in the outlying buildings that was being shipped all over the world. There had already been three planes that had landed, loaded up, and taken off. He didn't think it was care packages for orphan children. This country had sufficient poverty with a huge unemployment rate. *Radical juxtaposition* were the words that came to mind. Wealth right here, in the midst of poverty, and now justifiable homicide from somebody who wanted to live so much.

This Omar cat was a world-class idiot. He literally killed for sport. He had taken power on the backs of common people he had murdered, tortured, raped, and pillaged. Starting out as a type of common or local warlord, he had amassed power through deals with ex-patriots in the drug-trafficking world and in the ensuing vacuum of leadership had risen to take the country and hold it in a death grip. The only vice he didn't partake in was the one he wasn't doing at the moment. He had slaughtered hundreds in just the previous weeks, and now his regime was going to start moving out into surrounding countries. This guy was an enigma. Basically a thug, he was somehow able to amass all kinds of new technology and the latest weapons in his struggle to maintain power. The Intel out on this guy was that he was a finger on the hand of some unseen power that was using him to create chaos in this part of Northern Africa. The concept was to start cutting off the fingers and see if the hand starts to bleed. His newest criminal activity was, without question, the one that had put him on the radar. You can't start buying small surface to air missiles without all of the alarms going off in the geopolitical defense world.

As the car came to a rapid stop right in front of him, he saw the Suirillite literally jump out of the car and head into the house. Probably a little too much Jack Daniels on the car ride over. There were three other cars right behind the first car, and apparently, the dictator had forgotten his manners because he was not waiting for the entourage to catch up with him. The operative lay unmoved in his ten-inch water runoff and waited for the right moment to pull the trigger on the CEMEX explosives that was carefully hidden in the downstairs bathroom. The choice for the explosives rather than a simple sniper shot from an outlying spot was pretty simple. The ensuing chaos that would take place would allow for a pretty simple escape. He could have already been much farther away, but he wanted to be sure that he had the right guy in the right spot.

Time seemed to simply stand still at that moment as he watched through his eyeglass camera the door to the bathroom open. At the same instant, the most surreal thing happened that literally took his breath away. She was a long, tall wonderfully curved jaw-dropping beauty who stepped down out of the second vehicle. She was at least six feet tall and, without question, royalty. In fact, she was probably the princess from the neighboring country of Sudan and seemed incredibly out of context in this hole of human misery. The immediate problem was that if she was in tow with her young daughter and walked any closer to the house, they were going to be in the red zone.

The operative didn't even think. He just reacted, and he knew that it would blow his cover and make escape virtually impossible, but it was too ingrained in his nature to deal with innocent blood as a result of his collateral damage. And it would be a real waste of good blood if you thought about it. Obviously he didn't agree with the princess hanging out with this beast, but he didn't have the luxury at the moment to be judge and jury. He simply just called out to the princess to halt, and she turned to him with a bewildered look, but the pause in her step was enough to halt her progress as the blast erupted. The sound of the explosion caused everyone to turn, and the force of the eruption pushed the princess and her daughter to the ground. That was the last thing he saw as he was already running down the slope, knowing that he had maybe four or five seconds before this group of drug slugs was after him for obliterating their chief into a million tiny fragments.

There was a carousel of images pulsing through his mind even as he fled across the thirty-yard open space toward the fifteen-foot-high rod-iron fence. He had also heard a "What are you thinking, you are a crazy idiot" in his earpiece as Johnny was reacting to something. He immediately spotted the tree he had marked and with one jump caught the right low-hanging limb with his left hand, and then his momentum allowed him to swing up. He vaulted the top of the fence and reached for the rope dangling from the zip line he had set up on his way into the compound. The zip line was rigged to take him quickly down the hill and cut through all the red tape of something or someone or many someones giving him chase. There was an ugly group of leaderless men standing at the top of the hill shooting worthlessly at him, and then two cars were already making the first turn. But they were driving in vain because he already knew that his timing was spot-on, and as the zip line came to an end, he jumped straight onto the third-to-the-last car of a freight train. There were not too many trains in Northern Africa, but it didn't matter because this one was going his way. It was headed straight over the river via a bridge that maybe spanned sixty yards, which isn't that far, but the first car was going to have to travel twenty minutes south to get over the same river.

He felt like he was in the middle of a spy movie as he knelt down on the train and got ready for the jump-off. After rechecking his gear and updating Johnny, he walked carefully to the last car. Johnny pointed out that yelling and giving away his location just before blowing up the intended target was not on the best-practices list. Johnny said that saving the princess and her daughter was admirable but officially stupid.

"Dude, if you choose to hang out with the wrong people, it has unintended consequences. In the meantime, you have people looking for you, and otherwise, you would have slipped out of there without a chase."

"Yes, but now I can sleep at night," Clyde said.

"That was a really good point," Johnny responded, "but you play the game like that again, and you may not get to sleep at all. Now get to the plane, and let's get you to your target off the coast of Italy."

The last thing Clyde heard Johnny say was that the water temperature in the northern Mediterranean was fifty-five degrees. That might be a little chilly. A quick descent down the ladder off the last car, which looked pretty much like an old-fashioned red caboose, and then he stepped off into the gentle hillside. He made a quick tuck-and-roll procedure, and then bounced, slid, and skidded to a stop. The cargo plane had its back door open, and Clyde ran up and hit the back door. The plane started to move, and it lumbered down a typical third-world runway. It was a good thing they didn't need to make a fast getaway. But the cargo plane was handy, local, got wings without any strings (Johnny's joke), and dumped the necessary gear into the ocean, where Clyde was going to jump.

DON'T STOP BELIEVING

B LACK OR WHITE? In the game or on the bench? Was there no in-between? Was there not any room for two perspectives? Do you have to be on one side of the fence or the other? Why is it that the world never seems to be what you think it is?

As the hum of the plane's engine droned on and on in the predawn hours of a very cold and eerie night, the serene dark man wondered to himself how he could even ask that question. While here up in this bird, he was actually an entirely different human being than from what most of the planet actually thought. Dickens wrote about a tale of two cities; he was a tale of two men. Actually, just one man, or at least one body, that shared two very different sets of circumstances that drove him to lead completely separate lives. Clyde thought that he had at least two inner personalities, each fighting to be dominant. Struggling over complex psychological questions was more intense than he could ever have imagined. It was a weird boundary he had crossed. Had he crossed a boundary? If so, when was the boundary even crossed? He was employed by his government to do a job, same as before, but those guys were shooting back. Now he just snuck up on them and eliminated the enemy. *Eliminated* was a spin for *assassinate*. Well, it certainly wasn't hard to justify.

He thought about this night's activities and the ruthless despot that he had to deal with and the thousands of cold-blooded murders that his victim been responsible for. Maybe even thousands of innocent lives. Conscience—why did we even have one? These were going to be some late nights lying in bed, staring-at-the-ceiling kind of thoughts. But the good news was that he had come through clean albeit not yet totally done, but the adrenaline and escape had not created another episode.

Good, Clyde thought. *That part of my life is over.*

The headaches were stress induced. He was fine. While he was lost in his own thoughts, *whoosh!* The howling wind coming through the newly opened door of a nondescript gray C51 transport plane jerked him back to reality. That current reality was termed *parachute*. He was about to jump from 7,500 feet into the middle of the Mediterranean ocean. This never got to be old hat. Seconds seemed like minutes as he stared up at the red light, looking for the signal. It started to blink, and then the knot in his stomach tightened. This never became routine. Anybody who said jumping from an airplane was another part of the job, no big deal, was lying. Then Clyde saw it: 3:2:1:green—that was his signal. He hoped the navigator's GPS was accurate because he was jumping into sheer blackness. He leaped from the plane and into absolute nothingness. Down he went, cold in his face, picking up speed, wind shooting at him, his mind a blank. He raced toward the ocean. Free-falling was the most exhilarating feeling he could imagine. What an intense rush. At the very same moment, it was terrifying, because one's life hinged on a cord.

At that very moment, Clyde pulled his chute, and out came the safety net to allow his free fall to stop, and up he went. Now he was floating down to an empty void. Pitch black surrounded him in every direction, except far off in the distance a bright-white full moon gave off a pretty startling contrast. But there was nothing below him, except for, as he drew closer, an occasional flash of white as the waves crested and broke and the moonbeams reflected off them.

"Super," the newly minted assassin mused. Either the GPS is wrong and he is headed for the beach break, which could mean somewhere he does not need to be, or the surf is pretty heavy. He reached into his pocket and located the transponder, which was really just a software program loaded on his PDA. It showed him the location of the pod containing his scuba equipment to get him out of the Adriatic and back to dry land, where he had his car waiting and would drive back to the water taxi, which would put him within five hundred yards of the hotel.

Very cool, he thought as the red light blipped on his screen, and the yellow light showed where he was and the distance indicator was narrowing. From his distance now he should be able to see a light. Oh, that's right; he was supposed to activate the light on the pod when he was within five hundred feet. With his pinky finger, being the smallest on the glove, he touched the screen where he saw the red-light icon and looked out into the blackness and finally saw a very small red light. From the looks of it, he was maybe about a hundred yards from his landing spot. Well, it was about to get real cold, and he had maybe four seconds to get the phone back into his pocket and zip the pocket shut before he went into the water. Then he actually splashed into the freezing water.

Freezing was not the right word. Cold and wet, yes, but in this part of the ocean off the city of Punta Sabbioni, the Adriatic really never got to the point of freezing. Clyde came up for air and took off his parachute. He could not leave any trace of his existence, so he carefully pulled in the chute as he treaded water and stuffed it back into his pack. A wet chute was not so simple to get back into a pack, but he had practiced it many times before. He loaded on the pack and swam to the pod. Grateful that his pod had floated for the last six hours he was gone and nobody had need of its contents, he quickly undid the latches and grabbed the equipment. He put on the fins first so it would be easier on his already exhausted muscles to tread water as he put on the self-contained underwater breathing apparatus. *Scuba* was a much better name, he thought, as he slid the canister over his shoulders and into place. His mind was wandering again as meaningless information swirled about. He was exhausted, and this took its mental toll. He got out his mask and then finally pulled out the mini propeller that would gently guide him back to the dock he was going to come in from the ocean on. He latched up the pod and let it float. Nothing was left in it, so he figured that would be left behind, although details become clues to someone following a trail, but after all, it was floating two miles out in the Adriatic.

At that moment, Johnny checked in and asked politely with a hint of sarcasm, "How is the water, buddy? By the way, don't you worry about the pod. We have a boat coming to scoop it up in the morning. Well, I mean, later on in the morning."

Not finding Johnny humorous at the moment, Clyde went about his task of switching on the motor of the mini prop as he had already put in his mouthpiece and was ready to dive down. After he descended a fathom, he flipped on the light, confident he was far enough below not to be seen from above. His equilibrium was good, and he started north for the dock just outside the city. This was a public dock that had not seen too much use for a couple of years. He had a GPS transponder mounted on the mini prop, and that told him where to head. Otherwise, out in the middle of the ocean, it would be a crapshoot, as they said in gambling, to find his location. Clyde thought about it and realized that he had two miles to go at about eight miles an hour. Fifteen minutes was not too bad.

The ocean was pretty dark at night. The only thing he could see was just a few feet in front of him. Off to his left, he could make out a large mass of some kind. Could be a school of fish? He guided the mini prop through what looked like two jutting columns and saw a pretty good-size hammerhead shark off to the right.

It is pretty spooky down here in the depths of the sea, Clyde thought. *I can only imagine what Jonah thought inside the fish.*

That mass had come back around, and it was a large school of some kind of very large creatures. Clyde was really not in the mood for more sharks, but as they got a little closer, he slowed the prop to a crawl and veered off for a big rock and crept down behind it. Maybe out of sight, out of mind, and he won't be their early morning breakfast. It was a huge pod of dolphins. It had to be one of the most beautiful things he had ever seen. He was sure the sharks would be beautiful as well, but it was hard to see the positive when the negative was staring you right in the face.

Well, it must be okay to move on, Clyde thought. How Gray Eagle found these abandoned places and got him out of these situations was a mystery. She had been money on every single mission. He had never met Gray Eagle during all the assignments when he was in the marine special recon forces unit. It was a good thing, or he would not have been attached to her now. She didn't know who he was. He now had a new call name, Lone Wolf. That did not need much use of the imagination.

I think I will change that to Friendly Dolphin, Clyde thought. He felt like a person all alone at the moment. Yet Johnny was in his ear, and Gray Eagle was available to him at these "critical" times, and each detail was always worked out. She wasn't crazy about coordinating with Johnny, but she was simply a vehicle and a necessary-items liaison, and she wasn't involved in the actual mission. Jonathan Walker had been a friend of Clyde's since college. They had fought together in the military, and they had fought with each other more times than he could remember. Johnny had always said that if Clyde didn't marry Laina, he would, just for the cooking and the family. Johnny was intense, brilliant, and athletic. He had more willpower and motivation than any ten human beings Clyde knew.

Johnny had lost the use of both legs in a mission off the coast of Somalia five years ago, and it hadn't slowed him down one bit. He owned his own software company, and they made products for the disabled to use as well as an assortment of other things. Jonathan Sinclair Walker IV was, in Clyde's estimation, a warrior in mind and spirit, coupled with being maybe the greatest tech and gadget guru on the face of the earth. Inevitably there was this symbiotic link between Clyde on the field and Johnny in the war room, whereas the two acted as one, and it made for a superhuman force to fight the enemies of good.

Clyde was physically drained. The high of the mission was over, and the adrenaline was gone. He knew he needed be careful, but this mission was over. He would climb the dock, look like any average idiot water sportsman who was diving at three o'clock in the morning for a morning catch or treasure seeking, pack up his gear in the rolling wet case he had, and head for the car parked just on the other side of the street from the dock. Into his car, drive thirty minutes for the water taxi, walk quickly to the hotel, and then sleep for five hours until his 10:00 a.m. wake-up call. He did not have to be on the set or actually at the restaurant where they were filming until noon. They had quite a schedule today, two restaurants in Venice and then hopefully two more tomorrow.

As the exhausted agent threw his gear into the trunk and climbed into the Mercedes and waited for the engine to start, he began to contemplate. He had these dark moments after every exhausting mission, and his weariness let his thoughts fall back a few weeks ago from now, maybe almost a month when his entire world had collapsed. As he drove, it was hard to pay attention because the image of that man in the street was so vivid. Could he have ever been at a lower point? Even though he knew that all things worked together for good, this was truth in his head sometimes isolated from his heart. Losing people you loved and circumstances beyond your control had a way of ripping your heart out, destroying confidence, making others look at you differently, and then you were living in the pain.

Suddenly it dawned on him that this was going to be life on this side of heaven. Always some form of pain. It wasn't going to change. It was a world longing to be away from the tyranny of the curse, and Clyde was going to have to keep his eyes on his Savior to get through the pain of each day. As he drove down the streets, he realized that things in the last few weeks had become very different. Maybe, just maybe, Laina was alive. How could that be possible? Who would want to kill her? What did she know that possibly could put her in so much danger? Successful Mission Number One was under his belt, and that meant a wire transfer. Clyde needed the money. The few dollars he got for their interview lasted less than a week. He had gotten his first paycheck from the payroll company that handled all of Channel 6's contract work. It should have been around eighty-three thousand, but after taxes, it was much closer to fifty thousand. How can you complain, right? He had just gotten paid fifty thousand, but that was not the point. He just paid the government thirty thousand dollars. He would do the same thing for the next twelve weeks. That was almost four hundred thousand dollars.

It is so lopsided, he thought.

The other side of the coin was that his life was expensive. Running around incognito and using a net jet wasn't cheap. He had some credit bills to pay and the daily overhead. How to get the money from his new South African account into his current bank scenarios was a critical step in covert operations. An electronic trail is never good. Oh, look, Clyde Gareen just had five hundred thousand dollars wired into his account. Not that it is so rare it would pop up on the front page of the *Wall Street Journal*, but he knew that for a savvy hacker from the dark side, it would not take much. He had a numbered account without his name on the electronic side of the file, and with the right combination of passwords and codes, he could distribute those funds electronically to a Swiss account and then to his accounts. People would know that money came from his account in Switzerland, but no way could they find out from where.

Clyde had changed already into a pair of sweats and a T-shirt, so if anyone saw him this early morning, it would look like he was down to get a paper or ice or any other type of normal activity. Nobody was alive at 5:00 a.m. He didn't see a bellboy or a desk clerk. He grabbed the local Italian newspaper and headed for his room. He grabbed the go camera and transferred the data to his laptop. After logging on to a national-level secure website Johnny had made, he uploaded the data. Johnny was able to get this to Kirby Myles, and he knew it was secure. He didn't rightly know how, but he trusted Johnny.

Reb got the data to Myles, and Myles saw his phone beep for an incoming e-mail, and thought he might finish his dinner first. Clyde had told him to marinate the tri tip and how to cook it off the heat with the lid down on the barbeque, and his life had never been the same. Clyde literally fell into bed, and the world was dark until the phone rang at 10:00 a.m. Clyde didn't pick up the phone since he knew that it was a hotel call and it was to make sure he didn't sleep too late. He was up out of bed, showered, shaved, and changed within fifteen minutes. He drank his little cup of hotel coffee and read the newspaper and glanced at his laptop. The phone rang again, and this time, Clyde grabbed it.

"Mr. Gareeeen?" the hotel front desk asked with a very thick accent.

Clyde responded in Italian.

"I am very sorry to trouble you, but your room is scheduled for some maintenance. Would it be too much trouble if we gave you another?"

"I am sorry," Clyde said. "You want me to move?" The phone in his hand buzzed. He looked down at his cell. It was still strange to be talking on a phone and yet holding a mobile phone. An unknown number was on it. Clyde clicked on it, and the text was "It is okay to move to another location!"

Clyde changed his tone and said that would be fine. "What do you need me to do?"

"You do not need to do nothing" was the response from the concierge. "We will bring you the key, and you will have the room 335."

So Clyde hung up the phone and heard the knock on the door, surprised at the speed in which they had made it to his room. He grabbed the new key and signed the papers and gave the bellhop the old key.

"Mr. Gareen, just shut the door behind you," the attendant said. "It will self-lock, and you can move. Mr. Gareen, we also have dinner for you at a local restaurant, if you get a moment to come to the concierge desk."

Clyde tipped the attendant, and he was on his way. *Okay, so for a trip upstairs with my luggage, I get a new room, a view, and dinner.* Clyde put his luggage on the cart and hung some of his clothes, and made his way to the elevator. He hit button 3 on the inside, and in moments, he opened the door to his new room.

Ah, very nice, he thought. *I got an upgrade and a beautiful view.* He unpacked his items, put his disks in the safe, put his laptop in a locked attaché case, and slid it in the closet. It was eleven thirty, and it was time for work.

Not a bad time to start, he thought.

"Hello, Reb," Clyde said. "What is with the room change?"

"I have a little intel that there are some goons who want to know your whereabouts," Johnny replied.

"You mean you talked with Giorgio."

"Mr. Cart Guy is in touch with a lot of people," Johnny defended himself. "His son makes a couple of other things besides carts. You may like his knives. Clyde, you can't be too careful when big-game hunting. You never know who you run into."

MADMAN ACROSS
THE WATER

Y ERI DE ANGELO just got off the phone with Fritz and
Charles. For Yeri, the seeds of doubt were starting to sprout,
as the old rhyme says. In his long relationship with Charles,
the man had virtually never been wrong. Yet this was a much-big-
ger project than any of them had ever attempted. It was almost as
if the always-analytical Charles was giving sway to an overreach
of power. Yeri had said, though it had gone unheeded and he had
always known, that North Africa was a bad point to build the
third warehouse to develop the final element of P3. His argument
had been that there was too much access and a lot of bad blood
in the surrounding area. He had said that some of the old Soviet
countries were better, and Greenland was good. Having a facility
in deep South America and one in the Malaysian triangle, he had
lobbied for Siberia and or its now independent counterparts. This

was a setback. Well, as Charles pointed out, there was nothing wrong with the building. It was just that the facilities manager was out of commission, of course. Yeri asked if they had any idea who had done this.

"That is why Alberto is not on the call, Yeri. He is in the midst of dealing with a counterespionage unit out of Yemen that is quite adept at getting to the source. They had already tapped the satellite images, and they saw the explosions and the chase. They saw in the image at least one of the culprits escape via zip line down to an oncoming train. From there, the image goes out of range. Fritz thinks it is neither Eastern European nor Middle Eastern."

"It could be Chinese or American," Fritz chimed in.

Yeri asked if they had any information from their senior correspondent in DC.

"No, we haven't had the opportunity to ask yet, but we got a text message out of our contacts in China, saying they had nothing on the books for taking out Suirillite or any other midlevel despot in Africa. They didn't want to waste their resources.

Fritz answered another phone at the same time. "Thank you for calling, and I am hearing you say no on the books or off the books ops for this kind of attack! Thank you for that information." He looked at Charles. "The veep knows nothing. Of course that isn't the first time he was out of the loop."

Yeri looked at the satellite footage in his war room and again was very proud of his level of equipment and his staff. He saw the black image run and knew it was a futbol player. He ran side to side and not straight up, sprinting, and he was smooth to catch that branch and launch over the fence and then one more jump and onto a preplanned zip line. So this was preplanned, premeditated, cold-blooded murder, he thought. Well, it really was more like payback for the thousands this idiot had massacred.

Yeri had one of those aha moments. He was going to be just as bad on an entirely different level than what this criminal was doing in the local villages. In fact, it was the second same kind of self-revelation moment he had had in the past few days. What on earth was he thinking? Maybe his son was right. What did Ed always ask? Why is there evil on the planet? I mean, if there is no God and we all are here to survive, then why is it that there is good and bad? Who defines the bad? Maybe there is simply a right. In other words, he always went on to say, there was an inherent trait built in right into our DNA. Where did we get those standards? We simply have a built-in conscience. It tells us what is right and wrong. Even the worst criminals in death row have their lines they will not even cross.

What is wrong with me? Yeri thought. Why am I all of a sudden having all of these second thoughts?

"Yeri, Yeri," he heard the caller on the other end.

"Yes, excuse me," Yeri said. "I was deep in thought about this soccer player."

"Soccer player?" Charles asked.

Yeri responded by pointing out that the guy they had captured making a getaway ran like a futbol player from side to side. Sprinters run straight up and down. And then Yeri went on, "See how adept he is, grabbing the fence and then lifting up to the tree all in one motion? Looks like he has spent time with over-the-head kicks."

"Notwithstanding," Charles said. "We picked up the train on another satellite pass, and there is no one on the train. Possibly he went into the train, but the train ends up at the coast three hours later. We checked the unloading, and no human got off the train that wasn't accounted for on the manifest. So he got off somewhere else. If he gets off the train at some point, it means, quite frankly, there must have been a rendezvous with a plane of some kind. So the plane had to take off and land somewhere. We will check into it."

Charles was literally seething inside. He hated more than anything else when people interfered with his plans. He was going to find the person responsible for this and in his own special way would get his revenge. He thought about it: a revenge cocktail, and his own mixture of absolute torture, murder, and mayhem. And yet no one would ever know. Kind of like his little "accident" in Palermo, where the identified culprit was vaporized. So he said to Yeri, "I think you are right. Let's find a suitable replacement for the third element of P3 in another territory. This one can serve as a backup. We will immediately work with the leadership that is left in our North African facility and get a working dictator up and running." Charles paused and then added, "It isn't so easy trying to run the world, is it, Yeri?"

There was a moment of shared laughter, but if one listened closely, one would not hear sincerity from both sides.

PRESSURE

Kirby Myles was reviewing the data sent to him from the back ops technical guy of Clyde's. *Johnny Walker is actually pretty good. We can't trace him at all. How he can upload and transmit this data? That we have no idea where it is coming from is a little scary. We, after all is said and done, have multiple national-level counterespionage resources available, and we can't figure this out.* Myles rubbed his chin and felt his white Wolfman Jack–style beard, and it reminded him that he was not in the military. His thoughts turned to the word *multiple*. That was always the problem with government resources and especially in the current democratic environment: there were just too many cooks in the kitchen. The bigger the government gets, the less it actually does. Myles was no saint, and here he was in the middle of a huge black ops project that if it ever made the national news they all might get sent to Guantanamo for a tribunal.

No, that wouldn't happen, he thought. We would follow the 9-11 guys to Colorado and sit before some soccer moms, retired postal workers, and businessmen who keep checking their phones. No, that isn't the way it works. It will never go back to the source. There is too much bureaucracy here, and the sitting president, who authorized this— well, he didn't really authorize it, but his administration did, and these guys can do a tango with the mass media, and they will dance away until the clock strikes midnight and we all turn into a pumpkin.

Kirby went on thinking, *Well, this is a horse of a different color, and I am one guy who certainly can't cast the first stone. Okay, for the matter at hand, I can't believe I am seeing pictures inside the buildings. How did he do this? What do we have here? Mr. Gareen, you have found the candy store, and I am not talking about narcotics. This is a lab of some kind. Each of the workers is in a full hazmat suit. Well, if they're not producing narcotics, and I am sort of guessing because it is a clean room from start to finish, complete with double entries and double glass windows, if I didn't know anything at all, I would say chemical or biological, maybe.*

General Myles was reviewing the data. Funny that this was really what used to be called film, but in the digital age, it was all reproduced via computers. He was watching this on his tablet as he sat in his living room. Encrypted data sent over the Internet. He logs into a secure website and downloads the data. One would think any would-be hack could grab this data. But he couldn't find where it came from. He knew where to look because he was given particular information. Well, the next set of images was a little blurry. Looked like the guy inside had to crawl through some type of narrow corridor, and this next set of shots was coming from the floor. So it was hard to tell. Boxes, carts, big, giant what-looks-like-restaurant-grade refrigerators—and what are those, metal cases?

He automatically put his thumb and forefinger on the screen and opened up the image. *I have seen those metal cases before. Where did I see those? Some sort of cargo casings. I have seen that before. When was it?*

"Come on, old man, you need to think." He let out a sigh of exasperation as he spoke the words out loud. He stood up, walked around the room, hands behind his head. No, he couldn't place them. Okay, time for a little more coffee and a doughnut. His little friend Shelia had dropped these off this morning. She was a smart cookie. No, these were not cookies—he laughed—or doughnuts, for that matter. What did the note say? "Baked, not fried." *These are scones, and really good, I might add. I haven't had one of these since we did that joint training with NASA.*

Myles paused. *NASA. Bingo, that's it! I got it. I saw those metal cases in the NASA warehouse. They are built for rocket payloads. Somebody is going to take these private payloads and shoot them up into the sky. Shut the front door!*

He felt his pulse start to race a little bit and realized that this wasn't a setup to start nuclear war. It was some sort of strategy to inflict biological terror on a countrywide scale. Gotham nothing, they want the whole continent. He needed to interact with Ike on this. *Imagine if I told him the whole state of Texas was at risk*, he thought. *He might have an aneurysm right on the spot.*

Not a time to be joking around. He would reach out to Ian, pronto, and explain this data to him. He picked up the phone and called his secretary and told her that the guys from the seventy-fifth aero squadron were getting together in New Orleans this summer, and they would really like it if their lieutenant could be there as well.

"I realize he is not a lieutenant anymore, but we were all just lance corporals and PFCs at the time as well, but let me leave you my cell phone—"

"General Myles," the secretary broke in. "I have your cell phone, and I have all of your data right here on the screen. So you guys from the old flying-butane brigade are having a reunion? I will give General Kilpatrick your message, and you want him to call the house."

"That would be great, Iris," Myles said. "I appreciate it, and I wanted it to get on his calendar, so that is why I called you. Have him call my cell because I am grabbing a pastrami sandwich over at Carmines this afternoon with one of the guys."

"Well, General Myles, I will give him the message straight away," the secretary said. "I am typing an IM to him right now, pardon the pun. Oh, here is the response: 'My, you do have access, don't you? I guess because you did the job.' Also, that comes without saying, he said that is just an excuse to drink bad beer. Can you please get him the dates, and he will see what he can arrange."

"Thanks, Iris," Kirby said. "I wonder why I always have to set him up with a date."

Iris thought that was hilarious. "Good-bye, General," she said. *Oh, that man*, she thought. *And with the new beard, sophisticated, funny, and handsome.* Just then over the intercom, she heard Donna on the switchboard, saying, "Beverly is on line 2 from the VP's office."

"Hi, Beverly, this is Iris."

"Well, you seem to be in a really good mood," Beverly said. Beverly was about to ask why, and then Iris said, "Someone made a little joke, and it caught my funny bone," and then she returned to business.

Beverly was so nosy and always trying to get information out of Iris. The vice president was left out of a lot of loops. Beverly, in her nasal tone, carried on, saying, "The vice president is playing golf this afternoon with a PGA tour pro at the club and needed a fourth. He was wondering if the chief had anything on his plate, or if he could meet them at two o'clock."

"Let me get back to you on that," Iris replied in a business-as-usual sort of way. Knowing full well that she was not going to interrupt the chief for that, she went on to add, "I will slip him a note when he gets off the phone. He has his IM turned off at the moment, so he must be on an important call."

"Thanks," Beverly said.

As Iris unhooked her headset and left the desk to walk into the doorway of General Kilpatrick's office, she saw he was at the moment putting a few balls into a shot glass.

She relayed the message to her boss.

"No, thanks," Kilpatrick replied. "I have to go over to see my friends at Foggy Bottom." He was thankful now to have a 2:00 p.m. meeting with the CIA director, and he was really thankful that it had been scheduled at 1:00 p.m. and he was the only one who knew it got delayed. *Sometimes, we need a few windows*, he thought. And with Outlook and electronic scheduling, it got a little too precise for him. Suddenly he was feeling like pastrami.

"Would you like me to call you a car?" his assistant asked from the other room.

"No, that is fine young lady, I am going to take mine" was the reply from the voice in the next room.

Iris loved being called young lady. So she relayed the message to Beverly, who started to carry on like they were two schoolgirls chatting in the powder room at their high school prom. Iris acted like she didn't mean to interrupt, but she quickly did and said, "Look, he can call the chief directly if he wants. I am only a piano player here."

Beverly thought that was really strange. Apparently she didn't get the "Don't shoot the messenger" or "Don't shoot me, I am only the piano player" reference, and Iris knew that Beverly didn't get out much or listen to the radio or have anything downloaded on her MP3 player.

What a stiff, Iris thought.

All of this information was relayed from Beverly to the vice president's assistant, and all that information was relayed to Fritz Reckonboeder. He was able to loop him in via encrypted text messages from a phone that Fritz had given him. What a phone, by the way. It was military grade, satellite access. He could watch anything on the planet, and it had GPS like one couldn't believe. No phone bill. He could make instant contact with Fritz. He slid that phone into his coat pocket, and the other one was on his hip. Slick. He liked having friends in high places. He was probably going to be running for Congress in a few years and then chairing the Ways and Means committee, and then maybe the Senate. Or maybe he could just leapfrog right into the vice president's office. He didn't want to run the country. There was too much at stake. For now, he was just going to represent the district of San Francisco and be their guardian angel in the District of Columbia. The vice president loved to play golf, and he didn't care who came along. No, it was not in his best interest to know that he had been rebuffed by the chairman of the Joint Chiefs of Staff. Why did everyone call him the chief? He was the chairman, after all. And what was so impressive about him? Lots of idiots had flown in helicopters. Heath Kildrone was certainly not moved by all that heroic stuff. If he was the vice president, he would tell him, well, that probably wouldn't go over.

ROCKET MAN

KILPATRICK LIKED PASTRAMI. He had changed out of his uniform and put on a pair of jeans, a polo shirt, and a leather bomber jacket. He had actually worn one just like this in Vietnam. He loved it, and he couldn't care less about the style. He looked like any Joe just trying to get a sandwich and stood in line. He ordered his sandwich dipped along with a Diet Coke and chips. He loved the homemade chips. They were really fresh, super crunchy, and had just a hint of sea salt. He paid for his sandwich, and the owner came over and said, "This one is on me."

"Morris, you are not going to make any money if you give out free sandwiches," Ian said.

"Your money is no good here," Morris Plankey said.

"Thanks, Morris." Kilpatrick stuffed a ten-dollar bill into the tip jar.

Morris laughed. "Anytime, Texas. See you around."

Ian had written a commendation for Morris's son ten years ago. His son was now a lieutenant colonel in Japan.

Should be Plankeyson, Ian thought, *since he is living in Japan.*

Ian bowed Japanese style to Morris, who grinned with pride from ear to ear. As Ian made his way with his tray over to the back tables, he spotted Kirby Myles and casually approached his table. "Are you eating by yourself today or waiting for a date?"

"I see you got all dressed up for me," Myles calmly replied. "I see how I rank on your list of important people to see."

Kilpatrick looked at Myles. "Did you wake up on the insecure side of the bed this morning? Why are you taking your personal problems out on me?" He sat down and smiled at Kirby. "No, really, man, it is good to see you. Speaking of insecure, I feel like we are being watched by the whole restaurant. It is funny because your little reunion ruse didn't fool Iris for ten seconds, but she plays it off like she has rehearsed it. I can imagine if someone is listening in and thinks, 'I know that this is such nonsense, but what do we do with it?'" Ian looked at Kirby. "I am supposed to be at the CIA, according to my internal schedule, but Peter Thrush knows I am not coming until zero two hundred hours. So what do you have?"

"I realize meeting again so soon has its issues," Kirby said. "And while I would rather just order a beer and shoot the bull with you because I think we have earned it"—he was quoting one of their favorite movies—"but you have got to see these."

As Kilpatrick stuffed a huge bite of pastrami sandwich into his mouth, Myles let the image go and just laid out the photographs of the inside of the Suirillites warehouse building that housed what he thought was evidence of biological warfare, and then laid down the next room with the rocket payload containers. Kilpatrick was now choking on his sandwich. He took a drink of Diet Coke and then just let out a slow whistle. "Private rocket payloads filled with a chemical cocktail that will do who knows what kind of human terror and misery. Okay, Myles, first of all, this is outstanding work! Second of all, let me get this straight. You sent a guy into utmost northern regions of Niger and dealt with criminal target number one and in the same trip collected this data from his buildings. Your guy got inside the building at night and was able to get this information, slip into a remote area, set the explosives, trigger the explosives, take out the target—with very limited collateral damage, I understand—and then slip out of the country, and nobody but you and God know who this guy is?

"Pay that man, Myles. He is gold. I don't know how he did it, but it is, first of all, unbelievable, but second of all, he has hit the mother lode. We are dealing with Marvel level creeps here. This group is obviously well-funded, smart, under the radar, getting local criminals to do their dirty work. They are using guys that are already on the grid as bad guys, so in essence, we are not looking under the hood. Okay, I will take this up the food chain, and I am sure we will deal with that building. Sometimes we are a little slow to make up our mind, but one thing about our great country is, when provoked, we come out swinging like the Italian stallion."

Ian took a few more minutes to finish his sandwich and his chips, and Plankey came over and checked on them, and Ian got a refill on his soda. Myles asked if Plankey was good people.

"He is so proud of his son, and he thinks my letter of recommendation set all the wheels in motion," Ian said. "He would take a bullet for me right now. Little does he realize that I had nothing to do with it. We recommend guys all the time that either don't cut the mustard, or they choose another path because they know the cost, commitment, and the general toll it takes on our personal, emotional, and spiritual lives may not all add up to be worth it."

"That is the voice of experience talking," Myles said. "But once in a while, when you train a soldier and they pull off work like this"—he motioned to the pile of pictures already back in the envelope—"you realize that it is all worth it, and it makes you proud to wear the uniform and to represent the flag."

As Ian Kilpatrick got up and slid the envelope into his interior jacket pocket, he looked at Kirby Myles and said, "Be careful, or we're going to put you into a commercial."

"Why do you need to recruit senior citizens?" Myles said, still sitting down.

ROLLING IN THE DEEP

Y EAGER HAD SENT some of yesterday's footage to the producers back at Channel 6. Chuck Seger was reviewing clips that his team liked, and couldn't believe it. "Fifteen minutes in Venice, and we have a beautiful introduction and backstreet local interaction. The chemistry between CiFuentes and Gareen is undeniable. I don't know if it is of the two of them together or that they are both good. It is impossible to tell. I love the pull back then the close up, and we have the question Yeager asks and the immediate live response and then four or five clips of this transition, and we get it. Clyde knows Venice, knows his coffee, and takes us to 'Giorgio.' He is a master espresso maker from the art and science of cultivating this ritual. The shots of the crew enjoying the beverage and Anna and Clyde waiting on them is classic. It is so simple and so refreshing. Do you think we have enough materials to send to TFN for some promo setups?"

Merna Hansford was sitting opposite Bryce Rogerson, and they had two of the show's producers, Erin Donahue and Lars Clarkson, on speakerphone. Erin and Lars hesitated for a second.

Chuck rested against the credenza facing the conference table. "I am not asking you guys on location. That was more directed to Bryce and Merna, who have seen most of the material."

They both responded quickly, "Absolutely."

"These guys are really up on camera. They are casual yet look directly at times and, when they don't look direct, speak clearly, and Clyde is naturally hilarious. This Anna CiFuentes is really sensational. She is fluid, asks really good questions, lets her cohost have his way with what he is authoritative on, doesn't interrupt yet stays in the pocket and keeps everything moving forward, mostly because her questions are good. She is inquisitive, and it plays out well in their dialogue. We have plenty. They are going to want to air Venice before we even get to Qatar. So they have already had their first day of shooting since it is about 6:00 p.m. in Venice?"

"Yes, Yeager, has said that they were just going for about five or six hours today to kind of get used to the pace a little. Tomorrow they will start around 10:00 a.m. and work until 7:00 or 8:00 p.m. Saturday is another twelve-hour day. Sunday they will start in the afternoon and be able to get the lunch hour and the dinner hour." Erin paused for a moment and thought about Chuck Seger sitting there with his team and said, "I am sorry. I was rambling."

"No, you are fine," Chuck said. "And you guys are leaving Monday open for any follow up, etc.?"

That is the plan, so far," Lars responded.

"Hey," Merna quipped. "You might want to let Clyde plan your day on Monday. He tends to be pretty spontaneous from what we gather here, and he really knows Venice."

"He was talking on the shoot today about a little pasta ristorante, but I think it was in Palermo," Erin said. "That was nothing more than a shack with an awning and a couple of tables that he used to eat at when he was on a traveling soccer team, or something like that, when he was in high school. He actually was crying as he related the story. Well, tearing up is the better phrase. It was quite a moment, to be honest, but the boys would all go to this shack after their game, and his late wife was one of his soccer mates' sister. He said it was magical, because they had played soccer, and the home team would invite them to come eat, and it would be sixty or seventy people, players and families, and they would serve these huge bowls of spaghetti and big plates of meatballs. They sat around on eight or nine huge wooden picnic benches. They would serve the spaghetti, and he can't believe what they would eat, then he chimes in with the garlic bread. He said his wife would leave the game early and go help cook and get the tables ready. The garlic bread was how she helped, and the little ristorante still serves her recipe for that bread. He says it was hot, buttery, fresh, and with tons of fresh crushed garlic on long loaves, and you would just take a knife and cut off a huge slab—"

Chuck broke in and, almost screaming, said, "Erin, my mouth is watering right now, and I have to see that little place if it still exists. I know you said Palermo, but give me something just like that in Venice. Five-star food in a little local joint."

SHOW ME THE WAY

LAINA WAS SITTING in her room with Ricardo, and she walked into the next room and saw a magazine for boats. She thought that they had a magazine for everything. She suddenly had a thought. *Clyde reads that soccer magazine religiously. Could I put something in the magazine that he would read and figure out that I am not dead, and that Charles Walls is in league with some very dubious characters?* She thought that this could take another month, and she was literally crawling the walls to see her children.

What if I just get on a plane and find the guy and wring his neck myself? Laina, you have to pull yourself together. That wouldn't work, and even if it did, you are going to jail for a long time, and then you are back to square one. She knew that his call sign was Lone Wolf, but she couldn't reach out through that medium. She heard Tonya laughing in the other room, and she was thrilled to hear her happy. Tonya said she was talking on the phone with her brother who had just gotten out of jail, and he was doing really well. He was working as a cook at an all-night diner and was going to church. His church was down in Inglewood, and he said his pastor was a young guy but really had good things to say and was meeting with him once a week for discipleship.

"What is discipleship?" the fifteen-year-old asked.

"He just called randomly?" inquired an observant Laina.

"Oh! Tomorrow is my birthday," Tonya said. "I will be sixteen."

"That is it," Laina said. "We are going to the store. We are going to make a cake. What kind of cake do you like? On our way to the store, I will explain discipleship to you as our bus ride will be about twenty minutes."

"Can we take the subway?" Tonya asked. "There is a store at the end of the Hollywood Boulevard exit. We can just walk upstairs."

"That sounds perfect," Laina said. "But first, we have to get to the North Hollywood entrance, where it picks up."

They got cleaned up and got the babies ready and put them in the strollers and hit the busway. They grabbed the cross-valley connector and walked down to the subway. There was a really nice young man in his early twenties who carried the strollers down all those steps for them. Tonya noticed that Laina had an easy way to make friends and that she wasn't scared and, for a homeless lady, seemed very confident about talking with strangers. Tonya noticed that Laina wasn't homeless in reality but really seemed to be pretending. Spousal abuse is what she thought. Most likely she was running from the idiot. Tonya had seen it before. She didn't even know who her idiot was. That was the crazy thing about her story. It was ugly.

Tonya found herself telling Laina the whole story. She started with her mother, who was a mess, and she didn't know her dad, and then it was it was alcohol and school parties, and the next thing you know, she was having a baby. They didn't have the answers at school. It was stupid, and she was not about to kill her baby. That was stupid. It was murder. She didn't know how she was going to raise her baby, but she had a choice. She drank the alcohol, she went in the bedroom with those boys, and then there was a living human being inside of her. The counselors at Planned Parenthood should quit their job. "She had a right to choose," they said. "You have got to be kidding me" was her comment.

"This is the only advice you have. So if I murder my baby, then I can do it again. This is for crap," Tonya had blurted out. "You guys are really idiots. I am fifteen and I am stupid and I need some advice, but termination is not a choice. What is the difference if I take that letter opener on your desk and plunge it into your neck and you bleed out and die?"

"Tonya, you are upset, and you are really talking crazy, and I understand you are emotional." The counselor tried to respond in his best try-to-stay-calm voice.

"I am not emotional, Lawrence," Tonya said, using the counselor's full name. "I am mad, and I am sad. You tell all the high school girls to do this? What is wrong with you? You should be ashamed! You start at the wrong place."

Larry, whom she thought wasn't the cable guy with the hat but was all proper with his degrees, said, "Excuse me? What do you mean I start at the wrong place?"

Tonya went on, "Well, I looked right at that man and said, 'You think that you are the beginning and the end of what is right and wrong. We have been told what is right and wrong. I am willing to admit I made a mistake. I got pregnant. But I also know that there is a God who says killing is wrong. Human life is important. Each little life is important. Thank you for helping me understand that. I am sorry you think your life is more important than the one growing inside of me. But this baby deserves to live and breathe and have its life, just like you and I!' I stood up and slapped that man across the face and walked straight out of that building."

It looked like the subway was coming down the tracks, and Laina thought discipleship was oftentimes a two-way street.

You start out in one direction, and the next thing you know, the other person is actually making a disciple out of you more than the other way around. Then the nice young man who carried the strollers down the steps came up to them again and asked if they needed more help.

"That would be terrific," Laina said.

The three of them boarded the metro going to Hollywood. Tonya was having fun, and both babies were sound asleep, oblivious to the world. Tonya couldn't believe that schedule feeding her baby meant life would be so much more peaceful. Laina was a good friend and a big help. She was going to tell her, but she would wait until they were alone and the nice young man who had helped them had left. *What was his name?* she thought, and he was a talkative young man. Laina asked him his name and why he was going to Hollywood. He said, "Oh, I am sorry my name is Arthur, and I am taking it further downtown because I have a lunch date."

"Oh, check you out," Laina said. "You are helpful and friendly because someone has a hot date."

Arthur said that he had met a really nice young lady who, like himself, was in the military. She was working for the marines and worked in a high-rise office building, but that was all he knew. She was pretty tight-lipped about what she did, and as a reservist, he understood clearance and all that stuff. He was able to give all kinds of details about how they met and where they were going to lunch. Laina said that he was pretty observant, and most guys miss all of those finer points about their dates, especially after just a few. He recounted that he was detail oriented and that he remembered those items. Even down to the gray eagle on her phone background. "I told her that eagles were black, and I had never seen a gray one before."

Laina paused for a moment and asked what he said again.

"She wasn't supposed to tell me, but I think her call sign is Gray Eagle."

Tonya noticed that Laina's disposition changed.

"Arthur, I was married—am married to a military man," Laina said in almost a whisper. "Well, he is a former military man, and there is one thing I never ever did: I never mentioned anything at all that came out of our conversations that were related to his work."

Well, Arthur was embarrassed, and he apologized. He knew he had been scolded. Laina sat back and laughed. "Arthur, we want to know how your lunch date goes. Are you a regular traveler on the Metro?"

"No, ma'am," Arthur said. "Only because I am going downtown today. Normally I ride my motorcycle to work at the Vons on Devonshire and Sepulveda in the Valley. I am the night manager, and I oversee all of the stock. It is a good job while I finish my business degree at Cal State Northridge," offered the Midwestern transplant easily.

"Did you grow up in Los Angeles?" Laina asked.

Arthur said that his family had lived there for the last ten years in Chatsworth, which was in the northwest San Fernando Valley, but prior to that, they had been living in Iowa.

"This is our stop," Laina said. "Arthur, would you be so kind to help us again? I don't know what we would have done without you." Laina mentioned to Arthur but she didn't say was that she felt like her world had collided with another former world and she didn't know why. What were the chances? He had heard Clyde mention in one form of conversation or another with his friend Myles about Gray Eagle, and he also talked to his wounded comrade Johnny Reb about her as well. Well, in fact, Laina didn't know it was a her, but now that Arthur brought it up, she thought it was too much of a coincidence. There could be lots of Gray Eagles, yet it was the marines, and it was a remote location. Pretty unidentifiable. She seemed, well, like she had been in her job awhile.

"Arthur, you have a great time at lunch," Laina said. "Hopefully we will see you again sometime on the bus, or maybe at the grocery store since it isn't too far from us."

With that, they were off and looking for an elevator, which they found, and once they loaded in, Tonya looked at Laina and said, "Okay, I didn't think you were anything like a normal homeless person, and I figured you were on the run from a bad or mean man, but it didn't sound like that from your conversation with Arthur." She smiled when she said his name because it made her laugh.

Now it was Laina's turn to talk. The elevator was a nice place to spill the beans a little. She said, "He was a nice young man, wasn't he? And he is so excited about his lunch. Listen, I am running, but it isn't from my husband. I saw something I wasn't supposed to, and they tried to kill me for it. In fact, everyone thinks I am dead. It is a long story, but this homeless gig was the quickest thing I could come up with. I have to get this information to my husband, but I don't know how."

"Why don't you call him?" Tonya asked simply.

Laina looked at Tonya and said, "Because there is a one hundred percent chance his phones have been wiretapped. And the bad guys are listening."

"Laina, you watch too much television," Tonya replied.

Laina said that riding the train was a lot more exciting than she imagined. "Well, we came all the way down here, birthday girl, for some ingredients to cook you a dinner and a cake."

Tonya wondered when dinner had gotten thrown into this.

"Tonya, what do you like the most?" Laina asked.

Lasagna was the immediate answer. "I have only had real lasagna once," Tonya quipped kind of longingly.

"You are in luck because my husband is a chef, and he makes the best lasagna in America, and I know his recipe," Laina said.

"How do you know his recipe?" Tonya asked.

"Because he stole mine, and I got it from my mother, who got it from her great-aunt Zena," Laina replied.

"You are a complicated woman, Laina, but I like you," Tonya said. "But whoever heard of a name like Zaneyah?"

A few groceries and a couple of extras, and Laina still had the cash from her original stash. Everything was paid for in the halfway house system. They wanted you to get a job, but they weren't pushy.

FUN, FUN, FUN, TILL DADDY TAKES THE T-BIRD AWAY

L ATE-NIGHT TALK SHOW hosts can be enigmatic and charming or mysterious with a smile. You may not know where they are going to come from next, and that is part of the entertainment. Most of us are afraid to go on national television and come from out in the left field, so to speak, and they can do it with humor, sarcasm, and wit. On this particular evening, which happened to be the very same night that Clyde had dealt with Perpetrator Number One, the late-night show host decided to review the fact that they had extended what seemed like a career-making opportunity to have Clyde Gareen on the show and yet he refused. Reif—pronounced with a long *a*—Lemonhead called it the new segment, "Update on the Guy Who Stiffed Us." He was in his brand-new double-breasted Armani suit, complete with a white shirt, cufflinks, and a very nice red-and-blue-striped power tie. He moved easily on the stage, looking casually at the camera, easily interacting with the audience, and then he went on to recount the story.

"Well, like I was saying, we reached out in mutual camaraderie, and we get spit out. Just want to talk and find out what this new global food critic game is about, and like an oyster spitting out ocean water, we get it right in the eye. Our guy who stiffed us said, 'I don't like talk shows that are totally liberal biased, hate everything about our country that I stand for, and want to promote people who are willing to hand out taxpayer money for government largesse without any way of ever slowing down the outflow of good dollars. They support *Roe vs. Wade*, and they support the overturning of the biblical definition of marriage.' Good grief, that was a long quote. Well, you may not remember that guy who stiffed us, but hopefully, this jogs your memory. So we did a little research—actually very little research because we don't have the staff capacity to burn all those man hours—and lo and behold, he not only stiffed us, but he also has stiffed his landlord. Yes, that is right, he owes his landlord two months' rent. So his restaurant recently folds, and he owes people money. He is concerned about what now? We think a little differently, and so he says, 'Forget your kindness, your willingness to put me on a show of thirty million viewers. Okay, maybe twenty-five million. But what is a few million when you are going to be seen on a nationwide format. Doesn't this sound a little hostile to you? Have you never met a more lovable guy than me?' We just want to have a little conversation, and this guy goes nuclear. You know, sometimes, people can sit down and have a Coke or perhaps an adult beverage, if you know what I am talking about, and have a little talk.

"This is the problem with our country sometimes. Goodness I love this country, greatest place on earth, wouldn't you agree, and we want to have a little chat, and people get all hostile. Like the other day, I jump into this cab, and this young couple is already in there, sitting all cozy, doing what young couples do, and I said, 'Do you mind if I share the cab?' They told me to get lost. Are you ready for that?"

The musician, at that point, pipes in and says, "No? You have got to be kidding me. Why are people so hostile?"

Back to the host, and he says, "Just a conversation, that is all. We want to talk. We can't set aside a few differences for a few minutes and have a conversation? So we asked this guy's people, and nobody is for sure? I guess they are so busy right now filming this new show, a food show. We need another food show, I guess. We don't have enough at the moment that he can't come on sit in the chair, have a cup of coffee, and talk with me, dear old Reif. So you aren't going to believe this. My mom"—there was applause—"you have to love my mom, and she is just a little more conservative than me. Something about the Depression, making a dollar last. I think you know what I am talking about. Mom is on vacation in Italy, and she actually sat down and had a little chat."

Reif responded to someone in the audience, "No, sir, I don't know what anybody was drinking." He went back to the topic. "So my mom has a chat with the guy who stiffed us parents, and we have a little tape of that conversation." Reif then turns to the producers and says, "Roll the tape. And then on the screen you see Mrs. Lemonhead and she says, 'Hi Mr. and Mrs. Gareen. I wanted to say what a pleasure it was to chat with you in such a lovely place.'"

The camera pans around a little tratoria in a very cozy Italian countryside. "She continues, 'Well, let me just get right to the heart of it. Why won't your son Clyde talk to my boy, Reif? He is a very nice young man and won't harm a fly!' Thanks, Mom. That is it. I got beat up in school. This guy is a Navy Seal or Army Ranger or something, and you are telling them I won't hurt a fly! You might as well call me a pansy."

Now it was back to the footage, and the Gareens are talking. Robert Gareen wasn't raised by a dummy. He had been around the block, raised kids, stayed faithful to his wife, worked hard all his life, and was now enjoying grandchildren and semiretirement. Well, he looked straight at Mrs. Lemonhead and, without batting an eye, said, "Please, Mrs. Lemonhead, you must join us for breakfast. You have to try their omelets. It is remarkable what they can do with an egg." He stood up and called for the waiter, and an immediate Bon Giorno is being spoken to the new guest, and Robert said, "We have a person to add to our table, do you mind?" The waiter responded with kindness and said, "Oh, not at all," and then asks Mrs. Lemonhead if she would like a cappuccino, or perhaps and espresso? The order is taken, and Robert looked straight at his newfound friend and says, "I am sorry you were saying something about one of my sons. Which son is giving you grief? I tried to raise them right, but you know how it is with adult children. They do have a mind of their own. Although we did raise them to be independent, take the world head on, so to speak. It is a delight to meet with you as well. We hope you are enjoying Italy. We are here visiting family and having a great time, but the truth of the matter is that I don't think our son—and I say this with all due respect—I don't think Clyde cares much for having sit-down chats with anyone on the radical liberal left. He refused five or six other invitations as well, so your son should not take it personally. You have to understand Clyde. He has grown up with very strong conservative values. He spent many years in the military. So he is very strong on pulling his own weight and can't stomach the way liberals want to create bigger government from a fiscal standpoint. While on moral issues or the lifestyle issues, he is just shocked that our country has embraced something so far from the Judeo-Christian ethic that our country was founded on."

So the little clip ends on the late-night talk show with a closing music and a banner, and Reif Lemonhead comes back on and says sarcastically, "Oh, that is all? Why didn't you say so? Look, years ago I had my old friend, Mr. Jerry from Virginia, had that big Baptist Church and that college and all, and he was a right-winger from when the earth cooled, and we had a nice little chat. So the flyboy won't engage in a nice little chat with Reif. We will just have to continue to find people who can speak in his place. Stay tuned, kids, for another riveting segment of…"

As the music came on, one could see the words "Update on the Guy Who Stiffed Us" come up on the screen.

I WON'T LAST A DAY WITHOUT YOU

CLYDE WAS WAITING for the rest of the team to arrive in the lobby. He loved Venice. All of the endless canals meandering through twelve different islands, very narrow ancient stone paved streets, tourists pouring into the city from all over the world, and he couldn't help but think about those years and years of independence where the republic withstood conquerors and lived free from tyranny for 1,200 years. The imagination it took from the first inhabitants to drive stakes in the ground and figure out a foundation to exist in a lagoon where the tide flowed in and out two times a day was almost incomprehensible. As Clyde looked out onto the *calle*, he saw small groups of tourists following a guide and learning about this charming city. There was actually no place like this in the world. Sitting in the opulent hotel, he was looking over at St. Mark's Square. This was a world-famous landmark, and rightly so. The cathedral that surrounded the square was a centuries-old Gothic and Byzantine mixture of architecture, and it was still stunning. He could smell the saltwater and listen to people as they laughed going by on the gondolas. He also watched groups board the vaporettos, or the public water boats, that were a very inexpensive way to get around. He had three restaurants, maybe four or maybe a dozen tratorias in mind. Two of them were really on the outside islands. He loved Murano, where they made their world-famous glass, and he knew of some out-of-the-way little cafes there as well. The only way to get to these islands was by boat. He had a pretty long history here, and he had played for the local club team one summer between his sophomore and junior years in college.

What a great time he had playing soccer in the Stadio Penzo. The fans would cross the canals and come by boat to the far end of Venezia and the entrances of Fondamenta Sant Elena or Viale Sant Elena. He could remember the warm evenings and the people packing out the stadium to see a Serie C summer team train. It wasn't hard to get some of the best clubs in Europe to send their one of their teams from their training academies because who doesn't want to at least play a game in Venice? The group gathered, and they were all starving, and so they followed Clyde down a little calle, or small street, and he crossed over on a wooden bridge, and they jumped onto a vaporetto. They went down the Grand Canal and stopped off at a little *fondamenta*, or sidewalk, which also had a port for the vaporetto. They then went into a little café, kind of small, outside tables, and the waiter put on a bottle of wine on the table and what looked like a quesadilla, but it was a cheese-filled flatbread. Clyde ordered the gnocchi and carpaccio, and the feast was on. He also ordered the fresh tomato plate with mozzarella, and it was soaked in the regions balsamic vinegar. They were not far from where he had played futbol, and Anna asked him how he knew about this restaurant.

He replied fondly that he used to come here for lunch almost every day one summer, when he was playing soccer up the way.

Clyde pointed down the canal. He loved this spot because of the gardens located on Viale Trento. Clyde described the gnocchi and how it was made and the four cheeses that were in the dish. He said it is pretty common in Italian restaurants in America now, but this potato-flour-egg concoction somehow still tasted best in the city that was known to create it.

"So you spent a summer here, and how did you decide to leave?" Anna asked.

He knew Anna was prodding him to chat a little, so he took the ball and ran with it. "Well, I wasn't picked up by the local futbol club, and I needed to go back to finish college, since Laina and I had just gotten engaged."

"Wait a minute!" Anna interrupted enthusiastically. "You got engaged in Venice? The city listed by most—well at least in my book—as the most romantic city in the world? Don't tell me you were on a gondola and the guy was signing some Italian love song."

"Okay." Clyde laughed. "I will lie to you then." Anna was begging, and she knew it but she said, "You have got to be kidding."

Clyde recounted the story. "So I told you I was here all summer, and my friend Ivan and his sister came up to watch me play. It was actually a ruse because I had talked with Rico, who is Laina's father, and had already received his blessing and I had bought the ring from a jeweler who was a sponsor of the futbol club. So I played an evening game against Barcelona's B squad, and we got beat 8–0. They were pretty good. They had a twelve-year-old phenom named Messi, who you have probably heard of. So after the game, we decided to take a tour of the city. Laina didn't know anything about it, but we caught one of the vaporettos into the Grand Canal, and as we were unboarding, one of the gondoliers asked if anybody wanted a ride on this magnificent evening with a moon so bright it was begging for love. Well, that is a rough translation, and it sounds much better in Italian. I volunteered, and Ivan had already disembarked, and I grabbed Laina's hand, and we sat down.

"As the gondola moved out into the canal, he started to sing, and I got down on one knee and told Laina that I had spoken to her parents and asked their permission, and I was wondering if I had asked in vain because I was hoping that she would marry me. Well, she was absolutely stunned. We had been friends, and we had talked, and there was obvious chemistry, but you have to remember I lived in New Jersey and she lived in Palermo, Italy. Not exactly what you would call convenient. I looked at her, and she was still speechless, and I said I was hoping for an answer because with the boat swaying and all. I don't want to end up in the lagoon! She laughed and said, 'Yes, with all my heart, yes,' and then we kissed. Which was the first time I had kissed her, and I knew immediately that the engagement needed to be short. I was not going to be out of her arms for long.

"We took the gondola back to this restaurant, where we sit right now, and the owner of the restaurant, with Ivan's help, had put on an absolute feast. The boys from the club came over, and it was a smashing engagement party."

Yeager Bierson thought he had died and gone to heaven. He captured the whole story digitally, and he had gotten all of the tears from Anna, who had responded to Clyde with a hug, and he captured the film crew crying their eyes out. The other diners in the restaurant had listened to the story and were now standing and clapping. The owner of the restaurant then came out and recognized Clyde, and they talked and laughed and he served more wine, bread with what looked to Yeager like a dip, but Clyde explained that it was Venice's oldest dish, made from salted cod, olive oil, garlic, and parsley all put together and then blended to make an excellent dish, perfect with the fabulous breads they were serving in baskets.

The afternoon turned into evening, and the group from the *Seasoned Traveler* had charted a private boat and visited two other restaurants that evening. The food was incalculable, and it was such an amazing place. Clyde was able to show the group some of the out-of-the-way places, and the city took on a whole new charm as the lights came on and reflected off the canals. Yeager called it a wrap around eleven at night, and the entire team was exhausted but yet extremely well fed, much better for the experience, and nobody seemed to want to depart. Yeager thought Clyde was, in fact, the seasoned traveler.

"I am glad we chose Venice first," Yeager remarked to Clyde and Anna. "What a blast." He had been in Venice before but hadn't seen it "backstage" like this at all. He had seen a few of the tourist stops, but Clyde wandered through it like a local. Yeager was up until 4:00 a.m. with a few of his staff editing clips and adding different angles. He wanted to send a really good JPEG file to the team at Channel 6.

"They are not going to believe this," he said in his heart. "I can't describe it. I just have to send it."

GOING DOWN
IN A BLAZE OF GLORY

T WAS JUST before five in the morning, and Onturei was walking to work. He had a backpack where he carried his lunch. It was just rice and fruit and nuts and a container of water. He was fortunate to have a good job, and this job paid well. He was a chemist. He had received training out of the country and really liked biology. He was not exactly sure what he was doing every day because the directors of the compound were very private. He didn't ask too many questions, but over the last few months, there had been rumors and a collective concept of what was being planned. It was going to be an interesting day, he thought. Since Mr. Surellite had been accidently killed in an explosion, there was a lot of meetings and conversations taking place, and the rumors at the warehouse were that he had been killed by a spy. Kind of a real James Bond thing was what everyone was saying.

"Who is James Bond?" someone asked. When they found out he was an agent working for the British government hired to defeat underworld thugs, everybody said, "Then why is he working for the British government?"

For Onturei, his walk was not too bad, and he enjoyed the crisp morning air. It would take about fifty minutes to walk the route he liked best. It avoided certain areas, and there was enough width in the road to see if any predators were on the prowl as he did not want to be a jaguar's morning meal. Although if he didn't put any more meat on his bones, then he might get passed up in favor of something a little more substantial. As he turned the corner, he could see the warehouse up the road. There were a few bumps and valleys in between him and where he was going, but they were, for the moment, hidden. But he saw a flash from the sky and was able to see a rocket making a beeline to what looked like the compound structure. Then there was a terrible explosion as the compound went up in flames like a small nuclear mushroom cloud. The building was still burning as Onturei started to jog to the next hill so he could see better. Once he got to the top and was looking down at the building from maybe two miles away, he could see the blaze light up the surrounding area as it was still very dark just before dawn. Then boom, a second explosion took place.

Onturei wondered if anybody was still in the building, although he doubted it after the twin explosions, but with everyone going home around four in the morning, he was hoping none of his friends had still been inside. Most of all, he was concerned about Endewla. They were engaged to marry, and she was going to quit her job as a chemist. He decided at that moment that he needed a god to pray to. He had followed the ancient customs of his village for a long time, and at this moment, with poor Endewla needing a real god in her life that had the ability to interact in time and space and to have protected her, he decided that his friend Graham in school was right after all. He had spent four years telling him all about the God of the Bible and His Son who died and rose again and was willing to forgive sins and accept people not based on works but simply by faith. Onturei had always thought this rather trifling and a bit foolish that God would send God and people would reject God and kill him and then he would be raised by God on the "third" day and now was giving people the "Holy Spirit" to come inside of them and change them. But it didn't seem foolish anymore. Onturei knew he was in trouble and he was a sinner, and he needed nothing more than Christ. The one who created and yet came to save, the humble man who knew he was sick. Onturei knew he was a sinner, he was powerless, but God is powerful.

He knelt down on the road and simply said, "Please accept me, God, as a sinner. Take over my life, and let me, from this day, live for you." He stood up and started walking and was crying and knew his fiancé might not be alive, but he was no longer dead to God, he was now alive, and it was this moment he had been created for, to bring glory to the Almighty God.

Wow, I must have learned more from that soccer-playing white kid from the Middle East than I imagined, Onturei thought. *Well, he was relentless after all. I wonder what he is doing now. He would never believe that I bowed my knee to Christ. He would probably throw a party.* A sort of lingo he knew they would say in America. In the next few minutes, Onturei arrived at the hole in the ground. That was all that was left. A twelve-foot deep and maybe two-hundred-foot-wide hole in the face of the earth. That was powerful, he thought. Somebody didn't approve of what was going on here, can you imagine? What were we doing? Who has the ability to do this? England, United States, Israel, Germany, or maybe France, was his immediate reaction.

No, not the French, he thought. *They would have missed the target.*

"Looks like I have the day off," he mused and turned to walk away. As he got back to the village, he had been praying. He was hoping Endewla was alive and if she was alive what was she going to do with him now. He was a Christian. It could be a very lonely life as one of the few believers in Niger.

This will change everything, he thought. *No matter. Live or die, starve or prosper—it is who I am now. I need a Bible. Graham said I should read the book of John.*

Forty minutes later, as Onturei turned the corner to his village, Endewla came running out to meet him. She had been certain that he would have been the first to arrive at the building. "I was the first to arrive," he said, "but I was not quite there yet. I was still ten minutes away. No, it wasn't nuclear. It was just a big, huge explosion, and the building is gone. There is now a giant crater in the earth as a result."

After the conversation died down and he had a chance to talk with Endewla, he told her of his changed life and his new heart and his desire to seek the God who created the world. She was speechless. With tears in her eyes, she turned and walked away.

Onturei's heart broke in forty-seven pieces. He was shattered. He couldn't reach out to her. He knew he did not have the words. There was nothing to say. He was a new man. He had changed. *God had revived me and taken me from the dead to the living. I see the world different. I want to please God.* He walked away and said to himself and to God, *That was a sacrifice. Wait until my family hears. I will be thrown out of the village.*

They heard from Endewla's family later on that day. They packed Onturei's bags for him. He was already jobless, and now he was homeless. They were not going to have this "religion" come into their home or their village. This whole village, for the most part, was still caught up in the mystery religions of Africa. They had a shaman, or religious man, and they followed really just the pluralistic pagan religions of their forefathers. The younger generation, having been sent to schools out of the country, was changing the village slowly. They were, for the most part, either a very hostile atheistic crowd to all outside religions or just convenient followers of the religion of the home to not cause waves.

Onturei did not know where to turn. He had seen a Baptist Church in the next town. Forty miles away, though. It was going to be a long walk. He had money in his belt that he had saved from his job. He didn't put it in the town bank. He knew better than that. He had around four thousand dollars. Now the trick was safe passage. He prayed for guidance and saw smoke from a distance. It was not smoke; it was dust from a car. He hailed down the Land Rover and hitched a ride with an American journalist out to see the remote villages of Niger. The two talked until they got to the next village, and Onturei said his good-byes and thanked Roger for the ride. He prayed for Roger and said, "You never know when the missile strikes and God changes your heart." He knocked on the door of the Baptist Church, and that was a new beginning.

PLEASE COME TO BOSTON

AINA WAS AT the end of her rope. She needed to tell Clyde, and she needed her family. It had been almost four months, and if she had to deal with the devil himself, she was going back to her family. It was killing her. She sat in a pool of tears and watched Ricardo sleep.

What am I going to do? she thought. *I can't even leave the state. That will be a federal kidnapping charge.*

The roads were blocked, and she was frightened. She just sat down and prayed. "God, I am at a loss, but you are bigger than anyone. I need your wisdom and protection. I am not afraid to die, but I fear for my family." Then she thought of Gray Eagle. Just like that. Wow that was a quick answer to a short but truly authentic prayer. "Okay, Lord, I will reach out through this guy we ran into in the subway."

She continued in her thought process. *I don't want to get any-one in trouble, and I wonder if she will be offended by a small token of my appreciation. But she might have some kind of covert contact with Clyde. But that won't work. Clyde hasn't been on active duty for three almost four years. No matter. I am going to reach out to her, and maybe she can reach out to General Myles. If I do that, it would be picked up, I am sure of it.* Although she thought his lines would be secured. *Not if he is out of the military as well. Oh, I am so scared and confused. I don't know what else to do.*

Tonya walked in and asked if she was okay. Laina shared her frustration, and Tonya said, "Let's go to my brother's church. He has recently been released from prison, and now he is going to this church in Inglewood. He loves it. The pastor is a great guy. If my brother is going to church, I am encouraged and prayerful that it will begin to change his life."

"It is Saturday, so we should go tomorrow," Laina said. "Can we get down there in time taking the bus?"

"It is a little tricky, but my brother has offered to bring the family minivan and pick us up. What do you think?"

"I am game if you are," Laina said. "Let's go for it. But I have to ask you to keep all the information I have given you as private. My family's life is at risk because of it. I know it sounds crazy, but I can guarantee you the guy that I have information on is bigger than the Mafia, or any gang in Los Angeles, by ten times. He has access to the highest levels of any government on the planet, which comes with being a multibillionaire. I don't know what his plans are and why he is in league with the people I saw him with, but according to my husband, the man doing business with his second-in-command is a dangerous criminal: running drugs, selling arms, and doing all kinds of nefarious activities, considering maybe even nothing short of human trafficking."

Poor Tonya looked at Laina and said hesitantly, "I am sorry, but I do not follow what you mean by human trafficking."

"It is an ugly world out there, and sometimes they kidnap little girls and—"

"Oh, wow," Tonya interrupted. "I have heard of that, but I didn't think it was real. I get the picture. You don't have to explain anymore. You have my silence. How are you going to explain to people who you are and what is happening with you?"

"I will start from the beginning," Laina said. "Homeless, a little on the crazy side, and here I am."

"That is not from the beginning, and cleaned up, you look like a movie star," Tonya said.

Laina didn't respond to the movie star comment, but she said, "I will say little and keep my distance. It will be great to be in church, and I look forward to meeting your family. It sounds like they have had a little practice at forgiving."

"You can say that again," Tonya said. "We are experts in the craft. Between me, my brother, and not to mention the rest of the family, we have made a lot of mistakes."

Laina sat back down at her desk and penned a little note.

> Dear Gray Eagle,
>
> I am taking a risk, but the rest of the planet thinks I am dead, so I trust my secret will be yours. Do you have any way of reaching out to my husband, Clyde Gareen? Can you please tell him 'go Unione Venezia F.B.C., and to call this number (818) 635-8678 when able from secure line?

"Tonya, let's take the bus over to that Vons," Laina said. "Let's get a few groceries and say hi to our old friend that we met the other day on the subway."

Tonya knew something was up, but she was always hungry for something Laina was going to cook, and the grocery store was the beginning of all kinds of possibilities. Tonya realized that Laina was her first friend. Whatever the correct label was, she was not sure, but she knew that even more than a friend, Laina was a confidant, mentor, someone who actually cared about her. Tonya liked being liked. She liked being heard and listened to.

The four of them caught the 188 bus for Sepulveda and Devonshire and fifteen minutes later were deboarding a b.g, huge double–air-conditioned bus crowded with people from all walks of life and heading into the store. She didn't think Arthur, her newfound friend, would be at work since he was the night manager, but she was pretty convinced he had a locker. She had sealed the envelope, and nobody would understand the message, anyway.

FREE-FALLING

Nothing! Nada! Not one word anywhere. Charles Walls could not believe it. How could an unmanned aircraft carrying a rocket-propelled missile blow up an entire warehouse at five in the morning in Northern Africa and no one seems to care? It was impossible. Well, it wasn't like he was able to go in there and start asking questions. But this was preposterous. Somebody drops a bomb on a sovereign country, and not even a peep out of the United Nations. It seems like nobody knew. How could this be? Charles slammed down his coffee cup. It was lousy coffee, anyway. He was in a foul mood. Rico Del Amo hadn't returned his phone call, which was very unusual for his longtime friend. Of course, he hadn't been to church, and he had all the usual excuses. Except over the last few months, he really didn't want to go. Prior to the killing of Laina Del Amo, most of his plans were carried out by a third party, and he wasn't really responsible. But he felt like he had crossed a line with the operation of traffic vaporization. He had to admit that had gone off so smoothly that the Italian police did not even launch an investigation. He smiled for a half a second and called to his assistant to bring in more coffee. "Can you make a fresh pot with a little more ground coffee in it? On second thought, bag the coffee. I mean, forgot the coffee. I will take a pot of hot water and some of that black tea."

"Would you like some honey, Mr. Walls?" his assistant asked in perfect English. She was a college graduate from a school in England and had moved back to her hometown so she could attend Rico Del Amo's church. Charles had been shocked to learn that she wanted to go to his church specifically, and she had mentioned her friend in college, some boy named Graham who had directed her to visit the church since it was in her area. Apparently this Graham character had been on a mission trip to Argentina, where he had met a disciple of Mr. Del Amo's, and it had really changed his life as he headed off to Oxford. Charles was so bored with the conversation when he interviewed this young lady that he almost fell asleep. But the one thing that really caught his attention was how interlinked the Christian church was. Millions of followers all over the world, and these connections are made all the time. He had been traveling in Dallas, Texas, and he made connections with people in a church that knew some people in Los Angeles, who knew people from South Africa that he had done business with. It was a small community, but it really was not. The brotherhood seemed to keep track of each other.

Charles thought that all of these people were duped and that the community was about to get a whole lot smaller. Although this little setback in Africa was going to cost a little bit of time to get the final element of P3 up and running. He had studied the air streams, and despite Yeri's misgivings, he felt like the northern African/southern Mediterranean currents were better and quicker to mix with the two other locations, and he was confident that based on the best weather-pattern studies, this would be unstoppable once each element was released. He was not quite as confident about the northern Russian and/or Siberian air patterns. Like the continent, which broke into several people groups, the jet streams seemed to break up and go east and west and, at times, south to India. Charles knew it could be unpredictable, but Yeri had argued that the air stream in Siberia would go both ways and mix with the streams coming up from the Malaysian triangle, as they had called it.

The phone was ringing, and it was his friend and comrade Alberto Johnston. "Alberto, how are you today?" He was asking what was going on in New Zealand and that side of the world.

Alberto knew that, of course, on speakerphone, it would be a limited conversation, but he enjoyed the small talk like anyone else. Alberto had information, so Charles dismissed his assistant. What was her name again? And why was she so nice? Crabby—no, that was not it. Gabby.

"Thank you, Gabriela," he said. "And if you would shut the door as you walk out, I would appreciate it."

As Gabby left, Charles took a moment to size her up and then turned his attention back to Alberto.

Gabby shut the door and then sort of shuddered. She didn't know why. This guy just kind of gave her the creeps. Other adults called her by her given name. But in this case, she had made a point to use the shortened version, which was what she was used to. He had lots of household help, so she wasn't alone. There were people coming and going and deliveries and tons of phone calls. He had an executive assistant who handled the trips and planning and the business side of things, and she was perfectly nice, and this was a really good job with lots of potential and excellent benefits. But well, she couldn't put her finger on it. A guy with manners who spoke perfect Italian, German, Spanish, and, of course, English, and he was in his midforties, obviously a very wealthy man. He was a man who went to the church, but why was he not married? Why didn't he have children? Of course, he might have the gift of singleness, but he didn't seem to be uninterested in women, which she could kind of tell. These were a lot of thoughts for so early in the morning, and she had a lot to do. But this feeling had come on her for the last few days, and she had only been on the job for a couple of weeks. *Creeper* was the word her American counterparts used in school. Charles fit the description, and it made her skin crawl. This was going to be a short-lived job. She knew it right then and there.

Alberto was saying that he had gotten more information from that intelligence unit based out of Yemen. "These terrorists are getting pretty good at the technology game. They can track a dingo through the outback and tell you if he favors his left paw or his right." Alberto thought this was funny, but Charles wasn't sure if he saw the humor. He forced a little chuckle anyway, and then Alberto said, "We think he was American."

"Who was American?" Charles asked. "Oh, the guy who killed Suirillite you mean? That is interesting."

"We have a satellite image of a C-4 transport plane leaving northern Africa, heading northeast. We also have confirmed through our sources that a C-4 cargo plane—or transport plane, if you will—left the American airbase in Germany around 7 p.m. German time and returned around noon the next day."

"Did you find out where it had gone?" Walls queried.

"No, that is just the thing." Alberto was almost yelling. "We know it went nowhere, but it had to go somewhere for eighteen hours."

Charles was now adamant. "Let's press this with our people on the inside at the Pentagon. This is a huge deal."

Alberto took a big sigh. He knew his friend didn't like to back down. Alberto said to Charles "Hang on just a second. Let me finish. We actually had a conversation with the pilot of that transport plane, and he said they were testing the limits of fuel capacity. It was a test flight on the books. It looks like they refueled in midair somewhere over Cairo. We have no satellite tracking of this plane because the route they took was purposely to be off of the map, so to speak."

"We get an American guy to pick off Suirillite, and then we get an unmanned drone bombing our warehouse in the same location," Charles summarized.

"That our culprit must have gotten data on the warehouse before he blew up our on-site administrator."

"How is that possible? We have really good security on that building."

"Humans have to go in and out of them Charles," Alberto offered. He went on to add, "There are cameras and passwords, but a really good trained operative can bypass almost anything. This guy is top-notch. And he has resources."

Charles, who was deeply perturbed, responded, "So it is an operative with training, with access, with resources, and he is off the radar since nobody knows about it."

"We are working on it," Alberto said. "We have our people inside in Washington, both in the executive office, as you know, and in Congress and our new guy in the Senate. Who would have ever thought a senator from Arizona would turn independent and then be willing to come on the payroll? Boy, greed is a beautiful thing. So we know of only so many guys that can fit that description. We are counting out anybody over forty-five and anyone under thirty. And there has to be black ops go between who is off the books and has access to the people in Washington, CIA, and Homeland Security. We have our feelers out. Mr. CIA just had a meeting with the Joint Chiefs of Staff guy Kilpatrick, and our sources say that the meeting was at one o'clock, but we have his car showing up at two o'clock. So two days ago, he goes missing for an hour, and the next thing you know, we have a little pop rock in Niger."

"Do we know his bathroom schedule as well?" Charles asked.

Alberto laughed out loud. "The meeting, supposedly at one o'clock, was for lunch, but he didn't touch his crab salad. So that made us suspicious as to what he had been doing for lunch."

"He knew what he would be doing for lunch in Washington DC, and it didn't involve food."

"Charles, you should settle down and get married," Alberto said. "It is the best thing I ever did four times." He broke into laughter.

Charles appreciated that Alberto could make fun of himself. It was hard for him to do, but he was taking a few pointers from Alberto on that. But it was so hard to do when you are right all the time, Charles thought. He quickly mentioned to Alberto that he would get a transition team into Niger and get the best biologists out and move them to their new location in northeastern Russia. The Russians really wanted their business, and it would be perfect. No problem for a pharmaceutical giant like Zeuterfeld Labs to spend money in the Russian economy. They would wine and dine. All of which Charles thought would be terrific. He needed a little less stress.

"Hey," he said to Alberto, and Alberto knew that Charles had another thought. "Kirby Myles is your black ops guy."

"How do you know that?" Alberto asked.

"Do you remember when we had our team in the beginning track a meeting between Ian Kilpatrick and Kirby Myles? Kirby came in through the back door, and the president left a meeting with the vice president and the rest of the cabinet for about thirty minutes, and we are pretty sure that these all overlapped."

"Wow!" Alberto said. "That is super helpful."

"I am pleased to be of assistance," Charles countered.

"We can put our finger on the trigger of operatives that Myles likes. Get back to you soon. Thanks for setting up that transition team to Siberia. Anything you need me to do?"

"All good for now, Alberto," Charles said. "Talk to you soon." He walked out of his office and asked Gabriella if he could send her to Africa to help with sending a former team to Siberia. He knew how to play this. He had a humanitarian facility in Niger that had been blown up. If anyone said that there was compromising materials in that facility, it would be tied to the local people and their misuse of an Amnesty International–sanctioned facility. That bad guy has suddenly died, and the building has gone up in smoke. Well, somebody would have to answer for this. Someone was missing a rocket-propelled precision bomb. This was at least a three-hundred-thousand-dollar piece of equipment, maybe even more. There was accountability and a structure in place, and it looked like a soldier somewhere had missed math class in high school once too many times. Charles had his executive assistant, Marlene, send the pictures of the crater to his friend in the vice president's office. He would also ask the question why a Zeuterfeld Lab humanitarian warehouse got blown up to his contacts in Washington, DC. Did anyone know anything?

ALL I NEED IS A MIRACLE

C HUCK SEGER WAS watching the footage from Yeager. It was awesome. His director was really talented. He knew this was an art. Yeager was akin to Rembrandt and was putting together reality television done by professionals. *The Seasoned Traveler* was fun to watch, Anna and Clyde were a perfect tandem. Clyde knew Venice better than he ever would have imagined, and the footage from the live segments, together with the before-and-after outtakes, was amazing. Both Clyde and Anna were passionate about food. Because Anna had spent a few years writing articles, she was well-oiled in her side of the craft of asking questions, talking about the food, carrying on a very engaging conversation. But the ad hoc moment of Clyde's engagement, coupled with the fact that he had lost his wife abruptly, was totally endearing. You just wanted to stop what you were doing, reach out, and hug the guy and, at the end of the time, clap for what was actually heartfelt real romance done in a spectacular way.

This was the second time Chuck was watching it, and he was seeing things now that he hadn't seen the first time. The restaurant had kind of paused to listen to Clyde. While he was speaking in English, he would intersperse enough Italian to keep the conversation moving and his newfound Italian friends engaged. Chuck knew classic moments when he saw them. His staff loved it and had no changes. "Send it."

They responded with "If we keep this, the Food Network will kill us. Let's see their response."

It didn't take more than an hour for the CEO and her staff to call back. "Chuck, we don't want to wait," Barb Reiding commented firmly. "We want to air this as a special tonight. We will have one less chopped and one less triple D, as they called it, and set up Clyde and Anna for an hour. We will air this as a pilot, and it breaks new ground. It is a reality show hybrid, if you will. Actors on the move but interacting with the public and explaining authentic cuisine, and ultimately it makes us want to go to Venice, and when we go, we know places to visit. We haven't been this excited since Livee Lapay [*liv-e la-pay*] started her shows with us before moving to daytime talk. I know it preempts our contract a little bit, and we are willing to pay. We have got our three biggest advertising agencies coming in for lunch, and they will bid for their spots. I know they will be mad, but this is like trading Peyton Manning. You have to pay the piper if you want to hear the tune. So it will come back to you. I will have legal forward you a new contract, and if you like it, have your team authorize it and send it back.

"Chuck, you and your team have done good work. Yeager is brilliant. He was a great choice. He knows when to insert himself, and he knows when art is being made to let it roll. It is so exciting we think America is going to grab on to this tonight. We will show it this evening and then rerun it later this week."

Chuck thought this was a lot to say. Barb was truly excited, and that doesn't happen often with a serious veteran like Barb.

This wasn't her first rodeo. For her to be thrilled about a show was a seriously good sign. She shot out her next question, "When does your team go to Qatar? Clyde speaks Arabic as well?"

"We have our crew scheduled to go to Qatar in three days" was the response from Nina Pearson, who was also on the phone call.

"That is perfect," Barb said. "Let us keep the wheels moving here on our end, and we will reach back to you in a few hours."

"Thanks, Barb," Chuck said. "It is a pleasure, as always."

As Leah hit the off button on the speakerphone, she said to Chuck and the gang, "Well, that went well."

Everyone in the room started to laugh. They had all been holding their breath, so to speak, while on the phone with the network executives, and their response was a huge sigh of relief as well as celebration.

"I can't believe it," Bryce Rogerson said. "They are actually going to preempt regular programming for our show. I hope we are all correct and America loves it as much as we all do."

Chuck dismissed his crew and went back to work. No sense in getting all worked up. He had played enough sports to know that momentum can swing really quickly one way or the other. He had a local station to run the programming for. His bosses were paying him to keep this New York station sharp and fully profitable. His career had gone from promise to panic to upgrade. He had been sent to program a small local channel in Des Moines, Iowa. While he thought it was a panic to his promising career, he had really enjoyed his five years there. He turned the station around, made it number one in its class in the Midwest, and got promoted to this heavy hitter. So after three years, he had taken a running in the red, going downhill fast monster, and turned it around. Best local channel in the New York metro area, he had turned the ship around and it was biting on the network's heels. Especially since they were now doing the Knicks home games. That was a boon. And to top it off, there was nothing wrong with selling a show to the Food Network. He had a little shared expense with the fact that they were letting him produce it, which was amazing. In reality, he didn't have to add anyone or any hours to his bottom line. He didn't get the ratings increase directly other than the backdrops and vignettes they were able to add. But the revenue was virtually pure profit.

I WANT YOU TO WANT ME

RTHUR WAS SO excited. He was working from two to
ten. He had switched with Jose Portillo, the swing shift
manger, because he was going on a date with his newfound friend. Her name was Roxanne, and she didn't wear a red
dress, but she wore red pants on their first date, and Arthur like
her from the get-go. She was warm and kind and funny, and they
seemed to like a lot of the same things. He was picking her up for
a quick bite, and then they were going to see the midnight showing of the new film by that infamous British agent.

Arthur thought that Roxanne was all that. He had grown up
in Iowa, moved briefly with his family to California, and then
joined the military. Hard work and keeping his nose clean led
him to a nice career for eight years. He had been stationed in
California the last couple of years, and he became a resident. He
wanted to stay there and go to school. He was working on getting a business degree from the local university and had a great

job for a twenty-nine-year-old single guy. He had explained to
Roxanne on their first lunch date that he had a motorcycle. He
didn't date much, so it didn't matter. He was going to school,
working full time and in the reserves. Which was where he first
ran into Roxanne. She had to run down to Camp Pendleton for
some updated training. She was never exactly sure why she had
to shoot because she had a desk job. But they wanted her to be
up to speed on the latest equipment. Her instructor was a quote-
unquote reservist.

Great, she thought sarcastically. *This guy is going to be a real pro.*

But his name was Arthur, and he had been deployed and had
worked his way up to gunnery sergeant, and he was very young
for his rank, and he knew weapons. That was for sure. They spent
the day training, along with forty of their closest friends, and at
the end of the day, he walked over to her and said, "Hey, nice
shooting, Texas," as that was where she was from. "Would you
like to have lunch sometime?"

*Long and lean, with a friendly smile and an easygoing Midwest
style about him*, she thought. Secretly she said to herself, "I am all
in, soldier." But of course, she played it coy and said, "If I give you
my number, will you call me? I work in downtown Los Angeles,
and I know you are up that way, right?"

"I will call," he said. "You can bet on it."

She gave him her number, and he had called.

Lunch was terrific. They walked over to a place called Olvera
Street and ate tacos. He must have eaten six. She said he was
going to have to keep working out to keep his figure up with that
amount of food. Roxanne had agreed to a second date, and he
asked if she minded riding on the back of a motorcycle. He had
an extra helmet, and if she wore jeans, it wouldn't be a problem.
Did he mind picking her up, because she lived in a loft downtown? She had been very frugal with her money, and when the
real estate downturn came, she picked up a foreclosure at a song.
Most of the homes were currently selling new in the $500,000
range, and she bought a three-bedroom for $275,000. She did an

FHA loan and only had to put down $9,625. She had a fixed-rate loan and a payment that she could afford. But then the value had gone up, and her lender, a really nice guy who had his own mortgage company, called her back and refinanced the unit at no cost with a new fixed-rate loan at 3.5 percent, and she got rid of her mortgage insurance. She saved almost four hundred a month and thought she had died and gone to heaven. Her payment was $1,218 and with taxes, insurance, and association fees, she was out the door for $1,872 a month. She couldn't rent for that.

She was so happy, and she was given a military car to drive as part of her package. But she had to admit she was lonely. She had dated, but nothing had come of it. Growing up Catholic, she had her standards, and all of the guys she had met were vitally concerned about themselves. Arthur was different. Well, his name was Arthur, after all. He said it was a family name, and he didn't care. Lots of people called him Art, and he said, "You can call me Arthur or Art or anything else, but don't call me late for supper." She thought he was hilarious, and they had so much in common. He came down to her place in Los Angeles on his motorcycle, which was a very nice Harley Davidson. She sat very comfortably, upright on the back of the bike; it made her a little nervous that it would be street-bike style. But that was not how this guy rolled, and she was happy about that. He did look a little serious when she came down to the front.

"Okay, I have to ask your forgiveness," he said. "I made a mistake."

Oh no, Roxanne thought. *He is going to say good-bye right now. This would be a bummer. Okay, relax.* She took a deep breath. "What is it, Arthur?"

"At some point, I saw the Gray Eagle on your phone, and, well—"

Oh, he didn't have all the words. "I am sorry," he said. "I rehearsed this a couple of times, but I need to apologize, so just give me a second."

Second nothing, Roxanne thought. *This is like an eternity.*

"Okay, so when we were going to meet for lunch, I helped this homeless lady and her young friend get on the bus," he continued. "And I know this sounds strange, but it turns out the lady isn't homeless. She is actually hiding. I know, I know. It sounds creepy, but the reason why I am telling you now is that I told her I thought your call sign might be Gray Eagle."

Roxanne relaxed because, after all, it was on her phone. Not his fault, really. It was kind of dumb of her, actually. But only the ops guys knew the name, and they didn't know her at all. She actually didn't know any of them either.

"So as we were riding the bus and chatting a little, it turns out that she heard me say Vons in Devonshire," Arthur said. "And after, she scolded me for giving the name of your call sign because her husband was in the military before, and he knew a Gray Eagle."

Now all of a sudden, Roxanne's heart started to beat a little faster.

"I am so sorry," he said with his Midwestern drawl. "Will you please forgive me?"

Roxanne really liked his way of communicating. His drawl was certainly not a Texas drawl, but at least it was a drawl, and it made her feel at home.

Roxanne looked at him and said, "Mr. Lewis, apology accepted, and we have cleared your name before the board, and you are free to return to duty."

He laughed and gave her a high five. "I almost forgot. This note is from her. It was sealed with a *G*."

Roxanne's heart now stopped.

"What is it?" Arthur couldn't help but notice.

She opened the envelope and read the letter and fell down sobbing. Arthur's first thought was *Wow, I thought I had been cleared for duty*, then his second thought was, *That was quite a strong reaction.* "Roxanne, are you okay?" He helped her up, and she fell into his arms. It wasn't a romantic hug; it was just one person leaning on a friend.

So they sat down on the street corner, and she explained a little to him about whom this homeless lady was and her "death." Obviously she couldn't go to the funeral, but everyone in the military was shocked. They were all perplexed, to be honest. She didn't say what was going on currently, and there was really no accounting for why Laina would reach out to her. Although come to think of it, she is the lady who knew her call sign. Clyde could be one of the operatives, or the asset. But that was impossible. He was a big TV star now. She dismissed that idea. She thought there has to be some connection for Laina to take the chance and reach out to her. *But somehow, she must think that I can reach out to someone who knows Clyde, and she was smart enough to figure out that she might be able to communicate with him via encrypted message*, Roxanne thought. *I can go through my channels, and they can reach out to General Myles. Okay, that is crazy news, and to think I may be the only one on the planet who knows.*

"You know, Roxanne, I have always maintained that life is stranger than fiction," Arthur said. "You think you know something or someone and then come to find out the truth is different. We live in a strange world. Do you still want to get a bite and see the movie, or would you rather take a rain check?"

"No rain check," she said. "You got to try these hot dogs at Pink's, and then let's find out if *Skyfall* is any good."

BAND ON THE RUN

AN KILPATRICK WAS thinking that he was stuck inside these four walls and there was no way out. He loathed Ash Grafton. Whoever named him Ashton Grafton? He knew it was a family name, but really, one couldn't think that through first.

"I want to know who ordered this bomb to take out the humanitarian warehouse of Zeuterfeld Labs," Mr. Grafton screamed at General Kilpatrick.

There were a couple of other civilian stiffs in the room, and they were at about the same blood pressure level as Ash. Heath Kildrone, the slimeball from the vice president's office, was in tow with his partner-in-crime, Grafton. It was always someone from the vice president's office and/or the secretary of state's office who were questioning everything. They seemed to be out of the loop on a lot of current events. Kilpatrick couldn't quite put his finger on it, but he felt like a couple of people in these high places were on somebody's payroll. This was actually really good data, and they had put their fingers on quite a few items. They were trying to link the assassination of Surillite to this bombing, and they couldn't figure out what the tie was.

Just ask the guy who is writing your check, Ian thought. But the truth was that these suits were probably out of the loop on the mole. They were really just pawns being used by one or maybe two liaisons who could be totally unaware of each other.

Ian stood up and said, "Time for more coffee." He walked out of the room and filled his coffee and brought the coffeepot back to the doorway and asked if anybody needed a refill. This was almost enough to send four guys into cardiac arrest. The vocabulary coming from these guys was akin to some of the language he had heard during combat. He looked around the room and pointed to the group, saying that nobody was wearing combat boots but they were all talking like soldiers waiting to charge. They didn't find that funny.

"I have absolutely no idea what on earth you are talking about," General Kilpatrick said. "I am totally unaware of any executive order or military order to use weapons in North Africa. Surillite was a bad apple, and I can't say that I am sorry he is dead, but as to what the tie-in is between a bad guy and Zeuterfeld Labs's humanitarian warehouse, I have absolutely no idea. You know we are not the only guys on the planet with the ability to deploy bombs in the Mediterranean theater."

Ash Grafton looked at the general. "You are a liar."

Ian looked at the young punk. "Would you prefer to take this outside?" Ian sat down on his desk and crossed his arms, and he looked straight at Grafton. "Ash, I may be old enough to be your grandfather and I represent all of the armed forces in this uniform, but if you so much as insinuate again that I am sitting here not being forthright and if you insult me again, I am going to take off my coat, walk you outside, and give you an old-fashioned whipping. Do you understand?"

"Mr. Grafton," one of the counterparts said—probably Heath Kildrone, but Ian didn't remember exactly. "We don't need to get into name-calling here. Let's just stick with the facts." He had noticed that he hadn't ever seen the general show even the slightest bit emotion ever before, and these were pretty strong words. In relating the story afterward, no one really quite understood the actual sequence of events. Grafton started to say to the general to kiss his behind, and then Ash just hit the floor. The chairman of the Joint Chiefs of Staff hit the assistant secretary of state so hard that somebody commented he might not get up for a week. Well, the medical staff came rushing in, and it was a scene of extraordinary chaos. It was all they could do from keeping the press at bay as they realized something was going on. There were enough White House correspondents around to actually hear what was happening. Ian had actually anticipated all of this, and he knew that he might get in some hot water, maybe even asked to step down from this post that ultimately it would bring this inquiry to a grinding halt and allow for a little more time. Somebody was going to launch rockets with biological warfare in it, and he didn't want that somebody to know the extent to which they knew so they could catch him. But in the meantime, with what appeared to be a mole running on loose on the inside, he also couldn't bring all of the players in the government into the loop at the moment. So for now, chaos was actually a strategy.

Sitting on his boat with Kirby Myles a day later at a remote West Virginia lake near his one-bedroom log cabin, Myles said, "Man, if you would have called me into the meeting, I would have hit him for you. Then you wouldn't be in trouble." But they both knew that what Ian had done was allow for a little more time. What Ian didn't know was that their operative was now crossing into Qatar on somebody else's dime. Kilpatrick asked Myles, as he was reeling in a rather large trout, "How did your guy actually get in that warehouse, get out, get Surillite, and get back out without so much as…"

And then the question just kind of tailed off because the two men both knew the answer. There was no way on God's green earth that Myles was going to give up his operative. That would never happen. All Kirby said was "It is times like these we need superheroes, and the world may never know. Just like nobody is supposed to know that you stocked this lake with big fat trout so you can tell everyone you know how to fish."

Kilpatick laughed out loud and said it didn't go well the last time someone called him a liar.

WORKING EIGHT DAYS
A WEEK

A FTER VENICE, THINGS had moved quickly as they boarded a commercial flight for Qatar. Clyde had spoken to his father from Venice and apologized for the intrusion of the interview at breakfast. His dad said that it was no harm, no foul. Really quite delightful once you get past the camera crew, which must have cost them a few bucks to send four guys to Italy. Robert Gareen gave Clyde all the information Clyde needed in a few short sentences and then handed the phone to his wife. He knew she would say all the same things again, but moms need to talk to their kids, even if they were all grown up with families of their own. Robert never understood how his wife could keep track of seven kids and thirty-one grandchildren. Her calendar looked like a crossword puzzle with all the writing in it. Everything went into that weekly little book with pencil.

Grandma Gareen, as she was known, was actually pretty fast on the phone. As soon as she found out Clyde was okay and he was sleeping and eating, she told him the kids were great and having the time of their life. "They miss you, though. Clyde, you be careful now. That Anna is really attractive. Don't go falling into love. We know you are lonely, and—"

"Mom, don't worry," Clyde interrupted. "You have my word. Thanks for watching my back, though. I will call you guys from Qatar." He said good-bye in Farsi, and they said "Be careful," because that is what they always said.

Clyde couldn't believe how simple the flight was and how quickly they had moved through security. It was hot, and they were building everywhere. *A little early to be getting started for the World Cup,* he thought. He checked into his hotel room, and then he got out his earpiece and connected with Johnny Reb.

"Hey, Mr. Popular, how are you?" the Reb asked. "Dude, that show was sensational the other night. By the way, the bit about you getting engaged? Unbelievable. You are breaking hearts all over the social network, as we speak."

Clyde was still in shock. They had told him that the show was going to air and they had moved up the filming schedule a little, which was why they were already in Qatar, but he hadn't seen the show. They had a crazy agenda, and being in a foreign country doesn't always mesh with what is happening in the United States.

"We can't wait to hear Lemonhead tonight," Johnny said. "He comes out bashing you on one night, and two nights later, you are the sweetheart of the Food Network. You get a big sympathy vote for having lost your wife, and then you share with the world how you got engaged. In the context of traveling and eating, what did you call it? Baccarata? How do you make creamed codfish look appealing? I wouldn't ruin my mayonnaise with that."

"Johnny, there is more to eating than pulled pork and ribs," Clyde said, who was trying to antagonize Johnny just like a little brother.

"Look, if I can't slow cook it on a smoker, then it isn't worth eating."

"You can't judge the world's cuisine by MREs, Reb."

"That, friend, is a very good point," Johnny conceded. "Okay, enough. I have information you need. Ildefongwe from Hong Kong, and most recently from the Philippines, is in town. He is bosom buddies with that Thai bad guy who goes by Mr. K."

"You have got to be kidding me," Clyde said. "Right off of our little list."

"Yes, that is correct, in the same town as you right now," Johnny repeated.

Clyde wanted to ask how Johnny knew this, but it didn't matter. He was going to deal with this guy when they went to Singapore, but here he was in his lap. Clyde said to Johnny, "How fast can you send me a cocktail?"

"FedEx should be there within the hour," Clyde," Johnny said. "This isn't amateur hour, you know. I thought being in Qatar you would need the proper sandals to go under your tunic. Or were you planning on running around as a Westerner in Levi's and tennis shoes?"

Clyde didn't have to ask. He knew full well that the cocktail would be embedded in the sandals, and pulling out the toe thong would mean the release of a small little compartment able to hold the odorless, tasteless poison he could use to slip into this guy's food. Where and when was another question. Who was he visiting, what was the agenda; this was all stuff he needed to know.

"I think he is after helicopters," Johnny said. "He is growing his heroin on so many little islands in the remote part of the Philippines that he needs to be able to get around quicker, and so do his commanders."

"He can get those in Qatar?" Clyde asked.

"Yes" was Johnny's quick response. "The guys here have several contacts with old military guys from the former Soviet who are selling choppers, which you actually can't find on eBay."

Clyde thought out loud, "so if he wants *helipokters*, as my four-year-old says, then who is the seller and where will they meet?"

"I am thinking in the old town, especially where the harems are available for a price, if you follow me."

"Okay," Clyde said. "I have a great restaurant in that part of the city, which will at least put us closer, and we will see if I can find anything out if I keep my ear to the ground."

"Clyde, do you really want to mix business with business, if you know what I mean?" Johnny Reb asked.

"I know what you mean," Clyde said. "And I will get back with you. Hold on, the hotel phone is ringing." He switched to the phone. "Yes, this is Clyde Gareen. Great, I will be right down." He went right back to Johnny. "Johnny, FedEx is here. Thank you much, and hopefully, Qatar is as good as Venice, and you will see me on TV tomorrow night."

"Don't get your hopes up," Johnny said. "They plan on rerunning your show a couple of times, and I don't think your audience is going to spend their only summer vacation on traveling to Qatar."

"Talk to you later, pal." Clyde took out the earpiece and put it back in the container. He tucked it quickly into the lining of his leather satchel, which he could carry on his shoulder. A quick trip downstairs, and he got his package from the concierge. He tipped him and went back upstairs. Listening to the television in Arabic, Clyde saw that the problems in Egypt were not going away any day soon. *Good thing we went back when we did*, he thought. *It would be chaos trying to go back now, even if I did need the money.* Dark days those had been. Being broke was really no fun at all because one felt hopeless and worthless especially as a provider. As he opened the package, he thought he needed a little monkey. *That would be handy. But for now, I will get this little cocktail into a small amount of water and make it a lot more readily transferable. Don't want to disappoint the people that paid for their aperitif.* This, of course, wasn't the word they used here in Qatar as opposed to there in Venice, but the thought was the same. He had time for a quick little nap before they were to meet and discuss Qatar. Sleep when you could was a military habit. He was sound asleep in thirty seconds, and the phone startled him forty minutes later, but he felt like a new man.

MESSAGE IN A BOTTLE

C HARLES WALLS WAS a lot of things, and stupid wasn't one of them. He knew full well that somebody saw that rocket payload and was willing to take a big risk to blow it to smithereens. He had top-notch guys working backward on where that bomb came from. He had a mole deep in the American government who was handsomely paid for really good information. He also had some on the payroll in China, France, and England. Israel was a different game altogether. He had conspirators inside North Korea, Iraq, and Pakistan. The truth was you never could actually know what your money was going to get you in some of those regimes. This, of course, was a little bit of the gamble. Russia wasn't hard because they were still trying to figure out if they were a democracy, republic, or going back to the former communist era. Nobody on his payroll in any of these countries knew anything about him. He was not on the radar.

He already had his team back there at the site of the previous warehouse, and he was going to rebuild. It was a completely benevolent operation. It wasn't for money; it was a medical facility for the good of northern Niger and the surrounding poor countries. Vaccines were made and distributed, health care needs were met, and he was going right back and from his own money, rebuilding. Quite possibly he might become *Time's* Man of the Year. He had put out a press release through his African director for humanitarian resources that they were sure it was a mistake and there was no ill will meant and Zeuterfeld Labs was sorry for the delay it caused in getting medicine into the hands of the people who needed it. His executive assistant was there, along with that college girl he had hired, Gabriela, and they were rehiring, staffing, and, at the same time, pulling out some of the top-notch members to become part of a new group in Irkutsk.

He had been literally weeks away from rolling out the first element of Tierdon P53. The second biological component was eighteen days behind that. This final molecule would attach to the first two and then morph through the process of rain and evaporation into an undetectable deadly disease that would silently attack the immune system and make it look like people were dying from super strains of influenza and/or whatever was the virus du jour in their particular region. It was a foolproof strategy. He had built the components to it himself. He probably was more capable than Pasteur or Franklin when it came to biology and inventions. The amazing thing was that he would bring a cure and save the human race. What a shame that it would be 75 percent down—or, if really fortunate, 80 percent—he thought, but again, *Time* magazine Man of the Year. That would look really good framed behind his desk. It would make his morning coffee time so much more fulfilling.

As they were rebuilding the warehouse and already reestablishing their third facility, Charles swore he was going to find the individual and/or the government responsible. It would be helpful at this time to have maybe a nuclear meltdown, like Chernobyl, or a 9/11 to get the world to focus on how important each person really is, and then they can all come together and sing the perfect harmony song and praise each other for their resiliency. It was enough to make him gag. Not quite, but almost as bad as watching S11 on television. Boy, that had happened fast. He was in the midst of negotiating with a large hedge fund firm to buy a major position in that network so he could influence the programming. They were crazy to buy that garbage. S11 was so full of himself. Like anyone actually believed he had really surprised Laina with that insidious story of getting engaged in Venice. What a pail full of manure. She had known full well that he was going to ask her. He had talked with Rico, who had shared the story with him, and S11 said he had never kissed her before the engagement. What boy in his right mind would wait to kiss Laina? He would have kissed her the first chance he got. She would have actually still been alive and so much happier as a Walls instead of being part of the S11 family. Why would somebody turn down all of this to live like a pauper and run a restaurant? Working herself to the bone every day. And then they go and have all those loud and obnoxious kids. Why would he push her into that and make her give birth to all those dreadful human beings? Crying, whining, and driving you mad. No, they would have had one boy, Charles R. Walls II. He would never admit that the middle name stood for *Ransom*. Why would his parents have named him that? Did they intend to hold him for ransom? Charles was going to hold the world for ransom, that was for sure.

Oh well, he thought to himself. *It is hard to be right all the time.* He turned to the television and saw some group somewhere demanding more rights.

Nobody wants to work hard, he thought. *They all want more, they all deserve more, they can't go to school and get the grades and pay their dues, so they protest. It would be a lot simpler if they replaced the rubber bullets with real ones. That would put a quick end to the protest. Maybe they would get so outraged it would promote civil war. Oh, that would be fabulous. All of Italy engaged in a huge civil war. One can only dream. Things would be different if I was in charge. Well, I am about to be in charge.*

He hit a button on his computer and opened up a file. It was labeled Reconfiguring the World Systems. That was the simple title of the file. He had a couple of very bright minds working on this little project. It was going to come out of the hypothetical and into reality as everyone started dying. These guys at the think tank were, like, "Why would we want to develop this?" Charles said that he just wanted to get a series of steps in place in case there was a nuclear holocaust or worldwide famine. If there was a disaster of epic proportions, then what would be the steps to take so as to minimize downtime, maximize human life, and stop chaos from destroying the rest of the planet? Countries from all over the world would be collaborating, sharing platforms, linking at the macro level, giving each other critical information, and it would be one world working together for the common good of all mankind. They bought it hook, line, and sinker. *60 Minutes* wanted to do a piece on it, but he declined. This was the kind of thing that remained in the background until necessary, and hopefully, it was never needed. He thought now there was a reason to be on television. Not to cry over gnocchi. Venice was sinking, anyways. Why would you build a city in the middle of the lagoon? There were some things he just couldn't understand.

As he got up to refill his wine, he saw a little note sticking out of the corner of one of the bottles on the dresser. *What is this?* he thought.

Dear Mr. Walls,

Thank you so much for sending me to Africa to help with the transition team. It means a lot to me that you would trust me to part of such an important task. I realize, of course, that I am simply a liaison to help your administrators do their work, but I really appreciate the opportunity.

The good news is that I get to see my friends from college again. You may know Onturei and his fiancé, Endewla. I knew them both at Oxford. Our mutual brother in Christ at Oxford tells me that Onturei was saved five minutes after the explosion. It is amazing how God can bring such amazing sweet goodness out of horrible devastation."

Charles thought that it was his facility and it was devastating to his current plans. The letter finished with "I am thankful and look forward to see what transpires as a result of all of these things. God is good. Thanks again, Gabby."

Too bad she didn't know that Onturei was going to Irkutsk and Endewla wanted nothing to do with him. She was not about to abandon her family and give up her life for some stupid far-fetched story of God creating the world and then dying for it. Why would God ever do that? What is the point?

Well, I can't crush her dreams because they are part of the human spirit, Charles thought. *Making good from bad, pushing the clock back is all it did. Bad will come out of it, and they will all be gone. That is what I think, and I am in charge.*

At that very moment, Gabby was sitting with Endewla on a small hill, looking at five thousand stars, and Endewla was giving into the call of the Holy Spirit on her heart. She had initially rejected the Spirit, and Onturei had gone off to Irkutsk to start the new facility. She was brokenhearted, but more than anything else, she sat down and realized her world was empty. Christ had come, and she knew it. There was not any doubt that He had walked on the planet. The Jews crucified Him maliciously for claiming He was God. She knew it was simply man's way of trying to manipulate the circumstances. It never worked. This planet was here by design. Plain and simple. Mankind was evil, selfish, and bent on simply personal gratification. She knew this. She had grown up in a stern household without much love, and her humble mother had meekly served a cantankerous man for decades. Onturei was changed. His heart was soft. His demeanor was different. He had walked away from the one thing he loved with all his heart, and that was her. God had performed a miracle right in front of her eyes, and she knew it.

Gabby was such a dear sister and so gracious to sit and cry with her. Gabby said, "Endewla, I love you, but this is simply your choice. I can't make it for you, and the call is to give up your life, your ambitions and to follow Christ. It is a narrow gate and a high calling, and few are willing."

"I fully understand," Endewla said. "And I feel like a drowned rat with absolutely nothing to offer Almighty God."

"Well then, Endewla, you are ready because we have nothing to offer but simply just to accept His grace," Gabby said.

As Endewla prayed on that hill under the stars, the planet continued to spin in control, and the wheels of time moved forward, and those who thought they were in control were simply mistaken.

Charles was going to make a memo to keep his top scientists apart, but he knew that Onturei and Endewla would never see each other again. Onturei was already in Irkutsk and Endewla was going to head up the rebuild in Niger.

"I will talk with you, sister, in the morning," Gabby said to Endewla.

"I am resigning tomorrow," Endewla responded. "I don't want to run this rebuild. I want to be with Onturei, and maybe I can find other work in Siberia."

"Good luck with that." Gabby laughed as she walked Endewla back to her home.

ALL THE LEAVES
ARE BROWN

RESSED IN THE modest fashions of Qatar, Clyde and Anna were dining seated on pillows. The food was laid out in front of them, and the waiter was walking them through the delicacies in Arabic. Clyde was translating and talking about the food and allowing Anna to sample the food as he spoke. There were different kinds of flatbreads and olives, cucumbers, and fresh tomatoes. Along with what Clyde called a tabouli, which, of course, is grain and a fresh-vegetable type of salad. There was hummus, which was ground up garbanzo beans and then chicken and beef on skewers that you sliced off and got kind of like shavings. It was a feast. What Anna didn't know was that Clyde understood the history of the food. He was explaining how these dishes came about and why it was natural to sit on the floor. He also described the spiced rice dish with meat in the middle called machbous.

"It looks like a stew, but it didn't taste like any stew I had ever had," Anna said.

Clyde walked over to talk with the owner of the restaurant. As they were conversing, he followed him into another section of the restaurant. There were three gentlemen sitting on very short ottomans. They had food in the middle of the floor. But they were deep in conversation, and Clyde had not seen them before because they were behind a wall that separated the two rooms. He didn't move a muscle or any other muscle than the ones he was using to follow the owner. Clyde couldn't imagine why Ildefongwe was at this end of town and with these particular guys who looked every bit the part of local Qataris. It was everything in him to follow, but Clyde relaxed and stayed with the owner who was showing him a little bit of the prep that went on. In the kitchen were about eleven workers all wearing either the abaya or the thobe, as it was customary. There were large pots of various dishes being heated on wood-burning stoves. It was not exactly cool in the back room, but it wasn't terrible. Clyde conversed freely with the owner and asked how much time he spent in the restaurant. The owner said, "I am here from around 6 a.m. to 6 p.m. every day, except for Sunday." That was a rough translation, but it was about a seventy-hour workweek. It was a well-established restaurant with really good food, and there wasn't an open pillow in the place, as Clyde stated.

Clyde walked back to the section of the restaurant where the *Seasoned Traveler* crew was dining, and as he walked pass Ildefongwe and his people, he could hear them talking. Ildefongwe was speaking in the local dialect of the Philippines, Tagalog, and Clyde couldn't quite understand him, but his conversation was being translated, and it was fortunate for Clyde that there was a little bit of a backup right at this point and Clyde was waiting for the hallway to clear. But he heard the translation. The interpreter said, "I would like to get the helicopters tonight," and named the airfield and the time. Clyde thought the toxin he had inside his pocket would be easier, but he thought he might be able to get more information if he was to slip out and take a helicopter ride. He hadn't flown a copter in a while, but it was like riding a bike. The *Traveler* gang finished, and then Clyde walked with them through Doha to the ports. They boarded a small fishing vessel, and the sailing crew backed it out, and within a few minutes, they were sailing on the Arabian Sea. Fishing was a mainstay for the locals, and they derived much of their cuisine from the ocean. Yeager was thrilled to watch, to sail, to fish, and to catch it all in two languages, the interaction with Anna and Clyde and the locals. Qatar was central to many of the Arab countries, so there was a lot of interaction, explanation, and really superb under-standing of the culture—who these people were, what they ate, how they worked, how they participated in their religion, they were big on families, and they played a lot of soccer, and while it was still eight or nine years away, they were really busy preparing for the World Cup.

As they headed back to port, it was nearing sunset, and the temperature was dropping to around ninety-eight degrees. It looked like a cool evening ahead. Off in the distance, Clyde could see a few helicopters making a landing, and he was able to get a gauge on where the purchase would take place. It was a long way to fly helicopters back to the Philippines, so Clyde thought something else might be afoot. This was be a good brainstorming session with Johnny, he reckoned. Wouldn't mind talking with Myles as well, but that might be dangerous. As they were com-ing into the slip with the boat, Yeager was thinking that he had really gotten the most he could get from today's proceedings, but he just had a few misgivings about Qatar as a whole. No, he loved all that they were doing—the people, the food, the culture—and Clyde captured it like Ansel Adams captured Yosemite. But would it sell? Would America go gaga for it the way that Venice had exploded?

What Yeager didn't know was that the trip was about to get interesting. He had his crew off the boat, and they grabbed Clyde and Anna coming off the boat with the sailing crew and there was no way to hide it, with the sun in the background and Anna coming off the boat. She had class and style, and her costar, with his two-day shadow, came across almost as a local, and they were both stunning. It certainly didn't hurt the promos. *Well, if anyone can sell Qatar, it would be those two*, he thought.

Yeager said to the team on the wharf, "Great day again. Thanks for your hard work and cooperation. We appreciate you putting up with us and letting us stick our cameras in your face all day and shadowing you everywhere like stalkers. We will turn in for the night, take tomorrow off, and meet the following day at the lobby again at ten o'clock. Is that okay?"

Clyde turned to Yeager. "Can we make it nine o'clock? I might have a little surprise."

Well, that was enough to pique the interest of the whole crew. What kind of a surprise?

"It is not every day I find the talent asking for an earlier start time, so I say let's roll with it," Yeager said.

"Thanks," Clyde said, and he turned to Yeager. "I don't mean to keep you in suspense but I just have to confirm a few things."

"What have you got up your sleeve?" Anna asked.

Clyde responded with an innocent reply, "Who said I have anything up my sleeve?"

Little did Anna know he had enough poison up his sleeve to drop an elephant. A call was coming in from Conner, so Clyde excused himself and walked over to the van. "That will be perfect," said Clyde. "We will see you around nine the day after tomorrow."

The ride back to the hotel was quick, and the air conditioner in the car was helpful. Clyde was thinking about the last time he was out on the Arabian Sea in a boat, and it was with a squad escaping some pirates out of Karachi. Pirates, Pakistanis, Al Qaeda operatives—they didn't really wait around for identification. They had gone in, grabbed a soldier, literally shot their way out of town, and swam out to their rescue boat. Clyde had taken a round through his calf and still had the scar to show for it. He had held down the attackers while his crew swam to the speedboat, but when it became his turn, one of his new guys, Damon Wellbuilt, missed an attacker. Clyde got the shot that pegged the leg, and then Damon got the sniper on shot number two and said, "He might have a hard time breathing after that shot." Later on, Damon had said, "I am so sorry about the leg, but I needed an advantage in soccer." Clyde responded to Damon, "Well, it is a good thing you got him with shot number two, or I wouldn't have to worry about losing in *futbol.*"

As Clyde thought about this old interaction, it suddenly occurred to him the copters are flying to Karachi. That was it. They were going to pick up arms and then push on down to Southern India, and his guess was girls. It would be a three-for-one trip. They would buy the new birds; buy arms to smuggle, and then buy female slaves.

"Clyde, Clyde," Anna said. "You are a million miles away, friend." She leaned her head against his shoulder.

Clyde was certainly glad that they were about to turn into the driveway. "I wasn't a million miles away." He leaned down, which made her sit up, and for that he was thankful, and he rolled back his thobe, enough to expose his calf. He showed Anna the scar.

"That is ugly," Anna said. "What happened? That looks like a bullet wound."

"I got this souvenir just on the other side of this little bay we were sailing on today," Clyde responded. "My special ops unit was leaving Karachi in a hurry. Seems like they were a little upset with us taking one of our soldiers back without complete permission, and my man, Damon Wellbuilt, who, by the way could lift about four hundred pounds—that man was, is a monster, coaching high school football and soccer, of all things—well, he misses the sniper on his first shot, and that guy gets me in the leg. I was down for about two weeks after that, and I spent it loafing around Doha and hanging out with an old friend.

"What was her name?" Anna asked, smiling.

"We are going to meet him soon, knucklehead," Clyde said. He grabbed his gear and made for the lobby and got his messages. Rico had a call into him, as well as Conner. *Looks like Conner figured out to get me on the cell phone*, Clyde thought.

Conner was a good friend. They had known each other a long time. After high school, Conner joined the military at eighteen, and his girlfriend got pregnant. Conner didn't know about the child, and, in fact, since she was from Dubai, nobody knew. She was out of the country in school, and she finally told Conner at almost full term. Conner had a couple of weeks leave and went to England. He told her, "Whatever you want to do." She wanted to put the baby up for adoption because they thought it was not the right time for either of them to get married. Conner was sewing his wild oats a little bit and taking his leave from the faith, but he still trusted his parents. They said, "Conner, bring the baby home, and we will raise it." Well, Conner had been a good dad, and his parents had been great-grandparents.

Of course, no pun intended, and now Graham was off at Oxford. He was a brilliant student. He went to Oxford at barely seventeen. He couldn't be a day over twenty now. He fit in with the older students. He was an evangelist and was already a teacher's assistant in the chemistry department and had just finished his master's degree. But Conner had never married. He got his life together and was in the military for eleven years and then ran a business from Qatar, and he and Graham were inseparable until he went to college. Graham knew all about his mother, and they had literally kept everything a secret. It was just a lot simpler that way. Her parents would never ever have understood, and what they didn't know didn't kill them, which probably would have happened had they found out. Disgrace was a major deal in the Middle Eastern cultures. Later on, she could follow Graham on social networks and keep up with all that he was doing. Conner had kept his distance from the family, which wasn't hard to do when you are living the military life.

Clyde and Conner had been stationed together a few times and had worked on a couple of projects together, and they both owed their lives to Myles many times over. Conner threatened he was going back for one of Laina's younger twin sisters, and that would make him a *cunyado*, which is Spanish for brother-in-law. But as it turns out, he never went courting in Italy, or anywhere else for that matter.

"Brother, I am content" was all he would say. "I have a business, I have a son, and God brought blessing out of my bad, and I am not looking at trying to push the envelope."

Clyde hopped on the elevator to the seventh floor and went quickly to his room. He dialed Rico back, and from the tone in his voice, he said, "Hey, Dad, can I call you right back?"

Rico said, "No problem," and he knew the drill. He walked down the street to an old pay phone. It was a wonder this thing still worked. But Clyde had set this up years ago, needing a secure line, and it was easier with an unused or undedicated anonymous line.

Clyde grabbed the earpiece and clicked on the transmission to speak with Johnny Reb. It was around ten in the morning, and Reb was up drinking coffee.

"Hey, mate," Reb said. "What is shaking?"

"I need to chat with you in a few, buddy," Clyde said. "But at the moment, can you hook me secure out to that landline next to my father-in-law's?"

"Your folks mad at you, Clyde?" Johnny inquired.

"Probably, but by the tone of his voice, I could tell he had something on his mind," Clyde said. "He forgets that we live in an ugly world and the boogeyman is listening in on all kinds of insecure communication."

"He is a pastor, Wolf. What do you expect?" Johnny asked. "The man talks secure straight to the big guy all the time. Who needs encryption when you have those resources?"

"Reb, you are an anomaly," Clyde riled.

"At your service," he shot back. "One encrypted line to a beat-up old pay phone in Palermo. I am bugging out, no pun intended. Call me back when you are done."

"Ten-four" was the last thing Clyde said, when the phone started to ring. *What a world*, he thought. *Sitting in Qatar on a hotel bed, using an earpiece connected to a handheld cell phone, talking to a World War II leftover phone in Italy secure.*

"Hey, son," said Rico. "You are welcome to leave our grand-children as long as you want. That little girl reminds us of Ilyaina so much it is like reliving her childhood. I don't know whether to laugh or cry every time I talk to her. Do you know what I mean, son?"

Clyde took a deep breath and paused, and Rico realized that just the thought of it probably pierced deep within the soul of his son-in-law. "Sorry about that. No need to kill ourselves in the moment. I got to tell you a couple of things." He started speaking in Italian, which was funny because it was so natural to him that with something on his mind he didn't even think about it. But the translation was interesting. He had met Yeri de Angelo, and from what he could tell from Ed, Yeri was not only in business but also some of his business was probably illegal. "Now Ed didn't say that, but intuition tells me that Ed found out more than he wanted to." Rico told Clyde about the soccer game again and said, "I am sorry I didn't tell you this in LA, but in the recent weeks, I haven't heard a word from Charles. I am pretty put out with what he did to you in the restaurant, and I know he is an associate with Yeri. I always felt like Charles was a tare. A Pharisee, if you will. Living a life of the saints on the outside for all to see, but he had never bowed his knee to the Creator. Do you know what I am saying?"

"You are preaching to the choir, Dad," Clyde offered.

"He is a bad apple, I think, and I don't know what he ′s into."

"Well," Clyde said. "A couple of things back at you."

"He just lost a warehouse in Niger, and it wasn't because it was strictly a humanitarian medical facility," Clyde said and then continued. "He is blaming the locals for storing unsanctioned content in his warehouse, but I am not buying it. Charles is up to something, and I think he is knee-deep in it."

They spoke for a few more minutes and laughed and cried together, and then Rico prayed for Clyde, as he always did. "Now, Lord Jesus," he would always say. "Help my brother Clyde to walk in wisdom, give you the glory, and run from the bad guys."

Clyde thought Rico meant "Run from the evil one," but the translation could go either way. "Thanks, Dad," Clyde said. "I got to scoot, but call me in two days, please, from this phone."

"I am sorry, you don't have the number to the house?" Rico asked.

"I have the number, but if you call me, we can keep away the bad guys," Clyde said. "So it will be the same drill as before."

"Thank you and good-bye" was the last thing Clyde heard from Rico before he clicked off.

GROUND CONTROL
TO MAJOR TOM

C LYDE CALLED JOHNNY back, and they confirmed a few
things for tomorrow night.

"Rest up," Johnny said. "Tomorrow you got a big night in
front of you."

Clyde slept in, and it was nice. He made his way down in
the lobby by lunch and walked into town. He was keeping a low
profile, but people noticed him from the television show run in
America. He was actually quite surprised, but then he remembered people were watching Hulu and YouTube on their phones
from any place they were. Since he spoke the local language, it
gave him access to places off the main streets and away from
the regular tourist haunts. He found a cool little family-run
restaurant that had a big screen on the wall, and he watched a
rerun of the recent El Classico game between Real Madrid and

Barcelona. It was nice to relax, eat some super spicy hummus, fresh pita bread, and highly seasoned vegetables. It also gave him a few minutes to chat with Conner, set up things for tomorrow, and also to think through plans for later this evening. Clyde was sitting alone but having one of those conversations you can have with yourself. So they knew all along that Charles was in business with Yeri. That wasn't new. Yeri was one of the original investors in Zeuterfeld Labs. Along with Alberto Johnston, all three of them had become billionaires, which begged the question why they would be in cahoots with these known international criminals. It didn't make sense. You didn't take legitimate billionaires and get them to get into legal trouble for no reason at all. Why the need for rocket payloads in Niger? Did someone think they were going to shoot biological warfare into space or chemical warfare into the atmosphere?

Clyde suddenly thought of the diagram on the table of which Ildefongwe and his crew were hunched over. It was a building plan. Maybe these Qatari guys are going to help him invest in building a plant? Maybe he has a plant and the Qatari guys wanted to build something like it. But one guy said there were four plants like this already—well, now three because of the attack in Niger. *Wasn't that a thing of beauty?* Clyde thought. *I am sure they are paying the piper on the Potomac for unsanctioned hostile aggressiveness. Wow, I better check in with Myles on that and see what is going down. Well, Kilpatrick was pretty adept at the old DC two-step, as they called it. I would want to be in his press briefing. That is for darn sure.*

His thoughts went back to Charles for a second as he took a long drink of water and washed down a near-perfect bite of shredded lamb, yogurt, cucumber, and dill sauce. Why would a guy who has spent his life increasing the longevity of human life and enhancing the quality of those lives want to associate with people who were in the business of ruining lives through illegal narcotics, destroying small countries with the shipment of illegal munitions, and then finally denigrating young women and devastating families through sexual slavery? It didn't add up. Not even for a man who is as utterly consumed with himself as is Charles, who quite frankly, didn't care about any single person on the earth other than what he saw in the mirror and at the end of the day was not comfortable in his own skin. It still wouldn't make sense. Wait a minute. Charles was still mad at the world. He was mad about the respect and admonition he didn't get from—really, from Laina. He never could figure why she and/or any woman, for that matter, would not fall down and worship him.

"Clyde, you big fat idiot," he said out loud to himself. "You have been looking at the answer all along. This guy has a God complex, and if people don't see it, then they are going to have to understand that ultimately he will be the judge." Clyde relayed the same thought process to Johnny without taking a breath.

"I have to get my boys to track this man," Johnny said. "Although it won't be easy, because with his financial prowess, he will have mighty long fingers." Johnny went on, saying, "Money fuels the political machine, and you can make a lot of inroads and get a lot of your agenda done if you are contributing in the right places. What is it called now, Super Pacs or something?"

Clyde grimaced at the thought of Charles Walls. "It is painful. He might well be my public enemy number one. Thwarts the restaurant, potentially comes after my family, and could be responsible for the explosion in Palermo and all because he wants to rule the world."

Johnny spoke calmly to his dear friend. "Clyde. Listen, friend, I am going to give you a page out of your book. Remember, this is by design. You have faced nothing less than the fires of hell. The fires rage and burn far deeper than just the skin, but the pain that is caused comes from the reshaping. Keep your head down, and face the music, and remember I am there every step of the way."

"Thanks, Johnny," Clyde said. "That means a lot."

"I will talk with you soon."

Clyde headed back to the hotel and spent the evening talking and interacting with the crew and thoroughly enjoying getting the background on the people he was working with. Around 8:00 p.m., Clyde said he was going to turn in and would see everyone in the morning. At 9:55 p.m., Yeager called and said they were a little scared about not being prepared for tomorrow without any information on the agenda.

"Yeager, I am really sorry, but I think it will have much greater impact if no one knows the agenda," Clyde said. He gave Yeager a little more heads-up, but he begged him to please keep this under his hat. Yeager said that was terrific and he appreciated it because there was a little setup he could prepare for as well.

Clyde looked at his watch. That worked out well. There was nothing wrong with a late-night alibi when the fireworks start later on.

"Reb, it is Greenie," a suddenly very awake and alert Lone Wolf queried. "What is happening?"

"You are happening, my nocturnal friend," Johnny said. "Let's get it on. Listen, I got confirmation on that helicopter delivery. My contacts in Qatar tell me that we have big money being thrown around by this Chinese businessman doing all his dirty work in the Philippines, and he is at the top of the criminal hierarchy. I mean, he has his own Topps bad guy card, and you don't get the bubble gum. He is taking copters out to run his drugs from island to island. This is about a sixty-million-dollar transaction, and most of the money has been delivered."

"Does that end your diatribe?" Clyde questioned. "For the record, that is a serious amount of cash."

"Well, word on the street is that he is doing a few side jobs for a fat cat from New Zealand or Australia," Johnny went on to say. "And there seems to be a pretty good money flow. We set you up with the usual transportation. MB at the back of the lot, and it is 06-4-6-9 to get in. Take that to the wharf and find Adu-Riyaad 563. That is the slip. Keys for the dock and the boat are in the

Benz. Take the boat south to a private airstrip. It is about eleven miles, and it is a one-lane airport. Businessman is waiting to fly you to Dubai. Once in Dubai, you are going to steal an F-18 fighter jet. It is a UAE patrolling aircraft, and it won't have *USA* plastered all over it. You got to fly low and stay out of range from our carrier, which is kind of funny, and then on the other side, you will have to skim the water to fly underneath the Pakistani radar so you can maneuver around to take out those whirlybirds."

"Do we know which one our target is in?" Clyde asked, not wanting to know the answer.

"We do," Johnny piped up. "He is definitely in one of the eleven choppers."

"How many missiles do I have onboard the Super Hornet?"

"No worries, old buddy. You are fully loaded with eleven shots. So you don't have even one to spare."

"Thanks, I feel better now," Clyde said. "Hey, Johnny, are these sidewinders or something different?"

"Well, remember that this ship is part British, part USA, and parts unknown," Johnny said. "But we were able to secure Starstreak missiles. They are not heat seeking, so you need to actually aim and fire. They have three separate warheads on them, so you can hit a target, release a warhead, and the missile can keep going on through the initial target."

"Can you guys get me through the satellite seams so we don't put this up on Fox News? So once I hit the targets I just turn around and fly back to Karachi and take a little vacation?" Clyde's second question had more than a hint of sarcasm.

"Fly north, avoiding any Pakistani aircraft," Johnny answered. "Stay low. At the right moment, I will bring you south again and circle around our carrier. You won't be hot on the fly back, so the level of concern will be way down."

"That makes me somehow feel so much better. I am good on fuel?"

"It will be close, but I think you will make it if you don't hot dog around and try and show off in Abu Dhabi," Johnny replied.

"Business guy flies me back to Qatar?" Clyde shot back.

"We are working on that angle as we speak," Red Horse said without total conviction. Then he added, "We got a crop duster at the moment, but it is a two-seater."

"That is just great," Clyde said. "There are no crops within two thousand miles of this desert, and you don't have a plan."

"We have a plan, Batman, but we are just trying to get a little better return flight so you can come back into Doha unnoticed. Private air strip netjet isn't coming back till next week. So we have to get an unscheduled return flight back in there." Johnny used his best defense-lawyer tone. The banter back and forth was completely in sarcastic debate overload. But it didn't matter because they accomplished a lot and were not offended by the rhetoric.

"Doesn't someone need to stop for refueling before they head on to Riyadh or Kandahar?" Clyde asked.

"Good thinking," Johnny said. "And I will get Gray Eagle on it as well. We will bring you up to speed, but for the moment, I say you are a go. Mission green: Lone Wolf."

Gray Eagle came on the line. "You are a go from our vantage point here as well. Mission green: Lone Wolf, Gray Eagle out."

Clyde knew that by here she meant ops or operations, and he certainly didn't know where she was. Johnny was pretty sure he knew, but it didn't matter. In the meantime, Clyde really did feel a little like Batman. He thought of the song his older brother used to listen to by that old rock band from the 80s Whitesnake: "Here I go again on my own, going down the only road I have ever known. Like a drifter, I was born to be alone." Why his mind popped in the song from that band at this moment was beyond comprehension. It just was constantly working. But he was not alone. He had four kids to feed, and it would be really tough to do it if he didn't make it back from this mission. Trying to save the world and nobody really knows. Working clandestine for the government was a really weird job. He knew full well that the middleman can become the odd man out in one quick beat of the heart.

He slipped out off the balcony to the roof. He crossed over on a cable and worked his way out of the next hotel. It was 10:00 p.m. in Doha and finally dark. He slipped out of the hotel and went to the back of the lot. The white Mercedes was parked at the back, and he entered the code. Katarina was ten now since she had a birthday. At least he was there for that. This was the wrong gig to be moonlighting on. So Charles was in bed with some bad guys. Well, there is a real surprise because, of course, the billions he made running Zeuterfeld wasn't enough. *I knew it all along*, Clyde thought. *I should have knocked his teeth out the first day I met him. I was just a skinny little teenager but he was a bad apple from the get-go. He had eyes for Laina. Why did he pause? That was interesting. Okay, focus, friend.*

Looking for the right slip, he saw the number and parked the car. He grabbed the keys to the boat and locked the Mercedes. It was certainly dark, and he had his gear, and he shuffled along to the boat. "Red Horse, I am at the boat and making my way over to the plane. You are thinking about twenty minutes from here?"

"Cruising at around fifteen knots, you should be twenty-two minutes out. Watch out for cross traffic. Check in with me when you get on the plane."

"Roger that!" Lone Wolf cried out. Shortly thereafter, he pulled the craft into the slip. A deck boy came down, and Clyde threw him a rope. He tied it and grabbed the back rope and made a slipknot, as though he had been doing since he was born. He probably had.

"Mr. Smith, your plane is waiting," said the hand. "Call me Handle, because I can handle everything."

Clyde laughed out loud. There was no way the boy was a day over fourteen.

"Do you have a bag I can carry?" Handle asked. "Mr. Sebastionpol is ready for you to board and is grateful you are sharing the expense."

Clyde said "Thank you very much" in Arabic, and the boy smiled and started rattling a thousand things to him. Something about no white guys ever speaking the mother tongue. It was refreshing to have a Westerner who can speak the language, although he admitted he really liked to practice his English. "Sir, if I may ask, your bag is very heavy. What do you have in it?"

"I have ropes, pulleys, and all kinds of gear in case the bad guys are chasing me and I need a quick getaway," Clyde responded. In Arabic, he said, "You never know when your camel breaks down and you need a flare gun to hail a helicopter. Wouldn't you agree, Mr. Handle?"

Handle laughed. "I can't speak to that, sir, because I just have a license for a scooter." They had come to the plane. Clyde threw his bag in the open compartment and kept his backpack with him. He said hello to Ronald, who was doing business in Dubai and then on to Kuwait City. He worked for a telecommunications company, and they were dealing with cell towers, satellites, and all boring stuff. Actually, Clyde said that he was very interested in communications, and it was fascinating how he could still call from his handheld and the guy on the other line could be speaking on an old analog phone. Crazy you would think, right? The engineer explained that it was actually just a simple switch, and the connection happened seamless at a digital relay transfer station, and each phone company put them up all over the world. "Typically one in every large city," Ron said.

There was a very nice attendant who offered them a beverage, and they both declined. The flight was less than forty minutes, and they were good. The attendant said that Mr. Sebastionpol had already paid for the flight and if Mr. Smith wanted to pay him directly, then there was no need to log Clyde in as a passenger. Very nice, Clyde thought. All the world over, people are transacting business in cash. What one will do to avoid a few taxes.

Clyde slipped Ron five Benjamins and said, "I am grateful to you for allowing me to hitch on to your taxi."

They landed quickly, and that was where it got a little dicey. Clyde walked into the airport but went in through the men's bathroom and picked a side door that brought him into a private hallway. He moved quickly through the hallway and out the end door, which brought him to a series of outside hangars. The voice in his head said, "Lone Wolf, go over to the fence quickly, and watch for tower light. Guard dogs should be asleep by now. Travel down the dirt road, and keep low, and duck off if you see any oncoming cars. Third hangar is your target. Clip the fence on my count." He heard Johnny counting down. "Five, four, three, two, one, and go!"

Clyde heard the power go down on the electric fence. A programming glitch, and it would be around seven seconds before the backup generators kicked in. Clyde had his wire cutters out and sliced through that fence like a hot knife through soft butter. Just in time, as he heard the buzz from the electricity come back on, and he was through moving swiftly to the back door. No time for a pick, so he just put a little freeze on the lock and hit it with a hammer. He was in. Wow. F-18 all loaded and ready to go.

"How did we get those bad boys on there?" Clyde asked. "And if you got missiles up and running, how come I had to come in the back door?"

"It is a long story," Red Horse responded shortly. "Do you want it now?"

"Nope. Hangar is not on automatic doors, I am assuming?"

"No," Johnny said. "But if you get into the control room, I can give you the code."

Start the plane or pick the lock? Clyde thought. *Well, pick the lock.* "Okay, I am in."

"Right on the desk, push zero-nine-one-one-two-zero-zero-one," Johnny said.

Very funny, Clyde thought, and then a computer terminal slid out. "My company installed this for their crew operator who is disabled. Actually, he is very able but no use of his legs below his knees. You got to type in Arabic, big boy. Translate as I go. 'All good men need to come to the aid of their very favorite country, Emirates.'"

"You got issues," Clyde said. "Okay, the hangar is opening. Any word on getting into the plane?"

"No. If you don't know how to mount an F-18, we got more problems than I can even begin with." Johnny howled.

Gray Eagle wanted to laugh. Red Horse, whoever he was, was a whiz. Lone Wolf was, in her mind, a living James Bond. He operated like a world-class athlete on one level, and yet his mind was fully engaged. But these two guys were like brothers sharing a room. How they could be on such an intense mission and yet be so relaxed to actually chide each other and be in good humor. At this moment, Clyde chose to bypass the humor and flipped the step down and climbed up into the saddle. These things were more automatic than a Cadillac, and it was like starting King Kong with paddles. One mistake, and you had more power than you ever wanted in a building. Clyde ran through his mission controls in lightning speed and knew exactly what he was doing. He had a lot of hours in this bird, and his brother had given him more than he needed on advanced training and technique. Clyde was a quick study and loved flying. He couldn't believe what these machines were capable of, and he appreciated the engineering although, of course, it was the math he really loved. Now he was taxing forward even as he finished his flight check and saw that his fuel was not full.

"Hey, Gray, are you up?" Clyde asked. Referring to her tracking with the conversation, he knew she was but didn't want to presume. "Sorry you had to listen to all this garbage. Red Horse doesn't get out much anymore and decides to take it out on me. I am going to need a refuel at approximately zero two hundred hours, Dubai time. Do you copy?"

"Yes, sir, but I am not sure where we are going to get authorization to refuel a brown bird in that air space," Gray Eagle answered.

"Go Blue Ox on this one, and while Red Horse is figuring out exactly how to get me out of Dubai after I have test driven their little package here, have Blue Ox authorize that fuel transfer. On second thought, Gray Eagle, let me see if all the instruments are working correctly. I know we are dark and all that, but I have a little feeling we got friends in the right places."

"Roger, Lone Wolf. I am working full throttle on it right now. Don't worry about it for one second, and you take care of your wings, okay?"

"Assured, Gray Eagle." Clyde knew that if she was working on it, then there was a good chance a FedEx cargo plane might refuel him in midair over the Arabian Sea. She worked magic. *Gray Eagle has big medicine*, he thought. "Johnny, how are we looking for a go on this bad boy? All systems clear nothing but a few seagulls out there." Clyde throttled the stick forward, and the rush was incredible. This bird could literally shoot straight up in the air. He was moving at 100, 150, 200, 250, 300. This {bad} boy could move. At 350, and he was wheels up and still gaining. He cleared the runaway about 500 miles an hour and continued his climb. He was listening to the chatter in his headset from three different control towers, and they all wanted to know who he was. It was not going well for him when he was not checking in, so he started speaking in Arabic and claiming that he was a simple test run for and air show tomorrow. Nobody had any air shows on the books, so he played dumb.

Clyde hit the speed of sound and heard the boom. He was moving now at Mach 1, and he was flying so low he could fly fish if he needed to. It was blacker than coal on the ocean, and it was a still night, with nothing but stars above. He was listening to Johnny talk about the clear path in front of him, and he came around wide of his target for Karachi and didn't want anyone to misinterpret his intentions. He was hoping to not have to get to near Karachi air space, thinking that maybe the birds have already loaded and are heading south. It was nighttime, and while he didn't think they would have flashing neon lights on them, he could only imagine a few running lights to get quietly out of Karachi without waking up any of the Taliban or Al Qaeda. "Johnny, do you know which one the target is in yet?" Clyde probed.

"Sorry, Clyde," Johnny said. "You got a bad guy in every package, so you just have to buy the whole dozen. Red Horse and Gray Eagle, I have a visual on the targets. They look around ten minutes off Karachi, and I will be on them in around forty-five seconds."

Clyde realized his momentary crisis of conscience was over when he thought about what he was doing for a full second. They would immediately release a counterattack. At the moment, they were too far away, though, to strike him, and he was moving too fast. He flipped on his weapons and went hot, and he could hear a whole lot of cackle going on in his head, which he muted. He took aim and shot the first copter straight through the middle. He had immediately targeted one to the left and to the right and triggered two more shots. His sidewinder missiles couldn't miss from this distance, and the first three slammed home, and immediately there was a cacophony of explosions and a huge fireball. Clyde got a two-for-one special with his first three shots because the Starstreak missiles actually went so clean through the helicopters that they didn't explode until they hit the second birds. Six gone in three shots, and Clyde thought, *Nobody could beat this score, not even on PlayStation.*

Two copters shot low, and Clyde triggered his device and got the one on the right. He aimed missile five and pulled the trigger, and immediately, there was a slice right through hot metal, clean in the middle of the bird. Clyde instinctively went left and came around on the three remaining copters, which were lined up like ducks in a row, and fired point plank with his sixth shot. The missile tore through copter 1 then 2 and exploded in 3. Clyde veered back to the rear and could see off to his shoulder that copters

9 and 10 had exploded. All eleven were gone, and Clyde knew that the world at large was going to be chasing him all over the planet. Pakistan had already released their own counterattack, but it would be too little, too late. Clyde was making a low-flying beeline straight back to Dubai. He looked down at the fuel gauge and realized it didn't work because it hadn't moved. If his engines stopped running, he would eject and take it from there. This was a pieced-together machine, from probably a few spare parts here and yonder, and Clyde was guessing it was a goodwill trade and they were asking back for a little of that goodwill right now. The people who live in Dubai would play stupid, and there was nothing tracing back to the infidels—or, Clyde meant, Americans, so it would be anyone's guess. This flying ton of steel was every bit like the Super Hornets he had flown in Iraq and other necessary places on the planet.

His timing on the shooting had been impeccable, which was in between three satellite passes. And he was ten minutes away from his takeoff on the runway. He immediately contacted the air traffic control and explained that all was fine and he was coming in to land on runway 679. Dubai didn't have the capability to know that his missiles had been hot and launched. The *USS Lincoln* was in a tizzy, and the Saudis and Pakistanis were in full cardiac arrest. But Clyde landed the plane, turned it to the hanger, and shut it down as it was still rolling. He was down to virtually just eking forward and didn't think he would stick around for the after-cast party since the show was over. He went down the dropout ladder and waited another split second and rolled out before the wheels could hit him. He had been trained to do that under combat circumstances, and was off and running. He was back to the fence and shot his "Get me out of here" auto zip line cord into the nearest tree. It held taut about fifteen feet above the fence, and he clamped on the automatic zip pull, and he was up off the ground and over the fence and still climbing for the tree. Only Clyde stopped climbing, and his momentum swung back into the tree. He got a foothold and released the zip line gear. No time to keep the rope, and he shouldered the gear in his pack and shimmied down the tree. An old-time F100 was rolling his way, and Clyde hopped in.

"Heard you might need a ride," the driver said, who may have predated the 1956 truck by twenty years, and away they went. "I am part of the network, friend."

"What network is that?" Clyde asked.

The elderly ex-pat replied calmly, "'Get you out of a jam when you need it quick' network, friend. Johnny said to drive you to this tiny corner of the ancient desert not far from here. In between a few dunes, there is a twin-engine amphibious. Not as quiet as you like, but runs low, and you can turn out the lights. Nice bird over water. It should get you to your boat in about twenty-five minutes. Not as fast as the Netjet you had coming south but better than a swim in the Gulf of Oman, friend."

"I needed a friend," Clyde said. "And even though you remind me of a skinny Santa Clause, I would say that we are BFFs right at this moment."

"Think nothing of it," Skinny Santa said. "Do you ever get anywhere near Coeur D'Alene?"

Clyde looked directly at Santa and nodded his head in the affirmative.

"Well, I have a friend up there that is part of the same network, and his name is Norv Adkins, and I would sure like to have somebody tell him that Hal from Twin Falls said hello."

"Next time I am in the panhandle, I will look up Mr. Adkins and deliver the message." a bewildered Clyde said. "Thanks for the lift. Make sure you get your money straight up from Johnny."

One quick twin-engine Cessna back, and he saw the speedboat right where he left it parked in the docks yards from the runway. He dropped the plane down deftly, and just as he left the prop plane, he saw someone climb up, taxi the plane, and fly back the other way. Clyde took a moment to appreciate that literally between Red Horse and Gray Eagle there was no end to their ability. Creative, administrative, and with precision timing, there was no limit to their skills. They took an ad hoc mission like this and almost on the fly allowed him to pull this off. Well, he knew that there was a lot more preparation than they let on, but they only had about a full day to work with. Clyde took a breath and scurried to the boat and then ran that little speedboat as fast as it could go up the coast. He hit the running lights and stayed wide as there seemed to be a little extra search and patrol out tonight. He circled around and found the slip. Tied up the boat and found the car. Put in the code, and it didn't work. Clyde reentered the code with a 10 on the end and laughed hard as he climbed into the car. He drove back to the lot and reentered the same hotel. He took the elevator to the roof, his same gear still attached. *Nobody took my rope*, he thought. He clamped on his second and last automatic zip pull, and it shot him across the rope. He kept this mechanism this time, though. Much better than climbing the rope, he thought. Heavy little gizmo, though, and hard to travel with. Well, the good news was that was something he didn't have to arrange.

"Lone Wolf is back in the den," an out-of-breath Clyde said. "I am a little disappointed that I didn't walk straight into a massage when I got back though. All present and accounted for. My gear is stored safely in room 714. I am all out." It was 4:00 a.m., and he had to be on call at 9:00 a.m. *Who needs breakfast anyway*, he thought as he hit the sack. This was another extremely successful operation. These guys were good, and nobody knew. The cracks in the military regime would evaporate like an ice cube in the desert sun of Qatar. They could dig forever and not find the right people with the right information to call this tune. Gray Eagle was simply the drummer and kept the players in rhythm, but there was an entire band she didn't even know about.

FOOL ON A HILL

C HARLES WALLS WAS sitting in his laboratory absolutely
riveted. He was trying to understand why he could not
release his toxic chemical compound into water and why it
would not just work immediately through evaporation. His plan
of seeding the jet streams and all three meeting or colliding and
then raining the chemical into the world everywhere seemed like
it would work. It had been tested in every case that it would work.
Simply releasing this in water and having evaporation immediately absorb this into the hydrological cycle and, thus, producing
the deadly disease in rainfall would be so much quicker. He liked
speeding up the process because there were forces opposed to
the rocket payload facilities and/or warehouses. He knew that his
teams were, at this very moment, applying pressure on various
government agencies, and he would uncover this systematic deni-
gration of his plans without revealing the threat that was behind
all their vigilant work for the last few years.

Charles knew that at some point, as he looked at the complex makeup of this toxin and the three ingredients that had to come together to make this formula with its ugly side effects destroying the human capacity to fight off anything. There just had to be a simple solution to his chemical-cocktail-distribution mystery, and he was going to get to the bottom of it right here in his state-of-the-art cellar laboratory. Having worked for almost twenty-four straight hours when he finally saw the missing piece, he was fascinated by the energy created from the sun that turned water into the mist that formed the clouds. It was in this energy that was able to filter out the bad and only bring in the pure elements of water and transfer the liquid properties to the cloud, like mist in its purest form. Charles suddenly realized that instead of working against this process and trying to add to it, he needed to get in line with the properties of water that got diffused into the inner atmosphere while he needed to fool the process, in a manner of speaking, and allow for the substance of his poison to be engulfed into the energy field of evaporation and become part of the next rain cycle in that local area. Obviously, once it got into the rain cycle, it was out of his hands as to where that might hit.

Charles didn't care at this point, but soon, he had made the necessary changes to mask the impure properties and allow the process to take place. He immediately set out to disperse his findings into a local body of water. He sent his findings to his chief biologist in Singapore. He would have this done without notifying his comrades. He would get it done immediately and find out if this was going to work. If it worked, they could diffuse it into other bodies of water immediately. Yes, the consequences would be people potentially dying in out-of-the-way third-world environments. How long would it be before UNICEF or Amnesty International or some other would be philanthropic organization figured this out? In the meantime, they would be seeding all the largest bodies of water throughout the world, and the only people who would really survive would be those who had been inoculated.

ONLY THE GOOD
DIE YOUNG

THE SENIOR SENATOR from Delaware slammed his fist on the table in Ian Kilpatrick's office. He was not officially back yet, but he had made the necessary schedule adjustments to get back in today to meet with another fellow Democratic senator. The much-more junior senator was also now absolutely furious over the recent events. Both senators were screaming at Ian. "I am so irate at this travesty I can't wait to get the people responsible in the public square and flog each one you in their own set of stocks," he said. "This is so typical of the old boys' club. You just do whatever in the world you feel like without authorization and spend the government's money out their embarrassing us on the world stage and putting other countries' citizens in jeopardy. It wasn't bad enough to have an unmanned drone bomb a sovereign country, and now you shoot eleven helicopters out of the sky near Pakistan, of all places. That means at least eleven people died. You got eleven bad guys. Did you know that you shot people from the country of the Philippines, which is one of our allies? This is sheer lunacy, and I don't care if you want to punch me like you punched the assistant secretary of state. I am going to go one better than public flogging." He lowered his voice. "I am hoping you go to jail if you are responsible for this."

Ian looked at the senator. "Are you done with your little show? I have had enough of all the little temper tantrums running around here, and if you will calm down for a few minutes, I will have a lucid and honest discussion with you. I think you will find some merit in the recent events that have taken place." Ian knew full well that somebody in this man's immediate staff was on the payroll of the devil they were chasing, and it might be the senator himself. Ian didn't know, and quite frankly at this point, he didn't care. "I will remind you, Senator, that I serve at the will of the commander-in-chief. If he doesn't want to keep me on the job, he can let me go. I am not doing this for fun. I don't need the job. Politics isn't my bag, and military operations are my forte. You know this, and so do I. So before you go hopping around here and screaming at me, remember that I don't have a constituency like you do, so I operate to protect and to serve."

Ian stood up and closed the door, and then he turned on a device, which was an anti-bugging device. He had a manual one that he gave to the senator and asked him to run it up and down, covering the length of his frame. The senator actually complied without so much as a chirp. "Now I don't know who author-ized the bombing in Niger, and if I knew you know full well, I wouldn't disclose it, but let's make it perfectly clear. We have a list of about ten criminals that are deeply impacting the world with prostitution, illegal drugs, arms trafficking, terrorism, other kinds of crimes. They are regional warlords, and they are wreak-ing havoc on humanity. But we have recently learned that these guys are a front for a major player that might have a plan to start chemical warfare on a national scale. Meaning sending a rocket to the atmosphere, releasing anthrax or whatever chemical biohazard du jour, and wiping out Saudi Arabia or Guatemala or Nepal all at once.

"The reason why some of this had been done in secret is that this player has people in our government on his payroll. Now we don't know that for sure, but we have a pretty good idea. So we have moles located on the inside, and on the outside, we have country-destroying-level threats. If you want to be the one senator who is remembered for slowing down the wheels of maybe one of the most critical missions any of us have ever been part of, then you can keep on making accusations and wonder why the necessary people are fighting the exact battles we have been hired to fight, and in this case, it comes with some very un-politically correct and albeit very unsavory elements at the moment.

"The reason why that warehouse was bombed was because it had rocket payloads with what looked like some sort of biological agent. Now unless someone has recently discovered how to increase the rainfall in the Sahara, I, for one, figured that kind of threat to humanity was worth having a couple of armed services members or Homeland Security committee members coming in my office and screaming at me. And to be honest, if I am the fall guy for this, I will sleep at night knowing that the right people in the right places did exactly what they have been trained to do, and that is to protect our country. So when you go back and get on the Senate floor and make proposals to launch an investigation into secret operations outside of the realm of government sanctions, just remember that potentially every word you have typed up on that speech has been sent to someone who is on the verge of destroying mankind as we know it."

"Man, that is all just superhero stuff, making me to believe that I should let you guys do whatever is in your little military heart," the senator said. "Which is fighting wars as is no secret to anyone."

"Well, I hope they say, when I die, that I was one of the best ever at fighting wars and eliminating threats on a global scale,"

Ian said. "Well, I was candid with you, Senator, and you have a choice. If I am lying, then you can launch your investigation, and we can both join the dance and see how long it takes for us to tango. Or you can say just maybe this time Kilpatrick has only crossed the lines of authority because there is a real threat and people could die on a countrywide scale. Just this morning, we received documents showing that, like the warehouse in Niger, there are three more that are mirror images of the first one. Now if you believe the CEO of Zeuterfeld Labs that the humanitarian facility was compromised by local thugs and they literally did not even know there was any kind of materials stored in this building, then fine. Someone else is up to no good. But if, in fact, this company is, in fact, tied into the weapons, then we have a billionaire with tremendous resources, along with one or two of his original investors, that might be funneling money to these other local criminal despots and making Armageddon-type plans to destroy maybe up to a third of the population."

"I really find this very hard to fathom that we could be dealing with this kind of threat," the senator said.

"Well, Senator, I can't make you believe it, but I can tell you this much: if normal procedures had been observed as is protocol, then the right people would have not gotten that data on the rocket payloads in that warehouse. We wouldn't have documents showing us there are at least three other facilities. Last night, there was eleven helicopters eliminated that Jose Loo Ildefongwe paid sixty million dollars for. Now he has some cash flow, and I don't think he is short of making his mortgage this month, but sixty million? I don't think so. By the way, he picked up SAM's in Karachi and was on his way to Southern India and Bangladesh for underage females. I know it doesn't justify all that is being done, but give us a little rope, and we might just save the world from one of the biggest threats mankind has ever known."

MIDNIGHT AT THE OASIS
PUT YOUR CAMEL TO BED

CLYDE MADE HIS way down to the hotel lobby a little before 8:30 a.m. He was going to get a really good cup of coffee before he went on his way for the day. He pulled up Proverbs on his cell phone and read the fifteenth chapter and loved the whole conversation on anger. He needed to give a soft answer much more than he did. The coffee was excellent, and he managed what looked like a wedding cooking. Simple self-control stopped him from eating a dozen. He would save that for hot, fresh doughnuts. Everyone started to gather, and Anna came down in a traditional Middle Eastern abaya and a head covering. But it didn't matter if she was in a paper sack. She had a smile that lit up the morning, and Clyde took a long deep breath. It would be a lot simpler if his wife was alive. But as Anna walked across the room, he could see that she was looking the other direction. It was subtle, but Clyde was pretty perceptive. He turned to look at the same direction which would have been the door, and he was looking at Conner Griffin.

"Hey, dude," Clyde said. "When have you ever been on time?"

"That isn't fair, Colonel," Conner said. "I was on time twice just last month. It, of course, wasn't consecutive, but it was a 100 percent increase in efficiency from the prior month."

Clyde turned to the room. "Hey, gang, this is my longtime friend Conner Griffin. We have played soccer together, fought in the military together, got in all kinds of trouble together, and if it wasn't for Conner on at least two occasions, I can promise you I wouldn't be alive today. He is going to be our guide for the little excursion we have this morning, so if you will give a warm welcome, I would appreciate it."

They all clapped and hollered, which was a light crew of really only about twenty. Conner looked at Clyde. "Oh, you mean you haven't told them what we are doing? You are going to make me the fall guy." He turned to the crew. "Well, in that case, if you guys want to load up in the vans and follow me, we will get on with the surprise."

Clyde introduced Conner to Anna, and she asked how long he had been living in the Middle East.

"Let's get in the car before Conner starts to talk," Clyde said. "We don't have that kind of time."

As they got settled in the vehicle, Conner turned to Anna from the front seat and said, "I have been living in the Middle East all of my life. My parents were business people here in Qatar, and they have been doing missions work for a large church in Texas since before I was born. I met this young punk Gareen when he was fifteen in Italy, when we were playing soccer. What you don't know was that when he first got to Italy, he was a skinny little brat. So in one summer, he grows three inches and puts on fifteen pounds. By the time the summer was over, he was probably one of the best American soccer players in his age group."

"Oh, that is not true," Clyde said. "By the way, it was the pasta. It literally stuck to my ribs and thighs. I needed those fifteen pounds, that is for sure. Those guys were knocking me around a lot."

A few minutes later, they turned off in a remote area and pulled up to a huge camel farm. Anna just looked and said, "You have to be kidding me. That is completely insane."

As Clyde explained to everyone that they were going on a caravan and everyone was riding, Yeager had his camera guys prepped. They knew how to play this and keep the cameras still. They had brought special equipment that would mitigate the up-and-down momentum of the animals.

"My crew is a little nervous around these spitting horses with humps," Yeager said.

"Once you get a feel for them, you will realize that they are extraordinarily willing," Conner said. "They aren't big fighters. They can make some noise, but it is harmless."

"Have you ever been thrown?" the director asked.

"No," Conner said. "I have never come close, and I have been in races with these guys."

They made their way out into the desert, and it was hot. It was early in the morning, but it was like 105 degrees. Conner came back to Clyde and Anna. "Hey, do you feel the breeze?"

"The only breeze I feel is that of the camel breathing," Clyde said.

"Now there is a nice little breeze coming up the pass," Conner said.

Anna shifted her head covering and moved her hair so she could feel the breeze on her neck. "I am sorry, Mr. Griffin, but I don't feel a thing as far as cool air goes."

They went about another mile and came to a legitimate oasis. What a relief. Water, trees, and shade. It was like heaven in the midst of an inferno. Anna said that it was nice of Conner to take the day off to be their guide. "Thanks for the little tour through this paradise on these humble little animals." She laughed.

Conner said that not everyone who can say they have come to Qatar have gone on a real camel ride. "This oasis has served people for thousands of years."

"How far do we have to go?" Clyde asked.

"Just about three more miles after that hill." Conner pointed southeast. "We have already come around seven miles. So it will be short."

Everyone got wet and enjoyed what felt like ice-cold water, and then they got back on the camels. They rode for another couple of miles, and then Conner started running his camel, and all the rest followed. Everyone was screaming and holding on for dear life. But the camels settled into an easy trot, and most of the crew got the hang of it and were bouncing in step with the dromedaries. As they pulled into what looked like a football-stadium parking lot, people were laughing and crying and were pretty much hysterical. It was a fun ride.

"Welcome to Il-Reyanna, home of the Doha university soccer team and hockey team," Clyde said.

Well, that made everyone howl. Hockey? Almost like bob-sledding in Jamaica. "Well, today, it will look more like a soccer field, but we have a live outdoor cooking show going on."

"Who is the chef?" Anna said.

Clyde raised his hand. "I am. I am going to cook for about five hundred college students. My featured plate will be frozen yogurt date shakes."

When Clyde said that, the crew all cheered. "That is exactly what I need," Izzy, from wardrobe, said. "I used to get those as a kid in Palm Springs."

"Exactly what I was thinking," Clyde said. "But yogurt is a staple of the Middle Eastern diet. We will just freeze it, and mix it with dates, which there is no shortage of either."

Conner invited Yeager to come take a look at their setup, and Yeager said, as they walked into the main part of the auditorium,

"This looks great. Kind of like an *Iron Chef* setup, and you have cameras mounted and everything."

Conner showed Yeager the sound board and control center, and they were off and talking for twenty minutes.

"What does your friend do for a living here in the Middle East?" Anna asked.

"He actually produces television shows for all kinds of local television," Yeager said. "He does news shows, talk shows, and then he has other interests as well."

Conner came back to talk with them, and Clyde said, "Let me go and check out the food prep."

Conner introduced Clyde to the university caterer who had whatever resources Clyde was going to need.

"So you like living here?" Anna asked Conner.

"I love it," Conner said. "I have been in the military, so I have traveled and seen all kinds of cultures. I recently spent three weeks in England with my son."

"You are married?" Anna asked.

"No, far from it," Conner said. "But my Middle Eastern girlfriend got pregnant when I was seventeen, and my family and I raised Graham. He is a great kid, but you can imagine what would have happened to a young lady in this culture who got pregnant out of wedlock over twenty years ago. My son just graduated from Oxford. He is a scientist. It is crazy. That kid is so smart it is mind blowing. He is a good kid too. He loves the Lord and is a witness for Christ wherever he goes."

"I am not sure exactly what you mean," Anna said. "I mean, I am Catholic, so what do you mean witness for Christ?"

"Well," Conner said casually, "my son is willing to tell people wherever he goes that Christ is God and he came to earth to pay the penalty for their sin, and they need to repent, change their lives, and become followers after Christ, willing to give their lives, if necessary."

"Other than spending time with Clyde over the last few weeks, I have never heard anyone talk like that in the Catholic Church," Anna said. "I always thought it was the same as being a Christian, but you guys all talk about a personal relationship with Christ, and that is completely foreign to me.

"You know, Anna, you are a really honest person," Conner said. "I like that."

Clyde was watching the two talking from a distance and knew Anna had forgotten all about him, and he was glad, although it made him nervous for Conner. But Conner was a seasoned campaigner, and it would take a lot more than a pretty girl to upset his apple cart. Girls had been flocking to Conner since he could walk, and having raised a son for twenty years, Clyde was pretty confident Conner would be crystal clear on who he was and what his expectations were.

The crowd started to file in, and even for a tunic-clad crowd, they were college students, they were hungry, and they were a lot of fun. Clyde, of course, knew how to work the crowd, and Anna, having been a cheerleader, was no stranger in front of groups of students. So they interacted and took questions from the crowd, and Clyde let the locals correct him when he was wrong, and took their advice and put out all kinds of exquisite local food, but he always was working in a little American flair here and there. When they wrapped up the show with Clyde's frozen yogurt date shake—Clyde had added a little bit of goat's milk to thin it a little and blended in the dates along with honey and vanilla—you could hear the buzz throughout the crowd. Clyde ended the show by introducing Conner, who, amazingly enough, the crowd actually knew. He took a bow and asked them to thank the visitors once again, and the students roared.

Yeager couldn't believe it. It was mind blowing. Who would have ever thought? He was thrilled to send in the footage again. He felt like he was walking through brand-new, never-been-done-before television. It was fun to see the people and hear them talk. Their English was pretty good, and of course, talking to them in their language as well was an added bonus. Anna had played host and interacted with the students and always kept Clyde on track with really good practical questions. Yeager said that was a wrap, and Conner informed everyone that the camels were ready for the ride home. "No, just kidding. We had the air-conditioned vans brought over."

Clyde thought it was enough excitement for one day. So that brought Qatar to an end, and now it was back to Italy to see his kids for three days and then on to Singapore or Malaysia for round 3.

DEVIL IN A BLUE DRESS

C HARLES WALLS WAS in Washington DC. The reception was a little cold, and he knew it was because of the payloads found in his warehouse. He knew that was a mistake, but things turned completely around once there was a small hint that his support might get pulled. The good senator from Delaware was enjoying the good life at this point far too much to give up on his old friend from college. Charles was the smartest guy he ever met and was confident that this very small glitch was something he would be able to turn to his advantage. He had seen it dozens of times.

Charles was saying, "Senator, we have started rebuilding that warehouse. We have fired the entire staff, and we bought the property from the Surellite heirs, so we are not tied to them in any way whatsoever. We are seeing up to one hundred patients a day in our clinic, and it is all for free. We have also just made an agreement to do the same in Perm, which is in Siberia, and help out a large very poor group of indigenous people that are very hard to get to, especially in the winter. So we are going to make it warm and easy to get to."

"I was told," said the senior senator from Delaware, "that there are three facilities like it, and they have schematics that show all the centers are the same, and on top of that, they feel like you may be the one who is building a chemical release system that could destroy millions of people."

"Senator Cummings, may I ask you a question?"

"You already have," the senator said.

"Yes, indeed. I have, and let me throw out another one. Why would I want to do something like that? You have known me for years, and why would I ever do anything that doesn't bring me the greatest personal advantage? What is the benefit? If that is what they want to think, I believe our record shows that we have spent our lifetime increasing the longevity of all people groups, no matter what class, what race, or what country. We have spent countless millions improving the lives of thousands of underprivileged people."

All of a sudden, Charles changed gears midstream. "No matter. But I will tell you that if there is that kind of thing going on, we won't fight it, or, I mean, waste time defending ourselves. We will simply coordinate our resources to do what we can to be vigilant to help solve this challenge and apprehend this global villain."

Well, that could not have been a better response, Senator Cummings thought. *And it makes sense that someone is out there who is actually a criminal from the beginning and now is taking a step up in their criminality.*

"Senator, I really think at the end of the day, you have a few loose canons who love using all that hardware they have spent billions on, developed, and have available at the touch of a button. What good is an unmanned drone if you can't use it and blow something up? They have convinced themselves that there is a global threat, and there well may be, but how many times before have we heard, 'Quick, let's rally and save American lives by using the newest and greatest technology we have even at the cost of billions of taxpayer dollars.'"

The senior member of the Homeland Security committee shook his head. "I am sorry I ever doubted. Enjoy your meeting with the vice president's assistant. He is a smart chap and knows his way around the political landscape."

Charles sat down in the lounge area with a younger man who was having a cocktail. "A little early for that hard stuff, don't you think?"

The man was Heath Kildrone, the staff manger for the vice president. "Oh, excuse me, Dr. Walls. I didn't see you come in. You are looking dashing in your white summer suit, and you look casual without the usual power tie!"

Charles always got the feeling that young man was flirting with him. He found it a little odd. "How is the vice president doing today?" Charles asked, knowing the answer already. He was biding his time so he could run for president. It had to be the most boring job in the world, but there was really good access, and he was near the president on a lot of important items. The Democratic Party would start to push that more as the second term started to get past the midway point. They would want a successor. Charles got a flash message from Fritz, and he also wanted to get the latest information from his source here. Charles mentioned that he was fully supportive of the vice president's latest initiative to help raise poverty awareness in South America. They were going to increase the size of their medical facility in Rio de Janeiro as well, and Heath could tell the VP that if he needed anything, he could just ask. Charles knew this young man had information and was willing to sell it. But he was waiting for the right price. This man had been raised in the school of grease the skids with cash politics in San Francisco, where for the right price you could throw out a vote by the citizens with one little judge's decision on the circuit court of appeals.

"I have to fly commercial to my next stop, and my plane has to go back to Italy," Charles said. "It is scheduled to come back Sunday night and get me, but there is no reason you and a friend can't jump on it and spend the weekend at my villa outside of Milan, and since it is coming back anyway. Can you free up your schedule?"

"I think I can," Heath said. "And by the way, we have some interesting news out of California. We have found an ops center that is working with a certain liaison that has connections to our esteemed chairman of the Joint Chiefs of Staff. It is a funny little gig in a downtown high-rise, and we think it has connections going back to elite navy and marine units. For some reason, they pulled this one back in after it was dark for a long time. Which made our people on the inside suspicious. On the back of that napkin, under your ice water, is the address. That may help as you guys come alongside and try to find these reckless Musketeers who are unilaterally destroying the goodwill of Americans all over the world."

Charles gave a number to Heath so he could make all the arrangements for the plane and the trip to the summer cottage. He then thanked his younger comrade and excused himself and dialed Fritz on his way next door to his hotel. Fritz had put together some very interesting news. They had been doing research on a certain YouTube video on a homeless woman in Los Angeles. They had looked into the death of that man, and they had also found out it was true. The man had actually died although the video only showed him falling down. From there, Fritz explained that they had done extensive research on the tooth that was found, and while it was a real tooth, it had been connected to a bridge. Meaning it could have fallen out and have just been sitting in the car.

"I thought the explosion would have been too hot to even save teeth," Fritz said. "But this other evidence confirms our suspicions. Laina Gareen is still alive."

Charles was absolutely stunned. "Well, that is very interesting Fritz. Now I have a bit of information for you as well, and then we can discuss what to do about our problems in Los Angeles. I think that once again I was correct on my instincts to rid the world of S11. Obviously with how he handled that kill squad, he is still very skilled. But I have a little feeling that I will share with you next time we meet."

MORE THAN A FEELING

G RAY EAGLE'S SUPERIOR walked in. "We are being relocated. Site unknown at present time."

Roxanne knew this was a possibility because she had moved eleven times before, but this time, she really wanted to stay. She would have to explain to Arthur what the story was, and then he would have to understand that she couldn't tell him where she was, but she could come to him.

"We clear out tonight, so any personal items you have, please take them with you now. We have an elite technical team coming in and grabbing all of our items."

"Any idea on where we are going?" Roxanne said.

"You know the drill, Major."

Roxanne sighed.

"What?"

"Can I let a young man know that I am interested in? I don't want to just disappear."

"No problem, Roxanne, we understand," Roxanne's superior said. "It is a very gray area when it is not someone you would designate as significant other at this point."

"Or a spouse," Roxanne offered.

"Exactly," said the colonel, who had just recently joined this team and was thrilled to be a part of it. Roxanne was probably the best in the business, and it was fun to be off the grid.

"I would just tell him that he will have to hold on until you can come see him," the colonel said. "Attachments can happen, and Arthur is a good guy."

Roxanne didn't even blink when the colonel said that.

"You knew we would know?" her superior asked.

"It is protocol," Roxanne said. "I actually don't mind at all. I don't want to be dating the guy who sells our secrets to the Soviets or Al Qaeda. So I knew that you would check his background, follow up on his school, check his work, and make sure he wasn't sending coded messages. I am okay with that. It is the life I chose. I got a responsibility to ops guys out there who are risking their neck from the second I say mission is a go. Last night notwithstanding, that was unbelievable. He didn't even let those guys fire back. Well, he was in a Super Hornet, after all. It wasn't a real fair fight. Eleven to one."

"And you would think if those derelicts had a brain they would have armed one of those HAMs."

"I am sorry. HAM?"

You know it is usually surface-to-air missiles, but in this case it was—"

"Okay I got it," Roxanne said. "Kind of funny, Major." She grabbed her coffee cup and a few mementos that she put in the Trader Joe's grocery bag she kept in the bottom drawer. Her desk would be duplicated in who knows where. This was a smooth gig in Los Angeles, though. She liked the weather here and her loft downtown. She would rent it for now. They had been here for almost six months. This mission was in the critical stage, and the ops guys were heading for another destination, so they would have to be up and running by tomorrow morning. She had already cleared the message from Arthur to reach out, but she didn't know how to even start that process, and up until now, they had asked her to wait. But she was just now getting the green light.

The colonel walked over to her. "Hey, by the way, Roxanne, it is a go for operation Word of Mouth. You can reach out to a friend of the Gareens named Norv Adkins. He is one of our own. He served from the Second World War all the way through Viet Nam, and then he was a private contractor for twenty years. He is still very well connected with current and former members of the military. Here is his number. He has the ability to contact the family members of Laina Gareen. While this is unrelated to us, we appreciate you dealing with the breach of security and then bringing all this to our attention. In truth, it is one in a million, or maybe in a billion, that Laina connected the dots from your screen saver to your current friend. We are okay with it, and Norv is the right guy to handle the message. This center will be untraceable in fifteen minutes, and if they trace it, they will be selling sofas for Macy's, anyways."

Roxanne took a deep breath and dialed Mr. Adkins.

"Hello, this is Norv Adkins," the former two-star general said. "May I help you?" Norv didn't know where the phone call was originating from, which meant that he knew who was calling. He had already been given the information that someone was going to call him with a private message from Laina Gareen.

The young lady on the phone said, "Mr. Adkins, I am not exactly sure where to begin."

"Take your time," Norv said. "I was expecting your call, and I know you can't divulge much."

She said, "Thank you very much," and then related the contents of the note from Laina. It didn't really mean much to her, and while she knew that Clyde was a huge celebrity now, she just couldn't reveal her identity. Those inside of her unit must have a lot of trust for Arthur, or she might have gotten in real trouble.

Norv was very kind. "Ma'am, I realize your position is very tenuous. Having been a member of elite units over the years, we were not always at liberty to publish our current or former operations. I appreciate you reaching out. I will get this message to the right people. Thank you, and good-bye." Norv knew whom he would reach out to. He could call Robert Gareen, but if Laina was supposed to be in hiding, he needed a backdoor channel. Clyde had a very close friend in the military who was a beast in the tech world, and Clyde knew the two stayed in constant contact. Johnny Walker—the rebel, as Clyde would say—would be the one to reach out to. He was without the use of his legs from a mission in Somalia, as Norv had heard the story, but his mind and personality were working overtime. He called Johnny through his company, and when he explained a little bit about why he was calling, Johnny Reb said, "Mr. Adkins, I would like to call you back in two minutes, if you don't mind."

Norv knew the drill and appreciated Johnny's quick uptake. Norv heard his cell phone ring literally forty-five seconds later and gave Johnny the quick and precise information. Johnny was stunned. Johnny had an emergency shout to Clyde. It was a text message to his cell phone, but it was a little tricky to reach out to the cell and try and make it untraceable. Johnny used his computer and was able to bounce out of a few untraceable networks and text Clyde's cell. It was probably more of an e-mail, but the lines were blurred on the PDA's.

Clyde was on his way back to Italy, and he got a text on his phone. It was a signal to call Red Horse. So he reached into his pocket and pulled out the earpiece connected to his secure phone he used with Johnny. He hit the hot button, and after he heard the connection, he said, "Go, Red Horse. This is Lone Wolf."

"Hey, Lone Wolf, I know this is out of character, but I wanted to give you a message," Johnny responded. "It has been cleared, and we needed some downtime for this."

What on earth could this be? Clyde thought. He figured it was a rare but sometimes necessary kind of support team to operations intervention. He was waiting for Gray Eagle to come on the line and for Blue Ox and get the old "positive criticism." That was an oxymoron. He was ready for the "You are not allowing us to support you," or, other times, it was "Look, we work hard on a plan, and then you freestyle when all you have to do is stay on the chosen course of action." Clyde waited and listened, and his friend repeated, "I was given a note through unfamiliar channels, and it is from Laina."

Clyde heard that word, and it was like he just went into warp speed. It was an out-of-body experience.

"Lone Wolf, are you with me?" Johnny asked.

Clyde nodded, and then he said breathlessly, "I am nodding in agreement, but you can't see me. Give me the message."

"The message comes via Norv Adkins, and who knows where he got it from. It simply says, 'Go Unione Venezia F.B.C. and to call this number (818) 635-8678 from a secure line when you get a chance.'"

Clyde wrote down the number, and then he simply said, "Thank you."

"The message related that more could have been said from the source, but I think Laina should fill you in."

Johnny do you think this comes via from someone who knows who we are? Obviously, they know Laina."

"No, I don't think so," Johnny responded. "Because they went out of their way to contact Norv, whom they knew you were friends with. They wanted this to come via backdoor channels. Norv has his ear to the ground, so he reached out to me, knowing that I could safely contact you. Okay, big dog, you gotta to fill me in because obviously you didn't overreact, and I would have guessed that normally you might have blown through the top of the plane. You knew something?"

"Yes," Clyde said. "I had two clues already, but I didn't want to get too caught up in the hope. Ironically enough, it was Norv who had this information already, and he showed me in Idaho. She mailed her purse to me at Norv's address the day she supposedly died."

"Big clue!" Reb exclaimed. "Okay, and the second?"

"There was a YouTube clip of a homeless lady being accosted, and then she turned it around."

"Hey, they were talking about that here locally and in the office upstairs."

"I taught her that move, Johnny," Clyde said.

"But she had a baby, if I recall?" Reb questioned.

"Yes, that is the one piece that has kind of thrown me for a loss."

"Make that call, friend. Hey, and by the way, I think Eagle's nest is on the fly. They went black for about three minutes, and then everything was on a loop."

"Don't tell them you know, Reb, it will spook them," Clyde said. "I am off to another world, Johnny I will talk to you soon. Hey, wait a second, can you put me through to that phone from here, or is it too risky?"

"It is too risky, Clyde," Johnny answered. "Make the call from the pay phone near your in-laws' house."

"I will do, that and I will call you right before so we can set it up," Clyde said. "What time is it in Los Angeles?"

"It is about 11:00 a.m.," Johnny answered.

"Okay. I land in five, so see you in an hour or so. Lone Wolf out."

Clyde's plane landed without any fanfare, and he made his way through customs. People were smiling at him, and one little girl asked for his autograph.

"Are you sure you want my autograph?" Clyde asked.

"I am sure," she responded sheepishly. "You rode the camels in Qatar."

"That I did," Clyde responded in his best Italian. He knelt down and wrote on a piece of paper, "To my friend." He looked at her questioningly.

"Jennifer," the little girl added quickly.

But Clyde wasn't as curious about her name as he was about her already knowing about the camels. So he said, "Jennifer, how did you know I rode those camels so fast?"

She looked at Clyde like he was from another planet and said, "It was a news item on my homepage."

"Okay. 'To Jennifer, always bend your knees when you ride the camels. Clyde Gareen.'" Clyde wrote the same as he spoke. That was a first, he thought. He grabbed his luggage and saw a van service and jumped in with three other people.

"Palermo," he said, and gave the specific address.

The driver, hearing the address, asked, "Do you know Rico Del Amo?"

"I am his son-in-law," Clyde answered.

"No kidding," the man said. "I go to his church."

Clyde had a nice conversation with Patticio, the driver, and a quick ride home. He came in to the house, and it was late, around 10:00 p.m. The house was quiet, and he said hello to Rico and Marie and put his bags down. "Hey, I need to make a quick phone call from that pay phone down the alley outside the kitchen. I will be right back."

Rico knew the drill. Clyde was an old army ace, so he gave him his space. Marie questioned Clyde, saying, "Clyde, honey, are you hungry?"

"Starving," Clyde almost yelled. "I couldn't eat the chicken on the plane. It was kind of a soggy mess."

"That is okay," his mother-in-law said. "Not that the food was pathetic, but that I have garlic bread, meatballs, and linguini pasta ready to go."

"Yum" was Clyde's reaction, and then he added, "I will be right back." He put in his earpiece and called Johnny. "Red Horse, this is Lone Wolf, and I am ready to make that call."

"Sounds good, friend," Johnny said. "I think you are calling a boost mobile pay-as-you-go phone. They won't know you are calling, but the line won't be secure."

"How about my side?" Clyde asked.

"Well, sure, but it won't matter," Johnny Reb said. Then he added, "They will probably pick it up, but just make sure she tosses the phone, and get her out of LA, for goodness' sake! Okay, I am ringing you on the pay phone."

Clyde picked it up, and then Johnny said, "Okay, we are dialing her, and when it connects, I will hang up."

The phone rang a few times, and then a woman's voice came on the phone.

"Oh, dear Lord!" Clyde said. "I love you, I have always loved you, and my world fell to pieces when you were gone."

Laina reacted with tears, her voice shaking. "I am so sorry, Clyde, but the moment I saw Fritz meet with Jean Luc Renee and that ill-looking Ildefongwe, I knew that Charles was poison. And then my friend Karen borrowed my car as I was going to the dentist, and she went up like a cloud of fire. So I knew they were already after me. It was less than two hours."

"That explains the kill squad that Dad and I took out in Idaho," Clyde remarked.

"Clyde, you are really good on TV," Laina said. "I was afraid you would fall in love without me. How are the kids? I miss them so bad it is destroying me." She was barely whispering, and she was crying.

"Laina, sweetheart, how long have you been in LA?" Clyde asked. He had tears streaming down his face and wanted to talk more, but this phone call needed to come to an end. It was just too dangerous.

"Almost three months," Laina said. "It took me around, well, maybe almost four weeks to get here. That is all a very long story."

"Honey, it isn't safe anymore," Clyde added quickly. "They are going to figure out the YouTube video."

Now it was Laina's turn to be confused. "What do you mean?"

Clyde repeated her phrase. "That too is a long story, and we don't have long." He then went on to ask, "Do you have any means to rent a car and drive to Camp Pendleton?"

"I have a credit card, or would you rather I pay in cash?"

"No, they won't take the cash," Clyde said. "Use the card, but get out of Dodge quick. I am going to get you to me in Singapore via military cargo plane. Go tonight. I love you with all my heart."

"Clyde, can you forgive me?"

"You have done nothing wrong, Laina. You did what you thought ultimately would protect us. Thank you. The important thing is we are all still safe. I will talk with you very soon."

"I love you, Clyde." Laina hung up.

There was a ten-second pause on the line and then a click. "Clyde, this is Blue Ox. Sorry to butt in on this."

"Hey," Reb said. "Ten seconds, folks. Clyde, hang up the pay phone and call me back."

Clyde had been under authority far too long. He knew to obey direct orders. It didn't need to come from an authority. This was Johnny's delegated responsibility. Clyde hung up the pay phone immediately. He then clicked on his cell and punched the programmed key to Johnny and spoke to him via his bluetooth ear piece.

"Hold on for Blue Ox," Red Horse said. "Ox, you are on, please confirm."

"Thanks, Red Horse," Blue Ox said.

Clyde broke in and asked Blue Ox if he could please get a cargo plane to Singapore from Pendleton. Kirby Myles was Blue Ox, and while he was very limited on conversing with his ops in the field, this wasn't the first time Clyde had spoken to him during an ongoing ops.

"That is not a problem," Blue Ox said. "Work with Red Horse, and give him the details, and we will get an ancillary group working on this through your brother Brad and the navy. I will talk with you more about that, Red Horse. No worries, we will get Pendleton squared away. Also we have an airfield not too far from Singapore. So we can work something out. Clyde, Singapore might be dangerous. The top dog found the mole, and he took the bait—hook, line, and sinker. He then immediately met with the billionaire and your former investor friend Charles Walls. Based on the information we gave him then, we are confident that the mole subsequently transferred that data to Charles directly, and we are betting that Walls will probably try and protect his resources with a bit more security. Also don't think that they are not on to you yet. Obviously Dr. Walls is a pretty intelligent human being and a quick study. So your risk level might be pretty high again."

"Not for long," a resolute Clyde Gareen said.

"Hey, soldier, I know you have a lot at stake in this personally, and for us, it has come to fruition faster than we anticipated, especially based on your guys' outstanding work," Myles said. "But for the moment, we have to stay on course here. We have an internal network that this guy has built, and we are working with three other countries at the moment as carefully as we can, and we would also like to find out if he has partners in on this. And ultimately, we don't really know anything that we can prove. And, Lone Wolf, I have kept a pretty tight loop on your identity. Charles Walls obviously has a leg up because of your history with him, but I would prefer to bring this guy in and solve this crisis without revealing our ops guy."

"Simply put because you can use me again," Clyde chided. "Ox, are you familiar with the title of the Eagles last album?"

"Yes, I am," Kirby said. "I get it. It will be a very cold day before you ever sign on for this again."

"I just landed forty-five minutes ago, and I have two days here," Clyde went on. "Let me know the timing on this whole thing, but I would like to get to Singapore fast. I would prefer to fly commercial to Malaysia with the crew to be normal."

"Roger that, Lone Wolf. Carry on."

Clyde walked back into the house.

Rico was the first to see him. "She is alive, isn't she?"

"Oh, stop that, Rico," Mrs. Del Amo cried out. "You are going to drive us all crazy. That is just impossible." She looked at Clyde, who had tears streaming down his face.

Clyde just sat down on an ottoman and put his head in his hands, sobbing.

"Oh, dear Lord!" Maria Del Amo screamed. "What is it, Clyde?"

He put his head up, smiling through the tears. He stood up. "It is true, Mom. She is alive. It wasn't her in the car."

Now it was Maria's turn. She screamed hysterically, and she was crying. Clyde stood up and hugged her. Then the Gareens came running into the kitchen and said, "What on earth is going on?"

Rico turned to them and said, "My daughter is alive. She wasn't in the car. That is all I know, and that is all that matters to me."

Robert Gareen couldn't hold back the tears. "You have got to be out of your gourds. Clyde, is this true? Laina, our sweet Laina, is alive, after all these months? Oh, sweet Jesus, thank you from the bottom of my heart."

Crying, tears, laughter, joy, and hysteria were all present in that same moment. Katarina came running into the room. "What is going on? You guys are crazy. Daddy, what is happening?"

"Sweetheart, I have very good news," Clyde said. "Your mother is alive. She is in Los Angeles. I just spoke to her on the phone."

"But, Daddy, that is not possible," Katarina said. "She was in that car. She has been gone. She wouldn't leave us, would she? Where has she been?" Then she started to fall to pieces.

Clyde went over and grabbed his poor daughter, who couldn't seem to think and was just bawling. "I don't understand, Daddy. How is this true?"

Clyde, as calmly as he could muster through his own tears, said, "Sweetie, listen to me. Your mommy saw something that she felt like would have jeopardized—well, would have made it very unsafe for us if some very bad people knew she was alive. Everyone thought she was in the car, so for our safety, she let everyone think that. Now we think it is safe again, so she called me, or she sent me a note and I called her."

"Oh, Daddy, I am so happy," Katarina said. "I want to see her, please. Can I right now?"

"Well, we have a few details to work out, but it will be very soon," Clyde promised.

And then Cody walked in in his little New York Red Bull jammies with the footies cut off because he was growing too darn fast. "I can't sleep. Hello, Daddy, why are you crying?" He looked at Katarina. "Are you okay? You are crying too."

"We are crying, little man," Grandpa Gareen said, "because we are happy."

"That is kind of funny, Pappy," Cody said. "What are you happy about?"

Maria took Katarina and put an arm around her, hugging her. Clyde picked up Cody. "Well, we are happy because Mommy is alive."

"What?" Cody asked. "What are you talking about? She exploded, Daddy." He made a sweeping motion with his arms. "She is gone. That is what you said."

"It is what I said, and that is what I thought son, what we all thought," Clyde said. "But Mommy wasn't in that car. Everyone thought it was her because she left a tooth in the car. She was going to the dentist. It was her friend from high school who borrowed the car."

The light went on in Rico Del Amo's brain, and he mentioned, "Karen. That is why the article made note of the fact that she was missing. I saw it in the paper."

The two older children, ever so inquisitive, started to ask some questions and then Katerina asked, "So why didn't she come home, Daddy?"

Clyde responded again with the same patience as the first time and wondered how he would ever, if ever, be able to communicate this to his four-year-old. "She was afraid that the people who made the car explode would hurt you guys if they knew she was alive."

"How can they hurt us, Daddy? They don't know you are a soldier? You have a gun and a knife, and I saw the spears you made in Idaho," Cody replied matter-of-factly.

"Daddy, I want mommy to sing to me. I always fall asleep when she sings to me. Can she sing to me on the phone?" Cody Gareen, suddenly very tired, asked. This was one of those moments in the life of a family that one will never ever forget. The sorrow had turned to joy. Everyone was laughing and talking, and Cody was glad he didn't have to go to bed. Clyde related the whole story as far as he knew it to everyone.

"She had a baby in the YouTube video and a dog?" Clyde's mom asked.

"That part I don't understand," Clyde responded. "She is going to drive to Camp Pendleton in San Diego, and then they are going to transport her to where I am in Singapore. I am going to meet her in Singapore and then not let her out of my sight. Can you guys go six more days without seeing her, or do you want to all go to with me?"

"No, no," Rico said. He added naturally in Italian, "You go see your wife! Tell her we love her very much. You work hard, and as soon as you're done, hightail it right back here. We fully understand. I think you guys have some catching up to do."

THE CLIFFS OF DOVER

Tom Nelson was a fish-and-game specialist for forty years. He was going to retire soon, but in the meantime, he loved the outdoors, and he was happy to travel. He had graduated from UC Berkeley as a biologist, and he went to work for the USDFG and had been a lifer. He started back in 1973. He was, without question, odd, and he knew it. He had worn the same type of hat for all those years. Around year fifteen, the department bought him a new one. The next time around, it was a tradition every five years.

He was traveling in Malaysia, and he loved the back country and the simple way of life. Tom's life was not very complicated. He had been married to a good lady. But he was too boring for her, and she took off after ten years. He didn't begrudge her.

I might have left me too, he thought.

They shared a beautiful daughter, and Tom got the privilege of helping raise her. It was enough. He had his work and his daughter and loved to travel. She was in her late twenties, and Tom kept in touch often.

Tom, as a matter of habit, would test whatever water he was fishing in. He always took a sample of the water, and then he would run it under the microscope. Tom had been doing this same drill for forty years, plus a couple of years in college. To him, it was simply just amazing. A drop of water in between two sterile plates or at least two glass plates with nothing on them. Nothing could ruin your sample more than dirty glass. And then to look at that drop through the lens of a microscope—of course, it was around a magnification of 500—and to see the life in that drop of water. It never got old to him.

Today was no different. He had a simple little inflatable boat and his fishing gear and his work gear. He found a shady spot under a tree but still had excellent light. He would put down a flat piece of plywood and set his scope up on that, and then he would just look at the sample. He could identify almost anything he had seen in the last twenty years. He had one small book, which is like a biologist's dictionary for microbes. It would help him identify some specimens that he would come across from time to time. Today was no different. There was something in this water, and it was simply an out-of-the-way freshwater lake in the back hills of Malaysia. He had been here three times before in his forty years of travel. So he had seen this water before. But he wanted to make sure and wanted to know what he was eating.

Because the fish were living in the water, it was finding its way into all of the lake's inhabitants. For the first time in maybe five years, he saw something that he had no idea what it was. It was three separate microbes, and they were not fusing. But they looked related. Because they were separate, they were probably harmless. He looked up in his little bio dictionary, and he found the microbes. In and of themselves, they were harmless, but there was a little note that directed each time to a toxin that would inhibit human defense mechanisms.

Almost like giving people AIDS, he thought. *That is weird. Why would this be here in this lake?*

Tom lost interest in fishing. He needed to verify these samples and then alert the local agencies. He was a little worried that they wouldn't care, so he would send his findings to his director, and no doubt, Bart Sutterfeld would pass those on to the Center for Disease Control. Tom made his way back across the lake and took another sample. *Pretty big lake*, he thought, *and it would be a lot of this to be in the whole lake.* He got into his rental car and headed back to town and his almost hotel. They had electricity but no Internet. He would have to drive into the next city to find an Internet connection. He mapped it on his phone and found the nearest place with WiFi. It actually wasn't far away. Tom passed a jeep on his way down the hill and thought in all the times he had been here he had never seen another car. As it was, he would have hiked into this remote spot himself, but on the first day he took water samples, he brought the four-wheel drive to drop off the boat, and he didn't want to pack in his gear.

The car that passed him stopped up the road about a half-mile away. The driver got halfway out of the car and said to a very heavy young Asian man sitting in a chair with his eyes closed, "Hey, who was that?"

"Who was who?" the young man asked, trying to stretch and yawn at the same moment.

"The Subaru-looking car that just passed me, you lazy moron."

"Oh, that guy. Just an old man fishing."

"Did he catch a lot of fish? I didn't see him catch anything. So how do you know he was fishing?"

"Well, actually, I don't know for sure that he was fishing," the young man responded. "He was in the water and then out of the water, and then he rowed back across the lake, stuck his hand back in the water a couple of times, and then took off. So he could have been taking samples of the lake. He could have been doing anything."

The driver, by this time, came over to the young man and slapped him on the head.

"Hey, what was that for?" the young man whined.

"I was hoping that maybe I could loosen up the rock you have for a brain," the driver said. "We were told to report any suspicious activity. Well, actually, any activity in this remote lake. That was our job. I have to call this in and follow that old man. Are you coming? You got five seconds to get your fatness in this car, or you are going to walk, which might do you some good." He jumped into the car, and he turned around.

The large young man didn't like the sound of walking, so he made a beeline for the passenger door as the car came around. And they sped off down the road looking for the other car. In the meantime, the driver called it in, and the contact who hired the driver said, "Well, now that is interesting. An extra $500 if you make the old man go away. In fact, if you make him go away cleanly, like a car accident, I will make it a thousand on top of the $500 I have already paid you."

The jeep sped down the dirt road, and within a few minutes, they saw Tom in his rented Subaru Forrester.

Tom looked in his rearview mirror. The jeep was coming toward him like a baseball player trying to stretch a double into a three bagger. He was flying.

He is going to hit me, Tom thought. *I wonder what I ever did.* He thought about the toxin and said, "This is a very strange day, indeed." Tom was no dummy, and he had been driving mountain roads on the job for forty years. He had singlehandedly turned in at least a dozen pot farms. He had been chased before. He didn't even break into a sweat. The good news was that he knew this mountain road, and he had a pretty good idea where they would try to bump him off the cliff. The jeep was close enough to spit at him now, and they were about to take a sharp left. If one missed the left, it was about a thousand feet straight down. One might call that a very hard right.

The large young man was screaming at the driver and asking why he was driving like a madman down this mountain road. "You are going to go over the cliff!" he bellowed. *And that would be bad*, he thought, *because I would miss dinner.* "Man, you got to slow down. You are going to hit that old man."

"That is the plan," the driver said. He accelerated just before the turn to shove the Subaru off the cliff.

Tom Nelson had seen that move before in the hills above San Bernardino. It was a classic "I don't really have a plan, but I am going to surprise the old guy" try. Just as the driver in the jeep hit the accelerator, Tom pulled on the emergency brake and turned hard left. The emergency brake had just enough drag to allow him to start to slide and slow down enough so Tom could make the turn even if it was a little early. But unfortunately for the car behind him, it accelerated into nothing, and it was too late to change gears or slam on the brakes, and Tom watched the car behind him literally fly off the cliff. Tom had to stay focused because he was still sliding around the turn himself and coming out of a fishtail, so to speak. He had to overcorrect the other way and slow way down as well. As he brought the car to a stop, he heard the crash, the scream, and then the explosion. It was instinct to go see if he could help, but he overrode the instincts in this case because for whatever reason, these guys had tried to kill him. *I'll be darned*, he thought. *Not much hospitality in Malaysia anymore.*

He straightened his hat and got back into his car. Drove to the hotel and studied the other samples. His microscope connected to his laptop, and he downloaded the findings into a PDF file. Pretty cool stuff, he thought. He packed up his gear and headed for the rental car agency and figured it would be time to switch cars. On second thought, he drove the cafe with WiFi and logged on and uploaded his stuff to Bart. He always liked the names of the towns in Malaysia. Ulu Tiram was his best bet and easiest to get to from where he was currently. He wasn't too much in a hurry because he didn't think those guys in the car would have been in position to call in the missed opportunity to anybody else. Indisposed at the moment, he thought, and then he thought *incinerated* might be the correct word. He e-mailed Bart and told him it was super odd what he found and that someone tried to run him off the road. "It wouldn't have fazed me in the slightest, being at work, because I have seen all kinds of things out there in the woods, but here I am on vacation. Just wanted to make sure the fish I got didn't have something in it that might upset my stomach."

Tom headed down to the larger city and went to the district or area called Tamar Pelangi. He found a similiar rental car agency and traded in his Subaru. *Good car*, he thought. "You know what, I am going to not replace it."

"Well, Mr. Nelson, you have five days left on your rental you already paid for," the clerk said.

"Just refund it to my card, sir," Tom said. "I am going to take public transportation." Tom had always wanted to see the city of Singapore, and he thought he might do that now. A friend of his had told him that he discovered an excellent little cafe called Ya Kun Kaya Toast where they served Kopi which was Singapore's version of coffee. They filtered it through a sock, of all things, and their signature Kaya Toast was out of this world. Tom was dying to venture in and see this circa–World War II restaurant and what it was all about. He thought if they back trailed him here and somehow got his credit card information, they would at least have a tough time finding him wandering around in Singapore.

The bells were going off from the samples Tom sent in. Bart had forwarded it to the Center for Disease Control and had forwarded it to the Malaysian authorities. Tom had asked if Bart would do it because he didn't know whom he should forward it to. The Malaysian authorities were not as concerned because, of course, while it was strange to have all three compounds in that lake, it was harmless until they were combined, and that was impossible. But the Center for Disease Control had put the compound concoction into a database, and within minutes, the head of Homeland Security, the chairman for the Joint Chiefs of Staff, and the director of the CIA all called him in a conference call.

"I feel important," the director said. "And why is that the some of the highest leaders in the free world are all calling me today?"

Ian Kilpatrick took the lead and said that they were recently engaged in tracking a guy who might be playing with some new chemical-warfare capabilities. They were not exactly sure, but they had found rocket cargo payloads with parts of this same concoction and felt like someone might be trying to upload it into the clouds. Maybe to create like a toxic rain. The director was a biologist by trade, and he had a staff of highly trained competent biological experts in the conference room with him. He said, "We think it would take an immense amount of energy to fuse these and to make a toxin. But we are theorizing that it might be possible to let evaporation do the dirty work for you. I mean, it is just a one in a million that we had a biologist gather this data in Malaysia, and he had the capacity to recognize these microbes as part of a threat to the human anti-immune defense systems. Which is really what AIDS does." The director of the CIA added, "So we are too late. Are we going to see people die in Singapore?"

"Well, maybe," the head of Disease Control said. "But we have sent a team there, and from the samples we have, it looks like a test. Maybe your rocket scientist figured out a way to not need the cloud dispersion and was just testing to see if it would work from a lake."

The leading chemical compound biologist for the center said, "I can't believe it would fuse just through evaporation. If it worked, then people would just breathe it in when it rained, and it would be like AIDS was rearing its ugly head again all over the world."

Chance Summerhill, the director of the Center for Disease Control, said, "This is a major threat, and we have got to treat it very seriously. Do you know who, or do you know how? Well, if it doesn't work in Singapore, do we have a case? You bet your sweet apple pie we do. This stuff didn't show up from a spring-fed lake in the middle of Asia. This is manufactured compounds, and even if it doesn't fuse, the fact that all three are together—which make up the bacteria, really, that does the damage—is criminal behavior. Like if you guys came upon a guy uploading all the necessary ingredients for methamphetamines or all of the ingredients for a bomb, you wouldn't wait for him to put them together for a test run. It would be 'Hello, Guantanamo Bay' for terrorism, right?"

"Yes, sir, I get your point. Well, we feel like we are nipping on the heels of the guy who is responsible. We just have to tie him to the dispersion, right?"

"Not if you have already found the other substances. You would have enough to convict. This is too serious. Keep us in the loop, and we will provide any help we can. We are pretty good with the biology, if I say so myself. And right now, you guys need to be pretty good at catching the bad guy because if someone figured out how to make this work well—" Chance paused and looked at his staff, and three of them simultaneously gestured that they were slashing their throats. "It would be a bad, bad day for the human race."

"Thank you, and we will be back in touch," Ian said. But before he hit the off button, there were a couple of American leaders cussing like sailors.

"I hope they have the right guy tracking this monkey down," Chance said to his staff. "This is like something out of a Superman movie."

AND THE CRADLE
WILL ROCK

A LBERTO JOHNSON WAS really concerned. He said as
much to Yeri. He knew Yeri was already livid at some of the
decisions Charles was making. They didn't have absolute
proof that Tierdon P53 was going to work through the seeding
of the clouds and the energy created in subsequent evaporation.
Yes, they had seen the models, and they trusted Charles's science,
and they had been working on this for five years, and they all felt
that it was a 99 percent chance. The real breakthrough was the
vaccination against Tierdon P53. So there was really a lot they
had accomplished, and they had been patient. Time was on their
side because they were all very affluent, and none of them were
struggling. But Charles had really made some powerful decisions
in the last few weeks that jeopardized everything. He was pushing his operatives in DC too hard to get updated information. He

had sent a kill squad into the United States to eliminate Clyde Gareen. He had stored cargo payloads in the warehouse in Niger. And now, which made everything else look like stealing bubble gum from a newsstand when you are ten, he had gone into the hills of Peninsular Malaysia and had seeded one of their largest manmade lakes. Sure, it was a very long shot that someone had tested the water, but it doesn't matter. Someone had tested the water, and now the jig was up, as he had heard Americans say. The proof of the pudding was in the tasting. The water had been tasted, and it came up foul. It came in with all three elements of Tierdon P53. Well, now, there were worldwide dragnets being set for the person responsible for putting what amounted to eco-terrorism into motion.

Yeri had had it. "That is it, I am done with Charles."

Alberto reminded him that they all went a long way back, but Alberto knew he wasn't talking Yeri out of this. He was already on a plane for Italy. Yeri knew Charles's plane was heading back for Milan, which meant the summer villa. Charles had a summer residence like the pope. Charles was going to need the pope after Yeri was done with him. Yeri had grown up in the rough streets of Argentina. He was still a skilled master of the martial arts. He taught and sparred daily. He was fifty-eight, but he could still break through a block, jump through a window, and take on four men twenty years younger. He walked the streets at night in seedy parts of Argentina without a bodyguard. And now he was going to confront Charles. He might not kill him, but it was going to be really close. Charles was no fighter. He was a windbag, and he had thoroughly disgusted Yeri. This was it. He was done. He had already withdrawn his portion of the mutual funds in the Singapore account. The writing was on the wall, and it didn't look good for Charles.

Yeri drove up to the summer home of Charles Walls and saw Charles's personal car was in the driveway. *Good, Charles is here*, Yeri thought. He was so disgusted with what Charles had done he was ready to slash, maim, and kill if necessary. Maybe he was entertaining a lady friend or maybe another meeting with Fritz to further destroy the plans they had already laid. Well, he couldn't destroy much more. The cat was out of the bag, so to speak. Yeri's American idioms were flowing this morning. *Anger increases your English*, he thought. *I will have to look into this.* He meditated for a minute before he went to the door. He thought maybe to knock because, of course, that would be the polite thing to do. No, the element of surprise was what he was after. Ironically he was wearing a favorite pair of his Italian-made leather gloves. They fit skintight on his hands but were well-worn and didn't hamper his flexibility at all.

It was around 7:30 in the evening. The sun had set, and it was twilight. It would be dark in ten minutes. He didn't think any of these thoughts. He more instinctively was aware of them. He heard muffled voices from upstairs, and he went to the second level. Through the master bedroom, he saw a door slightly ajar leading to the patio. The second-floor patio, overlooking the infinity pool and the green hills and vineyards below, was spectacular. The talking had stopped, and Yeri saw the back of what looked like Charles looking over the bannister of the patio. As Yeri carefully stepped onto the patio to confront Charles once and for all, he stepped through very quietly. As he came through the open door, looking straight ahead, he caught something coming at him via his peripheral vision, and Yeri thought he was too late. He ducked, and the baseball bat went over his head. He turned and gave the would-be hitter a kick on his side, sending the hitter through the glass window. Yeri turned back around as a much-younger man than Charles, whom he did not know, fired a gun right at him.

Yeri never even hesitated. With catlike reflexes, he jumped left and felt the bullet burn his neck and then with both feet kicked the shooter full on in the chest. The shooter fell backward over the railing and into the yard below straight onto two garden stakes. The large metal stakes and the points, of course, were in the ground, but they were jagged edged enough on the top and the force was great enough as he landed facedown that they went cleanly through. Yeri had that image in this mind as he turned back around and scooped up the gun. The man who had gone through the glass was not moving either, and his head was at a wrong angle to his body. It looked like he had broken his neck on an end table during the fall.

Who were these guys? Yeri thought. *I killed them both. They certainly were not fighters. They must have heard me.* But he thought that was strange because the door was open and he had just walked in. Then he saw the security system, and he could see the front door. They left the door open for another person, surmising that they were expecting someone else.

Yeri sat down and started to weep. He had had it. He hated his life. He hated who he was. He detested the fact that he was so utterly despicable and profoundly selfish. It was over. He wanted to change. He wanted to be different. He was, in fact, simply sorry. He picked up the phone and dialed the local police. He was done running. Then he picked up his cell phone and dialed his son. He stated very clearly that he needed to change and his life was a mess and he was going to face trouble in Milan but would very much appreciate if he could come over as soon as possible and talk with him. "Ed, I want what you have. I don't deserve a second chance. I should go to jail for a long time, but I don't care, my conscience will be clean. Ed, here is my American Express card. It has a twenty-five-thousand-dollar limit. You can get your tickets on that. Bring your family and stay a couple of days here to help me through this."

"Dad, what happened?" Ed queried.

"Son, it doesn't matter," Yeri said. "I will explain when you come. Come to Milan and start with the police station. I am sure I will be there."

"Dad, we have a few things to arrange, but we will get on a plane in the morning," Ed said. "At least I will. Anna and the kids might be a little behind me, or they might not be able to pick up and leave, but I will be there. Okay, I love you, Dad. I look forward to talking to you when I get there."

The police came. Yeri was sitting on the patio with his head in his hands. He was bleeding pretty good from the bullet burn, but nothing life-threatening. The medic immediately started to treat Yeri's wound. The detectives walked around, and the coroners came, and they took away the bodies. The police got statements from Yeri. There was nobody else at the home, so there was no one to interview. After an hour, the lead detective said to Yeri, "It looks like self-defense. The first guy hid for you as you walked into the patio, and the second man took a shot at you. They saw you coming via the security camera on the front porch and actually were ready for you. How, in fact, they missed you twice is astonishing, and then they both got killed as you defended yourself."

Yeri was astonished. He said, trying to implicate himself, "I came here to confront the owner of the home, and I was mad. Who knows what I would have done should I have found him here?"

"Mr. de Angelo, I appreciate your honesty, and that certainly helps us understand why you came here and walked into the home unannounced, and that certainly proves to be hostile intent," the detective said. "But that is where it begins and ends for us. You had bad intentions and bad motives, but those never got carried out, mainly, of course, because your business associate is not here at the moment. So while I find you a threat and I recommend you don't act on those threats, you are an unwelcome intruder, but the door was open. I can't arrest you for being really mad at the owner of this home. Let me ask you a question: if these men had just sat on the patio and you would have realized that they were not the owner of the home but merely guests, what would most likely have transpired?"

"I would have left still angry, but I wasn't hostile to these guys." Yeri finally relented with a sigh.

"Exactly my point, Mr. de Angelo," the lead detective said. "So I have an ongoing investigation here, and I will need you to stay in the country for a while, so please don't leave. Your passport won't work, but I am sure you have other ways of getting out of the country. But don't. I need you to stay here."

HIGHER LOVE

L AINA CAME INTO the apartment. Tears were streaming down her face. Tonya asked her what it was. She had stated that she just gotten off the phone with her husband.

"That is amazing, Laina," Tonya said. "In fact, it is really all hard to believe." And then she started to cry.

"What is the matter?" Laina asked Tonya.

"I am really happy for you, Laina, but this has been the best few months of my life since I met you," Tonya said. "You are wise and kind and nice and encouraging, and somehow, you don't talk down to me. You make me feel like an adult, and you allow me to be a kid at the same time, since I am only sixteen, and I don't want to lose you." Now tears were pouring out of her eyes.

Laina went over and hugged her. "Tonya, you are my friend, and wherever I go you are welcome. You will be welcome with us for as long as you need. We can help each other. This isn't the end of the journey, this is only the beginning. I have not asked you, but how do feel about New York?"

Tonya said she would go anywhere as long as Laina was there.

"I wouldn't want to be anywhere without you either," Laina said. "We are not roommates, we are teammates. You too, Tonya, have been a fantastic friend, and I really appreciate all that you have done and helped me through in this dark time of my life. Now the plan is for us to go to Camp Pendleton, and they will fly us to Singapore, where Clyde is going to be. We are not sure what will happen from there. But it sounds to me like they are closing in on the guy who I have been hiding from." Laina got on the phone and called the closest rental car company and gave them all the necessary information. They said they could drop off the car in thirty minutes. She said that would be great.

Tonya said it will be easy to pack. The girls divided up the chores. Laina had around six apple boxes from the grocery store, and they quickly packed up the few meager items they had. Laina grabbed two large suitcases, and they put one on each bed.

"Tonya, put your clothes and James's clothes in here," Laina said. "I have boxes for things you need every day and things you don't need since we might have to ship those back to my in-laws in New Jersey for safekeeping. The military post office will help us. But I just used my credit card, so if anyone is looking for me, I will not be hard to find electronically for anyone who has the access."

They didn't have that many belongings, so they were making short work. In an empty townhome around South Glendale—which was a great location for just about being anywhere in Los Angeles in fifteen or twenty minutes, unless, of course, you hit traffic, and then it could be forty-five minutes to an hour—there were two guys sitting at a table working on laptops. Isaac, who was around thirty-five and had worked for Fritz Riedboecher all over the world, was a specialist in cyberterrorism. He was just as capable at tracking people electronically. He had never been caught and had breached the security of the KGB and MI6. He was close on the CIA several times. But this was a simple job: find one woman in Los Angeles. They had been close, but she was very careful. She hadn't used an ATM or a credit card, didn't use her cell phone, and was logging in different on unknown computers. The only real clue they had was the YouTube video of a homeless woman fighting off an attacker and then leaving him, running, while he choked to death in his own blood. She probably didn't even know he had died. They knew her kids were in Italy, and there had been no correspondence. They had just recently found out that she had gone to a homeless shelter then a halfway house for women and then a family shelter. They had been looking for a week and had found all this information out. It was down to three possible locations, but they were not close. Isaac and his coworker had just rolled the dice for locations one, two, or three. They preferred Pacoima because it was the closest, but Long Beach came up on the dice. So they were grabbing their gear and getting ready to shoot to Long Beach when Isaac's computer made a ding. Rental car purchase in Van Nuys.

"I can't believe it," Isaac said. "She finally used her card. She must be on the move, so she didn't care." Isaac told Oliver to drive, and when he called him Ollie, Oliver nearly hit him.

"Touchy, touchy, are we?" Isaac said in his very British accent. "You can't work for the man if you don't have a little play in you, Mr. Oliver."

"Let's go, Newton," Oliver said,

"You call me a nickname, and I don't get all huffy," Isaac responded. He was tracking the card purchase via his 4G network card as they drove. "It looks like she gave an address in Pacoima. Yes, that is the family halfway shelter. She is bumming off the state. I hope they bill her for a nice three-months stay."

Laina and Tonya strapped in the car seats into the car then Laina checked the last box, loaded it, and then shut the trunk. The rental car company sent two cars, so the driver went back in the second car. *Smart*, she thought. *For a couple of extra bucks, we get delivery.*

They pulled out and drove down the street. They turned the corner, and literally thirty seconds later, Isaac and Ollie pulled into their same spot. Isaac hopped out of the car and knocked on the door. A young Hispanic lady opened a little porthole in the door and asked if she could help.

"Yes, ma'am, I am sorry to intrude," Isaac said. "My wife's sister is living here, and she said it was, and he gave the address, but I must have written down the wrong apartment. I am looking for Laina Del Amo. I am sorry, that is her maiden name. I mean Gareen."

"Well, Del Amo was familiar, but Gareen didn't ring any bells," the lady said. "I know that Del Amo is in number 13, which is outside and around the back and second unit on the left." She knew that Laina had just pulled out and was going to give her a little more space. She sent him on a chase, and he was going to have to come back out and go all the way around to get to 13.

Laina jumped on the 118 and headed east. She was going through Pasadena and then down the 605 to Long Beach and then catch the 405 south to the 5 south to Camp Pendleton. There were easier ways, but she didn't mind a little extra drive, and she didn't want to be followed. It was a pleasant drive as the babies were sleeping. She was excited. Excited to shower, do her makeup, and get ready to see Clyde. He was hilarious on the show. It was as if he was born to it. She missed her children, and she didn't know what to do about Ricardo. She would have to deal with that from New York.

I wonder what happened to the restaurant, she thought. *Maybe Clyde hired a couple of good chefs and they are running it.* She missed the restaurant, the people, the pace, and most of all, funny enough, she missed the staff. They were like family.

I wonder how Katerina is doing, Laina thought. *Four long months. Did Clyde tell everyone I was alive? Tough call, because it creates huge expectations. Although my dad would have a heart attack if he knew.* She had no idea he was thirty yards from her in the gas station across the street when he spoke in Los Angeles. Tonya had a million questions, and most of it came from her street smarts and survival instincts.

"You have a serious job, and that is to grow your son," Laina said. "It won't be long before he is up and running, and you will be freed up a little more. I would really like it if you met a few of our friends who produce records. We have some connections back in New York. A couple of label guys ate dinner every Tuesday night in our restaurant. Veal parmigiano and egg plant parmigiano were their orders every time. We need to talk to them, and they need to hear you sing."

"Are you serious?" Tonya asked. "Do you think I can actually do it?"

"Tonya, when I heard you sing in church, I thought I had left the planet and was raised up to the third heaven," Laina said. "You sing gloriously, and I am not just saying that. You have a rare talent. You are young and raw and have lots to learn, but as they say, you could open the phone book and sing. Do you play any instruments?"

"I play a little piano and the guitar," Tonya said. "But it has been a while."

"Why didn't you tell me? We would have gotten you a guitar."

"You are too nice," Tonya said. She became quiet, and she said, "Laina, I don't want to put you guys out. I mean, I can't offer anything back."

"Yes, you can," Laina said. "And I know you are not a free-loader. We will extend kindness to you, and in return, you will later on have to extend that same kindness to somebody else."

"If I get on my feet, you know, I will have half my family living with me," Tonya said.

"Exactly, and after you are on your own, you will have known what it is like to have been shown a little grace in times of need,"

Laina said. "And you will understand what can be done to give back even when you are being given to."

"You mean like take out the trash, watch Ricardo when I can, help cook, do dishes?"

"Tonya, I have four other children, and there are clothes to buy, groceries, appointments," Laina said.

"It will be a real-life zoo in the Del Amo household."

"Gareen," Laina said.

"Oh, that is right, Ms. Homeless," Tonya said. "And I don't talk, I forgot you are married. To that handsome guy on the food channel. He is pretty funny, Laina. You better keep your eye on your man because I think his cohost has big eyes for what is his name? Oh yeah, Clyde."

"That is not what I needed to hear. I am half a world away, but the truth is now that Clyde knows I am alive, there will be no issue. I have known Clyde since he was fifteen."

"Are you kidding me?" Tonya said.

"Well, you heard the engagement on the show, right? That was exactly the way it happened, but Clyde came to Italy to play soccer with my brother Ivan. We had a couple of kids stay at the house all summer. There was a friend of Clyde's named Conner who was two years older and handsome as all get out, and Clyde was younger than me, and he had really not grown up yet. I mean, he did during the summer, kind of like bread in the oven. All the ingredients were there."

"He just needed to kind of"—and she made big arms— "fill out."

"Exactly," Laina said. They both laughed hysterically.

"But it was his personality that won the day," Laina went on. "He was sure of himself, and he started liking food that summer. He was funny and honest and didn't care what the other boys thought. They would tease him, and he wouldn't care. He just kept being Clyde, and then the next thing I know, he is leaving back for the States, and now he is six foot tall and had like a 180 weight, and he was tan from all-summer soccer, and his curly hair, and—well, I was really sad he was leaving, if you know what I mean. We started to write, and then Clyde came back the next summer. He started playing for a practice team that was in the Serie C, and then he went to college. He came and played for the semipro team in Venice, and we got engaged. We went to England, and he played for Aston Villa."

"Are you serious, he was professional?" Tonya asked.

"Well, he was on the team," Laina responded. "And we had a lot of fun living in England too, and the next thing I know, I was an army wife, traveling, having kids. He was gone for three months, but he has seven siblings, great parents, and then I would go home and be with my family in Italy. So it was actually a lot of fun. But I missed him awful."

They continued to drive, and by that time, they were just outside of Irvine. They stopped and got coffee and fed the babies. Tonya was really happy. She had never experienced a family with consistency and people who loved each other. This was a big world, and her little corner of the universe didn't tell the whole story. She was eager to learn, and she wanted to sing. They got to the marine base. Laina pulled up and put her driver's license out.

The man at the booth said, "Laina Gareen. We have been waiting for you. I need you to pull straight up this road and make a left and park in front of the PX. Gen. Brad Gareen is waiting for you."

"Thank you, Officer," Laina responded.

"My pleasure, ma'am, and it is good to see you in fine health. You had us all worried down to the rank and file, ma'am. If you don't mind me saying, your husband is a fine soldier, ma'am, and his brother is no sissy either."

"Thank you, Sergeant, and I appreciate it."

They drove off, and Laina couldn't believe it was Brad.

"As I live and breathe," he said as she got out of the car. "As you live and breathe, I should be saying. And who is this pretty lady who is with you?"

"This is my friend, Tonya," Laina said. "She has kept me going these last three months when times were a little frightful.

"I can't imagine," Brad said. "This is some kind of miracle."

Then they got the babies out of the back, and Brad just whistled. "Laina, you are more than a brother-in-law can speak to. Where did you get a child? He is like four months old."

"Three months old, but he is happy," Laina said. "No, I wasn't pregnant, because you know Josephina was only three months old at the time. Ricardo is only four months younger than Josephina. They will be like twins. No, when I was pretending to be homeless, I found a baby in a dumpster. I tried to turn the child in to the hospital and to the police, and they turned me into the shelters. No one would believe it wasn't my baby. That was it, a mom with a baby who has my same markings, although I think he is Hispanic, and of course, I look like I am."

"Yes, we know, Ilyaina, full-blooded Italian. Okay, here is the drill. I will call all this in, of course, but they are rolling out the red carpet for you. Clyde is not even in the military, and I couldn't get a transport like this for my family. I guess this is what happens when you are a big TV star like my little brother. We have a little place for you over here, and then we will leave at 9:00 in the morning. I am flying you to Hawaii and then on to Singapore. Tonya couldn't believe the apartments. She thought she had died and gone to heaven. They had breakfast at a little café on the base, and then they boarded a giant plane. It had all kinds of stuff in it, and it was kind of loud but super fun.

They landed in Hawaii, and it, of course, is paradise. The boys had been crying a lot, and Laina said that flying hurts their ears. Before they left, General Myles had—through, of course, a chief of staff liaison—the people at the base take pictures of Laina and Tonya and footprints of the child. Tonya's boy, James, had a birth certificate, and that wasn't hard. The base sent all the pictures and footprints to the Joint Chiefs of Staff office, and he forwarded everything to Myles, who sent it all to Johnny Reb.

Johnny was a miracle worker and put his staff on it and coordinated with some inside technicians he knew in Los Angeles. When you have the resources and the right people working the system, you can't believe how fast things can actually get done. Johnny also had some clout that came through Ian Kilpatrick's office via Kirby Myles. They were to upload the footprints to the Department of Social Services. As it turned out, Johnny's assistant had a sister who worked for the Department of Social Services. She was a lead social worker. Kim, the assistant to Johnny, had explained who she was and what the situation was, and they took the footprints and handprints and created a temporary birth certificate for Ricardo Gareen. Eventually, they would have to get a judge to sign off on it, but they didn't see a major problem.

Kim's sister was a fifteen-year veteran of the social service network in Los Angeles. She had come to America as a student at USC and started working in downtown Los Angeles. They were able to secure Clyde and Laina Gareen temporary custody of one Ricardo Gareen. There was a process and a time element that had to be followed. They published the need to have this child's mom come forward in the local newspaper and made some posters as well. They were trying to show the court that they had reached out. There was a good chance that the mother of the baby might not have known she was pregnant until late in the game, and then all of a sudden, she gave birth and freaked out. In the moment, she did something stupid, and in this case, it would have been better to drop the baby off at the hospital or fire station or the local police department. In fact, what she did was actually criminal. Which, if you think about it, is so amazingly ironic due to the fact that if she chose to abort the baby even up to the last ninety days, then there would no consequences.

But the department made attempts to get a hold of the mother even though they knew it wouldn't reveal anything. Laina's passport was updated, and they got a copy of Tonya's birth certificate as well as James's, and they were able to get passports for them.

All of these items were uploaded to an onboard laptop and were printed on the spot. Pictures, paperwork, and temporary visas were all included in the family dossier. Monster was the biggest problem of all. He was a good dog and had been no issue even in the cargo plane, but they didn't think they were going to get him into Singapore. He would have to go through Quarantine. Brad told Laina to leave the dog with him, and he would take him home, and they could figure out how to get the dog from DC to New York at the right time.

"He speaks Italian, so give him a little slack," Laina said.

"Italian?" Brad asked.

"He stayed with me since the first night I was down at the ports near Rome."

"That is amazing," Brad said. "He must have known you needed a little comfort to weather all of the storms that you were facing."

"Storms nothing," Laina said in almost a whisper. "It was more like the fires from the Valley of Gehena."

Brad paused, thinking on that last comment and the clear picture it painted of what this life can throw at you. But he skipped over it and just added, "So Monster has been from Italy to Mexico to Los Angeles to Hawaii, and now to Singapore. But he won't get off the plane in Singapore. Well, at least not off the base."

EVERY DAY I WRITE
THE BOOK

Chuck Seger and his team were sitting in the newly refurbished conference room of Channel 6. It had a stunning view of the bay and was very nicely appointed. Barb Reiding had come over from the local offices of The Food Network. The had just received the news that the most recent airing of *The Seasoned Traveler: Qatar* had beat all of the network and cable shows in its time slot, and it was number two for the week. They anticipated that the second showing or rerun—which aired tonight, Friday—might even be bigger than the first run. That actually never happened, except for *The Seasoned Traveler: Venice*, which, of course, took a huge run-up because of word of mouth. Chuck and Barb Reiding, the FTN president, didn't want to miss the opportunity, and the advertising dollars had gone through the roof. They also were going to send the show to iTunes once it aired again, and Netflix was buying it as well. Not a bad deal for a travel and cooking show. The decision to send Yeager was a brilliant one, and it was a joint decision by both Channel 6 and the Food Network.

"So what is next?" was the query from Barb. She went on, "You have kind of set us up now. We were supposed to film three episodes and start showing in the fall, and they are so good that we did a special. The next episode was just as good, if not better. Camels in the desert—who would have thought?"

"What are you going to do next, raise someone from the dead?" Barb's assistant quipped.

Chuck thought out loud, saying, "It is going well, and they are good, I will admit, but let's not get crazy. We started out with low expectations, and I don't want to increase the pressure."

"Well, okay, Chuck. Our weekend ratings will probably be around seven million, which is a 600 percent increase from a month ago. So we are actually going crazy. This thing is gold. So it isn't out of the question to get a little religious around here."

Everyone laughed, and Barb asked, "Can I get a hallelujah?"

After they stopped laughing, Chuck said that the plan was for Singapore. Clyde has only been as a soldier to the naval air base in the northeast part of the island.

"Singapore is an island?" someone asked.

"See, that is the stuff that we find so fascinating that when the show in Venice was done, you knew that the city was built on upside-down spikes. Where does Clyde get this stuff?"

"Well, I think for the most part, it is the inquisitiveness of Clyde's mind, as we are finding out, and really good questions from Ms. CiFuentes. So we have Singapore, and then what is the plan after that?" Asked the never ending methodical mind of Lars Clarkson.

"Well, we were going to end leg 1 of the filming and take a little hiatus. I mean, originally our goal was to bring you ten shows by the end of the summer."

"All right," Barb interrupted. "I have an idea. So let's give them a little break, but we could move up the next shooting for Quebec or Mexico City. Then can we do, like, a three-city tour in the countries of the former Soviet Union."

"Hold on for just a minute," Chuck said. "We have to keep in mind that the beauty of this show is that we have a dynamic duo. One of whom is a family man, and he has been through two huge personal crises in the last five months. Now on top of that, he is a budding international television personality. All of us on the production side of television have seen what the pressure of stardom can do to a seemingly normal human being. Am I right? Do I need to cite some examples? I will throw these ideas with the team, but I want to protect Clyde and Anna as well."

Barb's palms were sweating. "You are 1,000 percent right, Chuck. We love Clyde and Anna. Please keep them as they are. Thanks for stepping in at this moment. We will take our cues from you. We have really enjoyed the partnership. Put out your feelers, and let us know. How is Channel 6 with all this? Do they mind all of the publicity and the change away from their typical programming?"

"Are you kidding?" Chuck asked. "No, we love the publicity. It has increased our ratings, and of course, we are able to show little back vignettes and some takeaways that Yeager has sent us, and it is great material."

"I am a little jealous," Barb said. "Although I don't know if it would sell because we actually have the show running. No, we are good. The promos have been great."

Just then the intercom interrupted the speakerphone conversation. It was the receptionist saying that she had Barb's secretary on the line with Yeager Bierson was on the call as well. "Did you want to take it on the conference room speaker phone?"

"Are you okay with this, Chuck?" Barb asked. "I don't want to step on your toes."

"By all means, I am delighted that we talk to Yeager," Chuck commented.

"Well, I didn't think we could top Venice, so I was skeptical in Qatar," Yeager blurted out. "And then once we shot the camel ride and the stadium, with Clyde cooking, I thought we cannot outdo this. Hence, to be honest, I was kind of bored thinking about Singapore. Not that it isn't a great city and all, but I just got off the phone with Clyde, and things are going to get really interesting in Singapore. We have what is actually earth-shattering news, like, make the six o'clock headlines. Hey, I thought you were meeting with Barb in the local Chelsea Market Square offices?"

"We were, but we had a last minute change of plans and now we are waiting for your news, but I am sensing you are not at liberty to say," Chuck said.

"I am not," Yeager said. "And I am not sure why. But I have kind of found out with Clyde that he has pretty good instincts, and they seem to be proving to make surprisingly good film production. And you guys are able to deliver that and get the response you want from your audience, so I kind of feel like I roll with it. I wasn't in the dark on the camel ride, so I knew how to shoot it, but it was a surprise to most, especially Anna. I have a crew already there in Singapore because Clyde is getting there a little ahead of schedule, and we will film him getting off the plane, and he is doing a little scouting around. He wants to take us up into the mountains of Peninsular Malaysia, he calls it, where there are still some pretty primitive communities, and there are a lot of waterways that you travel via small boat where we will be fishing, eating, and cooking. But he wants to give us a lot of the back drop on where the really good cuisine comes from."

"The original concept of the show was so anyone can arrive in Singapore and find great places to eat," Chuck said. "But your crew has kind of turned it into a little bit of a travel, culture, docudrama, and so far, it is working."

"You typically cannot argue with success, right, Yeager?" Barb piped in. "Yeager, it seems like you are really enjoying yourself. I think it is a little different from the big Hollywood blockbusters."

Yeager's response was candid. "You couldn't be more correct. This is a lot of fun. That is the bottom line. We are traveling and seeing sights, Clyde and Anna set a great atmosphere, it is a team effort, and we give a few days' break after shooting so we can all go see our families, so it is a blast. Except when I talk with my dad, who thought my career was over directing a foodie show."

"I am sorry, Yeager," Barb said. "And by the way, how many television shows has your dad produced to date?"

Well, Yeager knew the answer, which was zero, but that wasn't the point. The point was, as Barb was pointing out, his father didn't have any experience with the high pressure and stakes of television and what went into every second of the programming experience.

"Hey, Yeager," Barb said. "Just as an FYI, coming from a grandmother who has been in this business since the early sixties. There was a guy named Michael Jordan who was never a superstar in baseball. Many successful people don't understand the television world, and I am still not sure I understand it myself."

"I am reading you loud and clear," Yeager said. "Thanks. Do you guys have any suggestions?"

"Does Clyde know anyone in Singapore, like he did in the last two cities?"" wondered Nina Pearson out loud.

"No, but they know him," Yeager said. "You can't believe the reception he gets from the military guys everywhere he goes."

"We have troops over there," Barb said. "I have a nephew who flies out of Sembewang, I think it is, and also Paya Lebar air base. It might be good to see some of that interaction. I know Clyde will be on one of the bases, so I will keep a crew with him."

"It sounds great, Yeager," Chuck said. "Thanks a bunch."

"This has the potential to knock your socks off, and I know I am overselling a little bit, but I actually don't think I can," Yeager said enthusiastically. "I gotta run. I will talk with you soon."

"See you later," Chuck said, and with that, the phone clicked off. He looked at one of his staff and shrugged and commented to Barb, "I don't know what he has up his sleeve."

"Well, when you have a town called Johor Bahru," Barb's assistant said, "it can really get kind of interesting very quickly."

"No," Barb said. "There is something going on. From what I know of Clyde Gareen and Anna CiFuentes, we have already seen the results of shows 1 and 2. We better call our advertisers and raise their buy-in. He makes for incredible drama."

Their thought process was preempted by a breaking-news segment on the television. *CBS News* was reporting that the vice president's recently promoted chief of staff Heath Kildrone and his friend Ash Grafton assistant to the secretary of state, were killed in self-defense by and unknown assailant at this time.

"This is a vacation home of Charles Walls, billionaire founder and owner of Zeuterfeld Labs and friend to the vice president," the news anchor said. "Charles Walls has not been available for comment, but it appears, according to the Italian police, that Grafton and Kildrone were on a little hiatus in Milan, and they were threatened by the man who killed them both. They were waiting to attack what they thought was the intruder, and Kildrone tried to swing with a bat, and then Grafton shot at the attacker. But the attacker fought back and prevailed in both instances. This is, at this point, sort of bewildering and beyond explanation. We are trying to learn the name of the man who killed these two American dignitaries, but they won't release it as of yet. The vice president is flying over to Italy, so I am sure there will be much more on this story."

Barb muted the television and looked at Chuck. "Isn't that the same guy who pulled his money out of Clyde's restaurant?"

"I think it is," Chuck said. "This is actually pretty bizarre. Do we need a comment from Clyde?"

"Is this the news that Yeager was talking about?" Nina Pearson asked.

"Well, if it isn't," Chuck added, "I can't imagine there could be anything more earth-shattering than this!"

There was a moment of silence as everyone kind of absorbed all of the information.

"This is cutting it pretty close to the edge," Barb finally said. "Talk about trying to protect your team, Chuck, and now we have this. We are in the entertainment business driven by culinary concepts, and I don't think this fits our wheelhouse at all. But it sure is remarkable, and those poor guys. I wonder what actually happened."

"Here is an angle," Nina threw in. "Channel 6 is a news station, after all. This is in our wheelhouse. Why don't we run with this from our side and you guys can pick it up and use it nationally."

Now it was the Food Network's time to make a call.

"Although it is a bad word at the moment, this is real synergy, guys," Barb Reiding said. "I like your plan. I am with Nina, Chuck. Run like mad and put this out as a news piece and give us a heads-up as soon as you are going to air the information concerning Clyde and Anna. We will run your news items on a scrolling ribbon or tag line, if you will, on our shows that are currently being aired."

Charles Seger motioned to his executive staff that they were staying as he hung up on the conference call. Nina, Lars, and the others pulled up a chair around his conference table.

"All hands on deck," said Chuck, and everyone in the room immediately knew it was time to cancel evening plans. This was one of those pitfalls of being highly paid executives in a demanding industry. "I am sorry," said Chuck, "and if you have something that can't be unbroken please talk with me in a moment, but we have got to get this segment out ASAP."

Nina, who was the most senior on the staff and had followed Chuck from the previous gig in Iowa asked, "If they could take ten, make arrangements and meet back for assignments?"

Chuck agreed as he knew he had to make his own phone call. When the room had cleared, Chuck hit button number one on the speed dial and the information line on the outgoing call read *Maureen.*

Maureen answered the phone, saying, "Hello, darling," and she knew what the call was all about. Chuck only called at this time of day from the office when he was staying late. He didn't do it often because his staff was strong and he could do a lot of work on the train and via the cell phone. Maureen Seger was no dummy. She loved her man and she knew he loved her, but this was a great big ugly world, and he was a handsome television executive in New York City. There were a lot of young ambitious women out there who were not concerned about her family.

Chuck said, "Honey, I am sorry we have a story that demands my attention that we have to air in an hour or so, and I need to stay at the wheel."

"No problem," chimed in Maureen. "Hey! I have an idea. The kids and I will jump in the car and head your way. Can you meet us for dinner in two hours?" Chuck really liked that idea. He would be starving anyways and the train would be a drag on an empty stomach. His wife continued and said, "Lily and Charlie don't have school tomorrow because it is an in service day so we are not rushed to get everyone to bed."

Chuck said, "That's perfect, honey. Thanks for the suggestion, and he mentioned a pretty kid friendly very upscale New York pizzeria that everyone loved."

Maureen loved having the twins home for kindergarten, and Chuck knew that she would make a note of this at some point in her conversation and didn't mind. "Chuck," questioned Maureen, "does your story have to do with what happened in Italy?"

I had a conversation with Holly (who was her cousin and the daughter of Bodimer Chance), and she said her dad was very concerned about this, especially as it related to the Food Network. All of a sudden, this conversation had turned the corner from being a casual discussion concerning arrangements and had become a source for Chuck as a news guy. Maureen's uncle was very well connected and was on the board of the parent corporation that owned the Food Network. He was very well liked of course but extremely conservative and many on the board felt like he was a pick to keep the masses of middle America and the huge population of still very conservative red states fully aware that they still had their proverbial eye on the ball.

Maureen said, "Charles Walls's home was being used by these two guys for a getaway and it was his partner Yeri de Angelo who was the culprit."

Although this information had not been released as of yet, his wife was already ahead of the curve. This, of course, hadn't been confirmed, but Holly via her father had this knowledge from Roscoe Watkins, very close associate of Charles Walls, and also fellow board member with Bodie Chance.

"Honey," said Chuck, "you may have just given us the lead in on our news segment this evening."

"Well now, I am glad to be of help!" Maureen responded with a little sense of pride.

Chuck was always amazed at how his wife, stay-at-home mother of four, could literally network all over the world, keep her ear to the ground, feed a hungry family, drive the Suburban to multiple places in a day, cook like it was no one's business and still look fabulous at forty-nine. In the last few years, she had started talking with her cousin Holly once a week or so. Holly lived on an acre just outside of Los Angeles. She raised chickens, had her own beehive, had seven or eight fruit trees (one for every kid that they had), and homeschooled all of them to boot. He had always thought she was a little extreme, but her influence on his wife was always good and at the end of the day he trusted in his wife because she was so wise.

Maureen broke in on his thoughts and said, "You know, this is a very small world, Chuck. Holly's son, Chance, who is finishing a very prestigious eight-year career in the marines was on an operation with his former Colonel Clyde Gareen, and he watched him free climb a five-hundred-foot cliff before he stole a helicopter and singlehandedly got them out of a pretty harrowing situation."

Chuck responded, "I knew he was ex-military, but he downplays being a hero and always says it was just part of his duty."

Just then he heard his assistant say in his ear that Yeager was calling in and had super important information.

Chuck said, "Hey, Maureen, I have a call from Yeager I need to take. I love you very much, and I will see you guys at the restaurant."

"Not a problem, sweetheart. See you in a couple of hours."

Yeager came through and said, "Hey, boss, this whole thing just got really interesting."

Chuck Seger was standing up, talking on his wireless headset, and looking out over the city. "Yeager, this is one ride that I don't think can get any more interesting than I already know? What have you got for me now?"

"Chuck," said Yeager, "you are not going to believe this. Laina Gareen is alive. What is more is that she has been hiding from Charles Walls. This whole thing is connected from start to finish, and our boy Clyde is smack dab in the middle of this."

Chuck asked, "Is this going to hit the mass media soon?"

"I don't think so," said Yeager, "I had to do some very fancy footwork to follow Clyde onto the airbase in Singapore where Laina is flying in, and I have some good sources for my information."

"If you are not careful," responded Chuck, "I am going to turn you into a reporter."

"We all have to do our background work," said Yeager. "It just happens in this case to be newsworthy as it involves our now infamous super chef."

"*Infamous* is the right word!" exclaimed Chuck. "This young man has literally come out of the burning fires of total destruction to sweep the nation as a brand new kind of superstar. Well, this adds a whole new element to the saga my young friend. Where is this Walls character? Is our costar at risk? Okay, Yeager, thanks for this new information and by the way. Great work."

"Thanks," responded Yeager. "Just when I thought Singapore was going to be dull compared to the Venice engagement episode and then the camels in Qatar, it looks like Singapore might just blow those two out of the water."

"Thanks, Yeager," said Chuck as he hung up the phone as his group was gathering. "Okay, folks, we have our work cut out for us. Here is the angle I think we should take. Good evening, New York, this is your number one local news station, and we wanted to bring you the latest on the developing tragedy happening in Milan, Italy. We have it under very good resources that the person responsible for the death of these two American Civil Servants is Yeri de Angelo, most recently from Argentina. He is a business partner with Charles Walls, who owned the weekend retreat that was the scene of this weekend's deaths."

The staff was speechless. They were all shocked. Lars asked, "Chuck where did you get this information?" I got it from a colleague of another business partner and friend of Charles Walls. It was one thing to have firsthand breaking information, and it was another to take it live to five million viewers. Just as they were digesting that information Chuck said, "Now are you ready for the biggest news of the day?"